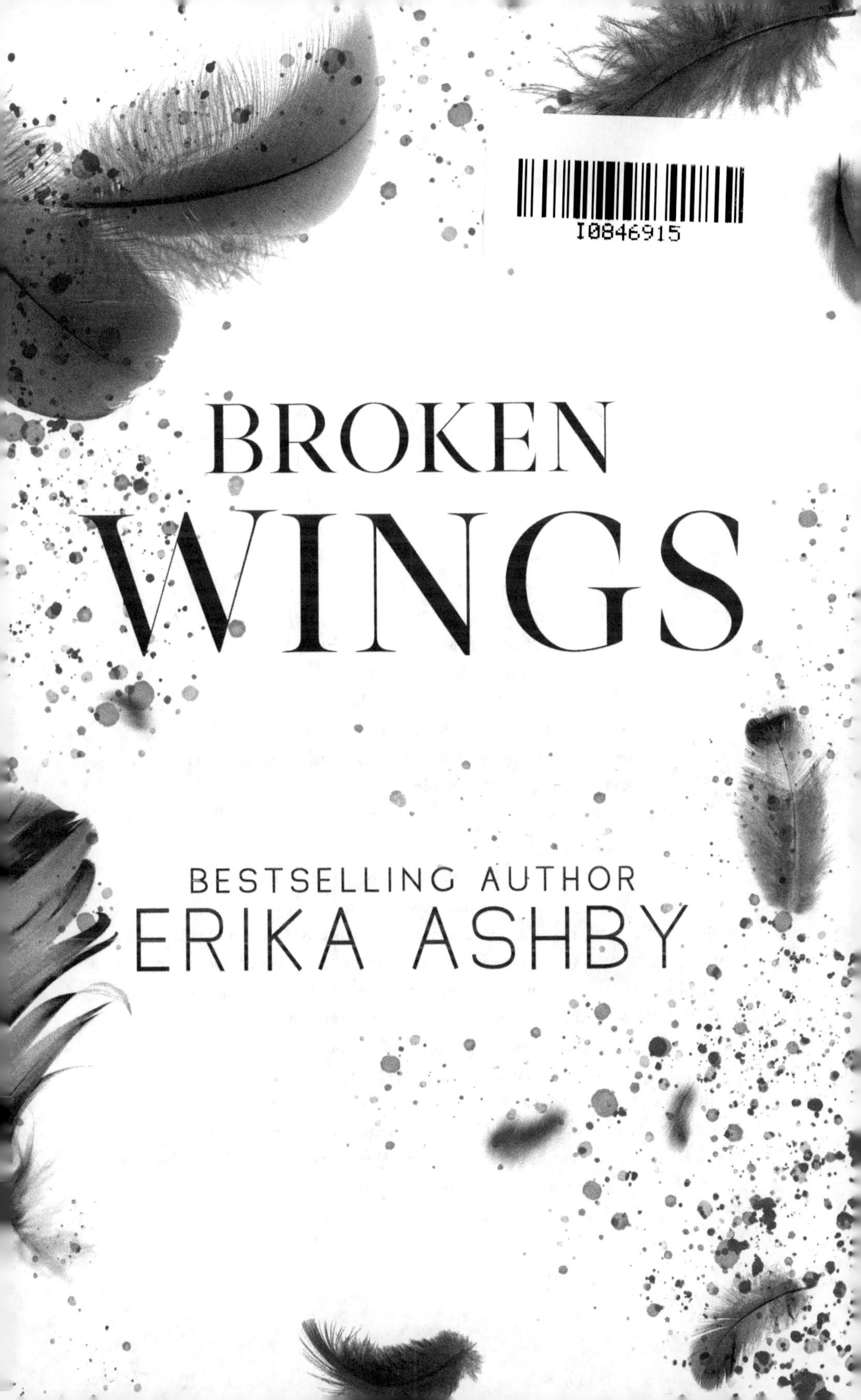

I0846915
BROKEN
WINGS
BESTSELLING AUTHOR
ERIKA ASHBY

Broken Wings:10th Anniversary Edition
Broken & Mended Series, Book 1
Copyright © 2024 Erika Ashby
Stock Image by Adobe Stock
Cover Design by Sommer Stein at Perfect Pear Creative Covers
Interior Formatting by Devin McCain at Studio 5 Twenty-Five
Developmental Editing by Megan Hand at Story Girl Editing
Copy/Line Editing & Proofreading by Emily A. Lawrence at Lawrence Editing

ISBN: 979-8-9902492-0-2

A NOTE FROM ERIKA

Ten years ago, I wrote Broken Wings.

Ten years later, I still have the same fierce love for this novel and its characters.

Broken Wings is a military romance novel. If you're triggered by tragedy surrounding the military and/or you're not into stories that rip your heart to shreds and then slowly piece it back together... the Broken & Mended series isn't for you.

Despite many words being deleted from the original edition, this 10th Anniversary Edition has been updated with a prologue and extended scenes.

As always, thank you for taking a chance on this book that holds so much meaning to me. Make sure to check out the acknowledgements for the backstory.

"When once you have tasted flight,
you will forever walk the Earth
with your eyes turned skyward,
for there you have been and there
you will always long to return."
—Leonardo da Vinci

*...to all aviation crew members that have
and will make the ultimate sacrifice
while doing something they love.*

Prologue

LINCOLN

SUMMER 2007

"Dude, this sucks." I sigh, plopping down on Dax's bed. Two years of fixed-wing pilot training together and my best friend is getting assigned to another base, states away.

"Such is life, man," he replies, seemingly unbothered, but I know better.

"Glad you're just as heartbroken as me," I mutter, and he drills me clean in the face with a balled-up T-shirt. The force of the blow catches me off guard, and I fall back on his bed. Like a ninja, I roll to my side, retrieving the dirty laundry, and sling it back, missing Dax as it makes a thud hitting the wall behind him. "Lucky throw on your part."

"Yeah, that's exactly what it was." He snorts.

"God, I'm gonna miss you. You're like my yang." I place my hand over my heart, clenching it into a fist. "You keep me balanced and from losing my shit. How am I going to keep from losing it without

1

you?" I'm being slightly dramatic, but moments like these call for such antics.

"I have a feeling you'll manage just fine." His words are reassuring as always.

"But what about you? How are you going to survive without meeee?" I drag the last word out with a high pitch.

Dax zips his suitcase shut, sits down beside me, and lets out the longest sigh I've ever heard.

"Tell me how you really feel." I cross my legs and pretend to doodle on a notepad, putting my imaginary shrink hat on.

He shakes his head, laughing, and pushes my shoulder...hard.

"Hey, you made me drop my notebook." I bend over, acting like I'm picking it up, and he pushes me all the way off the bed.

"There you go." He laughs. "Maybe you can find it better down there."

I quickly jump up onto the bed and pull out one of our famous wrestling moves from our childhood, putting him in a chokehold from behind.

"Tell me you're going to miss me, too." His hands grab at my arms, but I refuse defeat. He will show weakness. "It's okay to be sad," I coo, gently patting the top of his head. He relaxes his body, and I take the chance to give him a good going-away noogie, dragging my knuckles back and forth quickly.

"You win. You win." He slaps his hand three times on the bed, and I release my hold.

I plop down beside him and expel the sigh I've been holding. "In all seriousness, I am going to miss you. We've been inseparable our entire lives, and now it's our passion pulling us apart."

"Yeah, I think we've been in denial about the inevitable." He shrugs. "But I think it'll be good for us. Maybe the distance will bring growth and give us the ability to fully spread our wings."

"Tell me more, oh knowledgeable one." I laugh.

He glances down at his watch and stands. "Time for me to hit the road."

"Yeah, I know." I push myself off the bed, standing beside Dax. I tilt my head back, looking up at him as he towers over me. It's not by much, but he's always felt like a giant in comparison. He's got his normal Dax façade in place, and I can tell this isn't as easy for him as he's making it out to be. He has a girlfriend back home whom he's refused to let go of, and I get the impression this transition will also greatly interfere with that. The realization makes me feel like an ass for being so selfish.

"Dax, I'm sorry," I admit, placing a hand on his shoulder and gripping it tightly.

His hazel eyes finally connect with mine. "For what?" He raises a brow in confusion. Normally, I'd take this time to make a condescending joke, but I've done enough of that already.

"I've been thinking about how much this is going to suck for me. Haven't really considered everything you're giving up in the process, as well. And I'm not referring to me." I smirk. "How does this move affect things with Amber?" I usually don't like discussing his girlfriend because I don't particularly care for her. It's not because she's any sort of threat to our friendship. He just seems to have blinders on when it comes to her, and I can't figure out why. But he's my best friend, and just because I've avoided love to focus on my career, I can't hold his lack of abstaining over his head.

His shoulders slump, and he lets out an exasperated sigh, running his hand through his hair.

"Do I need to get my notebook back out?" I raise my brow.

He laughs and shakes his head, then looks away as if he's trying to piece together an acceptable answer. When his gaze meets mine, indecisiveness heavily weighs him down. "Honestly, I don't know. I'm supposed to stop by her apartment on my way to see my parents before continuing my trek up the coast."

I nod and offer a smile as some sort of reassurance. "It'll all work itself out the way it's supposed to. I have faith."

"Thanks, man." Dax pulls me in for a hug. "I'm going to miss you too, Lincoln."

He finally releases the words I've been trying to pull out of him. Victory is mine!

* * *

I THROW MY flight suit on, eager to get a head start on making a good first impression and personally introduce myself to my new commanding officer. On my way to the front door, I stop to take in the silence that surrounds me. I know it's temporary, but I already feel lonely.

"Suck it up, buttercup," I mumble, using the words I know Dax would say. He's right. This is an opportunity for each of us to fully immerse ourselves in our careers without our friendship possibly holding us back. I shut the door behind me, deciding not to be sad and lame, but to make the best of the situation.

The sun beats down on me as I walk to my truck. Almost as if it's a laser and I'm its target. I rest my hand around my door handle and lean my head back, reveling in the heat and letting it recharge me. *Here's to new beginnings.*

I make the short drive from the barracks to the hangar I will be reporting to daily. As I turn onto the mass of concrete sprawled out in front of me that leads to the enormous metal building, an over-whelming sense of emotion hits me. This is it. This is what I've dreamed of ever since I was a little boy. I'm a pilot—an aviation warrant officer. Life can't get any better than this.

I park my truck and walk in through the massive, lifted doors where mechanics work on a couple planes. These men and women are the true heroes. They work behind the scenes, making sure us pilots are operating safe flying apparatuses. I nod at those I pass, making my way to the offices on the adjacent wall. A nameplate reading Maj. Clark marks the third door down the corridor. Light shines through the half-cracked door and voices spill out as I inch closer.

A familiar voice says, "I think working at the salon in the PX will be a great start."

I can't help but wonder who Major Clark is talking to. Curiosity gets the best of me as I sidle up to the door.

A female voice replies, "Me too, Dad."

The conversation seems to be coming to an end, and I take the opportunity to knock, stepping into the doorway. Major Clark's eyes dart in my direction from behind his desk, and the brunette keeps her back to me.

"Sir." I clear my throat. "I hope this isn't bad timing."

He shifts his gaze from me to his daughter, then back to me.

"Not at all," the female says, standing. "I was just leaving." She glances over her shoulder at me and smiles. She rounds his desk and bends over, giving him a hug, then kisses his forehead. "Bye, Dad. I love you."

"Bye, honey. I'll see you at dinner."

I try not to keep my eyes trained on her, but I can't peel them off of her for the life of me as her petite stature saunters toward the doorway I'm standing in. She stops in front of me and glances down at my badge. Her green eyes slowly rise back to mine, and a smile tugs at the corner of her mouth.

"Fox." She drags the three-letter word through her pouty lips as if she's practicing it as her last name.

"Yes, ma'am." I smile with a nod. "Lincoln Fox." I stick my hand out, and she quickly accepts the gesture.

"Lynsie Clark." She smiles back.

The scraping of a chair jerks our heads toward her dad's desk as he stands. "Officer Fox, I've heard a lot about you." His tone is even.

"Sir, all good things, I hope." I chance a peek at Lynsie. She looks up and smiles, and I realize I have her blocked in. I shift to the left, offering her the space she needs to leave, and she mouths 'good luck' before walking past me out the door.

I straighten my stance and give my full attention to my commanding officer. I'm convinced I've just blown that good first impression I was after. Major Clark takes a few steps toward me, then crosses his arms and leans against the edge of his desk.

"Yes, all good things."

Redemption swarms within me. Maybe I haven't ruined it, after all.

"And how about we keep it that way?" he warns, raising a brow, and I don't have to ask what he's referring to.

I gulp. "Yes, sir." Clearly, his daughter is off-limits. Which is a shame since my career indicates that I like to push them.

Chapter One

LYNSIE

SUMMER 2013

"Dax," I yell as I lean back, peeking my head out the open bathroom door. "Now seriously, what was wrong with Tiffany?" I question, watching the back of his dirty-blond head from the upstairs bathroom that's directly centered with the couch. He better have a good excuse.

He won't.

He never does.

Dax shrugs, nonchalantly replying, "Her hair was too blond." He snickers, shoulders lightly bouncing up and down, always knowing how to rile me up.

I inhale sharply before marching downstairs. "Dax Lance Adams! That's your lamest excuse yet." I huff and drop next to him on the couch.

He tilts his head, scratching his jaw. "You sure about that, Lyns?" His left brow rises to a perfect arch, amplifying his doubt in my statement.

I sharpen my stare as he tries to suppress his amusement.

"Fine. You're right." I toss my head back against the couch. "You're like the King of Lame Excuses."

"I always knew I was royalty," he declares confidently. I half expect him to be eyeing himself in a mirror.

"Oh Lord," I mumble, rolling my eyes. "Seriously, though. I could rewrite 'Mambo Number 5', replacing it with each girl and your excuses."

Dax begins swaying back and forth, bumping into me as he does. He belts out his own rendition, patting the beat of the song on his thighs.

"A little bit of Amy with trust issues.
A little bit of Crystal who was Cuckoo.
A little bit of Jennifer who had big feet.
And a little bit of Tiffany with fluorescent hair."

He looks at me with his arms out and shrugs before continuing his song and dance.

"DJ Dax is in the hizz-house." I cup my hands around my mouth and yell, and then mimic the motion of a DJ scratching a record.

He shakes his head and laughs.

I lean up and angle my body toward him. "But in all seriousness," I say, my face void of emotion. "I now see why you're single."

"Hey now." He holds his hands up in defense. "You heard the song. I'm not the problem."

I shake my head, replaying his dating anthem debut in my mind. A grin tugs at the corner of my lips, and I suppress the laugh I've been holding. "I'm impressed you remember their names," I admit, slapping his leg.

"Hey, get your own drum." Teasing, he pushes my hand away. "And yes, I have a fantastic memory," he says matter-of-factly.

"I know. I know. You're like the boy from *Jerry Maguire*." I quietly acknowledge, still feeling a bit defeated in my matchmaking attempts.

A flash of humor crosses his face. "Don't go getting your panties in a wad about Tiffany. It only bothers you because you're the one who turned her head into a hundred-watt light bulb." Dax reassuringly pats my leg.

"Shut up." I playfully backhand his chest before I stand up, facing him. "Her hair is fine. You're the problem. You don't like anyone I try to fix you up with." I cross my arms, quietly studying Dax as he now intently watches TV.

From the side, his face goes serious momentarily before he shakes his head. "I disagree. When I find the perfect girl, she'll have no flaws. She'll be everything." He turns his gaze toward me, a dreamy look in his bright hazel eyes.

"Now that's where you're wrong, my dear." I ruffle his hair. "We all have flaws."

"I'm not so sure about that." He wickedly smiles and winks. "I'm pretty flawless. If I do say so myself."

"Well, that cast around your hand would say your basketball skills are lacking." I motion to his broken hand.

"Don't remind me," he mumbles.

"Maybe next time when the younger guys ask you to play, you'll say no," I offer.

"Age is just a number. The punk tripped me." Irritation fills his face.

"You ain't no spring chicken anymore, Dax," I tease.

He scoffs. "And I ain't no wrinkly rooster, Lyns." His Southern drawl is evident. "But yeah, I'm paying the price. I'd be with Lincoln, practicing for the air show, if I hadn't broken it."

"Well, lucky for you, I'm heading to work. So you don't have to suffer more than you already are."

"You know it's not even like that, Lynsie." He pauses the TV, focusing his full attention on me. "I'm a third wheel living here. I'm just trying to find a life outside of you and Lincoln. I'm up y'all's butts enough."

"Aw, we like you up our butts, Dax." We both laugh, and I clarify. "You know what I mean. We all agreed on you moving in with us when you got stationed here. There is no reason you should live on your own when we always hang out. You're family."

"Thanks, Lyns. You know I feel the same." He lets out an exasperated sigh. "I'm just really pissed at myself for ruining my chance to fly in the show. My cast literally comes off the week after." He laughs. "The timing is impeccable."

"I know you're bummed, Dax. Lincoln would much rather have you flying than Peterson," I joke, trying to make him feel better.

"That's for sure." He laughs, shaking his head. "I'm slowly coming to terms with it and telling myself I'm just not meant to do it this year." He shrugs, and I drop it.

AFTER I CHANGE, I jog back downstairs. Dax jumps off the couch clapping, hooting, and hollering at the TV. *Boys and their sports. I swear.*

I sigh, heading into the kitchen to grab my purse and keys.

He looks over at me, sitting back down as he jokingly whistles. "Hot date, Lyns?"

"Yeah, hoping to find you one." I stick my tongue out at him.

He groans, sinking back into the couch. "Lucky me," he mumbles.

I walk up behind him and prop my elbows on the back of the couch. "So while I'm at work today, what type should I be looking for?" I ask with determination.

Dax sighs and shifts uncomfortably. "Lynsie, you aren't gonna find her." He looks back with a pained stare that only makes me want to help even more. "Just let it be."

Chapter Two

LYNSIE

It's after 8:00 p.m. when I walk through the door, and I'm ready to pass out. Lincoln is lying on the couch, engrossed in some show. I take a moment to admire him. He stretches out, and I bite my lip as his shirt moves up his tanned torso. I quickly lock the door behind me, kick off my sandals, and stride over to him. I snuggle my way under his arm, lying sideways for him to spoon me.

"How was work?" He nuzzles his nose against my neck, kissing my sensitive skin.

"It was go-od," I stutter, melting into him. "How was your day?"

He drapes his arm around my hips, pulling me in tighter against him. "It wasn't bad. We're training for the Fourth of July show, so it's been a bit tedious. The extra hours we're having to put in anyways."

"Yeah, Dax seems pretty bummed about it."

"Bummed is putting it lightly." Lincoln snorts.

"Speaking of Dax, where's he at? I swear if he's trying to be a baller with a broken hand, I'm going to personally break his good one."

"Easy, killer." Lincoln laughs, tickling my side, causing me to giggle and squirm.

"Abort. Abort," I yell through laughs, and his tickles cease.

"I just love watching both of you do what you love. Just like in the *Pearl Harbor* movie." I laugh under my breath, knowing he hates it when I compare him and Dax to the Affleck/Hartnett duo. *Right, no resemblance there at all.* Best friends, both pilots, but that's where the similarities end.

"Yeah." He yawns. "He's pissed."

"We talked about it some earlier today. It explains him seeming off lately."

"That would be why. Not because he hasn't found Mrs. Right yet." He chuckles.

"She's out there," I mumble.

Lincoln's hand stills on my hip. "Babe"—he sighs—"give the love connection a rest for a bit."

"I'll try." I turn and wrap my arms around him, placing a kiss on his lips. Sometimes I can't help but get lost staring at my husband. I take in his features—from his deep brown eyes that always seem to soften at the sight of me, to his small cleft in the tip of his chin my lips always tend to gravitate to. His dark hair is thick and just the right length for me to wrap my fingers in and tug. And his face...his face is always smooth, just the way I like it.

"I know you're protective of him, but the only balling he's doing tonight is watching a game with the guys."

"Well, why aren't you?" I question, rubbing my arm up and down his side. Lincoln's hand tightens on my hip, pulling me into his body. His dark eyes hold my gaze before dropping to my lips.

"Because I wanted to spend the night with my wife," he admits, inching his mouth closer to mine.

He tells me all the time that he's the lucky one, but he's so wrong. It's me. I'm the lucky one.

Holding my chin, he trails his thumb back and forth across my cheek as we take each other in. "I hit a grand slam when I found you," he breathes against my lips before placing a kiss. "Let's go to bed."

I WAKE WITH a sense of urgency as I jump out of our empty bed, nearly tripping over the blanket. The sun is beaming brightly in our empty bedroom, and I hear the shower running. I feel like the rabbit from *Alice in Wonderland*. Quickly, I grab my phone from the nightstand and push the button to illuminate the screen.

"Crap!" Stripping my pajama tank and shorts, I almost trip over myself as I rush into the bathroom. I push back the curtain, startling Lincoln as I scoot into the shower in front of him.

His eyes widen. "Easy there, beauty." He smirks while scanning my naked body. He must be under the assumption that I'm eager for round two this morning.

I would be if I wasn't already late for work. I look down and gulp, seeing how ready he is for me. "Sorry there, cowboy." I squeeze some bodywash on my loofa and quickly scrub my body neck down. "But there won't be any rodeo this morning." I bite my lip, turning my back to him before I give in to what my body wants. "I'm so late." *I'm never late.*

"I must have worn you out last night." I hear the cocky tone in his voice.

I rinse off, turn back around, reach up, and place a swift kiss on his lips. "Yeah, something like that." I yank the curtain open and grab a towel.

Getting dressed in record time, I then sit on the edge of the bed to slip my tennis shoes on. They'll be more comfortable than my sandals from hell I wore yesterday. Lincoln walks out of the steam-filled bathroom. He's adorned in nothing but a tightly wrapped towel around his waist, outlining all of his delicious contours, leaving nothing to the imagination. He runs a hand through his hair, giving it a wet, messy look. My eyes take their time—*time I don't have*—raking over his wet body. He struts his way over, standing right in front of me as if I need a better view.

I swallow hard.

"Just one more ride?" He wiggles his eyebrows at me. I bite my lip, teasing it between my teeth. I'm tempted. I really am, but... He thrusts his pelvis. "I promise I won't *buck* you off."

I giggle, shaking my head.

He takes my dismissal in stride, his hand lingering where his towel is secured, and I know he's about to drop it to reveal all his hard glory. I stand up, placing my shaky hand over his. This husband of mine is making it dang near impossible for me to resist him.

The thought of ripping that towel off for him flashes by, but I quickly regain control of my disobedient mind. "No!" I tightly close my eyes, causing him to laugh.

With both hands, he grips the sides of my face and pulls me in for a kiss. His soft lips move perfectly against mine. The kiss is slow and sweet. Total opposite of what it'd be like if I had time to let him take me right now. I let it last longer than it should. Self-control is something I've lacked since I met him.

I pull back and look deep into his desire-filled eyes. "Be prepared. There will be plenty of *bucking* going on tonight."

I shimmy past him, but he grabs my hand, whirling me back around. "At least let me take you to lunch. I never get to anymore, and I actually get a break today." He rubs his hands up and down my arms.

Think, Lynsie. You're still capable of it with him touching you.

I smile at him, pushing up on my toes so we're eye to eye. "I should be free. I'll let you know. I love you." I kiss him once more and rush out before I end up calling in.

"I'M SO SORRY for running late, Miss Shirley." I rush in the door.

She looks up, bright-eyed, and gives me her always polite smile. "Now, sugar"—her Southern twang is evident—"you know it doesn't bother me a bit. I ain't got no better plans than seein' your pretty face." She waves over my worry with her dainty hand.

Whew! "So...are we just doing the usual today?" I ask as she takes a seat and I wrap my apron around my waist.

She fluffs her loose, white curls. "Yes. Just like my step needs an extra spring in it, so do these curls of mine." Miss Shirley pulls her glasses off and places them in her purse. "I like to stick with what I know best now that I'm older."

"I can't wait for that day." I pull out my drawer full of rollers. "I'm always trying new things." I lift a section of my hair, revealing the chunk of dark blue I had Echo put in last week. "I'm sure my hair will be happy when that happens. If I still have any by then. With all the abuse I put it through, I may go bald." I laugh.

"Now, honey, don't be wishing that life of yours away. It's far too precious." She grabs my hand, wrapping both of hers around it. "Just make sure you live this one like it's a gift, which it is." Her eyes pleading with mine, she holds my hand as tight as her dainty hands allow. "Live it to the fullest, no matter what comes your way."

I nod in response. Her eyes gloss over, packing more of a punch with her words—words that hold so much meaning. I can't even form a worthy reply.

After Miss Shirley is gone, I put the curlers up and check the rest of my schedule for the day. I happen to have an open window around lunchtime, so I shoot Lincoln a text, letting him know.

I GRAB MY broom and dustpan and begin cleaning up the hair before I head to lunch. Gathering it all in one good pile, I bend over to sweep it up. A whistle from behind startles me, causing me to drop the dustpan filled with hair. The plastic slaps the ground and hair scatters all around me. I grab the dustpan and stand up straight. I have the strongest urge to fling it at the culprit.

Lincoln's chocolate eyes stop me while his shoulders shake with laughter.

"*Ass!*" I swing the broom at him. He jumps back and I miss. Barely. "You startled me."

He cocks a brow as he approaches. "I wouldn't think a whistle would be scary." He grabs the broom from my hand and quickly sweeps back up the mess he caused.

I look around the salon, then back at my husband, who is now bent over. My eyes stay focused on his backside longer than they should. I have no control over them. I blame it on the sage green flight suit he's wearing, but I know I'd stare even if he were wearing a space suit.

He tosses the hair, then pulls me into him and places a kiss on my forehead. "I'm sorry I startled you. Where would you like to eat?"

"Anywhere." I give him one tight squeeze before releasing my hold on him. "Let's get out of here," I urge as my stomach starts to growl.

WE FIND A booth in the back of Lincoln's favorite burger joint and sit across from each other. I savor my fries, realizing I'm hungrier than I thought, while Lincoln unhinges his jaw to eat his burger.

"So what do you have going on the rest of the day?" I ask Lincoln between bites. I watch his mouth carefully as he takes a bite, licks his lip, and begins to chew. Something about his jawline and the way his mouth is working on that food has me mesmerized. I could watch this man eat all day.

With a mouthful of food, he still manages to pull off his sexy smirk. "Training. It's been a pain in my ass because we all have our normal jobs to get done, so we don't always get to train together. You'd think it'd be a simple formation that we just go over a couple times." He lets out a heavy sigh.

I reach across the table, covering his free hand with mine. "I can't wait to see it. I'm sure it'll be amazing." I smile proudly.

"Obviously. I'm always amazing." He winks, the frustration I saw no longer visible.

I smile and glance at the woman who just walked in. She's a gorgeous blonde, but it's not her amazing locks that capture my attention. It's the baby bump. The yearning mother inside of me is fixated on her perfectly rounded belly. She places her hand on her stomach, rubbing it lovingly, and jealousy instantly seeps in.

Lincoln follows my gaze, then groans once he notices what I'm staring at. Feeling his eyes on me, I pick at fries, refusing to look up. We've already discussed this. I know where he stands, and I respect it. I just don't know how much longer I can wait. I'm not getting any younger, my parents live here, and who knows how much longer we will even be stationed here. It'd be so much easier if it were to happen sooner rather than later.

Letting out a resigned sigh, I finally meet his gaze. He gives me a sympathetic look as he places his hand over mine on the table. "I know you want a baby, Lyns. And believe me, I want you to have my baby but not yet." His eyes plead with mine for understanding.

I nod, trying not to let my emotions get the best of me. "I know." I give him a genuine smile, though a little sadness slips in. "All in good time."

On our way back to the car, we pass Lincoln's favorite wood carving shop. He gets most of his wooden airplanes, helicopters, and basically any type of flying apparatus, short of UFOs, from this place. Full of excitement, he grabs my hand, pulling me over to the counter. The shop looks more like a pop-up booth you'd see set up at a carnival. The trailer is complete with wheels and a hitch, and I'm worried the owner will pack up one day, and I won't have another place to find my husband one-of-a-kind gifts. I stand, tucked under Lincoln's left arm as he uses the other to point out the new additions he's just itching to add to his ever-growing collection.

"This one is really cool." A lightness takes over Lincoln. "I love how the shades of the wood vary. It has this ripple effect." He not only admires the actual planes, but he also admires the woodwork and craft that goes into making them. I can't even begin to grasp the amount of time and precision it'd take to make. As Lincoln looks around in awe, I keep a careful eye on everything he picks up—which is almost every dang thing.

"I need to get back to work, babe." I urge, pulling him away from the wood shop empty-handed.

Lincoln gets me back across town in record time, pulling into the parking lot before my next client arrives. He wraps his hand around my neck and hauls me in for a goodbye kiss. I'm left breathless when he pulls away. "Love you to the sky and back, Lynsie Pearl."

I purse my lips. "You know, technically, the sky isn't that far away."

"Are you questioning the depth of my love?" he asks, throwing his hand over his heart like I just physically wounded him. "Who's to say how far away the sky really is? No matter how many times you were to travel back and forth, there'd be no way to cover every single inch of it. Just like counting every single grain of sand; it's impossible. There is so much blue up there, it puts the moon to shame." He stares out the window, eyes lifted toward the sky with awe spread across his face.

"Fine." I let out an exaggerated sigh. "Since you put it like that." I lean across the console, placing my lips against his. "I love you to the sky and back too, Lincoln Shane."

Chapter Three

LYNSIE

I sit in my chair, resting my feet and arms before I clean up and head home.

"Man, that lady had some hair." Echo glances over at me, wide-eyed.

I nod and laugh. "Yeah, it's just as heavy as it looks."

"It really could be a horse's tail." She flips another page in her book. "But softer," she adds.

The bell on the front door jangles and both our heads snap toward it.

Dax pulls his sunglasses off, tips his chin up, and takes long strides toward me. Echo's eyes are now focused on Dax. I can't place her expression as she eyes him suspiciously.

"Hey, Lyns." He leans his hip against the counter. "Any way you can squeeze me in?" He glances around, taking notice of the lack of customers.

I jump out of my chair and stand on my tippy-toes. I inspect his hair, brushing my fingers through it. Dax is at least a head taller than me, unlike Lincoln, who is half that.

"Has it even grown since your last cut?" I tease, ruffling my hand through it. He gives me a sheepish grin as I motion for him to sit. "Are you off early, or late lunch?" I ask, securing the apron around his neck.

"Late lunch. Connelly and I had to fly to Hunter Army Airfield this morning."

"Connelly's the super tall redhead, right?" I place my foot on the bar under the seat, giving it a few pumps as I adjust the height. Dax sinks back into the chair just enough to get comfortable without slouching.

"That's him," Dax replies.

"I've heard Savannah is gorgeous." I turn my clippers on, taking a smidgen off around the sides.

"It is. You know, growing up, Lincoln and I only lived about an hour away, right?"

I meet his gaze in the mirror, ready to reply, when a sudden noise jerks our attention toward Echo.

She appears nervous when she sits back up from where she was bent over. "Sorry." She waves her phone. "I'm so clumsy. I really need to get one of those cases for it. I'm going to end up breaking this one like I did the last three." She grabs her purse off the counter. "Gotta go pick Dylan up. See ya tomorrow, girl."

"Kay." Stunned, I watch her rush out the back door. It slams with a loud thud.

"That was awkward," I think out loud.

"Slightly," Dax replies, pulling me out of my thoughts.

I grab my scissors and start trimming the top of Dax's hair. I pull his soft hair between my fingers, blending it into the sides, and catch him watching me intently.

I smile at his reflection. "What?" I grab my comb, checking his hair one last time.

He shrugs. "I just like watching you. You make all these different faces while you're cutting my hair."

I cover my mouth with the back of my hand and let out an embarrassed laugh. "Oh God. I bet I look funny."

"Nah. Even when you look funny, you're still beautiful."

I stand silent for a moment, not sure how to respond.

My phone rings, followed by Dax's.

My father never calls when he's at work. Lincoln is training today and suddenly my insides twist into a knot.

"What's wrong, Dad?" I answer my phone, concern evident in my voice.

"Lynsie, I know you're at work, but I'm glad you answered." His soothing voice instantly eases my worry. I glance back over at Dax, who is now standing near the glass entrance, pacing back and forth on the phone.

"You're at work too, and you wouldn't call me unless something was wrong. Is it Lincoln? Is everything okay?"

Dax's eyes dart to me.

"Yes, Lincoln is fine." My father continues, "It's Travis Robinson." I know the name. I met Travis. He was at our wedding. Dax now stands in front of me and I take in the sadness evident in his features. He just received the same news. Because he also knew Travis. My dad continues, "He died today." The line goes silent momentarily.

I gasp, throwing my hand over my mouth. My stomach drops.

"He's been doing Recon training in Texas this past month, and something went horribly wrong during a normal routine." He sighs. "Anyway, I'm calling you because I know he and Lincoln were close... as close as you can get with one of your fellow pilots with all the moving around. I just want you to be prepared when he gets home this afternoon. I haven't told him yet but will as soon as he lands. He's going to need you, Lyns," my dad solemnly explains.

The heavy sadness in his voice reminds me of the time when I was younger and my father lost one of his dear friends. The risks that come with this job have never been a secret, but he'd always say, "Shit happens. You can't live your life in fear." I guess that's the truth, but sometimes I wonder why people purposely put themselves in dangerous situations, where the probability of something horrible taking place outweighs the likelihood it won't.

"Is it still hard for you?" I ask, wondering if after ten years, the death of a friend gets any easier to deal with.

"It doesn't hurt as bad, if that's what you mean." He exhales. "But every time I'm up in the sky, I think about him and everyone I've known who has died doing what we love."

It's times like these that make me frightened of my husband's job. Typically, the only time fear rises in us Army spouses is when the threat of war or being sent overseas arises, but that's not the case. Death could easily be creeping its way up our doorstep. It could be hanging out in our backyard, just waiting for the most unexpected time to strike.

I shake my head of that looming fear playing with my mind and pull my act together. My husband is going to need a supportive wife at his side—not a weak, scared one, who wants to second-guess his passion in life.

"Thanks, Dad. Thanks for the heads-up. I'm going to finish cleaning up so I can make sure I'm home before Lincoln gets there. Do you have any advice for me? Is there anything that could make him feel better?"

"Nothing can ever lighten this kind of blow, but you can listen. He'll most likely ramble. Bring up memories and reminisce about the times they had together. All you can do is share the moments with him. Laugh when he's laughing. Cry when he's crying. Be strong for him. We all handle these things differently. There's no right or wrong way. No direction manual for how to approach it. Consoling words don't tend to help. Keep that in mind."

I look up at Dax, who stands, nervously biting at his thumbnail. He's in a daze, and I can't even imagine where his mind is right now.

"Oh, Dax," I say, grabbing his hand.

Dax pulls me into his chest as my tears spill over. His body shakes against mine, and I know this one hit too close to home. It makes the risks my husband, father, and Dax face every day more real.

I MAKE MY way home in a bit of a daze. I've never had to console anyone before. What if I suck at it? Then I remember my dad's words. Still, I have no clue what I really need to do.

In our living room, I pace back and forth in front of the couch as I wait for Lincoln. I tried folding the laundry. I even attempted to scrub the lasagna pan from last night, but nothing is calming me down. I'm completely useless and nervous as I wait for the sound of Lincoln's truck to pull up. I'm worried. Worried I won't be able to comfort my husband.

The front door slowly creeps open, and instinct kicks away all worry and doubt as I walk up to Lincoln. His head hangs low, and I notice a redness in his eyes I've never seen before. I throw my arms around him, embracing him. I don't know what he needs, but right now, I just want to hold him. To let him know I'm here for him, without words.

With one hand pressed against my back and the other one on the back of my head, Lincoln holds me tightly against him. I feel slight trembles as this strong man of mine lets out silent tears. If I hadn't felt them, along with the movement of his body, I would've never known. I've never seen this kind of sadness in him until this very moment.

Pressing both hands against my temples, he holds my head in his hands and places a kiss on my forehead. I rest my hands on his forearms as we just stand in silence.

"I've never lost anyone I cared about before." His voice cracks. "I know it sounds stupid, but the idea never crossed my mind. We all know the risks, but...it just doesn't happen to someone you know." He swallows hard.

"I'm so sorry, baby. Whatever you need, I'll do it," I whisper, hoping there's something, anything, I can do for him.

Lincoln's brows draw together as he lightly shakes his head. Agony etches itself across his face. "I love you so damn much, Lynsie. When your dad told me, I was in shock, but as crazy as it sounds, my first thoughts were of you." He slides his hands down, cupping my face in his palms. "If anything ever happened to you"—he shakes his head as tears continue to stream down his face—"I don't know what I'd do."

I can't help my tears. The man, who is so good at keeping himself composed, is breaking my heart. "I'm not going anywhere," I reassure him.

He shakes his head. "There's no way to ever know, Lyns, but what I do know is that we have to live every moment we have as if it's our last. Losing someone just makes you put what's important into perspective."

A sensation of intense sickness and heartbreak sweeps over me. I can't even fathom losing Lincoln.

"I'd lose my way if anything ever happened to you. I'm not sure I'd survive." My breathing catches at the thought, and I drop my head.

"Hey, hey, hey," he says soothingly, using his finger under my chin to lift my face to his warm eyes. "As long as it's in my power, that's something you will never have to experience."

I let out a heavy breath. "I know, but you can't control everything. Look what just happened."

"You're right." He swallows hard. "But that's like anything in life. Shit happens and sometimes we don't have a choice in the matter."

He's starting to sound like my dad.

"I'm so sorry about your friend," I stammer. "Listen to me getting all selfish worrying about the what-ifs instead of being thoughtful."

"Don't apologize. I get it." He gives me a weak smile as a few more tears fall down his face.

We never think about these things until something forces us to deal with reality.

"What do you need from me? What can I do?" I search his eyes for the answer within their depths.

He shakes his head as he chokes back the cry beckoning its way out. "Nothing. I just need to be alone for a little bit."

I quickly drop my lashes to mask the hurt. I don't want him to be alone right now, but if it's what he needs, I won't question it.

"Sure." I reluctantly nod. "But if you need me for anything, you come get me, okay?"

He nods, placing one last kiss on my forehead before he heads up the stairs. I stand still as he goes up and turns left. The door at the end of the hall opens and shuts. His office. I guess being surrounded by his Army stuff in his normal place of solitude is what's going to comfort him.

My phone chimes, lighting up on the counter. I slowly walk over, not expecting to make it in time. But as soon as the last ring ends, the phone instantly starts buzzing again. Someone is persistent. I see the name across the screen and should have known it was him.

"Hey, Dax," I say, letting out a heavy breath.

"How is he?" Dax asks, his voice full of concern.

I will always be grateful for Dax. He's the most caring and loyal person to have on your side. Lincoln made out big time growing up with him. Maybe one day, I'll be able to have something like what the two of them share.

"He's in his office right now." I'm not sure what else to say. Dax knows him better. I'm sure he knows exactly how he's doing.

He sighs heavily. "Okay. Well, don't let him hang in there for too long, all right?"

"Why not? Is it bad?" I start to get nervous, wondering if I made the wrong decision by letting him shut himself in there.

"No. It's something he needs to do. I just don't want him to be alone, digging up and revisiting all the memories. He doesn't need to wallow in it."

"But what about you, Dax? What do you need?" I question through my sniffles.

Silence fills the line before he finally lets out a heavy sigh. "I'm fine."

"You don't need to be dealing with this alone, either. You should be here with him. You'd know what to do better than me." I cry.

"He needs you right now."

"I want to believe that, Dax. I really do, but..." I shake my head, feeling helpless.

Dax breaks the silence. "Just go check on him in a little while, okay?"

"I will." I nod, mostly to convince myself I can do it. "Thank you, Dax."

"Anytime, Lyns. I love him, too."

Chapter Four

LYNSIE

Thirty minutes later, I slowly creep upstairs.

I hear nothing but silence as I make my way toward the only closed door in the house. I take a few deep breaths, trying to talk myself into knocking. I'm having an inner battle. I don't want to bother him, but Dax's words keep playing over and over in my head.

I place my fist against the cool door before lightly tapping two quick times. No reply. I move my hand down to the doorknob, twisting it as I slowly push the door open. Lincoln is kneeling with his back toward me, facing the closet. A box is sitting open in front of him. All sorts of pictures, awards, newspaper clippings, and medals are scattered around him as he picks through the box. His chest quickly rises and falls as if he's crying, but there is no sound to accompany his grief. Heaviness centers itself in my chest.

Wanting to give him his space, I slowly start to back out when he says, "Did you know Travis is the only person I've ever heard of to receive the Broken Wing Award?" He lets out a laugh as if he just pictured a funny memory about his friend.

I stop and rest my hand on the doorway. It's taking every fiber within me not to move in from behind and wrap my arms around him. "I've actually never heard of that award before." As long as I've been around pilots, you'd think it's something I'd be familiar with.

"It's actually a pretty cool award." Lincoln turns his head back to me and my heart falls at the sight of his tear-streaked face. I'm not sure he wants my company, but it doesn't feel right to leave him like this. I make my way over to him, careful not to step on any of the items scattered about, and sit off to the side. I want him to have enough room to go through his things, but I want him to know that I'm here and whatever he needs to share, I'll listen.

"The award"—he picks up a newspaper clipping—"is only given out to one pilot yearly. It's basically when shit goes bad while you're flying...like really bad, and the pilot is still able to safely land the plane." He swallows hard, tears slowly streaking down his cheeks.

"When did Robinson get it?" I almost regret asking. The man just died in a plane crash. It's probably a touchy subject. But Lincoln's face lights up.

"He was flying a C-21 Learjet. The sky was clear, and everything was going smoothly. Then, out of nowhere, all control of his plane went out. He had nothing. No way to contact anyone or anything. So he pulled out his cell phone." Lincoln snickers. "He was able to call the control tower and tell them what was wrong, and he managed to fully land the plane."

He hands me the picture of Travis, Dax, and him. They look so young. Just like I remember from when I first met them all six years ago. "The three of you look happy in this picture." I hand it back to Lincoln, who stares at it one last time.

"We just graduated fixed-wing training and knew we were one step closer to our dreams. You can't help but be happy when it's your passion," Lincoln admits, making me feel like he's warning me that he never plans to quit flying. I'd never ask him to. I knew what I was getting myself into. I'll eventually get over the imminent fear in the days to come, once the freshness of this loss subsides, but it will always be a lingering thought.

"Do you think he was scared?" I blurt.

"I think the idea of dying scares everyone no matter how it happens."

I shudder at his reply.

"But do I think he would've rather died any other way? Nah. Something Travis always said was *'If I ever die flying, don't be sad because you know I died doing what I love and that should put a smile on your face'.*"

I scrunch my face at the thought. "I'm not sure that would put a smile on my face. I get that he wants his loved ones to take comfort in his death, but death is death. It's still sad and will be a huge adjustment for his family to move past. I'm not trying to be insensitive, but it's just hard for me to accept that anything about death could make me smile."

"You're right about that," he says in defeat, grabbing the stuff sitting around him and placing it back in the box.

I wonder what's in store for us next, hoping I didn't upset him by asking questions that were still too fresh. He stands up, bends down to grab the box, and sets it back up on the top shelf of the closet. There's a somber look on his face when he turns to me. I give him a weak smile. He reaches his hand out, and I place mine in his and he pulls me up.

"How about we take a bath?" he asks, looking completely drained.

I HAVE SO many thoughts swirling around. I'm sure Lincoln does, too. Sitting in this steamy bath with my back against his chest, I can't help the places my mind takes me. They bounce from worry to compassion, patience to anxiousness to confusion—I can't keep my mind still. I should be focused on consoling my husband, not going from being fearful for him to feeling maybe we should live life to the fullest since tomorrows are not guaranteed.

"What happened is bad enough, but knowing he left a wife and two small children makes it harder to wrap my mind around." He lets out a heavy breath, and my body moves in sync with his.

I swallow hard, hot tears streaming down my cheeks. "I can't even imagine what she must be going through." I link our hands together, crossing our arms over my chest. I want to be so close to him that I never have to worry about losing him. I need to shake these thoughts that are trying to consume me. I don't want to resent his passion or fear his career.

"You know I'm not going anywhere, right?" he whispers near my ear. "As long as it's in my power, I'm never leaving your side."

"But that's the thing that scares me, Linc." I take a breath, trying to steady my shaky voice. "It's inevitable."

"I know." His shoulders slump in defeat as he realizes nothing can be said. There are no guarantees. "But it's all part of life. I mean, people die all the time. All sorts of professions are dangerous. Hell, driving is dangerous. Sometimes shit just happens and there's no explanation for it, but all I know is that my friend died doing what he loved. That's got to count for something in my book."

Maybe he's telling me without outright saying it that to him, it'd be the ultimate way to go, or Lincoln could just be trying to convince himself, grasping for something positive from something so devastating. Maybe, just maybe, believing his friend died at the mercy of his passion somehow makes him feel slightly better about the loss. Personally, I'm not sure that counts. I'd like to think that picking something safe and staying alive for your family by not putting your life in unnecessary harm would count.

Says the girl who married a pilot.

He's right, though. Who wouldn't want to die doing something they loved? Like Lincoln said, knowing the thing that caused their heart to skip an extra beat is also what caused it to stop has to count for something, right? Dying at the mercy of your passion would be the ultimate way to go. Unless you could die in your sleep. That's how I want to go out.

"There's only one thing guaranteed in life," I mumble through a sigh.

"And what's that?" Lincoln whispers near my ear.

"Death." I shudder.

"I love you so much, Lyns." He wraps his arms tightly around me and kisses my temple. "I can't say it enough. I don't want to ever miss a chance to tell you. I want you to always know how much you mean to me. Life is too short for regret." My strong husband's chest shakes and I can't help the reaction it stirs inside of me. My heart pounds in my chest and I let myself melt into him as my head falls back, resting on his shoulder. He's not pushing me away; he's pulling me in.

THE NEXT MORNING, I wake to Lincoln staring down at me while running his hand through my hair. I smile and run my knuckles lightly down his jawline. He grabs my hand, places a kiss on each knuckle, then links our fingers together.

"How'd you sleep?" I ask as I take in his puffy eyes.

"Not very well," he replies, his voice husky with sleep. "I kept waking up. Had a bunch of crazy dreams." He gives me a sheepish smile. "About an hour or so ago, I finally gave up and decided I'd rather spend my time memorizing everything I can about you."

"I'm surprised that alone didn't bore you back to sleep." I snort.

"Nothing about you could ever bore me. Especially watching you sleep and listening to all the little noises you make. It's something I should've done long ago." His face is alert and serious, matching his tone.

I turn my head, hiding my silly smile. "So what's the plan for today?" I ask.

He falls onto his back, squeezing his eyes shut. "I need to find out when the funeral is. I'm sure it'll be in his hometown in Florida. So we might need to start heading that way today or tomorrow."

"Okay, just let me know what I need to do," I say, snuggling up to his side.

"Just stay where you are," he breathes against my neck, his hands rubbing up and down my back.

"Have you talked to Dax?" I pull back, and his eyes flutter open. Concern mixes with his lack of sleep.

"No," he says, shaking his head. "I don't think he came home last night."

"Well, he was worried about you, so maybe you should check on him." I push, a sense of worry seeping in.

"Dax is Dax, Lyns." Lincoln's shoulders shrug before he tucks his head back in the crook of my neck. "We all deal with things differently."

"I know," I whisper, relaxing back into his strong arms.

But I can't help but wonder if it's because no one pushes him to deal with things differently. Lincoln has me, but who does Dax have?

Chapter Five

LYNSIE

A sense of dread and sorrow instantly hits me as we turn onto the single-lane gravel road of the cemetery.

Lincoln pulls behind the line of vehicles already here, bumper to bumper in this small-town graveyard. Death has a way of making people realize what's important without giving them a way to atone for it.

Total jokester.

It's unfair for it to happen that way. We have this grand idea that our lives are measured in years, instead of by the lives we touch or the purpose we serve. Who are we to say someone is taken too soon when it isn't our call to make?

I grab Lincoln's hand and give it a reassuring squeeze before we get out of the car. "I love you," I tell him softly.

He bends over, placing his lips against my cheek. "I love you too, baby."

"I love you, too." I twist in the seat and look back at Dax, who has been abnormally quiet the entire car ride. Shutting himself off might be how he deals with things, but I don't like it.

"Love you, Lyns." The side of his mouth quirks up, giving me a slight smile before it falls along with my heart, seeing how hard this is for Lincoln and Dax. We get out of the car, and they straighten their uniforms. After they inspect each other, Lincoln holds his arm out for me to grab and we make our way to the graveside.

The place is packed. So many people stand around, filling the outside space. We find seats near the back and sit. Well, Lincoln and I sit. Dax stands off to the side, watching from afar. The air is sticky and humid, courtesy of the rainstorm that passed through earlier this morning. A gut-wrenching sob near the casket grabs my attention. There, sitting in the very front, is a woman I can assume to be the widow. Two little children are tucked under each of her arms as her body shakes while she sobs. I put one hand to my mouth to stifle the sob forming. The sight of the little boy and girl cradled against their mother breaks the barrier I had in place. My heart tightens in my chest and tears slowly begin to roll down my face. I can't fathom needing to hold myself together for the sake of my children.

She didn't want this. She didn't want to hear her husband died in a plane crash. She didn't want to tell her kids Daddy won't be coming home. But she signed up for the possibility of it. Just like me.

Different people take turns standing in front of the casket, talking about their memories with Travis. Most of them make me smile, bringing a lightness to such a heavy day. Seeing what an impact he had on the people he met throughout life hopefully brings a sense of comfort to his loved ones.

I lean into Lincoln's side and whisper, "Are you going to say anything?"

He shakes his head, replying in a low, tormented voice, "I can't." I weave my arm through his and lean into him.

After the shots are fired and the flag is folded, people stand and start paying their respects to the family. I'm not sure how I'd handle people I didn't know coming up to give their sincere condolences when all I'd want to do is crawl into a hole myself.

We stand and Lincoln grabs my hand as we make our way up front. He doesn't say a word as we pass people with tear-streaked faces. I have no idea where exactly we're headed until I see the older couple sitting. They both instantly stand, recognition in their faces as we approach, and they muster as much of a genuine smile as they can.

"Wings!" the woman exclaims, placing her hands on each side of Lincoln's face before hugging him. The older gentleman gives me a smile and rests his hand on Lincoln's back, patting it as they form a three-person hug.

My husband pulls back and uses the back of his hand to wipe away his tears. "Mr. and Mrs. Robinson, this is Lynsie, my wife." He gently wraps his arm around my shoulders.

This isn't how I want to be introduced to anyone, but life doesn't always give us that choice.

Before I can say anything, Mrs. Robinson pulls me in for a warm hug. "It's so good to meet you, dear. You take good care of this one." She pulls back, and I nod in reply.

Lincoln chats for a moment longer, then tells them goodbye, and I follow suit with a subtle wave. I don't have the words to say right now. I just keep hearing my dad saying over and over, "Words won't help." My mouth seems to agree.

"Oh, Lincoln," I hear as we make our way to Robinson's widow. She turns to my husband, embracing him. They hold each other, both weeping, and I watch him attempt to comfort her by rubbing her back.

When they pull apart, I hear Lincoln telling her how sorry he is and wishing he would've talked to him more. Standing here, I almost feel like an intruder. I look down at her two small children sitting in the grass, playing rock, paper, scissors with each other. I take a little comfort knowing they're both too young to feel the full effect of losing their dad.

"Lynsie." Lincoln's soft voice brings my attention back. "This is Rebecca."

Rebecca, a tall, slender woman, turns to me and tries to smile, extending her hand to mine. Her smile, though beautiful, doesn't sit well with me. This is her day. Passing out fake smiles shouldn't be something she feels she must do. I don't shake her hand. I walk right up to her and wrap my arms around her. I don't know what she *needs*, but I know it isn't a fake smile or a handshake.

"I'm sorry we had to meet this way, Rebecca." I lightly rub her back like Lincoln did. "I'd give anything if it could've been under different circumstances."

She sniffles and nods against the crook of my neck.

I continue, "I don't know what to say, but I just want you to know that if you ever need anything...to talk to someone or get away...anything at all, do not hesitate to reach out to me. I can't promise I'll be of much help, but whatever you need, I'll be it." I tighten my hold as her body shakes against mine. I rub her back with both hands and once the trembling eases, I pull away and look her in the eyes. "Anything," I say more firmly.

She nods in reply as she wipes her face with a balled-up handkerchief. She looks past me, recognition taking over her face. "Oh, Dax," she says, side-stepping me.

"I'm so sorry for your loss, Mrs. Robinson." He leans in, hugging her. "I didn't get as much time with Travis as I would've liked, but the time we attended training together were some of my best years." He pulls away, eyes glazed over.

"He sure loved you," she reassures, placing her hand on Dax's shoulder. "He loved both of you." Rebecca looks back and forth, giving them both a loving smile, and all I can think is how incredibly strong this woman is. The grieving wife consoling her dead husband's fellow pilots.

Chapter Six

LYNSIE

"Are you ready for tonight, gorgeous?" Lincoln asks as he walks up behind me, eyeing me through the mirror.

I turn around to face my clean-cut, handsome husband. He's decked out in his military uniform that's reserved for events such as this or funerals. It's only been two weeks since he last wore it. For the most part, he acts completely normal, but there are times I catch him staring off into space and I know he's thinking about Travis.

"Mmm. Mmm. Mmm. Something about a man in uniform." I beam, letting my finger trace over all the badges and ranks decorating his coat.

"You don't look too shabby yourself." He grins as he bends down, placing a gentle kiss on my cheek. "Are you ready for your dad's big night?" His finger glides along the thick strap of my beaded bodice, tracing its way along the fabric that covers my chest, leaving my other shoulder bare.

"I'm ready." I pat the chest of his jacket, swaying my hips as I walk past him before we head down the stairs. "I can't wait until the day it's you who's receiving a highly honored promotion." At times, I feel like I married a younger version of my dad.

"You and me both, babe," he says, leading us out the front door.

I stand on our porch as Lincoln locks the door, thankful it's not a typical blazing summer night in Alabama. I close my eyes, enjoying the slight breeze as it causes the flowy skirt of my cream dress to dance across my thighs.

Lincoln grabs my hand, pulling me out of my stupor, and we make our way, hand in hand, to his truck. "You know"—he pulls my hand to his lips, kissing each knuckle before opening my door—"I've been thinking a lot lately. About life goals and dreams. Ever since Robinson died, really. I don't want to waste any more time. The things that are important to you should be as equally important to me, and... I think I'm finally ready." His grin is so big.

I tilt my head, examining his face. "Ready for what, Linc?"

He closes the distance, touching his lips to mine. "I'm ready for this." He rests his hand on my stomach. "I want you to have my baby, Lyns," he breathes against my lips, claiming them in a tender embrace. My senses are instantly awoken as my heart starts pounding erratically. His nearness is overwhelming. His words, life-changing.

Pulling back, he cups my face. "And I'm also more than ready for all that goes into the baby making." He reclaims my mouth, and I push myself into him. His tongue traces the softness of my lips, sending my desire into overdrive.

I pull away, breathless. "We need to go," I groan. "But we should finish this when we get back."

"It's a date." He looks down at his watch to check the time. "Yep. We better go."

The banquet hall is packed when we arrive. Through the double doors, there's a circular stone fountain in the lobby. It's always brightly lit up, with beautiful plants on stone pedestals.

I hear my dad's roaring laugh over all the chatter and turn my head in his direction. He looks as handsome as ever, all decked out from head to toe. His usual crew cut, peppered hair that matches his mustache precisely is slightly styled to the side. I make my way over, watching him in his element—schmoozing the people around him. Lincoln is right behind me, his hand on the small of my back. Still laughing, my dad turns his head in our direction, and his eyes instantly light up as he swings his full body toward us.

"There she is," he says excitedly, extending his hands. I place mine in his and smile back. "You look beautiful as always, daughter of mine. I'd like to say you got your good looks from me but—"

"We all know that's not true," my petite mother chimes in as she walks up, sidling herself up against my dad's side.

"Yes, dear." He looks adoringly at my mom. "It's more than apparent she's the spitting image of her mom."

"Just because tonight's your big night, mister, don't forget who you're going home with." She playfully smacks his arm.

"Oh now, Brenda, you know better." He kisses her cheek. "Lincoln." He extends his hand out. "It's good to see you, son."

Lincoln nods, shaking his hand. "It's good to be here, sir. Congrats on your upstanding accomplishment. You truly are the man I look up to."

"No need to suck up. You already got my little girl," my dad teases, knowing Lincoln's words have nothing to do with me. "You kids know where our table is?"

"I have no idea," I reply, shaking my head. "We haven't even tried to make our way in there yet."

"Well, it's one of the tables closest to the left side of the stage area. That's all the help I can offer."

I bend in and hug my dad, kissing his cheek. "I love you, Dad, and I'm so proud of you."

"Love you more."

His words warm my heart. *He's going to be an amazing grandpa one day.*

We make small talk with people we've come to know throughout the years, everyone giving their congrats to me on behalf of my father and patting Lincoln on the shoulder, believing this will happen to him one day.

"Babe." I tug Lincoln's arm, pulling him down a notch. "I'm going to run to the bathroom before we go in there."

"Want me to walk with you?" he questions, holding my gaze.

"No, I'm fine. Stay right here so I don't lose you." With his head still lowered, I kiss his cheek. "I'll be right back."

When I come out of my stall, I notice a woman at the end of the sink area. She's checking herself out in the mirror, making sure every hair is in its perfect place before reapplying some lipstick while talking on her phone. I try not to eavesdrop, but she's in a public space using speakerphone.

"You know me better than that." She giggles. "You know I always get what I want. This guy can play hard to get all he wants, but he has no clue what I have in store for him once we leave this stupid ceremony thing."

I glare at the mirror, wishing her gaze would shift in my direction. It takes everything in me not to walk over and yank her blinged-out phone from her hands and flush it down the toilet. How dare she complain? She's lucky some dumb guy invited her in the first place. I release the scowl and return my face back to neutral as I make my way toward her, grabbing a few paper towels to dry my hands.

I push out the bathroom door and head back to where I left Lincoln, but he's not there. Shocker. He's always getting sidetracked or wrangled by someone.

"Lynsie," someone hollers, and I turn to see Dax standing near the fountain, making his way toward me.

"Look at you!" I exclaim.

"Yeah, figured I'd get dressed up tonight. I mean, it is for a good cause and all." He gives me a half grin. His dirty-blond hair is tamed with a comb-over, giving him a more grown appearance. A look I'm not familiar with.

"I'm glad you could make it. I'm not sure you had a choice, though." I laugh.

He slides his hands in his pockets as he bounces back on the heels of his feet. "I wouldn't have missed it for the world. Your dad has taken me under his wing, literally, since I showed up here. He deserves all the praise and respect he'll be receiving tonight."

"I swear, it's like you and Lincoln worship the ground that man walks on."

"More like we worship the sky he flies in," he openly admits.

I nod before reaching for his hand. "Well, let's go. I'm sure you're seated with us anyway."

"Just a minute." His hand slips from mine. I turn back, wondering what the holdup is. "You'll be proud of me."

"Why's that?" I prop my hand on my hip.

"Because I brought a date." He looks toward the bathroom door and the chick who was on the phone saunters our way.

Chapter Seven

LYNSIE

Dax and Lincoln sit next to each other, leaving us ladies sitting on their opposing sides. Through a side glance, I intently examine his date... Haley. If I didn't personally know Dax, I would suspect she was hired through an escort service. Her dress, if that's what it's called, is sparkly red, skintight, and strapless. The way it clings to every inch of her milky skin with her breasts spilling out the top has me believing it belongs in a club, not a military ceremony. I want to be impressed that he even brought a date, but he could've found a classy one. I'm not one to deny beauty. Of course she's a bombshell, but that's as good as it gets. Knowing Dax isn't looking for long term, I get why personality isn't a top quality.

Lincoln leans in, whispering in my ear, "What's going through that pretty mind of yours?"

"Nothing." I smile, unraveling my napkin and placing it on my lap. "I am eager to get home and start making some babies," I quietly admit.

He kisses me gently. "Me too, baby."

"All right, lovebirds," Dax groans.

Salads are served during small talk. After the main course of parmesan-crusted chicken, sided with garlic baked potatoes and crisp green beans, the announcer makes his way to the stage.

"First," the man dressed in the same hunter-green dress attire as my father says, "I'd like to thank everyone who was able to make it out to share in Colonel Clark's big night."

As applause erupts around the room, I chance a glance to the other side of my husband to see Haley roll her eyes as she stifles a yawn. The thought of tossing my half-eaten roll at her crosses my mind.

The announcer continues, "We have a few guest speakers in line for tonight's event. So, without further ado, I'd like to welcome Chief Warrant Officer Lincoln Fox. Being under his command for the last few years on base and off," he jokes, "we figured he'd be the most capable of gathering Intel on Colonel Clark's career path that led him to receive such an accomplishment."

I give Lincoln's leg a quick squeeze as the clapping begins. "Get 'em, Wings."

Lincoln smiles as he pushes his chair out and makes his way to the stage. Standing proudly at the podium, he speaks, "Let me just start by saying how privileged I am to know Colonel Clark. I don't just say this because he's my father-in-law. He's also responsible for a lot of good things that have happened in my life. Along with the direction my career has taken, I thank him every day for allowing me the chance to prove I was good enough for his daughter and for giving me the opportunity to love her. I expected him to run me off the moment he found out I was dating her, but he didn't. So thank you for that."

The crowd lets out a collective laugh, and Lincoln goes on to talk about my dad joining the Army at the ripe age of seventeen, following his high school graduation. How he was bound and deter-mined to break away from the Virginia town he grew up in and see the world. Like most pilots, if not all, my father was a helicopter pilot before he transitioned to airplane after going to Fixed-Wing training. And from there, his passion continued to bloom.

Hearing about my life and the life my dad lived before me makes me proud. Having it broken down the way Lincoln is telling it gives me an insight that I've never been able to see by simply growing up in it. My husband's words about my father's career give me a glimpse as to what it might sound like to an outsider—admirable.

"That was amazing, babe," I say with adoration as he takes his seat next to me. "And how very sneaky of you to keep the whole thing from me." I nudge his side with my elbow.

"I wanted it to be just as special for you as it hopefully was for your father." He grabs my hand, brings it to his lips, and kisses my delicate skin.

"Well, it worked." I look toward my dad, who's grinning from ear to ear. The smile hasn't left his face all night.

As the ceremony wraps up, the rather large crowd stands, clapping to congratulate my dad and the others getting promoted. I quickly give him and my mom a hug before trying to make our way out. Dax and his date are close behind us as we weave our way through the people standing around talking. A few times we're stopped by someone wanting to talk to Lincoln. Dax knows everyone Lincoln does, so they both chat, while Haley and I stand off to the side.

She pulls her phone out of her clutch, moving her fingers across the screen at record speed. I roll my eyes when she lets out an audible yawn. Dax looks my way, trying to stifle his laugh at my obvious distaste for her.

"Fox, how many more days do we have to get the show down for the Fourth?" a man asks, walking toward us. I take in his dark features as he struts up. His dark skin is a natural contrast to his buzzed black hair and deep brown eyes shadowed by thick brows.

"As many as it takes, Peterson." Lincoln clasps his shoulder.

From the corner of my eye, I see Dax's smile disappear and his body stiffen. I remember Dax isn't flying in the show this year, and Peterson is the one taking his place. It must be a sore subject.

I tug on Lincoln's arm and push up close to his ear. "Hey, we're going to wait for you up front by the fountain, okay?"

"Sure, I'll be there in a minute."

I link my arm through Dax's and lead us away from what I know would only irritate him more. Once we're on the other side of the wooden doors that separate the dining area from the lobby, I release Dax and lead the way toward the fountain, carefully sitting along the edge. The coolness of the stone seeps through the fabric of my dress. He sits down next to me as his life-sized Barbie doll shimmies into the bathroom.

"Thanks for that," he says, not looking at me as he keeps his gaze straight ahead.

"Anytime. That's what friends are for." I smile and he finally turns his eyes to me.

"I've been trying not to let it bother me, but I was really looking forward to it. I know I can be cocky"—he smirks, and I let out a laugh before he continues—"but I know I'm a better pilot than that Peterson guy." He sighs. "It just sucks when something you've been looking forward to for the past year suddenly gets yanked away from you." He holds his broken hand out in front of him and shakes his head.

"I get it, Dax. I'd much rather see you up in the sky with Lincoln."

"You're good people, Lyns. Thanks for being you." He looks around and then back at me. "By the way, how is Lincoln doing these days? He hasn't really mentioned anything to me about Travis."

"He seems to be doing fine," I reply. "When we got home from the funeral, he basically told me he didn't want to talk about it anymore. So I haven't brought it up. How are you doing with it?" I eye him, knowing he's the one who's a pro at hiding how he feels.

"I'm good." He gives me a slight grin.

"You don't always have to play it cool and be the one worried about everyone else." I place my hand on his, giving it a squeeze.

"I know. We all just deal with shit differently." He shifts to the side, digging into his pocket. Dax turns his body toward me as he maneuvers the quarter between his fingers before flipping it into the fountain.

"Uh, Dax." I watch the quarter as it splashes into the water and sinks to the concrete bottom. "This isn't a wishing well."

"Welllllll," he draws out with a laugh. "I just turned it into one. Others will now follow my lead." His lips curve upward, finally awarding me with the smile he's been lacking. "But anyway, why do I get this feeling you don't really care for my date?" He raises a brow, smirking.

"That obvious?" I ask with a shy smile.

"Oh yeah." He chuckles, rubbing the back of his neck.

"About that... I mean her. Do me a favor." I inwardly sigh, realizing I'm about to become a cock block.

"Anything," he says without hesitation.

"Please don't sleep with that woman." I plead with my eyes.

He bends over, laughing as she walks out of the bathroom, eyeing us suspiciously. I start giggling as he rests his hand on my knee in reassurance. "That's the easiest thing you've ever asked me to do."

Lincoln walks up to us with an inquisitive look. "What's so funny?" He holds his hand out to me, pulling me up.

"I'll tell you in the car." One last giggle escapes me as I think about what Dax said. I give Dax a hug. "See ya later." I pull back and give Haley a little wave. "It was nice to meet you." I say *nice* so faintly, I'm sure I'm the only one to notice.

Dax glances at me from behind her and shakes his head as he silently chuckles.

"You didn't like Dax's date, did you?" Lincoln asks as we make our way to the car.

"Was I that obvious?"

"To someone who doesn't know you?" He pulls my door open, tilting his head to the side as I slide in. "No, but since I'm your husband and know you better than the back of my own hand, yes."

Once he's seated inside, I explain where my dislike stems from. "Her only motive for the night is to get in Dax's pants."

Lincoln laughs. "Good, he needs someone in his pants. Maybe that will get him out of the funk he's in."

"I'm all about him getting laid, but the thought of it being with her makes me want to vomit." I scrunch my nose up at the idea.

He shakes his head with amusement in his eyes. "You want him to date, but when he brings his own, you don't like her. Woman, you are maddening sometimes."

"It's a female thing." I shrug, pawning it off on my gender. "I just want the best for him, and she's not even close."

"I don't think any woman will ever outrank Amber," he says sadly. "It's hard to replace your first love."

"That name makes me want to vomit, too." I mimic the gagging sound before changing the subject. "Oh yeah, so I left you there with Peterson because it looked like Dax wanted to grab the closest salad fork and jab Peterson's eye out with his good hand. He has to be a spectator this year. It can't be easy."

Lincoln shrugs helplessly. "Dax did this one to himself. I'm sure you'll be able to keep him in good spirits while you keep each other company from the sidelines."

"Independence Day is right around the corner. Are you guys going to have it perfected in a little over a month?" I intertwine our fingers together as our arms rest on the middle console.

"There are a few more parts that need tightening up, but yeah, I think we should be all good by then."

I rest my head back. Thoughts of tonight's event and what's to come when we get home flood my mind, and I shove away all worries about Dax and his trampy date.

WE LIE IN bed, wrapped around each other. The only noise is our breathing.

Lincoln runs the tips of his fingers across my bare belly. "I really can't wait until you have my baby growing inside of you. The more I think about it, the more excited I get. You're going to look so gorgeous with a pregnant belly."

I feel him smile against the top of my head as I snuggle closer to him, resting on his chest. "You're going to be the most amazing father. Our child will be so lucky to have you."

"You're pretty amazing too," he says softly, lightly trailing his hand up and down my back.

"That must be why we work so well together." I let my fingertips roam over his lightly haired chest.

"Must be. Good night, Lyns. I love you," he whispers against my neck.

Chapter Eight

LYNSIE

I wake up with Lincoln pressed against me from behind, hard and ready to go. "Can we just stay in bed, making love and babies all day?" Lincoln's voice is low and husky as he tries to pull me on top of him for round two.

"Whoa there, mister." I wiggle out of his grasp. "Some of us actually have to work on Saturdays." I try to roll out of bed, but his strong arm clamps down, swallowing me. Before I know it, he's pulling me back against his chest in a tight embrace.

His face is playful. "I actually have to work today too, missy. I was just testing you." He places a kiss on my forehead before letting me go and hopping out of bed.

"Testing out what exactly?" I chuckle as I follow him into the bathroom.

"Your resistance levels." He shrugs.

With my arms crossed, I prop myself against the bathroom doorframe. "What resistance levels?" I ask, still confused.

"Your resistance to this." He motions down his naked body before stepping in the shower.

I climb in after him, and we stand face to face as he rests under the spray of the showerhead.

"Just because I can't stay in bed with you all day doesn't mean I can resist you." I bite my lip as I let my hands trail down his wet body.

I MAKE MY way through the salon doors with an extra pep in my step. A full smile lights up my face as I replay last night and this morning in my head. Such good, good visuals play out before me.

"Umm, girl," Echo says as we pass each other.

I shake my head, ridding it of all the delicious thoughts. "Yeah?" I stop and spin around, facing her.

She quickly glances over at her customer who is sitting with a magazine in hand under the hair dryer then back at me. "Don't get me wrong, you are typically a very happy person, but what the hell is up with you today?" She props a hand on her hip, staring at me.

"I have no idea what you're talking about." I attempt to play cool.

"Yeah right, woman," she whisper-yells, rolling her eyes. "We will be talking as soon as we both get a break." She looks at her watch. "For me, that will be thirty minutes. If you make me wait any longer, it's very possible I will combust."

I laugh at her. "Fine. How about I just tell you now? I'd hate for one of my favorite people to combust." I look around, making sure we're clear of prying ears. "Lincoln and I are trying to have a baby." I can't help the excitement in my voice as I surprisingly manage to keep myself from jumping up and down.

Her face beams bright with joy. "Oh my God, girl! That's so freakin' amazing." She pulls me in for a hug, doing the whole *bow-chicka-wow-wow* as she pulls away and walks backward. "Now I know what that look was about." She winks before turning around, giving her customer her full attention.

I sit my purse down at my station and pull my phone out. I have a missed text from Lincoln. Just the thought of him has a lovestruck smile plastered on my face. I sit in my cutting chair and slide the screen to read his message.

> Lincoln: You have ruined me. All I can think about is you. It's on when you get home. You have been warned.

> Me: Bring it, babe.

Sounds to my left bring my gaze away from my screen. I look over at Echo, who has gone from her *bow-chicka-wow-wow* moments ago, to now singing "Let's Get It On". I can't help but laugh. Her customer looks over the magazine she had been fully engrossed in, trying to act like she's not eavesdropping.

"You got it bad, girl." Echo snickers and shakes her head.

I sigh dreamily, not even ashamed. "No, babe, I've got it good. Oh so good."

* * *

"WELL PLAYED, LYNSIE. Well played," Dax says behind me, clapping.

"Whatcha talking about, Dax?" I say innocently, turning around to face him while I finish separating the bag of Jelly Belly's I have, dropping the ones I like into the bowl. While everyone is outside drinking, I've been inside getting all the side dishes ready for our cookout. Dax's grubby fingers are dipping and tasting everything I have sitting out on the counter. With each taste, he gives me his nod of approval.

"Okay, Gordon Ramsey," I joke.

"Drop the innocent act." He laughs between bites. "I know you all too well." He shakes his finger at me. "You didn't invite these girls over so you could play dress-up. If that were the case, they'd be in here helping you instead of outside with all the guys panting over them."

I raise my brow. "Guess they don't have alllllll the guys panting. Seeing as you are in here." I cross my arms. I don't clarify that I didn't invite any of them. The guys out there have their own social circles and did all the inviting on their own.

He shrugs, grabbing another chip. "Not that I have a problem with any of them. I don't, but I'd rather hang in here and help you. I know you want me to be happy and you think my ex ruined me, but I don't need a woman to be happy, Lynsie," he openly admits.

"Did she ruin you?" I softly ask.

"I don't know." He shrugs, and I see a glimpse of residual pain in his eyes. "I mean, at first, it obviously felt that way, but now, I'm over her."

"So what exactly happened? If you don't mind me asking." I've tried not to pry, but I feel like our friendship has grown so much over the years, and it's now safe for me to breach the topic. Plus, when I asked Lincoln back when it happened, he summed it up as just a bad breakup.

He glances outside where everyone else is enjoying themselves and probably wishes he had stayed out there. "She cheated on me," he quietly admits.

"Whaaaat?" I shriek in disbelief. Dax lets out a low chuckle.

"I know you think I walk on water, Lyns. But I don't." He shrugs.

I scoff. "I wouldn't go that far, but if you could, I'm sure you'd make it look just as good as you do walking on the ground."

He raises a brow at me, and I wave his expression away.

"Oh, hush. You know what I mean. The point is nothing you could do would make cheating acceptable."

"Yeah, I know. I just think sometimes when those situations arise, you always tend to look back and try to figure out what went wrong or what you could have done differently. Feeling like you messed up somewhere along the way." He leans back against the counter, crossing his arms over his chest.

"And did you figure out what went wrong?" I continue to pry.

"Yeah." He looks directly at me, holding my gaze. "She wasn't the one." I enjoy these moments when Dax is forthcoming with me. He continues, and I lean in. "Yes, the revelation of it all hurt like hell. Yes, it took me time to get over it. But I'm a firm believer that things happen to put you on the course that's meant for you. Sometimes when you aren't looking, you find what you've needed all along without ever knowing it was what you wanted." He casts his eyes downward, speaking above a whisper. I hear sadness in his voice. "Sometimes there are things you want but know you'll never have... because they aren't yours to have." He looks up, offering a weak smile.

I carefully ask, "What do you mean?"

Taking a seat on the barstool across from me, he loosely explains, "It's always easier to want what you can't have. It's human nature."

"I get that," I say as Dax watches me throw a couple Jelly Belly's in my mouth. "But what I think is we don't want what people have, necessarily. We want the end result, the product of what they have." I pause to finish chewing.

"Explain," he says, grabbing his own handful out of my special stash.

"Well, someone with a nice house for instance. You may want their nice house, but you don't want their work ethic that got them there. Same with any possession. Even works with families and love. You see someone who's happy and instantly think it's because of who they're with. You think, to reach that level of happiness, you'd need to be with that person, but just because it works for that couple, doesn't mean it'll work for you. Yes, it's human nature to want what you can't have, but also by changing up the variable, the result would change as well." I reach over, placing my hand on his forearm in a comforting manner. "You might buy that house and the foundation could be unstable. You might get that girl, and all her little quirks that you didn't see drive you mad. Everything looks prettier from the outside looking in."

Dax lets out a *humph* as if I've stumped him. "When'd you become so smart, Lyns?" He grabs more of my candy, and I playfully smack his hand.

I give him a little smirk. "Honey, I've always been smart." Then I pat him on the cheek. "And quit eating my candy," I jokingly say as I head for the back door. "There's a half bag full of the colors I don't like sitting on the counter."

"Selfish much?" he teases before his voice goes serious. "What's this?" he asks.

I turn around and see him pointing to the folded invitation. "It's nothing." I try to snatch the invitation away before he can open it, but I'm not fast enough. "I'm sorry," I say, sitting down next to him.

Dax looks down at his hands spread on the counter. "You got nothing to be sorry for, Lyns." He lifts his head up, offering a half-hearted smile.

"I'm sorry you had to see it. I meant to trash it. I mean, it's not like we're going." I hop up and grab the stupid wedding invitation, rip it in half and toss it in the trash.

"It's not like it's a newsflash." Dax's shoulders sag. "I figured they'd get married. I don't get why in the world she felt like she should invite Lincoln."

"Yeah, she's stupid if she thought we'd go. Our loyalty resides with you." I put my arm around his shoulders, side hugging him.

"I know." He smiles. "I'm lucky to have you guys in my life."

The back door opens, letting a burst of sunlight in. I shield my eyes, allowing them to adjust to the change in light.

"Lincoln wants you, Lynsie," a petite redhead says, holding the door open. Bethany, I think.

Once she sees Dax, she heads straight for him, and I pass her on my way out. At the door, I turn around and mouth, "She's hot," to Dax.

He fully smiles as he rolls his eyes.

"Hey, Grill Master," I announce. From behind, I slide my hands up my husband's defined chest.

His low chuckle is sexy as hell. "I'll show you master." He looks back at me and I stand up on my tippy-toes to kiss him.

"I look forward to it." I drop a few kisses on his shoulder blade as I hold him. "How are the burgers coming along?"

"About done. Everything ready inside?" He turns around, wrapping his arms around me.

"Yep. All done." I give him a playful grin. "Not saying there'll be any left. I did leave Dax inside, and he was already munching around before I came out."

Something catches Lincoln's eyes, causing him to turn his focus away from me. "Well, well. Looks like one of the girls struck an interest with Dax."

I turn my head, meeting Dax's gaze. He gives me a nod before returning to the conversation he's having with some of the guys, Bethany clinging to his side.

I hesitate, torn by the conversation we just had. I'm not sure what to think. "I'm pretty sure she's friends with the girl who's attached to Peterson's side. But it's not like it'll go anywhere."

"Why does it need to go anywhere?" He tilts his head. "Some people just aren't the settling down type, you know?"

I look up at my husband, who seems to have it all figured out.

He's so right. Some people just don't have commitment laced into their DNA. That may be the case for Peterson, but I feel Dax is most definitely the settling down type. He's just not willing to settle. There's a difference.

They make their way over to us. Dax's arm is loosely wrapped around her waist. "Do you guys have anything planned for the night?" He looks back and forth between Lincoln and me. I'm trying to read his features. He gives me a light smile, a smile I feel is asking, *this is what you want, right?*

Guilt forms in my throat, keeping me from responding. I have been pressuring him about dating. Or maybe this has something to do with the invitation. From when we first talked in the kitchen to now—fifteen minutes tops—he's done a complete one-eighty.

I look up at Lincoln.

He just shrugs his shoulders, replying, "No. None that I can think of. Why?"

Dax coolly smiles down at me. "Bethany mentioned we should all go out tonight. I thought it was a good idea. Wanna join?"

I clear my throat. "Sounds great."

With Lincoln's crazy schedule these last few months, we haven't been able to do squat. There's no way I'm passing up an opportunity to go out with our friends.

"Don't burn the burgers, Wings." Dax nods at my husband before he suddenly pushes Bethany into the pool. She lets out a loud yelp, then he quickly dives in.

"Peterson, make yourself useful," Dax hollers from the pool.

"I'm always useful." He all but whines, walking over to the grill, and grabs the pan for Lincoln to stack the burgers on. I walk in front of them and hold the door open. "Thanks, Lynsie," Peterson says as he passes me, giving me a genuine smile. Then he winks and the idea of sticking my foot out and tripping him crosses my mind, but the burgers in his hands keep me from doing so.

They sit the burgers on the counter and Lincoln walks over to me, draping his arm around my shoulder as the rest of the company spills inside the house. "I just want to thank you guys for coming over and hanging out with us today. It's good to finally be able to relax together. I appreciate you guys. We should do this more often." He looks around and smiles. "All right, let's eat up."

He's right. It does feel good to all come together. This right here is one of the things I've always loved about the Army. It's like one big family. You grow unbreakable bonds throughout the years.

Chapter Nine

LYNSIE

Our five-year wedding anniversary is right around the corner, and I have one particular errand to run while my husband is occupied. I bounce down the stairs and walk into the kitchen, grabbing my sunglasses off the counter.

"Where are you boys taking your little remote-control planes today?" I ask, teasing them about their toys. They fly real planes, yet in their free time, they play with miniature ones. I guess a passion is a passion, no matter the size.

"Ahem." Dax walks up behind me. "Wing Dragon is anything but little, Miss Thang."

"Is that what you call it these days?" I giggle.

Dax's cheeks redden as he begins to stammer momentarily. He then shakes his head and turns to walk back outside. I rendered him speechless. Score one for Miss Thang.

Still chuckling, I hug and kiss Lincoln goodbye. "I love you. You boys have fun."

"You know it," he says, smacking my butt on my way out.

I pass Dax sitting on the front porch. "Take good care of Wing Dragon."

"Of course I will." He rubs the top of it like it's a pet. I half expect it to start purring. "It's my pride and joy," he says with delight.

"That's what they all say." I wink and get in my car, loving how easy it is for me to fluster him.

I FIND A parking spot nearby and make my way to whom I've started calling 'The Woodman.' I need to find that plane Lincoln saw and raved about the last time we were here. I look over the assortment of helicopters and planes he has placed out strategically from smallest to largest.

"Can I help you find something, miss?" He looks up from the folding chair he's sitting in as he chisels away at a piece of wood with his special tools.

"My husband and I were here a week or so ago and you had this plane. It was about that size." I point to the medium-sized planes. "But he loved the coloring of the wood. It was a mix of light and dark."

Recognition dawns in his aged brown eyes. "Oh yes. If I remember correctly, it sold that day, but you're in luck. I have a plane at home I've been working on. Same color pattern. It's a little bigger, but from what I remember your husband liking, he will thoroughly enjoy it."

I clasp my hands together to keep from clapping with excitement. "That sounds perfect. When should I come back for it?"

"It should be ready in about a week." He stands up, digging out a piece of paper. "If you want to give me your name and number, I can call you when it's ready."

After our exchange of information, I get in my car and head for the park area where Lincoln and Dax typically fly their toys. The park is lively with its share of Frisbee throwers, joggers, and people who just like to lie out in the open and enjoy the outside air. If I had thought better of it, I would've grabbed a book and taken advantage of the day. Instead, I'm making my way to the goofballs, who seem to be trying to take out each other's planes—the pricey planes.

"Don't be crying to me when you destroy your toys." I laugh as I walk up behind them.

"Oh no, she caught us." Dax glances over at me, smiling before returning his bright eyes back upward.

"Who's going to let me fly one?" I ask, knowing the answer. The idea of a woman flying one frightens them. They both look at each other in silence. "Just kidding. I wouldn't want to scratch your pride and joy. I'll just have to buy my own sometime."

I walk up to Lincoln's side. "Give me a kiss. I'm going to go get stuff for dinner."

He leans down, giving me a quick kiss without taking his eyes off the sky.

"You gonna eat dinner at home tonight, Dax?"

"Dude, watch out." Dax yanks his arms to the side quickly as if his body is synchronized with his plane. "You're flying sloppy all up in my personal air space."

"Bullshit. You crossed the imaginary line. Not me." Lincoln holds his remote steadily as his fingers move with fluidity, much like his plane.

I love how competitive the two of them get. They truly act like brothers.

"Ahem," I interrupt. "Did you hear me, Dax?"

"Oh sorry, Lyns." He flashes me an apologetic grin. "Yeah, I'll be home." He quickly looks back up, making sure not to lose control of his plane.

I roll my eyes at the lack of attention I get when they do anything related to planes or flying. It takes over, consuming them to the brim.

That's what a passion is supposed to do, right?

* * *

"I'M TWO DAYS late," I say, holding the unopened box in my hand.

"So you bought them all?" He laughs, seeing the extra boxes stacked near the sink.

"Well, I didn't know which one was best. You can never be too sure." Suddenly, I feel silly for buying five different pregnancy tests.

Lincoln quickly kneels in front of me. Looking up, he says, "I know you're excited. I am too. I also know you're probably a bit nervous and even scared. I am too." He smiles as he takes my hand in his. "But, baby, we got this. I'm going to be by your side through all of it. No matter what this test says, or the other ten you bought"—he laughs, and I join in with him—"I got you and you got me...and in the end, Lynsie, that's all that matters."

"How'd I get so lucky?" I ask. His words warm my heart as I swallow back the tears threatening to form. I drop my head down, placing a kiss on his sweet lips.

We both sit on the bed, hand in hand, waiting for the three-minute timer to go off. Bolting up as soon as my phone chimes, we look down at the stick together.

Negative. My heart drops.

"You know what that means?" Lincoln asks in an overly cheerful tone, winking.

"That I'm about to start my period most likely." *Ugh.* I whine.

"Umm, that's not where I was going with that." He chuckles. "I was going to say we have more time to practice." He cocks a brow.

"At the rate we've been going, I think we have the practicing thing down." I huff, feeling slightly defeated. "Is it okay if we just cuddle and watch a movie tonight?"

"Only if you promise me one thing." His face is full of sincerity.

"What's that?" I ask as he pulls me in close to his body.

"That every time you take one of these tests, you only do it with me here."

I start to nod, but he stops me.

"And you don't go getting all sad each time we get a negative. This could take time...lots and lots of time," he says seductively, kissing me just underneath the ear. It gives me goose bumps. "But don't let it get you discouraged. Got it?" He rubs my back in comforting circles.

"Got it." I take in his words, letting them soothe me.

"Good." He kisses me one more time. "Now go get comfy and I'll order us some food." He smacks my butt as I walk out of the bathroom. I let out a yelp and give him a glare that he can see straight through. "You better watch it." He raises his eyebrows. "There's more where that came from."

Chapter Ten

LYNSIE

The sun creeps in through the blinds, and I roll over and face my handsome, sleeping husband. Sometimes I like to just stare at him, remembering things we've shared together and all we have to be thankful for. Although, I can never get away with staring for long. He always catches me.

"Busted," he says as he cracks his eyes open, trying to fully focus.

"Guilty as charged." I place a kiss on his forehead and inch my body closer to him. "So my mom asked me if we'd meet them for lunch today. I never gave her an answer because I didn't know what our schedules would be like, but I'm going to go. If you have stuff to do today, I understand. It's not like I gave you any notice."

"It's cool, babe." He drapes his arm around my side. "Anything I have planned can wait until we get back. I'll go with you."

"Sounds perfect. I'm gonna go cook us some breakfast." I give him one more kiss before scootching out of bed.

"Now that sounds perfect," he mumbles, not moving one inch from where he's resting comfortably.

A little bit later, he strolls downstairs, wearing nothing but a pair of gray sweats. I instinctively lick my lips, watching his taut muscles move as he reaches into the cupboard for a coffee cup. He catches me and shakes his head, letting out a deep chuckle.

"So," I let the word drag out as I flip his omelet over. "I'm kind of wanting to tell my parents we're trying." I hear the chair drag across the floor, followed by the crackling of the newspaper.

"If that's what you want." He continues looking through the Sunday paper.

"It is," I say with absolute certainty. "I don't want to one day be like, surprise, we're pregnant."

"Honestly"—he folds the paper, sitting it down in front of him—"I'm shocked you haven't told them yet."

"It's been rough," I say with exaggerated desperation as I grab a plate, scooping his omelet onto it. "The only person I've told is Echo. I couldn't hide it. She has like this radar, I swear."

He laughs. "What kind of radar?"

"I'm beginning to think it's like a sexdar." I wave the spatula in the air.

He chokes on his coffee. "Umm, what is a sexdar, and why do you think she has one?"

I set his plate down and sip my coffee, taking the seat across from him.

"I walked into work the other day extra happy, and it was as if I had *baby maker in training* written on my forehead. I told her we were going to start trying, and now every chance she gets, she's singing every sex song under the moon to me at work."

I laugh as I remember her serenading me to "Push It" in the break room the other day. "Yeah, it's even better when she says just parts of the song in the most casual way in front of customers. Hearing her say, 'Hey, push it real good, Lynsie,' while I'm with a customer makes it impossible to keep my composure."

He laughs. "I vote you start bringing her around. Why haven't you tried hooking Dax up with her?"

His question shocks me since he's never been team *Love Connection*. I frown at him, holding my coffee cup under my nose. I've always loved the smell. "Well, she's married and has a son."

"Okay, what about someone like her then?" he asks before shoving the last bite in his mouth.

"Oh, honey," I scoff. "There is no one else like her. There is only one Echo."

"No, there's not." I raise my brow at him in defiance, and he adds, "See. Listen. Echo...echo...echo...echo." He thinks he's clever, like Echo's never heard that before.

"You're so funny," I say sarcastically as I stand to fix my own omelet.

"I know." He grins, all too pleased with himself. "That's why you married me."

"Something like that." I whisk the eggs in a bowl. "Speaking of Dax. Do you know if he made it home last night?"

"At your service." I hear groaning and my head darts to the living room. Dax slowly sits up, dropping his head back against the couch.

"Yep, he made it home." Lincoln snickers.

I walk to the dimly lit living room and stand right in front of him. He looks like shit. I put the back of my hand on his forehead, feeling the clamminess.

"You should've come home when we did." I try not to scold but hate seeing him with a raging hangover. "How many times do I have to tell you that you aren't a spring chicken?" I lightly pat his cheek, and he rewards me with another groan.

"I know, I know, mom." He peeks one eye open and tries to smile before slumping over on his side.

"You'll be thanking this mom later," I murmur, returning to the kitchen to get him some pain medicine and a Gatorade. I whip up some scrambled eggs and a slice of toast for him and place it on the coffee table in front of him. "Here's some food and medicine. It should help." I ruffle his hair.

"That feels good," he hums. "Thanks for taking care of me, mom."

I hear the smile in his tone. I shake my head and laugh.

"Anything for you boys."

MY PARENTS ARE already seated inside when we arrive at the Mexican restaurant for lunch.

"This place is nice." I look around, admiring the bright colors and sombreros decorating the walls.

"Wait until you try the food," my dad exclaims.

"I've heard nothing but great things," Lincoln chimes in, scanning the menu.

"So we have some news," I say when the waiter walks off with our food order. Lincoln gives my thigh a reassuring squeeze. I look over and smile as all nervousness seems to dissipate. "We're trying to have a baby."

Pure happiness washes over both of their faces and I swear I even see tears brimming in my dad's eyes. I know without a doubt I see them from my mom as she stands up to hug me, telling me how happy she is.

She sways us back and forth. "I'm finally going to be a grandma."

"I'm not pregnant yet," I say to my mom, who's holding me tightly—a little too tightly.

"I know." She pulls back and gives me an adoring look. "But the fact that it might happen soon has me so happy."

My dad stands, followed by Lincoln, and he gives my husband a manly hug, telling him congratulations.

As we sit back down, my mom continues to rave nonstop, and

now I get why Lincoln thought it was a good idea to hold off on telling people.

After lunch, we're standing beside our cars as my mom says, "Oh, I can't wait to start shopping for my grandbaby." She claps her hands once, an excited, dreamy look on her face.

"I love you too, Mom," I tell her as Lincoln tugs my hand in the same fashion my father is doing with my mom.

When we're shut safely in the car, I ask him, "Why did I want to tell them again?"

He chuckles. "It was your idea, babe."

"We both know that not all of my ideas are good."

He laughs even harder as he starts the car.

"So what're your plans for the rest of the day?" I ask, placing my hand over his.

"Dax mentioned going to the gym."

"I'm guessing it's leg day for Dax." I snicker.

"Every day is leg day for him until he gets that cast off his hand." Lincoln laughs. "What about you? Do you have any plans?" He briefly looks my way.

I shrug with indifference. "I guess I can run some errands while you boys are working out."

I see Dax sitting on the porch when we pull into the driveway. He ends the phone conversation he was having, sliding his cell into the pocket of his blue basketball shorts.

"You didn't have to rush your girlfriend off the phone," I tease, swatting his arm as I pass him.

He laughs. "Please. I was talking to my mom."

"How are your parents doing?" Lincoln asks from behind.

I unlock the door and make my way over to the couch.

"They're doing well." He pauses momentarily. "Well, besides not hearing from Dustin for a few months, but what's new with that."

"Who's Dustin?" I twist my body around on the couch to face him, curiosity getting the best of me.

"Just my brother," Dax says matter-of-factly.

"Why am I just now hearing about this brother?"

"I'm going to change." Lincoln runs up the stairs as Dax walks over to the couch, plopping down on the opposite end.

"My brother and I have a rather difficult relationship." He shifts uncomfortably, then leans forward, resting his elbows on his thighs. "Meaning, we don't have one. Therefore, I never talk about him." He looks over, offering a weak smile.

"Oh," is all I say, feeling I should leave this topic alone for now.

"I'm ready," Lincoln exclaims, reaching the bottom of the stairs.

"Later, Lynsie," Dax says, throwing a couch pillow at me.

"You're lucky you're already injured, boy." I wave my fist at him. "Because I got a knuckle sandwich waiting for ya."

He laughs and rolls his eyes.

"All right, all right. Break it up, kids." Lincoln laughs and leans over from behind the couch, giving me a kiss. "I love you, Lynsie. Be back soon."

MY PHONE RINGS, an unfamiliar number appearing on the screen. "Hello," I answer. Excitement hits me as soon as I hear his voice.

I pull up to the little shop on wheels and cannot wait to see the finished project this creative genius has made for me.

The older man spots me walking up. "Just in time." He turns around, bends over, and picks up an old shoe box. He places it on the counter and lifts the lid off. I let out an audible gasp as he pulls the beautiful hand-carved wooden plane from the wrapping.

"Oh my. It's gorgeous." I gawk.

"This, my dear, is a Mohawk. Also known as the Widow Maker."

He sounds like he's in awe as he appreciates his handiwork one last time before handing it to me.

"I have to ask. Why is it called the Widow Maker?"

He scrunches his brows, deep in thought. "Because back when the Army still flew these planes, that's exactly what they did. The Mohawk was a two-engine aircraft they called the Widow Maker because of the design and operations equipment. If the pilot lost engine one, or the critical engine in a two-engine aircraft, they'd most likely lose control and crash. Since the potential for disaster was inherent, they were the only airplanes that had ejection seats."

"Thank God they retired them then," I think aloud.

He nods in agreement.

"Well, thank you so much." I pull the bills to pay him out of my wallet. "My husband is going to love this!"

"SO WHAT'S THE deal with Dax's brother?" I ask.

Lincoln is totally into the movie but still manages to answer me. "Not fully sure, to be honest. I just know his brother is in the Army and they aren't close."

"So is this brother older than him?"

"Yeah, I think Dustin is about four years older. I never really saw him when we were younger. By the time we hit high school, he'd already taken off and joined the Army. Haven't heard anything since."

"And you never think to ask?" I ask in disbelief.

Lincoln just shrugs. "No, if Dax wanted to talk, he'd bring it up."

"Humph," I say as I take the information in.

Lincoln pauses the movie and turns to me. "What's on that pretty mind of yours now?" He grabs my hand.

"I just always thought having a sibling would be great. You know, with me growing up an only child and all. It kind of makes me sad to hear Dax and his brother aren't close. I mean, they're blood. That should count for something." I sit and think about how family is supposed to be everything. At least, that's how I feel about mine.

"Being related to someone doesn't mean you have to like them. Sometimes people go through stuff or deal with it differently. I'm pretty sure the reason for the distance in their relationship is because of Dustin. I bet going to war jacked him up. From what I hear, it does a lot of soldiers."

"I'm not sure I could handle it if you had to go to war. If you ever had to go anywhere for a long period of time without me, it'd be hard to handle. I mean, Echo's husband is over there right now, and I don't see how she does it, staying here and raising their son. She's way stronger than me."

"Sometimes we don't know how strong we truly are until we have no choice." His words, intended to bring a sense of comfort, bring about a dull ache of forewarning instead. I quickly push the feeling aside.

"War and work and everything aside, promise me one thing," I request.

Lincoln laces our fingers together, gripping my hand a bit tighter. "Anything."

"We will have more than one child. I know what it's like to bounce around, having to always make new friends and face it alone. I don't want that for our child. I want there to be a sibling. I know they won't always be best friends, but I want at least two, so they can endure it together. I mean, I know you didn't have to move around like I did, but how did you handle being an only child? Did you like it?"

"I did like it." Lincoln's words stir a thought within me. "I was spoiled, but I had Dax. I think we both helped each other make it through those awkward stages."

Realization dawns on me. Maybe it wasn't being an only child that kept me lonely. Maybe it was the Army and never being in one place long enough to form meaningful bonds.

I nod decidedly. "That's what I want for ours one day."

"I know what I want," he says, giving me his sexy grin as he pulls me to him. "All this baby talk is making me want to *make* babies."

Chapter Eleven

LYNSIE

I wake up with a huge smile on my face, knowing what today is. When I roll over, my smile triples in size. Sitting on my end table is a vase of a dozen colorful roses. I grab the little card that's tucked in between the flowers and roll onto my back.

Two o'clock sharp. Be prepared to spread those wings of yours and fly.
Love you to the sky and back, Lynsie Pearl.

— Lincoln

Today marks our five-year wedding anniversary. Five years ago, on a small private beach alcove, we said *'I do'* with twenty of our closest friends and relatives in attendance. I don't know what he has up his sleeve for the day, but I'm excited.

Lincoln sneaks up behind me while I'm standing at my dresser picking out earrings. "Happy five-year anniversary." He snakes his arms around my waist, and I warmly lean back into his inviting chest.

"Happy five-year *'best day of my life'* back atcha." I twist in his arms, facing him.

He's glowing with happiness as he grins from ear to ear. Before I can even question the source, I'm looking at a rectangular box in his hands. My eyes widen, as do his when I realize what this gift is.

"Open it," he says excitedly.

I stick my hand out. "Whoa. You need to turn your excitement down a notch, Wings. I'm the one who's supposed to be all giddy," I say jokingly, barely being able to contain my own excitement.

"Yeah, yeah. Hurry up. Open it," he urges.

Not wasting another second, I pull the neatly tied ribbon away and lift the top off. I gasp as I take in the beautiful necklace. A gorgeous white gold chain, finished with a pair of wings that says, *'When you feel like you're falling, don't forget to spread your wings.'*

"It's gorgeous," I breathe as I trace my finger over the etching.

"Only the best for my best." He pulls me in tight, placing a kiss on my forehead before stepping back and taking the necklace from me. "Turn around."

After he clasps the chain, I pick the wings up and place a kiss on them before resting the charm right under my collarbone.

"Come with me if you want to live," he says, and I laugh as he grabs my hand, dragging me down the stairs behind him.

I break away once my feet hit the wood floor.

"No, seriously. Come on," Lincoln urges me with his hand.

"Can I at least put some shoes on first?" I giggle at his impatience.

He stops, turns around, and looks down at my feet like I was lying about not having shoes on or something. That causes me to giggle even more.

"WHAT ARE WE doing here?" I press a hand to the window and look around, trying to place this airplane hangar. It's one I haven't been to.

"Well"—he leans back into his seat, turning his head toward me—"I really wanted to bring you here and show you the planes some of the guys will be flying next month." His face lights up. Seeing how excited he is about including me makes me just as excited.

"I'm all about getting some VIP treatment." I grin as he opens his door. He quickly jogs around the front of his truck, opening my door before I even have a chance to get out. The smile on his face is contagious.

"Good," he says, taking my hand to help me out. "Because what I have planned for you goes above and beyond VIP, baby." He winks.

We make our way inside the metal building, and I slowly take in the row of planes lined against each side of the massive opening. They're all smaller and look like they should be sitting in special glass cases to keep them from being damaged. They're so intricate in color and design that their age is apparent. They scream vintage and valuable. It's hard to believe they still take these planes in the air.

"They're actually letting you guys fly these planes this year? Are they crazy?" I walk ahead of him, fully captivated by the history all around me. I'm my dad's girl through and through.

I walk up to the ones with the colorful details painted on the nose. I remember when I was younger, my dad told me all about them. How during War World II, all sorts of themes were used, usually something the crew picked out. Most themes being women—like the Memphis Belle. It's crazy to think, during those times, something as simple as nose art was a good distraction from the reality of what was going on.

He laughs. "What's that supposed to mean? You think we won't take care of them? We're used to handling very expensive planes."

I take a moment before turning to face him. I admire the yellow plane closest to me and let my hand lightly trail its belly. "That's not what I meant. I know you'd be more than careful. It's just they seem too fragile and historical to risk something happening to one of them." *Or the people flying them*, I think to myself.

"Pretty amazing, huh?" Lincoln sounds in awe as he grabs my hand. "Two of the planes we'll be flying aren't here, but I really wanted to show you this one," he says with a bright smile and a gleam in his eyes. He walks us up to a gray two-seater. "F-14A Tomcat." He looks up at it like a kid in a candy store, rubbing his hand back and forth along its side. By his silence, I can tell his thoughts are elsewhere. They might be on the upcoming show, or he could be picturing himself flying this plane. It looks like some sort of fighter jet. Either way, he's completely in the zone, with a look of total contentment on his face.

"So," I say, shaking him out of his daydream, "I have to admit, I'm glad you're not going to be flying this." I'm now hoping he's flying one of those pretty, but almost fragile-looking planes I was drooling over a minute ago.

"No worries," he assures me. "No one will be flying this." He holds his hand on the plane, feeling the cool metal. Probably dreaming he could become one with it. I snicker to myself as he says, "I just figured you'd want to get some close-up action with a plane similar to the ones in *Top Gun*."

My mouth drops. He knows I'm Team Maverick.

Lincoln walks off, telling me to stay put near the wings of the plane. As I gaze over its gray body, I can see the place it used to hold its weapons underneath. It makes me wonder if it has been in a war or ever had weapons mounted on. Has this plane ever killed anyone or taken out a tiny village of innocent people? My mind instantly goes there with planes that look more like full-fledged weapons than a source of transportation. That's exactly what most military planes are—weapons.

I hear the squeaking of something moving across the floor and turn to see him pushing a tall set of metal stairs on wheels. He stops in front of me and clicks the safety locks into place with his foot.

"After you." He directs me up the stairs with his arm. I make my way to the top, the side bars keeping us safely secure. There's more than enough room for the two of us as I move back, giving Lincoln space to do whatever he has planned.

He opens the canopy, showing me what the inside looks like, telling me about the different controls as he points to each of them.

"Wanna sit inside?" He holds out his hand for me.

I take one long look at the intimidating interior. "Am I allowed to?"

Lincoln knows better than anyone that I will never pass up a chance to take a seat in a plane, especially a once-in-a-lifetime chance like this.

The side of his mouth quirks up into that sexy smirk of his. "VIP, baby."

That's all he has to say to convince me as I step down into the back seat. He keeps a firm grip on my hand as I do. After I'm seated, he sits in the front and continues explaining the history and inner workings of the plane, even going into detail about the ejection seats.

"You see"—he points to all the nobs and dials that surround the cockpit—"the person in the front has all the controls. Meaning that if they tell the back seat pilot to eject and they don't do so themselves, it's left up to the person in the front."

"Why wouldn't they do it if they were told to?" I curiously eye all the buttons in the back, careful not to touch any.

He shrugs. "Not real sure. Probably nerves. Last-minute freakout. I'm sure those happen in moments of duress."

I nod. "Yeah, that makes sense." I swallow hard, my heart sinking at the thought. "So why'd Goose die during the ejection?" I ask, wondering how Maverick survived, yet he didn't.

Lincoln gets out of the cockpit and lends his hand to help me step out. We stand at the top of the ladder as he places his hand on the canopy.

"From what I understand," he starts, "it has to do with the type of spin they were in." He leads me down the ladder, then finishes. "When you hit eject, your plane usually has enough forward airspeed that helps push the canopy away from the plane. But when you're in a flat spin, like they were in the movie, the air above becomes sort of a barrier, keeping the canopy kind of hovering." He grabs my hand, threading our fingers together as he continues to look at the plane before us in awe. I can't help but do the same, but at him. "In that type of emergency situation, you are supposed to manually release the canopy, giving it enough time to pull away and then eject. There's also a delay between each seat being ejected to keep them from colliding." He finally looks down at me and says, "So that's why Maverick survived."

Now I almost regret asking.

THE REST OF our day goes just as perfectly as it started. We made our way back home after having dinner at my favorite restaurant. Once we walk through the front door, I realize I haven't given him his gift yet. I see the nicely wrapped package sitting on the bar in the kitchen, and I make my way over to it. Lincoln is quick on my heels, wondering what I could be up to since I'm not rushing up to the bedroom like he assumed I would.

All in good time.

I pick up the wrapped square box and shove it into his hands. "Here." I smile, anxious for him to open it. "You must've really caught me off guard today. I forgot all about it."

"You didn't have to," he says with a look of surprise as he tightly holds the box. Lincoln places a kiss on my lips before tearing into the package. "This is awesome, Lyns. Thank you." He holds his wooden plane up to the light, inspecting all the chiseled details hand-carved into it. "This is the plane I'll be flying at the show. How cool is that?" he exclaims as he walks it over and sits it gently on the shelf in the living room with the rest of his collection.

"The Widow Maker," I whisper. Saying it out loud sends a chill down my spine.

"Yes!" His eyes widen. "How'd you know that?" He eyes me suspiciously. "I'm guessing Harold told you?"

I raise my brow, asking, "Who's Harold?"

He adds, "The guy who owns the woodshop."

"Oh, yes." I smile. "Woodman has a name."

He laughs and shakes his head at me.

I turn and make my way to the counter. "One more gift." I hold out the gift bag with colorful wrapping paper poking out the top.

He takes the bag with a playful smile. "Oh, I see. You're trying to outdo me, are ya?" he teases.

"Never," I say gently as I move closer to him. "This is hopefully more of a gift for both of us." I smile up at him as he pulls the pregnancy test from the bag. Not wasting time, we both hurry upstairs, hoping for a sign. A sign that comes in the form of a plus sign, but it's another negative.

I slip into bed with a heart full of love and a sense of longing from the disappointing news. I instinctively place my hand on my flat stomach. I physically ache with disappointment as I hold myself together. I need to remember that this can take months to happen. We'll have our baby one day—someday soon...hopefully.

Lincoln tightly wraps himself around me. "It will happen, Lyns. All in good time." He nuzzles into my neck, and I let myself melt into him. He always knows just what to say.

Chapter Twelve

LYNSIE

The Fourth of July air show is in a week, and tonight I'm getting news I would rather live without.

Lincoln kneels down beside the couch in front of me. He grabs my hands tightly and brings them close to his chest. "It's only going to be for three months, babe. It'll fly by. Literally." He chuckles like that last part was super clever.

"It might *fly* by for you," I say mockingly, "but you're not the one stuck here, alone. You'll be so busy with your training, it won't matter. Not to mention, you'll have a lot of copilots keeping you entertained."

"You'll have Dax," he reassures.

I roll my eyes and huff, crossing my arms.

I don't want him to leave me. Even if it's only for three freaking months. Not when we've been trying to have a baby. I don't want to be apart from him for that long. I know I've been lucky compared to most Army wives. He hasn't been deployed overseas or anywhere that I haven't been able to go with him, but this—training in Fort Hood, Texas—is putting a curve in our plans.

I don't want to be whiney about it. This has always been Lincoln's dream and even if I held some sort of power, I'd never keep him from it. If that means putting our baby-making sessions on the back burner, then so be it.

"Come on, Lynsie," he says soothingly, wrapping his arms around me, trying to comfort me, "it won't be that bad. Hell, maybe there will be a time here and there that I can come back for a weekend or something." His eyes are full of hope.

"You're right." I sigh in defeat. "I'm spoiled. I've just never had to go without you for more than a week. I'm not sure I can do it," I whisper.

"I'm going to miss you, too," he assures me as he rubs his hands up and down my back.

I let out a heavy sigh. "When do you leave? How much longer do I have?" I pull away from him, leaning back on the couch.

His facial expression is void of any smile, and I dread the answer.

"We're supposed to leave mid-September. We don't have an exact date set in stone just yet." He looks at me, his eyes tight with sadness, knowing that's way too soon for me. Lincoln leaving a year from now would be too soon. I guess it doesn't really matter when. The impact would be the same.

We sit in silence for a moment. He doesn't try to make me feel better and I have time to take it all in. Which is good because it gives me a moment to gather some clarity. More like me grasping for any piece of optimism I can find within myself.

"I guess that means you'll be back sooner, and then, we can pick up where we left off." I smile, trying to feel better, not wanting to make my husband feel like shit. I knew what I was signing on for. It just sucks that I finally have to face it.

Lincoln pulls me onto his lap and grabs my face, drawing it to his with his strong hands. I feel his breath on my face, his voice low and husky. "Baby, I plan on being inside you so much the next two months that your body is going to be screaming for a three-month vacation."

"Baby, you could never be inside me enough." I close the distance, pressing my lips to his, and beg him with my tongue to deepen the kiss. I desperately want my husband to ravage my mouth and then my body.

With one arm around my back, he curls the other under my legs and scoops me up as he stands, taking us to bed.

I WALK INTO work like a child who has lost her puppy. I'm a sap. I know it. I'm not going to lie, the idea of him going to the same place where his friend recently died in a crash has me freaking out. I can't tell him that. I don't need him going with that riding heavy on his shoulders. I don't need him to be reminded of the buddy he lost, or to even have that idea in his mind every time he takes off on a plane while he's there. That could mess him up. Instead, I keep it to myself.

Well, I try to. Echo notices I'm not my normal self as soon as I walk in. I continue to the back of the building, and she quickly says something to her customer before feet pad against the linoleum floor behind me.

"Girl, what's wrong? You look like a fat kid whose cake got stolen."

I give a little smile because that was funny and cake sounds good right now. "Lincoln has to leave for training mid-September." I sit down in the break room chair and keep my eyes down. "I've never been away from him longer than a week or two. I know I sound like a spoiled brat." I hunch my shoulders, feeling the weight of despair pushing them down.

"How long does he have to go for?" she asks, and I suddenly feel bad for complaining when her husband is sometimes gone for years at a time.

I couldn't do that. I could not be the wife of a soldier who goes overseas for war, or anything, for that matter. I'm on pins and needles as it is.

"Three months," I groan. "I shouldn't be so upset about it. I mean, you have it worse than I do." I gulp, looking at Echo.

"Yes, I do," she says with complete understanding. "But it's what I signed up for. I knew when I married Brian that he'd be getting shipped off shortly after. I didn't care. I loved him and that's all that mattered to me. Not saying it isn't hard because it is. And honestly, it doesn't get any easier."

I sit up straighter. "How do you do it, then?"

She shrugs, though I still see uncertainty on her face. "I stay busy. That's the only thing I can do. Between work and Dylan's sports and school, I don't have much downtime. It wears me out but keeps me from sitting around sulking."

Her words give me a sense of hope. It's only three months, not years like she endures. "Maybe it just upsets me more since we've been trying for a baby. I keep getting disappointed with each negative test and now with him leaving, it's only going to prolong it."

"You feel like his job is getting in the way of your dream to become a mother."

"Yes," I admit, shocked by my own admission. "After Robinson died, it made Lincoln realize life is too short. It made him want to start a family, and now his damn job is putting a freaking twist in our plan and a thousand miles between us." I swallow hard, biting back the tears.

Echo scoots closer and rubs a hand down my back. "It will all work out, Lynsie. I'll be here. You can tag along with me."

I smile, feeling a little better about everything. "I'm more than sure I'll be taking you up on that offer. I don't have many people around here I consider a friend, but you're one of them."

"HEY, LYNS. WHATCHA got cooking over there?" Dax bobs his blond head toward the sizzling skillet on the stove as he takes a seat on the bar stool.

"Fajitas. Ole," I sing, doing a little salsa shimmy with my hips. "You eating dinner here or you got a hot date?" I eye him as I rest my hip against the counter across from him.

"Eating here as long as you never do that little dance of yours again." He laughs, ignoring my hot date comment.

I grab the dishrag and throw it. "Shut up, Dax. You're just jealous of my skills."

He holds his hands up in defense. "You're right. You're right. I'll suffer through your dancing as long as I get to eat."

With Lincoln running behind, I take the chance to ask Dax about the training. "Hey, umm, are you going to the training in Texas?"

His smile vanishes and he looks down at his hands, then gathers his composure. "No. I didn't get in. What else is new?" he grumbles with bitterness.

"So you put in for it and didn't get accepted?"

He nods.

"Did they tell you why? Your cast will be off by then."

"Yeah." He sighs. "Something about it being full or some shit." He shrugs, downplaying it, but I can tell it bothers him. "That I'd get to go next round."

"Don't be mad, but I'm kinda glad you aren't going," I say, a little hesitant. He looks at me with furrowed brows and I explain, "I'm going to need company when Linc's gone. It'd double suck if you both were going. It'll be nice to at least have a roomie here while he's gone. Hopefully, you won't get tired of my company." I let out a short, nervous laugh.

"I'm with enough guys every day at work." He makes his way to the fridge, opens a can of soda, and takes a long drink. "You're a much-needed distraction from those knuckleheads." Dax places a reassuring hand on my shoulder as he walks back to his seat.

"Good point." I let out a worried breath and bite my bottom lip, leaning back against the counter by the stove. "I'm worried about this training."

He glances down, unable to keep eye contact with me. "I'd be lying if I said the thought hasn't crossed my mind. It's only because of what happened with Robinson. It's still fresh. The statistics are on our side, I guess." He shrugs and looks back up. I can see worry in his eyes.

"Yeah, but statistics don't ease my mind. We can't base our lives off them."

"True." He nods. "But we can't live in constant fear and worry either. We have to let it go and pray for the best. Same with everything in life."

"When'd you become so smart?" I smile warmly, using words Dax previously spoke to me.

His face lights up with recognition. "Ah, you know"—he winks—"I've been taking notes."

Lincoln walks through the front door as soon as I'm done warming up the last tortilla. "Something smells good." He walks up behind me and kisses my neck. "Well, other than you." I feel him smile against my skin, and it makes me shiver.

"I'll feed that appetite of yours later," I say, twisting around in his arms.

"It's never ending." He twists his hand in my hair, bringing his mouth near my ear. "Are you sure you're up for the challenge?" My knees weaken as desire floods me.

"Man, am I hungry," Dax moans. I glance over to see him rubbing his stomach.

Lincoln doesn't take his eyes off me. "Dude, there's a Taco Bell around the corner."

"Screw that." Dax dismisses him. "You know I'd much rather eat at Casa de Fox. Even if I have to put up with your gaga looks and bedroom eyes."

"Fine." I chuckle, not feeling quite as embarrassed. "We'll save the bedroom eyes for the bedroom." I give Lincoln a quick kiss and grab the plates out of the cupboard.

"Thank you, Jesus," Dax hollers as I hand him his plate.

I sit back and wait for them to stack their plates before I get up and scavenge what they leave behind. They both head to the living room and make themselves comfortable on the couch, watching whatever game is on.

"Dinner is great, baby." Lincoln looks my way with a smile.

Dax follows with, "Yeah, much better than Taco Bell."

After we're done eating, Lincoln runs upstairs to shower, and Dax stays put on the couch, watching TV while I clean up the kitchen.

I'm about done with the dishes when Dax suddenly struts into the kitchen, singing, "Hey, Lyns, what does the fox say?"

I stare. He stares. We both stare at each other.

I'm about to state the obvious—foxes don't speak, but before the words come out, he waves a hand at me. "Never mind," he says, exasperated, leaving the way he came. I shake my head and dry the last plate in my hands. Must've totally missed the punch line for that one.

"YOU READY FOR tomorrow?" I ask Lincoln as we all sit on the couch. I shimmy my way to lie down, resting my head on his lap. He begins to stroke my hair softly. If he keeps this up, he'll lull me to sleep in no time.

"Baby, I was born ready."

"Cocky much?" Dax laughs, reminding me he's still here. Sometimes he gets so quiet that I wonder what goes on in that mind of his.

"When you're good, you're good," he teases. Lincoln is anything but cocky. Confident, yes, but never cocky. A couch pillow smacks him in the face, causing Lincoln's body to move beneath me. "Hey, man, don't start something you can't finish." I quickly sit up, wanting to avoid being collateral damage.

"Enough, boys," I half tease, feeling like a ref/mom most days. "Seriously, though."

They drop their pillows and look over at me.

"Is everyone all set for tomorrow? Got everything down?" I'm usually not paranoid, but something I can't explain changed inside after what happened with Robinson. It opened my eyes to how everything I'm so certain of can instantly be taken away.

"Yep. The show tomorrow night is going to be amazing. I even have a surprise worked up for you." He tries to suppress a smile but fails miserably. I look past him at Dax, who shrugs his shoulders, feigning ignorance.

"Oh yeah?" I raise my brows. "And what would that be?" It's useless to ask. He won't tell me. I always crack under the slightest pressure, but Lincoln...no way. He can keep stuff on a Code Red lockdown.

"It wouldn't be a surprise if I told you." He taps the tip of my nose with his finger. Duh, Captain Obvious.

I glance at Dax one last time, seeing if he'll crack.

"Quit looking at me like I'm the weakest link, Lyns. It ain't gonna happen." He slowly enunciates the last part, then pretends to zip his lips.

"Fine, but y'all are both lucky I don't have very long to wait for said surprise." I narrow my eyes at both before giving them a sly smile. I lay my head back in Lincoln's lap with him wrapping one arm around my side, and his other hand finding its way back to my hair. Their conversation and the TV slowly become background noises as I drift to sleep.

Chapter Thirteen

LYNSIE

I arrive early at Lake Tholocco, beating what's sure to be an insane-sized crowd here this evening. I want to make sure I get the best seat in the house for tonight's show. With my plaid blanket laid out, I sit the mini cooler in the corner to keep it from flying away. Usually, my mom would be with me, but she's at home with a migraine. I promised her I'd take plenty of pics, but it's hard to remember when you're mesmerized by the show. Knowing it's my husband up in the sky, making everyone *ooh* and *aah*, causes me to burst with pride. I want to brag and yell, *'Yeah! That's my husband!'* But for his sake, my sake, and the sake of those around me, I always refrain from doing so.

Lincoln makes his way over, giving me the chance to see him one last time before the festivities begin. I soak him up as he saunters right up to me, pushing his Aviators to the top of his head and smiling brightly. He rests his hands on my hips and glances around in approval. "Looks like you got us a good spot to watch the fireworks." He practically bounces with excitement, and I know it's not because of the fireworks. I can't help but admire him as he stands in front of me, wearing his Army flight suit. The olive-green one-piece does nice things to his firm body, leaving no room for imagination.

"There's a more important show I want front row action to." My excitement mimics his as I push up on my tippy-toes and kiss him. His arms wrap around me, pulling me into him as his lips stay trained on mine for a heartbeat longer than I anticipated. Regaining control of my composure, I slowly land flat on my heels and tilt my head back. "Be safe, Lincoln." I search his silky brown eyes for reassurance.

His arms tighten around me as he leans in closer and grins against my lips. "No need to worry, Lyns. I'm doing what I do best. Plus, look." He motions out above the lake. "Blue sky, babe. It's perfect. You know what I always say."

"Yeah, yeah." I press a hand to his cheek, loving his chiseled face and enthusiasm. "Nothing more beautiful than a blue sky."

"Well, that isn't entirely true." His voice stills my heart while his strong hands hold my face in place. "There's *nothing* more beautiful than my Lynsie Pearl." He kisses me deeply and passionately this time as he takes my mind elsewhere. I temporarily forget my surroundings until I hear a throat clearing. I look over Lincoln's shoulder to see Dax standing there, running his good hand through his hair as he purposely looks away, leaning back on the balls of his feet.

"Hey, stranger." I grasp Lincoln's hand, swinging it between us.

Lincoln smiles and gives Dax an upward nod. "Hey, man."

"Thanks for saving me a spot." He glances around at the view. "Looks like you got the best seat in the house."

"Darn skippy." I pat Lincoln's chest. "My man's going to be in that sky. You better believe my butt will be sitting front row."

"Well, I'm glad I'll be in good company." He tries to give a genuine smile, but I can tell he's still bothered.

Lincoln looks down at his watch. "All right, time for me to head back."

"Get 'em, Wings." I hug him before placing a soft kiss on his lips. "I love you, Lincoln Fox."

One side of Lincoln's mouth quirks up. "I love you too, baby."

"Good luck up there." Dax places his hand on Lincoln's shoulder, giving it a squeeze.

"Thanks, man." Lincoln grips Dax's shoulder back, then pulls him in for a hug. As he starts to strut away, he whips around. Walking backward a few steps, he extends both arms, pointing at us. "I'll see you guys soon." His face beams and I wave, laughing at my husband. His energy is contagious.

Dax and I take our seats as the space around us starts to fill in. Families and friends laughing and having a good time put a smile on my face. I watch kids around us play Frisbee and catch with whatever ball they brought. Every now and then, one of the balls lands next to us, and Dax quickly grabs it and tosses it back.

"Why don't you go play with them?" I extend my legs out, crossing them at my ankles.

He laughs with playfulness in his eyes. "Ah, those boys don't want some old guy playing with them." He holds up his broken hand as a reminder.

"Right," I drag out. "I think you're safe with them." I laugh.

"I don't know about that. If I remember correctly, you told me I'm no spring chicken." Another ball lands right by us.

"I think them boys beg to differ. They keep *accidentally* throwing the ball over here."

"That's all on you, Lyns," Dax says.

I lean over, bumping his arm with my shoulder. "What's that supposed to mean?" There's no time for him to answer. I hear the rumbling of the first plane and quickly hop to my feet as if it will give me a better view.

"Okay, which one is the Widow Maker?" I ask, causing Dax to choke on his water.

"What?" he coughs out.

"The guy at the wood shop told me that the Mohawks are called widow makers."

His eyes are wide as he looks left and right. "Wow, I never heard that. Um, it doesn't look like it's out yet." He points up. "That one is Peterson. I believe Lincoln should be out shortly."

I keep my eyes focused upward, watching in delight. I see another plane in the distance join in the airshow. This plane looks like one of the ones we saw at the museum—too old to be in the sky. I glance over at Dax, and he nods. The sun slowly starts to set, painting a beautiful sky filled with pinks and oranges. The canvas the planes now fly against is breathtaking.

When the show is about halfway through, I eagerly watch for Lincoln's surprise.

"Hey, girl," Echo says, wrapping her arm around my waist as she comes up from behind.

I turn to her, giving her a full embrace. "Thank you for coming." Looking past her, I see a boy wearing a ball cap with his gaze fixed upward. "And this must be the baseball stud I'm always hearing about."

"This is him," Echo proudly exclaims as she tucks him up under her arm.

"Okay, okay, Ma," he mumbles, trying to pull away from her. Her arm grips even tighter around him in response.

I giggle. "It's nice to finally meet you." I extend my hand out and he politely accepts the gesture. "This is Dax," I say, elbowing Dax to get his attention. He looks at me with a bit of confusion and then notices Echo.

"Oh hey, Echo." He leans in, giving her a quick hug.

"This is Echo's son, Dylan."

Dax extends his hand to shake Dylan's. "Hey, man! I hear you're quite the baller."

"You heard correctly," Dylan replies as he pulls his hat off, flipping it around backward before placing it back on. Dax's laugh is cut short when the two finally make full eye contact with one another. He stares a bit longer than he should, almost as if he's seen a ghost.

"It's good meeting you," Dax says, turning back around. I smile and do the same.

"What was that about?" I look up at him, trying to read his expression. He's staring off into the distance, not paying attention to the show. I nudge his side, pulling him from his stupor.

He shakes his head. "What?" he asks, looking down at me.

"What was that about?" I repeat quietly.

"Oh, I don't know." He chances a quick peek behind us where Echo and Dylan are, then glances down at me. His brows are pinched in deep thought. "Her son really reminds me of someone. Where did she say she was from again?"

I want to pry and dig deeper, but more planes begin to take flight and my attention returns to the reason why we're here. I see Lincoln and it takes everything within me not to jump with joy like a toddler.

"Oh look!" I point with excitement. "He's doing the wing dip. That must be the surprise he told me about."

"Actually, that's not the surprise. I'm supposed to tell you what it is," Dax says, shoving his hands into the pockets of his shorts, looking over at me.

His mouth opens and shuts as we hear a loud pop in the distance. Our heads snap up to the sky. Smoke is billowing out of the front of one of the planes. It dips to the side before seeming to straighten out. Relief washes over me as the pilot seems to have regained control of the plane.

A thunderous boom fills the sky, followed by gasps from all around us.

My heart drops and my stomach clenches tight. "Please tell me that's not Lincoln's plane."

"No." Dax watches in disbelief. "I'm pretty sure that's Peterson's plane." He's still as a statue as he barely whispers, "And it's heading right for us. People need to start clearing out just in case he can't get it under control."

We watch in horror, frozen in time. It feels like it's come to a halt and moving at the speed of sound all at once. I cover my mouth and stare, feeling as if I'm paralyzed in place. A parachute shoots out the top of the plane and Peterson is blown around by the wind like a plucked feather. For an instant, relief washes over me, and I release the breath I'd been holding.

Dax grabs my hand and squeezes. "This isn't good, Lyns, we need to go." He eyes Echo and her son, telling them to leave before the max exodus occurs. Turning in the grass, Dax addresses the spectators in a loud, authoritative voice, "Everyone go! Get as far away as you can." It all sounds like white noise as the sound of planes and the crowd screaming fill our surroundings. This can't be happening.

With our hands joined, he tries to yank me forward, but I can't move. My thoughts tear at my insides, a mixture of hope and fear. My legs feel weak, but I stand firmly in place, my feet feeling like they are being held in place by quicksand.

My eyes are fixated on the sky. They must be playing tricks on me. I feel Dax looking at me, but my eyes are glued upward. The smoky plane in the distance is indeed heading straight for us, but there's something else. It's Lincoln's plane...heading straight for Peterson's.

Dax is silent for a heartbeat, then he's screaming. My hand slips from his as he waves both arms high at the sky. "No, no, no!" he screams over and over.

I drop to my knees, my body numb.

This isn't happening. He's safe. He'll eject. He'll be fine. I tell myself over and over, even in my shocked, numb state.

The noise is deafening as the two planes collide. The sky is no longer filled with a myriad of pretty shades. It is filled with a fireball of debris. I throw my hand over my heart, clutching it as I feel it eviscerating itself apart within me. Smoke and fire consume the sky, and I lose sight of the parachute. Debris spirals in every direction, splashing into the lake below, and my throat closes completely. Somewhere inside myself, I find the sense to say a prayer.

Keep him safe. Suddenly, a feeling of hope takes over. He's going to be fine. He has to be. Lincoln knows what he's doing. He told me himself before the show. He would never take that kind of risk, knowing he'd die doing so.

I quickly stand to my feet and yank on Dax's arm. "We have to go. We gotta get to the other side of the lake. We have to make sure they find Lincoln before it gets dark. He can be anywhere." I frantically pull on his arm, but he's not budging.

"Lynsie," he says, his throat thick. When he turns to me, I see tears streaking his face. "Only one person ejected from that plane."

I nod. "Yeah, I know. Come on, we have to hurry."

He grabs me by my elbow, but I yank away from him. If he won't help me, I'll go by myself. I turn, walking away, and Dax yells, "Lynsie! That was the surprise," he chokes out. I hear the agony in his voice. "Lincoln and your dad were both on that plane."

Chapter Fourteen

LYNSIE

A grave sense of loss washes over me. My feet halt on the grass and suddenly I can't breathe. My voice comes out low and shaky. "Well, maybe they both ejected in time." Tears begin to fall. I know we only saw one. My body trembles as heartbreak wretches through me. A scream claws at my throat, beckoning to be released. I swallow hard, pushing down what feels like shards of glass.

"Lynsie." He tries desperately to pull me in, but I yank away from his hold.

"No. We have to go." Peeking through my tears, I look back over the lake and watch the last bits of fiery debris fall from the sky. I stare out in disbelief. I refuse to accept that I just witnessed my future crash and burn in front of my very eyes.

The noise of emergency vehicles shakes me from my frozen state. I look up to see Dax staring at me, pleading. He extends his hand once more. I slowly ease my hand into his, knowing agonizing pain awaits me. He turns on his heel, pulling me behind him as we weave through the crowd.

"My car is over here," I yell.

He looks back over his shoulder. "We have to go by foot. We'll never make it through all the emergency vehicles." We run along the side of the road, careful not to be in the way of the ambulances and fire trucks screeching past us. They do nothing but make me push my feet harder into the ground. My heart pounds faster the closer we get, the sound deafening my ears.

The area is blocked off, only allowing emergency vehicles and military personnel in and out. Panic sets in as I realize they might not let us enter. I cling to Dax's hand as he pulls us through an area not being watched. I feel sick. I yank Dax's hand, stopping us, and turn around and heave. The run and the absolute terror get the best of me. I can feel the cracks in my heart expanding, just waiting for the right moment to explode. The tears won't stop, leaving the scene around me blurry.

I look out over the lake where they have rescue boats combing the water. Two helicopters fly from above. People are shouting from every direction. All I can do is stand, completely numb, feeling helpless as I watch.

I tightly close my eyes, letting the scene play over and over in my head. Each time, I pray I'll catch something I didn't notice at first. Another chute—there had to have been another chute that was clouded by the smoke, but each time, I see nothing.

I stand as close to the shore of the lake as I'm allowed and wait for some sort of news. My entire body shakes. I ball my hands at my sides, hoping the biting of nails into my flesh will offer some sort of distraction. But no amount of physical pain can lessen the emotional turmoil coursing through my body.

No one knows who made it out, or they're just refusing to say. Everyone who happens to make eye contact with me does so with pity. I'm *her*, the woman who either lost her dad or her husband. As of right now, it's a toss-up.

Dax stands right next to me with a glazed look of despair. He doesn't attempt to comfort me as we stand side by side in silent disbelief. I look down at his hand, seeing it trembling at his side. He's just as terrified. I grab it, lacing our fingers. Right now, I need him. I want to tell him it'll be okay, that Lincoln is fine, but I can't. And if I could, that'd mean my dad wasn't. We watch the boats out over the lake. It's starting to get dark, and the helicopters turn their searchlights on from above in attempts to help Search and Rescue. Not sure how much of that rescue part is true because, in all reality, there are no guarantees that both even survived.

I watch as men dressed in flight suits walk up, pushing their way to the shoreline. A momentary silence seems to take over with their presence as if they know whose fate has been sealed.

"Dax."

I look up and see Peterson at his side.

"I'm so sorry, man," he chokes out. His eyes make their way to mine, and I can see all the answers I need to in them as he drops his head, shaking it.

I hear some commotion off to the side and a few claps as one of the smaller boats bobs to the shore. From here, I can make out the flight suit I've known my whole life, and I see the helmet still on his head that hangs low. I swallow hard as tears start to form. A nauseating feeling of agony sinks in the closer the boat gets.

Look up, Lynsie, I say in my mind over and over. I need to know. I need to know what my future holds...or who it doesn't.

The boat comes to a stop and EMTs and firemen surround them, pulling the man to safety. I try to run up to get as close as possible, but so many people are in my way. I need to see. I push through two men in uniform, and I'm met with a pair of soft brown eyes. A flicker of hope I didn't realize I had is quickly doused. Sad, sad brown eyes. The same brown eyes I've seen my entire life. The ones that always made me feel better with each scraped knee or broken heart. Those eyes won't be able to help my destroyed heart now.

As I look into these brown eyes, I know I should be happy, but all I feel is my heart exploding into a million tiny pieces. I should be happy my dad survived, but my mind is frozen, and my spirit is broken. Red hot, fiery pain shoots out from my heart and encompasses my entire body until I'm engulfed. My other half is gone. Lincoln is gone.

"Lynsie, I'm so sorry." My dad comes toward me, weeping.

"No!" I scream, collapsing to my knees. The soft ground welcomes me. "*Noooooo!*" I press my hands to my face, rocking back and forth. The noises around me become a blur. My entire life becomes one as all the memories of Lincoln flood my mind in an instant.

Strong arms wrap around me, and I know it's not my dad. I'm sure if I could see Dax's face through my own tears, he'd look just as wrecked. I don't even hear what people are saying all around me. My life is over. My husband is dead. I can't stop replaying the crash and hearing the horrible sounds. Now knowing he was part of it...that he felt it. I will never recover from this.

"Let me take you home," I hear Dax murmur.

I finally look up and take in his red-rimmed eyes and tear-streaked face. Not only did I lose a husband, he lost his best friend. His lifelong best friend.

"Oh, Dax," I whimper as I turn and throw my arms around him. "I'm so sorry," I say more, mostly rambling, unable to stop myself as we both hold each other and cry.

"We should go." He swallows hard, biting back the tears.

I pull back enough to look up at him, my eyes clouded with tears. He turns his head away to compose himself, and I place my hands on his face, forcing him to look at me. He doesn't need to hide his heartbreak from me. He can hide it from everyone else, but not me.

I glance out at the now quiet lake, despite the people still rushing around, and my lip quivers with another round of tears. "I can't leave. Not yet. What if he's out there? What if...just what if there's a chance that he—"

"No, Lynsie." Dax solemnly shakes his head. "You saw what I saw. You know there was no chance. They aren't out there searching for Lincoln right now. They're searching for the debris and... remains." He barely chokes out that last word.

Remains... I squeeze my eyes shut to shake the visual, but it doesn't help. They're out there right now looking for my husband's remains. My worst fears have come true. I'm alone. He left me all alone.

Chapter Fifteen

DAX

Getting Lynsie to leave was damn near impossible. I was quite certain the night would eventually end with me picking her up and carrying her to the car, but much to my surprise, she willingly stood up and took off in the direction of the car without another word to her father.

I gave him a sympathetic look before turning back to follow her. It's still packed over here with every type of emergency vehicle known to man. And by the looks of it, every Army official from base as well. I'm still in shock. My mind feels numb, unable to process anything. This has to be a nightmare. One I'll eventually wake up from.

The car ride to Lynsie's parents' house is silent. What is there to say? What we both just witnessed. So many questions are flooding my mind. *What? Why? How?* I can't make sense of any of it. Tears constantly prickle at the backs of my eyes, but I hold them in.

I have to be strong, I keep reminding myself. *You must be strong. Lynsie's going to need you.*

I see fireworks lighting up the night sky. Everyone else going about their Fourth of July celebrations without a care in the world, all while we're here, left to mourn this sudden, devastating loss. It's not fair. My world has fallen off its axis, and it will never be the same again.

Lynsie's mother is waiting at the door, along with Echo. I'm not sure what she needs, but being around loved ones is the only logical thing that makes sense. As everyone walks in, I sit on the steps of the front porch. Lynsie turns around, noticing I'm not behind her, and gives me a panicked look. "You aren't leaving, are you?" Her voice is scratchy, barely audible.

"No. I'll be in in a bit." I let out a shaky breath. "I need to make a call."

Her body stiffens, and she nods, letting her mother guide her inside.

I'm dreading this phone call. I'm not sure if they've been notified yet. The officials will most likely wait until the plane has been recovered. Either way, it's a call I need to make no matter what. I can't chance them finding out from someone else. This is going to be the hardest damn call of my life.

My finger lingers over the call button as an inner battle wages war inside me. Where do I even start? How do I possibly tell them their only child was just killed doing what he loved? I can still barely come to terms with this myself.

Three rings in, Mr. Fox picks up. I hear the laughter in his voice. "Dax. How's it going? How's the show?"

That's all it takes for me to break down. I silently cry and feel the air on the other line thicken. He knows something's wrong.

"Dax," he whispers, "what's wrong?"

"Something went horribly wrong. There was a crash at the show." Saying it all out loud makes it real. Painful. "Lincoln didn't make it." My voice cracks as I finally release a sob and the line goes silent.

I hear him scream as he tells his wife. Their despair squeezes everything inside of me. It's too much for me to bear. Pushing end, I let my phone fall to the ground. I sit out here and take in the loss of my best friend, my brother. The horrible, horrible loss. *What the hell went wrong?* I lose track of time replaying the event over and over. My phone begins buzzing from the ground, but I don't have the strength to answer it. Headlights pierce my eyes as a car turns into the driveway, letting someone out and reversing back out of the drive. I make out the slouched and sad form of Lynsie's dad walking toward me. He looks rough. I can't imagine what he must be feeling. He was the last one with Lincoln.

Dan sits down next to me and gazes out at the road. "It should've been me," he whispers.

I stay silent. Shameful as it is, it's a thought that crossed my mind.

I can't say he's wrong, but I can't say he's right either. This is something he's going to have to come to terms with, and talking about it might help him, so I just listen, even though I don't really want to.

"It was my idea." Dan rests his forearms against his legs, hunching over. "When I heard Peterson's plane had engine failure and was heading right for the crowd, crashing our plane into it over the lake seemed logical." His body shakes as he cries, and I breathe through my nose, trying to keep my bearings. "Both seats were supposed to eject. Both of them," he yells. "I would never have made that call if I thought this could happen. The idea never crossed my mind." He shakes his head in defeat, letting the blame sink in. "Now look. My daughter lost her husband. You lost your best friend. I lost my son-in-law. The Army lost a damn good pilot. The world in general lost a good man, and I'm to blame." Another wave of sobs rolls through him.

My hands tightly grip the edge of the concrete step. "I don't know what happened up there, but I know without a doubt that it wasn't your fault. Whatever happened was out of your control." My voice is unsteady, barely recognizable.

I doubt my words offer him any comfort. Words don't fix things. He'll forever be traumatized by this. He was on the plane. He was front and center to the action. He made the call. And more than anything, it could've just as easily been him who didn't eject.

"What exactly went wrong?" I finally ask as uncertainty eats at me.

The front door slowly opens, allowing the light from the inside to shine on us. I'm sure the light exposes how broken we both are.

Mrs. Clark steps onto the front porch, and Dan stands to face her. He looks defeated. With his shoulders bent and head hanging low, he shoves his hands in his pockets as he takes slow strides toward her. His body shakes with tears that refuse to run dry.

"Oh, honey." She rushes over to him with open arms, enveloping her broken husband. Her attempts at comfort only fuel the emotion engulfing him. I have a feeling it has more to do with Lynsie. The responsibility for her husband's death eating away at him.

I wasn't even up there, but I find myself wishing I had been. Surely, a quick death would feel better than this excruciating pain in my chest.

I follow them inside, glancing at the couch where Echo holds her tightly while she sobs uncontrollably. She cries with her. My heart breaks even more just watching and knowing. The numbness of it all is settling over me.

Lynsie's sobs grow quiet like she's given all she has, but I know the reservoir has yet to be tapped. As Echo slowly pulls away, I watch Lynsie from the side, gauging her. The emptiness now etched across her face hurts me in more ways than I can explain. The fun, witty, lively girl I've grown to love over the past few years is gone. Replaced with a solemn look of emptiness. Hearing her dad's voice seems to spark something. She stands and stalks to where her dad and mom stand near the kitchen.

"What happened, Dad?" she asks without a shred of emotion. Her voice and face are empty.

"I don't know what exactly happened, Lynsie." He reaches out for her arm, but she yanks it back. He flinches and I see pain flash in his eyes. I see the guilt wash over him, again.

"I need to know what happened," she demands a little louder. "I have to know why my husband is dead."

"It's my fault," he weeps. "Peterson's plane was going down. I made the call for Peterson to eject, and Lincoln agreed we'd take the plane down with ours. It was heading right for the crowd. Right for you." He looks at Lynsie, pleading for understanding.

She stands there, stock-still, fists clenched at her side and mouth frozen in anger.

He continues, "We were both supposed to pull at the same time. We counted to three. I'm the only one who ejected. I don't know why. I wish it had been him." He falls to his knees and drops his head into his still dirty hands.

Lynsie stands, arms crossed, with a stone-cold look on her face.

I want to shake her and yell your dad's alive. It's not his fault Lincoln didn't survive. I want to tell her to show the man the love he desperately needs right now. Don't let him blame himself. She needs to cling to those she loves. Those who love her. And not push them away.

After a minute, the Lynsie I know reemerges. Emotions she's been holding break through the numbness that was settling in—the numbness that is sure to return later. She falls to her knees in front of her dad, pressing her hands to his cheeks. "It's not your fault, Daddy," she whimpers, throwing her arms around him.

Echo comes up to me, offers her condolences, and gives me a tight hug before she leaves. I walk into the living room and take a seat on the empty couch. I'm itching to get back to the lake in search of answers, but my main priority is Lynsie. She eventually joins me, stepping over my outstretched legs to climb to the other end. She grabs my hand, intertwining our fingers as she leans into me and rests her head on my shoulder. She's taking comfort in me and giving me comfort as well. I let out a heavy breath as my erratic heart begins to even out. Her nearness does something to me...it calms me. I wrap my arm around her shoulders, pulling her in even closer. She sniffles and shakes against my side. I run my hand through her hair, hoping to offer her some sense of calm.

Lynsie soon falls asleep, propped up against me. Her mom helps me lay her down, and I pray she stays asleep and gets some rest. Mr. Clark walks out from his room, showered and changed. He's still a mess, but it's a state we're all going to be in for a while.

"I want to go back to the lake." He looks at me, his eyes blood-shot from all the crying. "I feel like I need to be there when they pull the planes out, or what's left. I need answers. No one is answering their damn phones." He glances over at the couch where his daughter lies. I see the indecision on his face. He's asking himself if he should be leaving her.

I glance at Lynsie, then back at him. "I'll go," I tell him, my voice heavy and exhausted. "I'll stay on top of everything. Bug whoever the hell I need to. And I won't be back until I get the answers we all need."

His eyebrows tighten, like he wants to fight me on it. Then he takes one more look at his broken daughter and his defiance dissipates. "Are you sure you're up to it, son?" he asks, gripping my shoulder.

"Yes. I can't sit anymore. My mind is going crazy."

He nods sullenly. "Call me as soon as you know anything. Oh, and hey, if anyone gives you any grief, call me."

Let someone give me a hard time. I'll show them grief.

Chapter Sixteen

DAX

The area is still complete madness. Just as I expected, news crews cover the road, each wanting to catch the gory details when the search ends. None of them really care it was my best friend who lost his life. Lost his life to save so many in the process. I doubt that will even be the story they air.

I'm nearing the edge that's being guarded. A mixture of police and Army personnel roaming around. As I try to pass, a man in fatigues stops me, pressing a firm hand against my chest. "Sir, you can't go in there. This area is closed off."

"Yes, I can." I fist my hands at my sides to control my anger. The guy is only doing his job, but his job might get him a bloody nose. "I'm a pilot for the Army," I snap and pull my wallet out of my back pocket, opening it to show him my military I.D. He glances down but doesn't care. "It was my best friend's plane that went down. Our Colonel sent me here to find out the details while he stays home with his daughter, who just lost her husband. So if you'll excuse me."

He gives me a sympathetic nod, releasing me. I adjust my shirt, pushing my way past him.

It's complete chaos as I make my way toward the shoreline. I notice most Army officials standing together around the water. Some are barking orders, others just watch, hoping for news. I don't recognize any of them. They must've sent Peterson and the rest of the pilots home. I wander over to who I assume is in charge by the lines of frustration on his face as he yells orders. If he can't tell me something, he'll know who can.

"Colonel"—I quickly look at his badge—"Walker. I'm Chief Warrant Officer Dax Adams. Colonel Dan Clark sent me here to gather information."

He eyes me suspiciously.

I explain further, managing to keep my voice level, "He was in the plane that crashed. Chief Warrant Officer Lincoln Fox was his son-in-law. Colonel Clark is at home with his daughter. He asked me to come in his place."

He gives me a sympathetic nod. "There isn't much going on yet. We're working on getting some boats out here to pull in the wreckage. We had divers in the water earlier before it got too dark. The only thing I can confirm is that there's evidence of remains in one of the planes."

My jaw tightens, but I keep my face rigid, warding off the emotion threatening to spill out.

He can read my eyes like a pro as he clamps my shoulder. "I'm truly sorry about your loss, Officer." He opens his mouth to say something else but stops himself, giving me a wary look. Then he shakes his head. "I'm not supposed to say anything, but I've heard they're looking into the recording that the control tower has." He scratches the back of his neck. "I'm sure a copy has already been sent over to your unit, under the circumstances. I haven't listened to it yet, so it might not be something you want to hear."

The recording? Of course they have a recording. I give a single nod, then turn to leave. Once I make my way back to my car, I slam it in gear, speeding my way to the base. I screech to a halt right outside the hangar our offices are located in. I hear faint chatter down the hallway near Colonel Clark's office. Inside, Peterson sits with the rest of the pilots who were in the show. They're all solemn, sitting with their heads hanging low. I'm sure they've each been silently playing it over in their minds, realizing how easily it could've been one of them instead of Lincoln.

Something we usually don't think about—how easily shit can go wrong, shit beyond our control. Shit some might call fate.

Peterson slowly lifts his head. When he spots me, he quickly stands. Before I can even take in what's happening, they all surround me, hugging me at once and telling me how sorry they are, but they aren't just sorry for me, they're sorry for themselves too. We all loved Lincoln.

I pull up a chair and let out a heavy sigh as I rub my eyes with the palms of my hands. All this crying is giving me a headache. "So have you guys heard anything? I went back to the site and they're still working to pull the planes out of the lake. The only information I got was about a possible recording."

They all look at me with intense sadness and dread in their eyes before glancing in the direction of the computer.

"The recording is on the computer." Connelly looks up from where he's sitting behind the desk.

I quickly stand and make my way over. He stands, allowing me access to sit and play it. I take a moment, letting out a heavy breath as my finger hovers over the button.

"Peterson's plane. Peterson's plane is going down. The engine just went out," I hear Lincoln panic.

"Peterson needs to eject," Lynsie's dad says.

"But his plane is going right for the crowd. It's headed right for Lynsie and Dax." His voice is shaky, a tone I've never heard before.

He wasn't just worried about his wife. He was worried about me as well.

With complete calmness, Dan says, *"What if we use our plane to take his down? It'll happen over the lake, and no one'll get injured. Direct our plane just right and we'll both eject."*

I can almost picture Lincoln nodding as he agrees. *"Okay. Sounds good."*

I hear General Clark telling Peterson to eject. Peterson argues at first. Says he can land it. He quickly realizes he can't when a loud noise thunders as his engine gives out completely.

"All right, Lincoln. On three, pull to eject. One. Two. Three." I hear the wind whipping through the cockpit as the canopy flies off, allowing for ejection.

I hear Lincoln. *"No. No. No. Come on."* His voice is full of panic.

"It's not working. The ejection isn't working." His breathing becomes erratic. I hear his sobs. *"I don't want to die,"* he whispers. *"I'm not going to make it. Tell Lynsie I love her,"* he cries. *"Take care of her, Dax."*

Those are the last words I'm able to make out as the sound of the crash erupts in the office, burning its way into my soul. My best friend's last wish was for me to take care of his widowed wife.

After the recording ends, we all sit in silence, constantly checking our cell phones. We all want answers and need to keep our hands busy. I take this as an opportunity to call Lynsie's dad. I need to check up on her and let him know about the recording.

"Dax." His voice is shaky with concern.

"Sir, I'm at the hangar right now with some of the pilots. I went by the scene first, but they were still working on getting the wreckage out of the lake. Colonel Walker is who I spoke to. He informed me of a recording from the control tower. I listened to it in your office with the rest of the guys." I pause to choke back a sob.

Dan's voice is almost frantic. He's a father right now, not a colonel. "We can't tell Lynsie. If she knows there's a recording, she'll want to listen to it, and there's no way she can handle that."

I nod in agreement. "Yes, sir."

A FEW HOURS have passed, and it's just me and Peterson now. He's only staying out of guilt. I know he feels it's his fault, but it's not. It was his plane's fault. We sit in silence as we wait. Silence sucks. When everything around you is silent, the only thing that isn't is your mind. When silence surrounds you, your mind screams the loudest, making you think about things you'd rather not.

"I'm going to go grab a coffee." Peterson stands, stretching his back out. "You want me to grab you one?"

I know Zack doesn't have any family around here. He shares an apartment with a few other guys. He's trying to be here for me, or anyone he can, when he has no one to be there for him. I can't run him off, even though I just want to be alone more than anything.

"That'd be great. Thanks." I give him a weak smile.

He turns and I bend over, resting my head in my hands. I stare down at the floor, focusing on all the scuff marks. Anything that will temporarily pull my mind from reality. A few moments later, I hear footsteps and look up, expecting it to be Peterson, but it's not. It's Colonel Walker.

He's holding an envelope and has an indecisive look on his face as he slaps the yellow envelope against his hand. "The divers recovered this from the plane. I wanted to personally bring it to you. I know you'll get them to who they now belong to." He hands me the envelope and turns on his heel to leave.

"Thanks," I mutter, and he stops in his tracks.

He looks back over his shoulder and says gravely, "Don't thank me, son."

Once I'm alone again, I open the prongs holding it shut. Dread sits on my chest like a heavy boulder as I pull the flap back, tilt the envelope sideways, and let the contents slide into my hands.

Lincoln's Army tags land on my shaky palm. I let the chain dangle between my fingers while I tightly grip the tag and stare at it, reading his name over and over until it becomes blurry and unrecognizable through my tears. I'm holding the only thing that's left of my best friend. Dropping my face into my hand, I sob. I cry for my friend, who I'll never see again. I cry, letting the pain I feel consume me.

Chapter Seventeen

DAX

The sun peeks on the horizon as I drive back to Lynsie's parents' house. I really have no news to offer besides all that remains of Lincoln. The only thing I have to show is something that'll put to rest any hope Lynsie may still be clinging to. Knowing I'm going to be the one to extinguish it kills me.

I lightly knock twice, not wanting to wake anyone still sleeping. Within seconds, Lynsie throws open the door, her mother standing behind her. Lynsie's almost hopeful expression crushes me. When she fully registers it's me, that little bit of hope slowly drains away, leaving her silent and defeated. My heart breaks even more. She moves back, allowing me entrance, and then shuts the door. I head for the kitchen where the smell of coffee and bacon beckons me.

She follows me to the kitchen, leaning against the counter. "Did you find out anything?" she asks, her voice fragile.

"No," I lie, not mentioning the recording. "When I left, they still hadn't recovered anything, except this." I pull out the folded envelope, swallowing hard as I reluctantly hand it over. I can't keep it from her. I can keep his last wishes and what happened before he died hidden, but this is something she needs to see. She needs to face the reality of it all.

"What's this?" Her voice shakes. She looks fragile, a look I'm not familiar with.

"The colonel in charge brought it to me."

I carefully watch her and wince, hearing the chain sliding against the paper. Then the tags lightly clank into her hand. She covers her mouth with her other hand and falls back against the wall, choking on the sob forcing its way out. Regret washes over me, but they belong to her now. Anything left of Lincoln belongs to her.

I reach for her. My gut is churning. I want to pull her in close and hold her, but before I can, she runs off toward the bathroom. I hear the retching as she vomits, and my eyes clench shut. I shouldn't be here. I won't make things better.

Maybe I can't help Lynsie through this, after all. That thought tears at my already destroyed heart.

Her mom rushes past me to help as her dad comes into the kitchen and grabs a coffee cup out of the cupboard, filling it to the brim before setting it in front of me.

I take a few sips, not trusting my voice to come out even. "Is she okay?" It's a dumb question.

Dan barely looks human right now, eyes bloodshot, face drawn and haggard-looking. I've never seen him like this. "She will be," he murmurs, his emotions still on the surface. "You didn't do anything wrong. It's just all setting in. Nothing else to do." He pats me on the shoulder. "You really need to get some rest. You look like hell." He offers a weak smile, trying to lighten the mood just a tad over black.

"I can't." I tightly squeeze my eyes shut, running my hands over my head to the back of my neck. "So much to figure out. Arrangements need to be made. I'm not sure how much of the funeral planning Lynsie is going to be able to do. I don't even know where she wants him buried."

"Not here," she says, pain lingering in her voice. She wipes her face with a washcloth as she makes her way back to the kitchen. "He needs to be buried in his hometown. Where his family is. Where you guys grew up." I can see the glint of a chain around her neck that wasn't there previously. She notices me eyeing her neck and instinctively grabs at the tags dangling under her shirt.

I shake my head, attempting to regain focus. "Okay." I nod, my voice going scratchy again. I swallow a few times. "I'll call his parents later to start working on it. I'm sure they'll be happy about that."

"I already called them," Lynsie's father says. "They'll be here later today."

I eye Lynsie to gauge her reaction, but she's completely zoned out as she tightly grasps the tags. I look back at her father, who's watching his daughter with concern.

Finally, he grabs his mug and heads for the computer in the dining area. "I'll start getting an idea on plane tickets."

"I'm not flying." Lynsie finally looks up, dropping her hand. I see her chest rising and falling, more rapidly with each second. She places her hands on the counter. She's panicking. "There is no way you will *ever* get me on a plane again. Ever." She starts to cry, shaking her head quickly back and forth.

Again, I feel my heart crushing. I can't stand this. I hate seeing her cry. I hate seeing the fear in her eyes just from the thought of being on a plane.

I quickly chime in to put her at ease, hoping to offer some sort of comfort. "I'll drive her." All eyes are abruptly on me, and I wonder if I overstepped some invisible line.

Lynsie calms, her hands loosening their hold on the counter. A sense of peace seems to take over. "Are you sure, Dax?" she whispers. "I'm not trying to make it harder on you. Just the idea of flying..." She grips her stomach, looking like she might hurl again. "It makes me sick. I can't," she stutters, shaking her head, "I just can't do it."

"I will gladly drive you." I'd drive her to the end of the world if that's what she needed. "It's been a while since I've made the drive anyway."

Both of her parents look at me with a sense of relief as they realize I'm doing this just as much for Lynsie as for myself. I need comfort just as much as her. I can't face this alone.

She walks up to me and palms my cheek, eyeing me with concern. Being this close to her and not being able to hold her, comfort her, hurts. I want to hold her so tight that all her pain seeps into me. I would gladly take it all away if I could.

"Get some sleep, Dax."

"I'll sleep later." I shrug.

She swallows, blinking back tears. "You don't have to be so strong. Especially around me. Remember?"

I feel the tears coming, but I blink them back. She's wrong. I do have to be strong. Lincoln needs me to stay strong for her. It was his last plea.

She brushes her own tears with the pads of her thumbs. "Come on." Lynsie grabs my hands, not taking no for an answer.

I let her drag me through a door in the kitchen that leads to a lower-level living area. Where there would be a couch, the floor dips and is filled with all sorts of cushions and pillows instead. The big TV plastered to the wall tells me this is where they have movie nights.

We sit down and my body melts into the comfy cushions. Almost instantly, I feel my eyes getting heavy, begging to close. Lynsie turns the TV on and changes the channel to something she knows won't interest me—The Cooking Channel.

"I know you're worried about me," she says softly, with a slight tremor to her voice. I turn my rested head toward her, and she adds, "But I'm worried about you, too." She grabs my hand, linking our fingers together like she did yesterday. "We both need to get some sort of rest, Dax." She looks down at our hands. "Maybe if we're resting together, we can sleep. Then I won't be worrying about you so much."

Worried about me? The last person she needs to worry about is me. Because the only person I'm worried about is her.

She yawns, causing me to yawn.

"Yawning is contagious," I say, and she turns on her side, facing me as she closes her eyes. Our joined hands rest between us. Her dark hair falls over her face. Her beauty is still evident but masked by such deep sorrow. Lincoln should be here comforting his wife, but instead, I'm left to pick up the pieces. I feel the weight of everything taking over as my eyelids slowly shut.

FAMILIAR VOICES AND weeping wake me from my nightmare, but as soon as I wake, I remember I'm living one. I feel alone before I'm even able to open my eyes. The space next to me is cold. Lynsie's gone. Panic sets in as I jump up to find her. I'm wide-eyed and worried as I dash to where I hear crying. With each hurried step, my senses start to gain full mobility and I realize it's not just Lynsie I hear.

"He loved you so much, Lynsie," a woman says, instantly twisting my insides.

It's a voice I've heard my whole life. I stop in my tracks before anyone sees me. How am I supposed to face my best friend's parents? I can't do it.

The bathroom door to my left opens and out walks Lincoln's dad, wiping his face before looking up. When I see his face, the typical smile that has always resided there is nonexistent. Over-whelming emotion hits me. We meet in the middle, clamping arms around each other. My chest vibrates as we both sob.

"I'm so sorry," I choke out, feeling like I should've been able to do something—anything. Even though I know there wasn't a thing anyone could've done. I look over his shoulder and see Lynsie and Lincoln's mother, Julie, holding each other. We've lost an amazing person we all loved, leaving us completely shattered in death's wake.

Jim doesn't speak. I don't blame him. What is there to say anyway?

Chapter Eighteen

DAX

Three days later, we're heading to my hometown in Georgia. A town that holds so many amazing memories, along with a few I'd rather forget. We agreed to leave before sunrise this morning, giving us plenty of time on this six-hour drive to stop by my parents' house to change before the service.

"Are you sure your parents won't mind us using their house?" Lynsie asks after being on the road for a couple hours. She spent the last two snuggling with her pillow against the door. I was glad she fell asleep. She needs the rest. I do, too, but my needs aren't important right now.

"Yes. They're fine with it." I grab her hand, giving it a tight squeeze before releasing it. "They're really upset they can't make it to the funeral." My parents are stuck on their annual week-long cruise in the middle of an ocean somewhere. If they had been anywhere else, they would've moved hell and high water to make it back in time. "If you don't want to stay the night, we can stop by before we head home and change back into our traveling clothes to get comfy for the ride home."

I begin to fidget with the radio to find something to fill the void of silence. Then I remember I brought something. I look over at her tired face, covered in sadness. "Hey, would you be up for listening to an audiobook?"

"An audiobook?" She shrugs. "Sure, I've never actually listened to a book before."

"It's the only *reading* I ever do." I smile. "Can you reach back there in my backpack and grab it for me?"

She turns in her seat and fiddles with the zipper. "What's this?" she asks, holding up my worn notebook.

"Umm, that's my journal. It's personal," I falter. Without another word, I watch through the rearview as she puts it back and pulls out the disc.

She lets out a laugh as she turns back around. "Stephen King, really?"

I smile. "Well, to me, the purpose of reading, or in my case listening, is to be taken somewhere else. I want to be transformed and placed in another reality. I don't want to hear about stuff that can happen in real life. What's the fun in that? And Stephen King is the man of all things scary. He's what nightmares are made of."

She rubs her thumb across the case. "Lately my real life has been a nightmare," she whispers as she slides the disk in.

"Mine too, Lyns." I place my hand on her knee. "We'll get through this. Somehow." I hope she doesn't hear the doubt in my voice.

"Yeah," she breathes out, settling her hand on top of mine to reassure me, but I can see uncertainty written all over her face.

WE PULL INTO town, driving down the main street. Somberness seems to have settled over the old homes and shops. There are ribbons tied to the trees that line the sidewalks. Every now and then,

I catch some sort of remembrance of Lincoln. Most are banners that resemble the ones cheerleaders made for the football teams and taped all over town—all bright and glittery.

Lynsie is staring out the window, abnormally silent.

A few turns later, I pull up to my childhood home. It's a two-story, older brick home with a wraparound porch.

"I love your parents' house," Lynsie says, stretching as she gets out of the car. "It has that Southern charm thing going on."

I open the back doors and pull out my suit, along with the hanger her dress is on, and I grab our bags.

I glance around, taking in all the memories. "I've always loved the houses around here. Of course, I'd never want one as big as this. There's no need for so much extra space."

"I agree. No one wants to clean more than they need to." Her smile doesn't reach her eyes as she attempts lighthearted conversation.

As soon as I push the door open, I'm hit with a familiar smell I haven't smelled in years. My mother has always been big on her scent warmers for as long as I can remember.

I hold my arm out toward the stairs, directing Lynsie where to go. "We can change up there."

She takes my lead and heads up but stops to take in every picture that lines the wall. As I look at them, I realize most of them I've never seen. Many from around my graduation, one of the last times my brother was home.

She touches the old wooden edge of one of the photos. "You and your brother look so much alike, just like your dad. How much older is he again?" She looks over at me.

"Four years. As soon as I hit high school, he signed up for the Army and headed to war. I've only seen him once since then." I try to keep the resentment from my voice, but with everything else I'm feeling, I can't.

"Wow," is all she says before taking a few more steps, stopping in front of me and Lincoln in our graduation robes. She's silent for a moment, but I see her eyes glazing over. "I love this picture," she says softly, letting her finger glide across Lincoln's face.

I step up behind her to take a closer look for myself. My mother must've put it up after I joined the Army. "This is the first time I've ever seen it," I say before pulling it off the wall and tucking it under my arm. Lynsie looks at me questioningly, and I tell her, "I'm taking it with us." Then I step past her, encouraging her to continue up.

I open the computer room door and set her bag on the floor, then hand over her dress. "I'll be in that room." I point to the door across the hall. The room used to be mine, but it's now a guest bedroom. "I'll be done before you, so I'll wait downstairs."

She nods, glancing once at the frame under my arm.

I gulp. "I'll see you in a bit," I say as I turn away.

Chapter Nineteen

DAX

How can you be there for someone when you're just as equally broken? You want to comfort them, but where's the comfort when you don't have the words to say? Aren't words supposed to make everything better? I always thought of them as a source of hope and understanding, but in times like these, they're nothing more than a slap to the face. They don't minimize the pain or sadness. They damn sure don't fix it. Nope, they're just noise. Noise to fill the emptiness because people can't stand silence.

Silence is a reminder of what is lost.

Words of wisdom won't heal what we're going through. So instead of torturing ourselves, and each other, Lynsie and I try to avoid them. We don't tell each other time will heal because we aren't sure those words hold any truth.

Lincoln's dying wish haunts me. His words were filled with love and terror. The thoughts of what he must've been feeling in those last moments consume me. As a pilot, I often unwillingly visualize myself behind the controls and wonder if I could've self-sacrificed myself the way he did. Or would I have harshly pulled up in those last few minutes, hoping to save myself. Lincoln still had time to do just that, but he was unselfish. I don't know if I would've been.

I find myself getting mad at him, knowing he chose to die. I don't want to be angry with him, but sometimes the anger is far more bearable than this aching emptiness. When I'm strong, it's not because I want to be. It's because there are people counting on me.

As I walk Lynsie down the grassy aisle to our seats at the very front, I try everything not to think of the empty casket laid out before us. Being there when it was picked out, I know it's a matte, black finish underneath the American flag draped over it.

Lincoln's remains were never found...not any identifiable remains, at least. The crash, followed by all the debris landing in the lake, didn't give hope of finding much. His dog tags are the only remaining evidence of him from that day and Lynsie clings to them like they're some sort of lifeline. She's constantly squeezing them, pressing them to her heart, or kissing their rough surface.

Lynsie's parents sit on the other side of her as I tightly hold her hand. Her body's shaking, she's crying so hard. My eyes begin to prickle as the onset of tears begins to form. I listen to the stories of adoration for his passion that fellow pilots speak about, calling him a hero. He is a hero. Why do people usually have to die to become one, though?

Peterson makes his way up, shocking me. "Umm." He coughs, clearing his throat. "I've never met anyone like Lincoln. He's always put me in my place but did so in a loving way." He wipes his face and continues. "Truth is, I shouldn't be here. I know it was an accident, but it doesn't lessen the burden of guilt I carry. All I can say is a good one is gone far too soon." He sniffles, making his way back to his seat.

I wasn't going to speak, but words came to me as I was sitting in my room last night. I give Lynsie's hand a squeeze and release it before pushing myself to my feet. I make my way to the pulpit, feeling both heavy and light, almost as if I'm not really with my body. I keep my head down, gripping both sides of the wooden stand, and silently pray for strength. Shifting my weight to stand straight, I clear my throat and look out into the crowd.

"For those who don't know me, my name is Dax Adams. Lincoln and I grew up together. He was my best friend." I pause. "No, he was my brother. He's the reason I joined the Army and he's the reason I became a pilot. Now that reason is gone." My bottom lip trembles. I close my eyes tightly, willing my composure to return.

I take a slow, deep breath to calm my fast-beating heart and open my eyes. I look at Lynsie. Through her tears, she holds my gaze and gives me a nod of reassurance. I slip my hand into my pocket, pulling out the folded paper I ripped out from my journal. I unfold it and pray again that the chicken scratch in front of me doesn't sound like gibberish as I read it.

"Lincoln, I never told you, but I hope you knew,
Ever since we were little, I looked up to you.
Many times, I felt like your shadow; that I'd never be as good,
Yet, you always encouraged me and told me I would.
You were big on destiny and doing the right thing,
I wish I could wake up and this just be a bad dream.
I've done everything beside you my whole life,
How am I supposed to pick up the pieces you left me and your wife?

My heart is broken, now there's a gaping hole,
To be honest, man, I'm not sure how to survive
this big of a blow."

I stop, trying to still the unsteadiness I feel in my voice. My fingers dig into the wood they're gripping, and I take a deep breath, then continue.

"I want to be selfish and scream, be mad as hell,
When you did the most selfless thing; a story you'll never get to tell.
You made the ultimate sacrifice, the final transition,
Aviator wings to now Angel, I envy the position.
You were one of a kind; we could never replace you,
Until we meet again, brother, I'll find you in the blue."

I fold up the now tear-stricken paper and tuck it back into my pocket. Slowly, I walk back to my seat, keeping my head down. The sounds are hard to hear, making it difficult to keep myself together. I know once I make eye contact with the front row, I'll lose the tiny shred of restraint I still have. Lynsie swiftly grabs my hand, grasping it tightly. She pulls it to her face, pressing her lips to the bare skin. She rests our joined hands on her leg, and I chance a glance at her.

"Your words were beautiful, Dax." She takes a deep breath, steadying herself as she angles toward me. "You are beautiful, Dax."

Lynsie reaches over with her free hand, placing it on my heart before moving it to my face. I close my eyes, resting my cheek in her hand as the resolve I've held begins to crumble.

After the chaplain resumes his position, finishing out the service, the folding of the flag begins. With each precise fold and tuck-over, memories of growing up alongside Lincoln hit me hard. I'm trying my best to be professional and strong, but it's too much to handle. My best friend is gone, and we have nothing to show for it. An empty casket that holds absolutely no value. A tombstone that will hold none either. There is nothing left of him. I wrap my arm around Lynsie and tuck her into my side as the finality and significance of it all hits us.

Once the flag is only a small triangle of red, white, and blue, Lynsie eases her trembling hands out of my grip and holds them forward for the officer. After he sets it in her arms, she presses it tightly to her chest, then bends over in hysterics. Her mother and I are on both sides, trying to comfort her as we each break down ourselves.

I faintly hear the tune of "Taps" being played before the sound of the three rifle volley shots are fired, signifying that Lincoln has been laid to rest, which isn't true. Lincoln was flown to rest when his plane collided with another. The only thing that gives me any sort of peace about the fact that we just buried an empty casket is knowing without a shadow of a doubt that he died doing what he loved. And with that, I know it will make this journey more tolerable.

"Lynsie, it's time to go," her mother says.

Lynsie shakes her head, faintly saying 'no' through her despair. The trembling tapers as she tries to catch her breath. Her mother makes one last attempt as she pulls on Lynsie's arm, but that only makes Lynsie more upset.

Her face reddens with anger, a feeling I'm all too familiar with lately. "No!" she yells, ripping her arm away from her mom.

Her mother gives me a worried look.

I just nod in response, reassuring her that I'll take care of her.

Mrs. Clark nods solemnly. I know she only wants to help her daughter and be there for her. I feel bad that Lynsie's taking her pain out on her. I'm not sure I'll be able to convince her either, but I'll try.

"We'll be by to check on you tomorrow, Lynsie Pearl. We love you." Her father bends down, kissing his brokenhearted daughter's forehead, and I watch them walk away, her mother glancing back every so often.

"It shouldn't have been him," she weeps, finally looking up at where the casket had been.

"What do you mean?" I ask cautiously.

"It shouldn't have been Lincoln who died, Dax," she grits out, finally looking at me, still hugging the flag tightly to her chest. "There were two pilots in that plane. Why'd it have to be him?" Then she falls into my side, crying. I try to shush her as I rub her back, but she's inconsolable. "Is it horrible feeling this way, knowing I'd be burying my father instead?"

"Not at all," I tell her gently. "I can't say from experience, but I'm sure it's a natural reaction. It's okay to feel what you're feeling. It's okay to be mad. It's only not okay when you stop feeling altogether."

She shakes her head. "I'm not sure I'm ever going to get over this or be myself again."

"You and me both." My voice breaks, showing the difficulty I'm facing being strong.

She throws herself into my arms. "Promise me you'll always be there. I need you." Panic is evident as she pulls away, looking at me wide-eyed.

I pull her back in, rubbing my hand through her hair. "I'm not going anywhere."

She lets out a shaky breath. "We've lost so much. I just can't lose you, too."

"Let's get out of here, Lyns." I put an arm around her shoulder and begin leading her away.

Her face contorts with a pain I've never seen. "I can't leave him, Dax. I can't go home and leave him here. He's all alone, and I just can't leave him." She starts to freak out, shaking her head at me, dropping to her knees by the grave.

I kneel down in front of her. "Lynsie, look at me." She continues shaking her head, shutting out the world around her. "Lynsie." I grab her face between my hands, forcing her eyes to mine. "Lynsie, he's not here." My voice cracks with emotion. "Even if there were a body in that casket, he wouldn't be here." I grab her hand and place it on her heart. "This is where he is, and here," I say, moving her hand to my heart. "He lives inside us."

She squeezes her eyes shut for a moment, then finally takes my hand and I pull us both up.

"Let's get you home."

Chapter Twenty

DAX

"We really need to go say bye to Lincoln's parents. Are you sure you don't want to stay the night at my parents' house?" I personally don't care, but I'm hoping she'll agree to stay. She needs to rest.

"I'm not sure." She yawns. "I'm kind of numb. I need to spend some time with them, but I'm not sure how well I'll handle it."

"Well, just know you don't have to handle it alone." I grab her hand and we head over to where Mr. and Mrs. Fox are standing.

They're trying to be as stoic as possible while people hug them and give their condolences. For the most part, they're holding up well on the outside. I'm sure, just like us, they're dying on the inside. Dying to get away from here and mourn the loss of their son without everyone paying their respects. Respects don't make you feel better. Words can't fix things that are broken. Only time will, and that's even debatable.

Lincoln's mom excuses herself when she spots us. "Lynsie, darling." She pulls her into a full embrace. Jim does the same, turning his back to whomever he was talking to, and pulls me into a tight hug.

"How you holding up, son?" he asks, holding me tightly. I love how they've always been so accepting of me and completely took me under their wing when I was young. There's nothing better than your best friend's family treating you as if you're one of their own.

"It's still hard to process. I'm trying hard to be strong." I nod over at Lynsie as Jim pulls away.

He follows my gaze. "I know you were all close. She's going to need you, Dax. No one else will fully get what you both are feeling."

I nod in agreement as Julie and Lynsie step closer to where we stand.

"Lynsie has agreed for you both to stay the night tonight." Julie smiles, relief flashing in her eyes.

I look down at Lynsie, who gives me a faint smile, her way of convincing me she's okay with this.

"Okay, sounds good," I say with ease, trying to convince myself and reassure Lyns at the same time.

As we're heading to where I parked, we both stop in our tracks as we hear someone behind us, yelling, "Lynsie!"

We turn around to see a tall, slender woman quickly walking toward us—Rebecca. Lynsie quickly pulls away and meets the woman halfway. I don't even think any words are exchanged before they both embrace, leaving me to question how they know each other.

After they pull apart, Rebecca walks straight up to me, wrapping her arms around my back.

Discreetly, she whispers, "I'm sorry about your loss, Dax. If you or Lynsie need anything, anything at all, get a hold of me." I feel her slip something into my pocket before pulling away. She looks me dead in the eyes, and I give a quick nod, letting her know I will.

WALKING THROUGH LINCOLN'S parents' front door—a door I've walked through so many times—a sense of heaviness settles over me. The only reason for me to ever be in this house was Lincoln. I feel like I'm here without a purpose—without permission, like I'm an intruder and I no longer belong.

"Are you guys hungry?" Julie asks, heading into the kitchen. "We have so much food. Neighbors and church friends have been bringing things over for days. There's no way we'll be able to keep it all from going to waste." She stands at the open fridge, a small smile on her fragile face. She's attempting to play pleasant hostess to keep from showing that she's a broken mother.

We all have our moments where we pretend. Where we try to show some type of emotion besides the one weighing us down.

"I'm not hungry," Lynsie says as she studies all the pictures of Lincoln hanging on the wall in the living room. Of course there's every school picture imaginable, along with prom, Basic Training, graduation, and every Army ceremony thereafter.

She lightly smiles as she passes each one, letting her hand graze over each frame, but she comes to a standstill when her eyes land on a picture of her and Lincoln's wedding.

I freeze, ready for whatever reaction. I see her body start to shake and rush over to her side.

"How, Dax?" she whispers. "How am I supposed to live without him? He was my life. I'm not sure I can do it."

I turn her to me, wrapping my arms around her, allowing her to cry into my chest as I just hold her silently. "It's going to be so hard. So damn hard, Lyns, but we'll make it. I promise."

She just nods against my chest, but I wonder if she really believes me.

AFTER BEING HERE for an hour, I'm finally able to get Lynsie to eat. It's only half of a chicken salad wrap, but right now, anything is better than nothing. I sit on the couch with her propped up against me. She's been yawning nonstop as we all sit around watching TV. Everyone is quiet and gloomy—the shock of the day still evident. It's now dark outside, matching the heaviness we all feel. Emotionally drained, Lynsie's more than ready for bed. I'm pretty sure she hasn't slept much since the day we lost Lincoln. As tired as she is, though, I don't know if she'll be able to sleep. If I'm having trouble sleeping—nightmares taking over once I'm able to find sleep—then I'm sure she isn't sleeping well either.

"Let me go get the guest rooms ready for you guys," Julie says with a light smile, continuing to play hostess.

Lynsie turns to me on the couch, her eyes wide with fear. "Can you sleep with me?" she asks in a hushed voice.

"Of course." My hand grazes the side of her cheek. "I'll just have Julie give me a pillow and blanket so I can make a pallet on the floor."

She shakes her head, looking up sheepishly. "No, can you sleep in the bed with me? Or at least just lie next to me until I fall asleep?"

"If that's what you need," I say without hesitation, knowing that being next to her is what I need. I made an unspoken vow to myself and Lincoln that I'll be whatever Lynsie needs. If it's in my capabilities, I'll make it happen.

I WAKE UP alone. Instantly, a mini panic attack sets in. Bolting straight up, my tired eyes scan the room. It's highly possible Lynsie just went to the bathroom. Impatiently, I sit for a couple more minutes.

"Screw it," I mumble, throwing the covers back. Quietly, I open the bedroom door. Besides the nightlight in the hallway, the house seems dark. It isn't until I hear the sniffles down the hall that I notice Lincoln's old bedroom light on. The door is closed.

I slowly push open the door, not wanting to startle anyone. Just as I had suspected, Lynsie is on the floor, clutching something tightly in her arms as she rocks back and forth, crying. I know getting shit out and dealing with your emotions head-on is supposed to be therapeutic, but I'm really starting to think coming here was a bad idea.

I don't say anything as I kneel down behind her, pulling her back into my body. Wrapping my arms around her, we rock back and forth. I don't say anything. Once her breathing evens out, I cradle her in my arms and silently walk her back to the guestroom as she tightly holds on to some sort of stuffed animal.

A few hours later, I wake to the bright, warm sun beaming down on me through the window. I look over and see Lynsie wide awake, her eyes red-rimmed. I'm honestly not sure if she even fell back to sleep when I brought her back in here.

"Morning." I lie still, wanting to reach out and touch her, but refraining. I don't dare say *'good'*. Nothing is good right now.

She glances over, giving me a weak smile before turning her gaze out the window. "Can we leave?" she asks, plucking at the fuzz on the stuffed airplane.

I couldn't tell what it was last night, but seeing it in the daylight, I recognize it right away. Lincoln's dad won it for him at the fair one year. Lincoln thought it was the best thing since sliced bread.

"It's not that I don't want to be around Lincoln's parents. I know they're hurting too, but being in this house"—she lightly sniffles as she runs her hand under her nose—"it's just too much. I'm not strong enough to be here. One day, I will be, I hope, but today...it's too soon." She looks back at me with pleading eyes as if I wouldn't sympathize or understand.

I run my thumb down her cheek. "I'm ready when you are, Lyns."

Julie walks out of the kitchen with a look of disappointment as she sees us fully dressed with bags in tow. "Leaving already?"

"Yeah," I say apologetically. "We have a long drive and I'm going to have to head back to work soon." I look back at Lynsie, who isn't fully paying attention, but still tightly holding on to that stuffed airplane.

Julie notices her holding it, and a flash of sadness washes over her before she places the spatula down and walks to where Lynsie is standing. "He used to love this thing." She lets out a feeble laugh. "He wouldn't ever admit it. At middle school age, it wasn't cool to sleep with stuffed toys anymore. But that boy sure loved anything and everything to do with flying."

"Can I have it?" Lynsie squeaks out, trying to keep her tears at bay.

Julie nods, placing a dainty hand against Lynsie's cheek. "You can have anything of his you want. I always hoped one day it would belong to a future grandchild of mine," she admits, brokenhearted.

Lynsie's face suddenly crumples with pain. I knew they had been trying the last few months. No one else knows that I'm aware of. I don't even think Lincoln was supposed to tell me, but he was so excited.

Wiping tears away, Julie turns back and heads into the kitchen. "I'll put something together for you both to eat on the road." She packs us a paper bag with a couple breakfast sandwiches and snacks for our trip home. Standing by my car, everyone is quiet, waiting for the other to say their goodbyes first.

Lynsie speaks first, shocking me. "I just want to thank you guys. For making such an incredible son. He was the best thing that flew into my life...literally." She lets out a short laugh. "He meant the world to me. I loved that man so much and I just want you both to know I'll never stop loving him. I'll never forget him."

I stand off to the side with tears of my own falling down my face as Jim and Julie collide around Lynsie in a tight embrace. Through the muffled cries, I hear them telling her how much they love her and how much Lincoln loved her. How they want her to stay close and to never forget about them either.

Lynsie gets into the car, and Jim and Julie pull me in for a hug.

"We love you, son," Jim says. "Don't ever forget that. You're still family. Don't be a stranger." His voice is shaky.

I nod against them both. "I love you guys, too." I pull back, wipe away my tears, and give them my best convincing smile.

Chapter Twenty-One

DAX

We pull into the driveway, and I'm amazed by all the plants and arrangements sitting on her porch. The ones from the actual funeral were delivered to the Foxes' house. These must be from our surrounding community in support of a fallen soldier.

That's something I admire about the Army—when something bad happens to one, it hits us all. We're all affected as one when tragedy strikes.

"Wow." Lynsie's eyes go wide. She gets out of the car with her stuffed plane and folded up flag tightly in hand. I need to get her a glass case to put it in. She'd be devastated if it ever came undone.

"You have a lot of people who care about you, Lynsie." I walk behind her as she looks at all the different types of foliage decorating her front porch.

"I know." She turns to look at me, hesitating as she pushes open the door after unlocking it. "But none of them can make me feel better. I appreciate them, don't get me wrong, but I just don't want to always have people looking at me with depressed eyes and knowing looks. I'll never be able to heal or feel somewhat better if everyone looks at me like I could break at any moment." She stands in the doorway, not walking in.

I walk up behind her, placing a gentle hand on the small of her back. "It's just in people's nature. In their own way, they hurt for us. No one knows the right or wrong way to handle situations like this. And everyone deals with pain differently, so there's no right or wrong way. All you can do is deal with your struggles and emotions the best way you can." I follow her inside.

She takes a few steps before turning to face me. "I don't know what the best way is." She looks at me helplessly. "Crying every day and closing myself off from everyone seems best, for now." She looks around her house as tears spill down her cheeks. It's hard being in this house—a house that holds so many memories...all centered around Lincoln...the three of us. With slow, debilitating steps, she makes her way into the kitchen. She gently places the flag on the counter, careful not to disturb it. Then covers her mouth with her hand, muffling a sob.

"If that's what you have to do, Lynsie, then do it," I tell her, deep conviction in my tone. "But promise me one thing."

She gives me a doubtful look as if she's unsure she'll be able to keep any promises.

"Shut the whole world out for all I care, but promise me"—I swallow—"promise me you'll never shut me out." I walk around the counter until I'm standing right in front of her.

She nods, a few tears trickling down her cheek. "I promise."

I pull her into my arms. "Good, because I need you just as much as you need me." I take a step back, putting some space between us as I place my hands on her shoulders. "How about I get a bath going for you?"

"Are you trying to say I stink?" She lightly laughs, wiping the tears away.

I smile. "No, I'm trying to say you need to relax. You're tense. You haven't been sleeping. You haven't been eating. You just really need to step back and take a breather."

I don't know if a bath will help at all, but it seems like maybe it could somehow comfort her. Maybe loosen her up so her body and mind will allow her at least one restful night's sleep.

Her arms are tightly crossed as she glances around, feeling Lincoln's noticeable absence. "Okay," she complies.

I squeeze her shoulders. "All right, I'll go get the water ready."

After filling the tub, I walk out of the bathroom and see Lynsie sitting on her bed. "I don't think you're going to be able to take Jet in the bath with you." I smile, but she looks up at me, confused. I point to the stuffed airplane she's holding, and explain, "Lincoln named it Jet Fox." I shake my head at the memory of us as kids. So many good memories.

She laughs sadly. "He was always silly like that. I should've known." She places the airplane down and walks past me into her bathroom. "I'll be out soon. You aren't leaving, are you?" Worry is evident in her voice.

"I'm not leaving until you tell me to, Lyns. You're going to get tired of seeing me," I lightly tease.

"I doubt that," she says softly as she closes the door.

I turn the TV on downstairs and plop my shoeless feet on the coffee table. I'm hoping there will be something on that can temporarily distract me. I search every ESPN known to man, looking for any sport that will engulf my mind, at least until Lynsie comes back down. God knows sports won't be any sort of distraction for her.

Thirty minutes later, I start to worry. I'm sure there's plenty she could be doing up there. Surely the water is cold by now, but I don't hear it draining either. Once the hour mark hits, I set the remote down and climb the stairs.

"Lynsie?" I knock on her bedroom door. There's no reply, so I slowly push it open. As I get closer to the bathroom, my soul is pierced by sobs I hear coming from the other side. I want to rush in and be by her side, but I can't just barge into the bathroom even though everything in me is screaming to do so.

I knock. "Lynsie."

No reply, but her sobs grow deeper.

I slowly twist the knob, pushing open the door as I do. There, wrapped in a towel, is Lynsie, lying in a fetal position on the floor. She's holding something in her hand. I can't tell what it is. In two quick strides, I'm at her side, pulling her into my lap, careful not to jostle her towel.

She's cold and her body is covered in goose bumps. I run my hands up and down her arms to warm her up.

"Lynsie," I say, trying not to panic. "Tell me what's wrong."

"I promised him I wouldn't," she cries out.

"You promised him what?" I ask, feeling helpless as I rock her like I did last night.

"I promised Lincoln I wouldn't find out without him, but he left me no choice, Dax. I had no choice." She looks up at me. The pain in her eyes breaks me into a million pieces.

I still can't tell what she's talking about. I'm about to ask her again, but that's when I see it. What she's tightly holding in her hand. That little white stick tells me everything I need to know.

Lynsie's pregnant.

"I thought I could be," she whimpers. "I was two weeks late. I was going to surprise him the night of the show. I kept my promise that I wouldn't take a test without him. So I waited. Then he wasn't here anymore. And it didn't matter. Nothing mattered. I forgot about it, to be honest. Then, the few times I was sick..." Looking back down, she lets out a bit of a crazy cackle. I continue rubbing my hands up and down her arms, trying to console her while warming her up. "I thought it was just from the overwhelming sadness and me not eating. That type of stuff happens, you know? Then today it hit me. When his mom mentioned grandchildren. Something in me clicked. I wanted to have his baby so bad, Dax." Her face and voice are filled with such grief. "I can't have this baby without him. I don't know the first thing about being a mom. He was supposed to be here for this. How am I supposed to raise our child without him?" Gripping my shirt, she pulls herself into me, sobbing louder.

I want to comfort her. I want to have magical words to make her feel better, but I've got nothing. Nothing but what I believe to be true.

"You'll be an incredible mom," I say softly as I run my hand through her cold, wet hair. She always seems to calm down when I do this. "You have so many people who love you and they'll love this baby so much."

I continue rocking her as I tell her what she needs to hear right now. "You're never going to be alone. Not through any of this. There will be plenty of times you'll feel like you are, but you never are. And now you have a piece of him growing inside you. This is a miracle, Lynsie. It might seem scary right now, but it's amazing." I take her head in my hands and kiss her forehead, then continue rocking her against me. "I know you aren't fully ready to deal with this, but you have to. You need to make a call and set up an appointment tomorrow."

She shivers against my body. "Will you go with me?"

"Of course I'll go with you if that's what you want."

She nods.

"We need to get you dressed, Lyns. You're freezing." I pull her up with me.

Once I know she's okay to get dressed, I head back downstairs. I grab a couple blankets from the hallway closet on my way down. A few minutes later, I hear her door open, followed by her footsteps lightly padding down the stairs.

She turns the kitchen light off and joins me on the couch. Throwing her legs up on the cushion, I grab the blanket and cover her with it. I prop my legs up on the coffee table as she gets more comfortable, moving her body down just enough to rest her head on my leg. I let my hand move through her hair, hoping to lull her to sleep. My own eyes are getting heavy.

"I'm never going to be able to sleep in my bed again." Her voice slightly trembles.

"I know," I agree.

"It's hard enough being back in this house," she chokes out.

"Everything is going to be hard for a while," I tell her softly, brushing her hair back.

"Thank you, Dax," she murmurs through a yawn.

"For what?" I ask, resting my head against the back of the couch.

"For being you," she says sleepily as we both find slumber.

Chapter Twenty-Two

DAX

Lynsie didn't sleep well last night. She hasn't slept well since the accident, but it seems even worse since finding out she's pregnant. Every night, she wakes up screaming. I know because I've been beside her every night. It hurts that I'm able to comfort her while she's awake, but my presence does nothing for her subconscious mind. More than anything, I want to carry every ounce of pain and sorrow for both of us.

She's going to have a baby—Lincoln's baby. Even though it's such a sorrowful time, I want her to find some kind of joy and peace in it.

For obvious reasons, she's nervous. She keeps coming downstairs, then running back up, changing clothes like it matters what she's wearing to her first appointment. It doesn't, but there's no way I'm telling her that. She can change as many times as she wants.

"Lynsie." I pull her into my arms. "You've looked fine in every-thing you've tried on so far. Change as many times as you need, but we're eventually going to be late. There's no need to be nervous. I'll be right by your side." My words seem to calm her...just a notch.

She pulls back and sighs. "I know it's dumb, but I'm nervous." Which is evident in the way she looks away, chewing on her thumbnail before looking back at me and continuing. "What if I'm not really pregnant? I'll look stupid. Or what if I really am? I don't know how to be a mom." Her mini freak-out escalates as if some sort of anxiety is about to take over.

I grab her shoulders, forcing her to stand still. "First off, I'm pretty sure you're pregnant. At least, that's what the five different pregnancy tests said." I chuckle, attempting to offer some relief. "There's no way it could be some sort of fluke with all of them."

Lynsie looks up at me, and I lightly push back the hair along the side of her face. "And second"—I look deep into her green eyes while holding my hand against her cheek—"you'll be the most amazing mom. I have no doubts about that. You have the most beautiful heart I've ever known, and you love fiercely. You're loyal to those you love and would move heaven and hell if it meant helping a loved one. You got this." I smile down at her, and she lets out a heavy breath, though I see the war waging in her eyes.

She wants to be excited, but she's in a season of grief. Down the road, I know this baby will make her heart feel like it's going to explode with joy, love, and excitement. But right now, she feels guilty. I know she's questioning when it'll be okay to be excited about bringing his child into the world with him no longer here to experience it.

THE NURSE LEAVES the room, instructing Lynsie to change into a paper gown behind the curtain as we wait.

"Uhh," I stutter, pointing toward the door. "I'm just gonna wait in the hall." I turn away.

She peeks around the curtain. "Don't be silly, Dax. Sit down. If I was worried about it, I wouldn't have had you come in with me.

Unless you don't want to be in here." I hear the question in the statement.

Instead of replying, I simply take my seat near the wall and fidget with my phone as I hear Lynsie undressing behind the curtain. I'm trying to keep my thoughts clean, but it's hard.

I really should have waited in the hall.

She yanks the curtain back and props herself up on the bed, covering her legs with the paper draping the nurse left sitting on it.

"Um, they aren't going to be...you know?" I rub the back of my neck, unable to find the words as I point to the stirrup-looking things. I feel my face turning red and eye the exit with the desire to flee.

Lynsie laughs. It's the most genuine laugh I've heard since the accident, and it causes me to laugh as well.

"God, I hope not." She cringes, her face turning the same color as mine. "I might have you go into the hallway for that."

I burst out with a nervous laugh, and she joins me.

The knock at the door sobers us as the doctor walks in. "Hi, Lynsie. It's good to see you." She smiles and shuts the door.

"Hi, Dr. Marx." She looks over at me and I stand to extend my hand.

"I'm Dax, Lynsie's friend," I clarify, hoping she doesn't pry.

"Nice to meet you. I guess congratulations are in order for the both of you."

We look at each other and I see the sadness taking over Lynsie.

I give her a quick smile and move closer to her, grabbing her hand for support. I squeeze it, silently telling her we got this.

"So how have you been feeling?" Dr. Marx asks as she wheels her chair over in front of where Lynsie sits.

"Pregnancy-wise, I've felt fine." She covertly hides everything else she's dealing with. The doctor continues to probe Lynsie with questions, asking her when her last period was, to which Lynsie gives her an estimate. The doctor decides to do a transvaginal ultrasound and puts in an order for blood work. When I hear what the transvaginal ultrasound entails, I attempt to book it out of the room, but Lynsie grips my hand tighter.

"Stay." She looks up, her eyes pleading. "Please."

The very distinct sounds of life beating inside her play in the room, and I'm entranced, gripping Lynsie's hand just as hard. The fact that I almost missed out on something so incredible has me wanting to kick myself. It makes me sad that I'm the one experiencing this and not Lincoln, but it makes me happy too.

"I'd say you're about six weeks along." Dr. Marx looks at her grid. "Putting your due date around the first week of March. We'll get a better idea of an exact date once you have your ultrasound." She writes something down before standing. "I'm going to step out to set up your next appointment. Go ahead and get dressed." She smiles.

I follow Dr. Marx out, allowing Lynsie privacy to get dressed. When Lynsie gives me those wide, wondering eyes, I lie and tell her I need to use the restroom.

As soon as we're far enough away from the door, I address the doctor. "Dr. Marx."

"Yes." She turns around.

I shove my hands in my pockets. "I need to give you some information. Lynsie's husband died recently. About a month ago recently." Saying that aloud hurts. My stomach rolls for a second. "She didn't even find out she was pregnant until afterward."

"Oh my," she says as shock settles in.

"Lincoln was my best friend. I've been friends with Lynsie since they got together, and I plan on being with her through this. If that's what she wants anyway." I'm suddenly second-guessing myself. I've never actually asked Lynsie what she wants. I've just assumed.

She nods. "That's good of you. She needs someone like you.

Thanks for the heads-up." She takes a quick glance down at Lynsie's medical record. "Looks like she put you down as emergency contact."

My mouth gapes open. "I didn't know that, but that's fine."

"Well, if anything comes up and I can't get a hold of Lynsie, I'll give you a call."

I nod and thank her before returning to the room.

ON THE RIDE back to Lynsie's house, I come up with a brilliant idea. At least, I thought it was brilliant.

"Why don't we stop by your parents' house and tell them the news?"

She starts shaking her head as fresh tears stream down her face. She's held it together longer than I expected today. I didn't mean to upset her. I'm kicking myself now for bringing it up.

"I can't tell them, not yet." Her wide eyes are begging. "Dax, please. You can't tell them. I'm not ready for anyone to know. Please."

I inwardly sigh.

"If that's what you want, Lynsie, but you'll have to tell them soon. Someone, at least."

"You know. That's good enough for now." She relaxes into the seat as we drive the rest of the way in silence.

I unlock the front door and push it open, allowing Lynsie to walk in before me. She's quiet. She looks around the brightly lit downstairs, then back at me.

"I'm going to go lie down for a little bit." She drops her gaze to the ground. "I just need some time to take this all in."

I don't want her to be alone to process everything, but I'm not going to tell her how she should and shouldn't heal.

I close the distance between us, pull her in for a hug, and drop a kiss on the top of her head. "I love you, Lyns. I'll come check on you in a little while."

"Okay," she murmurs and heads for my room. She still refuses to sleep in hers, and I don't blame her.

While she sleeps, I find myself in the living room for the remainder of the night, watching TV and jotting in my journal, which mostly consists of random feelings and life questions, many from today. Like, how am I supposed to raise my best friend's child? Does Lynsie even want that? Will she want me around at all? If she asked, could I deal with stepping in as a father figure?

The answers are simple. They all revolve around what I feel and have felt for a long time now. I've accepted the constant war my heart and mind wage against one another, but for now, everything my heart wants must be put on hold. The war isn't over. It's just a battle I'll have to face another day.

Chapter Twenty-Three

DAX

It's been a month since Lincoln died, and it still feels like yesterday. I'm not sure the shock and disbelief I carry around will ever lessen, and I'm not sure which part is harder; returning to the job I love so much, knowing my best friend won't ever be there again, or leaving Lynsie each day to do so. No matter where I go, memories of Lincoln surround me. I have no escape from the pain. My only option is to hit it head-on, suck it up, and be strong for Lynsie.

For the most part, Lynsie seems a little more at peace being in their house. I wasn't sure how well she'd handle it. Sometimes I sit here, expecting him to walk through the front door or run down the stairs. Then reality smacks me hard in the chest, causing what's left of my heart to splinter even more.

I hear Lynsie tinkering in the kitchen as I jog down the stairs. She still isn't sleeping through the night, so her being up early isn't surprising...but her being in the kitchen this early is. I stop at the entrance, not wanting to startle her as she fills the coffeepot with water. I watch as she carefully pours the water in and flips the switch.

"Whatch—"

Lynsie jumps, letting out a shriek, stopping my words.

"Shit, Dax!" She turns around with her hand over her chest. "You scared me." She laughs.

"Good thing I waited until you put the glass pot down," I tease. "So whatcha doing up and about?"

She looks down at the fabric between her fingers as she rubs her robe belt. "Well..." she stammers, tying her robe closed. "I thought I'd make you some coffee for your first day back." She finally looks up, meeting my eyes.

I walk over and pull her into me, giving her a tight hug. She lets out a deep breath and finally wraps her arms around my waist. "Thank you, Lyns." I hold on longer than normal, knowing today is going to possibly be a doozy for both of us. "Hey, listen," I say, pulling away from her. "You aren't going to stay here alone today. I'm taking you to your parents' house."

She stands up straight, tensing. Then defeat settles in as her body relaxes against the counter. Lynsie crosses her arms and looks out to the side. "Fine. I'll go get my shoes, but I'm not changing."

She points a finger at me. "But don't think this day of me bonding with my mom while you and my dad are at work is going to make me tell her I'm pregnant. I told you I'm not ready," Lynsie snaps.

I keep my mouth shut and roll my eyes, refusing to argue with her just because she's being stubborn. I'm not trying to pressure her into telling anyone she's pregnant. I just don't want her to be alone while I'm working. Plain and simple, but not to her. She apparently thinks I have some sort of ulterior motive. That's her own guilt eating at her.

The drive to her parents starts off in silence, but to my surprise, Lynsie is the first to break it.

"Umm, Dax."

"Yes, Lyn?" I glance over, seeing her with her gaze fixed out the window.

"I just wanted to say thank you for giving up your bed for me."

"Well, of course—"

She stops me from continuing.

"I'd feel..." she starts to hesitate, then looks over at me with determination. "I'd feel more comfortable if you'd just sleep in there with me. You've been so respectful, falling asleep on the couch, but with my nightmares, you've ended up in your bed with me anyway." She glances down at her fidgeting hands. "Something about you beside me at night brings me comfort."

I reach my free hand over, draping it over her hands, halting her fidgetiness.

"If that's what you want." I gulp, holding back emotion. *I bring her comfort.* Little does she know how much she brings me.

I put my car in park, and we silently sit in her parents' driveway. I sit back against my seat and turn my head toward Lynsie. "I'll be back when I get off. Well, that is, if you want me to pick you back up."

Her nose scrunches, and her lip curls. "If I want you to pick me back up." She mocks, looking out her window before leaning her head back against the headrest, eyes pinched closed. I study her features. Her bottom lip slightly trembles as tears slowly start seeping out of her closed eyes.

"Hey, hey. What's wrong, Lyns?" I place my hand against her cheek. She tries to look away, out toward her window, but I turn her head back in my direction. Still, her eyes flicker everywhere but at me as she tries to regain control of her emotions.

"We've barely spent a second apart since it all happened, you know?" She finally looks up, the tears spilling out rapidly.

Gripping her face with both hands, I bend over, pulling her to me as I rest my chin on top of her head. "We'll make it through this,"

I promise. "You need other people around who care about you, not just me. They love you. You can't shut them out, okay?"

She nods against me, then pulls away and wipes her face dry. She looks composed for a few seconds, but she quickly loses control as she asks, "What if you have to fly, Dax? I can't even fathom you being in a plane. After watching Lincoln..." She covers her mouth with her trembling hand. Flinging the door open, she jumps out of the car.

I throw myself out and run to her as she doubles over, puking what little she has eaten. Her mom dashes out of the house, concern etched across her features. Lynsie tugs up the bottom of her shirt to wipe her mouth clean.

She takes a deep breath, wiping away the tears before her mom reaches us. "Please pick me up as soon as you get off. It's not that I don't want to be around my parents right now, but they make me sadder. They walk on eggshells around me. You don't."

I know exactly what she means, and I have a feeling what she feels here, I'll soon feel once I return to work.

ALL EYES ARE on me as I walk into the hangar. Some full of pity, like I expect. Others look at me with respect. I'm sure most are shocked I'm even here. I can say that getting on a plane is the last thing I want to do right now, but it's my job. I have no choice, but it won't be easy.

I heave a huge breath and stand straighter. No way to get over fear except to take it head-on.

"Dax," Lynsie's father yells for me. It's informal in front of the rest of the guys, but he quickly rights his mistake, correcting, "Adams. My office, please." I follow him into his office and close the door as he motions me to take a seat.

"I was happy to see the medical release come through." He motions to my hand that's no longer in a cast, and I ball it into a fist, flexing it. "I need your assistance today." He runs a hand through his short salt-and-pepper hair. "I'm scheduled to fly today. Not that I don't trust any of these other guys, but right now, I trust you most. Do you mind flying with me?"

I see the unease in his eyes. This will be the first time he's been on a plane since the crash and he's asking me to be the pilot on standby.

I don't even hesitate. "Yes, sir."

Relief washes over his face as he and I stand to our feet and shake hands.

"Thanks, son."

I nod, though I really hope he's not trying to replace Lincoln. There's no way I can fill his shoes.

He steps around his desk. "I'll meet you in the flight briefing room shortly so we can go over our flight plan."

Walking back to my office, I check my phone to see a text from Lynsie.

> Lynsie: Be careful.

Not only is she reeling from the loss of Lincoln—as we all still are—she's also highly worried about me being anywhere near a plane. I'm not going to tell her that her dad and I are about to take flight for the day together.

> Me: Always.

What happened with Lincoln was horrible, but it was a freak incident. He didn't die at the helm of the Widow Maker because of its namesake. He died trying to prevent a catastrophe. Every single what-if still roams my mind daily. The thoughts I don't write out in my journal, I keep airtight, locked in my mind. No one needs to know where my mind takes me. More importantly, no one needs to know that the what-ifs always end with the same conclusion—sometimes shit is just meant to happen. Feeling as if it was Lincoln's time to go will never make it any easier. It will never fill the constant ache I push down daily.

After two hours, we have our flight plan. We've checked the weather and double-checked the airspace and the airport we're planning on landing at before filing the plan with the tower. We make our way out to the Beechcraft C-12 Huron we'll be flying, and I search for the numbered tail we're scheduled to take.

"I think it's best if we both go over the interior and exterior preflight together instead of doing it separately," Colonel Clark says.

"Sounds good to me." I feel he's trying to calm his nerves by having two sets of eyes comb through it. "Everything out here looks good. Let's do one final walk around."

He nods in agreement.

After climbing in, I shut the door and check the locking pins before strapping into my seat. We go through engine checks, call tower to get clearance and an instrument flight rules flight plan, do taxi checks, call ground to taxi for run-up, taxi to an area, and go through all the run-up checks.

It isn't until everything is all clear and good to go that Colonel Clark asks me if I'll be lead pilot.

"I'm just a little shaky still." He stares straight ahead as he rubs his palms up and down his thighs. "I'll take full control on the flight back. I'd just really appreciate it if you'll take lead this round."

"You're the boss," I say.

I make my initial address. "Chief Warrant Dax Adams to ground for taxi for takeoff."

I taxi over, just short of the runway, then call tower for takeoff. Once we're cleared onto the runway, we do our takeoff checks before departing. Pulling back on the controls, we pull off the ground and ascend into the air. More checks take place as we reach the altitude we flight planned for. Everything is good and checking out normal.

"How are you doing, Dax?" Colonel Clark asks through the intercom in our headsets.

"Better than expected," I admit. My heart begins to slow to a steady beat.

I hadn't realized how terrified I was of getting back on a plane until now. Thankfully, flying was never on my agenda for the day. If I had been scheduled to, it would've given me too much time to dwell on what could go wrong. Instead, I did it without a second thought because duty called, and I was needed. And when I'm needed, all my inhibitions are gone. It's just my nature.

"Indeed. You're doing very well," Dan boasts, "but that's not what I meant."

"Oh. Well, I think for the most part, I'm handling it well."

"Don't hold it in because you feel like you have to be strong for my Lynsie. She's stronger than you think, but she wouldn't want you trying to be tough for her."

I glance over. "You heard that recording, right?"

"Yes," he says quietly.

"I plan on keeping Lincoln's last wishes until Lynsie doesn't need me any longer."

That idea alone causes my heart to constrict.

"Thank you for that," he says, looking my way with soft eyes. "You don't realize it, but you being around helps her tremendously. You both shared a love for Lincoln that no one else could touch. She seems more peaceful around you."

"She helps me, too. I guess I feel bonded to her."

"You are."

That's as deep as the conversation gets as we contact our scheduled airport, requesting to approach. As we fly in, dropping in altitude, we do a descent arrival check, set up the navigational equipment for the approach, and do a before-landing check. The checks are endless as we do a landing check while taxiing to parking before doing a shutdown check and finally a post-flight check. I grab the logbook and fill out our time flown, jotting down that we had no problems.

We unbuckle, but before we're out of our seats, Dan starts to speak. His words keep me seated.

"I've lost friends before. Some were close, others not. I've never lost a best friend like you just did. I cannot even imagine. I know you love to fly."

I keep my hands closed together in my lap.

"I didn't want what happened to Lincoln to take away from that. I, on the other hand, have dealt with the after-effects already, many times. I put together this flight today for you, not me. I've already been back in a plane since the incident."

His admission has me shocked and speechless.

He claps me on the shoulder. "I know what type of person you are. You didn't hesitate to hit the air with me today when I told you I needed your help. I wanted your first time back on a plane to be one without fear or worry. You did great today, Dax." He pats my shoulder and steps out of his seat. "Now let's go grab some lunch."

I sit, dumbfounded at his admission. Everything was planned and he knew I'd say yes. Suddenly, I laugh out loud, feeling a goofy smile spread across my face. It's almost as if Lincoln had planned it himself. Maybe in some way, he did, but it makes me proud of myself.

Chapter Twenty-Four

DAX

Just after dusk, I pull into Lynsie's parents' driveway. When I knock, I'm shortly greeted by Mrs. Clark.

She gives me a weak smile. "How was your first day back?"

I have a feeling she knows what my day entailed.

"It went pleasantly well, actually." I give her a genuine smile as I shut the front door.

"That's good to hear. Are you hungry?" She heads toward the kitchen.

"Ahh." I hesitate, unsure if Lynsie will be willing to stay. "I could probably eat. Where's Lynsie?"

"She's down in the movie room, asleep the last time I checked." She pulls a plate out of the cupboard.

I step in close to her and gently take the plate away, setting it quietly on the counter. Keeping my voice just above a whisper, I ask, "How was she today?"

Looking everywhere but at me, she fidgets with an oven mitt. "As good as can be expected." She makes eye contact with me briefly before turning to open the oven. I know Mrs. Clark is at odds with how to be there for her daughter.

"I'm going to go see her."

She smiles and nods, giving me the go-ahead.

Taking off my boots, I tiptoe down the stairs to where she lies, sound asleep. I quietly sit next to her, my fingers itching to brush the hair away from her face, but I restrain myself. All my effort doesn't pay off, though, as she stirs awake.

"Hey, sleepyhead," I murmur, smiling down at her.

"What time is it?" She sits up, rubbing her eyes.

"Around six. Your mom cooked dinner. Your dad hasn't made it home yet. He told me I could leave once we landed back at base." I cringe, realizing what I just said.

"What?" she shrieks. "He took you flying today?" Her eyes are about to bug out of her head. "And on your first day back?"

We hear the front door shut, and she wastes no time jumping to her feet.

"Lynsie, wait!" I yell as I get up to chase after her.

"Hey, Lyns." Her dad smiles at her, clueless that a shitstorm is headed his way.

"Are you trying to kill everyone I care about?" she yells, fisting her hand against her hip.

"Lynsie, it's our job. You know that." He walks up to her with a sincere face, not letting her words affect him.

Her shoulders sag and she sighs, letting her head drop. "I do."

He rubs her shoulders. "I know from personal experience that the best way for Dax to get over the dread was to get him back in the sky, behind the controls, as soon as I could. Even though he wasn't a part of it, it was a fear he needed to face. One that he took on and conquered." He glances over at me with a genuine look of pride in his eyes.

Lynsie calms down, relaxing into my side. I'm hoping we just made some progress. Maybe she won't worry as much.

I'M NOT AN expert on death or how long it takes to recover from the loss of a loved one, and I don't pretend to be. The only time Lynsie isn't holed up in my room, alone, is when I'm here with her, or I force her to go to her parents' house while I work. Every now and then, her mother comes here, but Lynsie doesn't talk to her much. Her mother is so worried—we all are—but Lynsie has to deal with this in her own way.

For the most part, I act as normal as possible around Lynsie. It's what she wants and needs, but that line is still blurry. I hate that my return to work is hard on her. I can only hope one day she has the strength to return. Even though I thought it'd have the complete opposite effect, being back at work has helped me. Being around people who care about me as a fellow pilot and person in general is comforting. The guys joking around and including me, instead of treating me like I'm damaged, helps as well. A sense of normalcy is slowly resuming at the base, and it feels peaceful, yet makes me feel guilt-ridden at the same time. I'm not sure when this sense of guilt will ease up, or if I'm going to bear it for the rest of my days. I come down from the room, eager for a cup of coffee before I head to work. Lynsie is already up and sitting on the couch.

"Morning, Lyns," I announce. As I head for the kitchen, I run a hand through my crazy hair. It's becoming borderline untamable. I'm really in need of a haircut.

She doesn't reply.

I call out to her from the kitchen, "You want me to make you a cup? I know how you like it—a little coffee with your creamer and sugar." I laugh.

Still no reply.

I put the empty cups down on the counter and step into the living room. She never ignores me...intentionally. As I inch closer, I see she's wearing headphones plugged into her cell phone. I ease my way around the couch, careful not to scare her as I sit down.

Lynsie peeks up and smiles. "I'm listening to a book," she says loudly.

I laugh and move my lips, acting like I'm talking.

"What?" she asks, moving her hand to pull one side of her head-phones away from her ear.

I move my lips again, this time making it overly noticeable that I'm not really talking. She lets out a giggle as she taps a button on her phone.

The brown, messy bun on top of her head bounces back into place as she pushes her headphones back, resting them around her neck. "You're funny." She smiles again.

"Anything to get that smile." I grab the TV remote, turning it on to check the weather. "So what book are you listening to?" I glance over at her. She's looking down at her phone, messing with it.

"I'm not sure of the name, but it's some paranormal-type book." Lynsie crosses her legs under her and grabs a pillow, placing it in her lap.

"I didn't peg you for the spooky type." I stand back up.

"It's not any scarier than real life," she says, barely above a whisper.

I swallow, feeling a sharp pang in my gut. "Right," I agree gently, quickly retreating from those sad eyes of hers. "Want me to make you a cup of coffee before I go?" I yell back from the kitchen as I begin pouring both cups.

"Please," I hear. "I can only have one per day. So do it right. Extra cream and sugar."

I roll my eyes. How does she think I don't know? And I'm pretty sure the amount of sugar and creamer she uses counteracts the caffeine in the actual coffee.

I set her huge, polka-dotted mug on the coffee table in front of her, holding mine in my to-go cup. "Is your mom still coming over?" I take a sip of the steamy brew, enjoying its freshness as it hits my taste buds.

She grabs her cup, takes a sip, then peeks up at me over the rim. "No. I asked Echo to since it's Monday and the salon is closed, and Dylan will be at school."

I sit my cup down and gently take hers from her hand, setting it next to mine. Kneeling in front of her, I grab her hands. "Lynsie, I don't care who comes over. You can have the Pope here for all I care. I just don't want you to be alone, not yet. Not until you can tell me truthfully you can handle it." I watch her as her eyes shift with uncertainty. "Can you tell me that yet?"

Her voice is timid. "I'm not sure I'll ever be able to tell you that, Dax, but I won't ever get used to it if I never face it. I mean, isn't the best way to get over stuff to hit it head-on? Just like you had to?" She eyes me. "I'm not going to break any more than I already have."

She pulls her hands from mine and grabs both sides of my face. I want to close my eyes and lean into her touch, soaking up every emotion soaring through me. Instead, I keep my careful eyes trained on hers.

"I know you and everyone and their dog are worried about me, but I'm as broken as I can get. The damage has already been done. Now it's all about me slowly piecing myself back together." She looks away for a moment, then her deep, green eyes return to mine. "Some of that will have to be done on my own. I can't depend on you to do it for me." She gives a weak smile.

I wonder if my heart is in my eyes as I tell her, "If I could, I would." She has to know I'd do it in a heartbeat.

"I know you would." She runs a hand through my already messy hair, pulling the length between her fingers. I can see her eyeing it. My hair has noticeably grown. "But you also need to start living again. Lincoln wouldn't want you to be my babysitter."

Clearing my throat, I pull away from her and stand. I can feel the hurt on my face as she stands in front of me, searching my features. I don't want her to see this, but it's hard to hide. "You think that's what I'm doing? That I'm here just to babysit you until you're all better, and then go on my merry way? Because it's not, Lynsie. Believe it or not, I need you too. Just because you can't see it, don't think you aren't helping. You do more than you'll ever know."

Her expression softens as she thinks about what I just said, internalizing it. I need air before I say more or do something stupid. Bending down, I place a quick kiss on her forehead, grab my coffee, and leave for work.

"DAX, I JUST got orders for you to take Lincoln's place at the training in Fort Hood." Are not the words I want to hear as soon as I walk into work. The Army doesn't waste any time, apparently.

"So soon?" I bolt to my feet and stand directly in front of Dan's desk.

"The Army doesn't stop when a soldier dies." His chair squeaks as he leans back. "It's the main reason I got you behind the controls as quickly as I did. I knew the chance of you filling Lincoln's place in training was a high probability. I didn't want your first time back on a plane to be while you were away and with someone unfamiliar."

I nod, appreciating the thought he's been putting into all of this behind the scenes.

"Shit," I mutter, turning my back to Lynsie's father. "This is bullshit. Total bullshit." I sink back down into my chair. My heart falls to the pit of my stomach. All I can think about is Lynsie. How is she going to handle this? "Does Lynsie know?" I glance up. Of course she doesn't know yet.

He gives me a sympathetic look as he shakes his head. "No, and I'm worried this could destroy her. You're the only thing getting her through right now." This time, I get to be the bearer of bad news. I'm sure her dad is more than tired of being labeled the bad guy.

"I need to tell her. Somehow." I brush my hand through my hair in frustration. More like despair.

"Tell her soon, son," he warns me quietly. "You leave in a couple weeks."

I nod and with an uneasy stomach and a wounded heart, I leave his office. For the rest of the day, my mind plays out each scenario, how this could go. They all end with Lynsie breaking down. I try to focus on work and scheduling flight plans, but I can't. All of this seems mundane compared to the big picture.

I don't know how it happened, but somewhere in these past few weeks, Lynsie became my bigger picture. I know one day my feelings for her could backfire. For now, all that seems mundane as well.

Chapter Twenty-Five

DAX

"You can't go, Dax." Lynsie paces back and forth in the kitchen. She stops in front of me and grips my arms. "You're the only thing keeping me afloat. I will sink without you." Her eyes plead with mine. Can she not see how desperately I want to stay?

"No, you won't, Lynsie. So many people will fill my place while I'm gone." I want my words to reassure her. Wishful thinking.

She clutches her hands near her heart. "I was wrong. When I said I'd have to do some of this on my own. I was wrong. I can't do this without you." She stutters the last part. Looking up through tear-filled lashes, she whispers, "You're my life raft, Dax. Three months is too long. What if something happens?" Suddenly, her eyes fill with panic. "Oh my God, oh my God." She gasps, throwing her hand over her mouth as she begins pacing again. "What if something does happen?" she quietly whispers to herself.

I abruptly stop her and spin her into my arms. Hers quickly wrap around me as I hold her and let her cry.

"I can't live without you too, Dax," she weeps. "I'm barely breathing without Lincoln here."

"You won't have to," I promise her, even though I know we aren't promised tomorrow.

"You make me feel closer to him," she tells me through her hiccupping cries.

"Remember what I said?" I lean back and tilt her chin up with my finger. "He lives in our hearts. We will always feel closest to him being near the ones who loved him most."

SITTING ON THE couch—with more space separating us than I'm comfortable with—I write in my journal as Lynsie continues giving me the silent treatment. She may be looking at the TV, but I know she isn't paying attention to it. This is the perfect time to jot down how I'm feeling in this exact moment. I'm not thrilled about leaving for training, but it's part of my job. This is the first time being sent away has ever bothered me. Before, I was chomping at the bit to be shipped off. Now, all I want to do is stay right by Lynsie's side. I'm only getting into training because Lincoln isn't here to fill the spot. I don't want to be his replacement in any capacity.

I purposely drop my journal on the wooden coffee table with a loud *whop*, but Lynsie doesn't move. Her silence keeps my stomach in knots. I sit back on the couch, waiting for her to say anything. To scream at me, curse at me, cry to me—*anything*. I can't stand the silence. This must be how she typically is around everyone else. I'm finally getting my own personal dose of what she's been spooning them, and it sucks.

"Don't shut me out, Lynsie." I sit up straighter, running my hand through my hair.

She doesn't shift, make a noise, or show any difference in facial expression as she blankly watches the TV.

I get up and kneel in front of her, forcing her to look at me. Her chin lifts an inch, and my jaw clenches. She's playing games and it's pissing me off. I shake her by the shoulders, and I yell, "Dammit, Lynsie! Look at me!"

She sharply cuts her eyes to me, showing the pain she's been trying to hide, but her hard face quickly softens as she stares into my eyes, causing hers to overflow with tears.

"I'm so scared, Dax." Her lip quivers before she throws her arms around my neck and leans into me as she lets out all the emotion she's been holding in since I told her I was leaving. "I'll always be scared. What happened to Lincoln has ruined me forever. One day, it won't hurt as much and I'll be able to move on, but I'll never get over this fear. I feel like it's choking me. Every second you're gone, I'm going to worry."

I press my forehead to hers. "We can't keep living in fear. That's not living." My grip on her shoulders tightens. "We'll talk every day. Just like we do now." My voice is hopeful, trying to reassure her.

She nods against me as she sniffles a few more times. "Promise?" Lynsie pulls her body away from mine just enough to look me dead in the eyes.

"I always keep my word, Lynsie."

She leans back into the couch, crossing her legs Indian-style, and glances over at something. "What all do you write in that journal?"

Pushing up on the edge of the couch, I stand and grab my journal from the table. "Anything that's on my mind. I don't have any set rules." I grip it tightly to my chest. If she ever saw what was inside...I could never let her. It's too raw, too personal. I'd be too vulnerable.

"Will you ever let me read any of it?" Her cheeks redden a tad as she looks away.

"One day." I swallow hard.

She tosses the pillow to the side and stands in front of me, extending her hand out. "Come on."

I drop my journal on the table and follow her as she leads us upstairs. Instead of turning to the room we sleep in, she goes in the opposite direction toward her and Lincoln's room. My feet begin to falter, and she turns around, noticing my reluctance.

"Trust me." She gives me a weak smile. I nod and continue letting her pull me in, following her to the master bath. Lynsie releases my hand and bends over, digging under the sink. "You can sit on this chair," she says, grabbing the chair tucked in at her vanity area, and sits it in the middle of the open space.

I sit and watch her pull out a pair of clippers. She sets them on the counter, then opens a drawer and pulls out a pair of cutting sheers and a comb. "You're in desperate need of a haircut, Dax," she says smoothly, but I see the uncertainty in her eyes. She hasn't done hair since Lincoln died. This is a big step for her. One I'm thankful to be taking with her.

"I know, but I wasn't going to let just anyone do it," I whisper.

She lets out a soft laugh. "Yeah, you're stubborn like that." She wraps a towel around me, securing it in the front with a clip. As the sound of the clippers fills the bathroom, I tightly shut my eyes. They'll give me away. My heart is pounding so fast, I'm scared she'll be able to see my body trembling. Knowing that I'm leaving soon, I soak in her touch—her caring, unselfish ways.

* * *

I WAKE UP to a cold, empty bed. Panic sets in as I see it's still dark out. I didn't hear her get up. I always hear every little movement or whimper she makes throughout the night, but for some reason, tonight she snuck out without stirring me. Which means she was being extra sneaky. Which worries me even more.

The house is dark as I jog down the stairs, calling her name. "Lynsie. Lynsie, where are you?"

Nothing but silence. Then I hear it—a noise I'm all too familiar with as I come into the kitchen. The back door is cracked. I open the door all the way, watching in shock as Lynsie attempts to fly Lincoln's remote-control plane. She's doing a shit job. If she isn't careful, she's going to end up wrecking it. Her body shakes as she cries and gets pissed off, cursing at the plane she can't fly.

"Stupid plane," she yells as she cries.

"Lynsie," I say calmly, so as not to startle her. "Let's get the plane down." Stepping beside her, I try to coax the remote from her hand, but she yanks her hands away.

"No, Dax! Lincoln promised he'd teach me. Now he'll never get to!" Her wild hair whips a little around her frantic face.

Her finger slips, and the plane sharply turns. "This passion for planes took him away from me. He chose dying over living. He chose to die. He chose to leave me. And now you're leaving me, too. Alone."

She collapses to her knees, and I quickly grab the remote to regain control of the model aircraft, but I'm too late. It hits the tree and falls to the ground in pieces. The scattered pieces resemble my heart, and I wonder if they're equally fixable.

I throw the remote down and sink to my knees next to her, pulling her into my lap. Something I've grown accustomed to. "You're not alone. I'm not leaving you by choice. It's work. I'll be back."

"You don't know that," she whispers through a yawn as she snuggles deeper into my arms. I smooth back her hair from her face and rub her arm up and down. I hate how much pain she's feeling.

* * *

I GRAB MY bag and head downstairs, anxiety sinking in as I realize I'm about to say goodbye. She's already been down here for a while. The smell of bacon makes my stomach growl. I drop my bag as I hit the last step and see her nervously waiting at the table with our plates already made.

"You didn't have to fix me breakfast, Lyns." I pull my chair out and sit down across from her.

"I know." She smiles nervously, tightly grasping her coffee cup. "I haven't cooked in a long time. It just felt right this morning."

She rolls her paper towel between her fingertips as she eyes me, waiting for me to dig in. I fork up some eggs and take a bite of bacon at the same time. I add a bite of my toast, swallowing it all down. Lynsie watches me in amazement as I tackle my plate like I haven't eaten in years.

"Man, that's the best breakfast I've had in I can't even tell you how long." I sit back, pooching my full stomach out and rubbing it.

She laughs at my silly display. "I'm glad you liked it. I wanted to do something nice before you leave." Giving me a weak smile, she stands and grabs her plate, heading for the trash.

"Lynsie, you really need to eat."

Besides feeling queasy here and there, she hasn't had any bouts of sickness except a few times.

She places her foot on the pedal at the bottom of the trashcan and I hear her food fall into it. "I did. I ate a piece of toast and drank a cup of orange juice while I made your breakfast. Eggs sounded good." She drops her plate in the sink, then turns around, leaning against the counter. "Until I started cooking them. Then the idea of eating them nauseated me." She cringes.

I wipe off my mouth and push out from the table. The chair scrapes loudly against the tile. "I got something for you." I rush over to my bag before she has time to reply.

I pull the neatly wrapped gift out of my side pocket, then quickly zip it back. Lynsie stands where I left her, almost in shock. I hand it over and watch as her eyes dance back and forth between me and the flat, square gift in her hands.

She slowly pulls the paper apart, gasping when she realizes what it is. "It's perfect," she breathes, tracing her finger over the single bird on the cover.

"I know I won't be here, but your thoughts, feelings, concerns, resentments...anything—they're all safe in here." I tap my finger on her new journal. "It does help, Lynsie. It sounds silly, but getting these feelings off our chests, no matter how we do it, really does help."

"If it works for you, I'll give it a try." She grips it, hugging the journal to her chest.

"Now this doesn't mean you get to shut yourself off. I still want you to be able to tell me anything. Okay?" I search her eyes, hoping I didn't just give her a reason to close herself off from me.

She nods. "You'll still be my number one journal." Lynsie looks past me over at where my bag is sitting and gulps. "You ready?" she asks, trying to be strong.

Not knowing how long it'll be until I see her again, I rub my thumb down her cheek, memorizing every single feature of her face. I'm not sure how well I'm going to handle it when her fractured shell cracks as soon as I get on the plane and take off.

"I'm not ready," I admit, letting her know I'm affected by this as well. "But it's time to go."

Chapter Twenty-Six

LYNSIE

I hold my breath, watching Dax walk toward the plane. He's always so strong for my sake. It's my turn to be strong for him, knowing how difficult the past month has been for both of us. He takes a few steps up, handing his bag over to the other pilot on the plane. Slowly turning back in my direction, he gives me a slight smile and wave. It's taken every fiber within me not to run to him and beg him not to go. Instead, I put my selfishness to the side and smile back, praying he can't see the tears falling down my face.

Standing on shaky legs, I watch the person who's been keeping me together the best he could, take off—on a plane, no less. My mom wraps her arm around me, and I lean into her, knowing I'm going to need to start relying on her more now. They've been trying to convince me to stay at my parents' house while Dax is gone, but I refuse. Heaven forbid I'm ever left alone. They think I'll break, but I'm already broken. Some pieces of me are more shattered than others. So much so, that at times, I think once I'm able to pull the pieces back together, I'm going to look like a starry night sky. I'll either be brightly lit, or barely flickering as darkness attempts to consume me.

The car ride to my house is quiet. Sometimes I feel guilty for the silence, but never enough to do anything about it. While my outside demeanor may appear calm, my mind is anything but. I just wish I could shut my mind off like I've shut out those who love me most—like the flick of a switch.

There are times when the memory of that day comes back in full force and drags me to my knees. Those days, thankfully, are becoming few and far between, but sometimes I still yell out to Lincoln—blaming him. He had a choice. He could've lived. On those days, it takes me until I'm done trying to scream out the pain in my heart before I come back to reality. He thought he was saving me. He thought he was saving Dax. He thought he was saving others. My husband died a hero. He could've saved himself at the last minute, but to him, there was no choice. He was always selfless like that. And sometimes I hate him for it.

"Lynsie, we're here."

I hear my mother's soft voice as my eyes fly open and I jump in my seat.

"I'm sorry." She pulls the keys from the ignition. "I didn't mean to scare you."

I study her face as she looks at me. Her green eyes are so tired and full of concern. She gives me a weak smile, causing a pang of guilt to course through my body. Why have I shut my own mother out? I've asked myself this question many times. And just like now, it's an answer I simply don't have.

"It's okay. I must've dozed off a minute." I unbuckle my seat belt and get out of the car. I make my way to my front door as she gets her bag out of the back seat.

We step inside and I'm hit with an overwhelming sense of emptiness. I'm not ready for a mother-daughter re-bonding experience. I inhale a deep breath and slowly let it back out, calming my erratically beating heart.

I point upstairs. "Umm, you can sleep in Dax's room on the nights you stay. I'll need to wash the bedding." I trudge up the stairs without looking back.

"Lynsie, you don't have to do it. I'm capable." I hear her from the bottom of the steps.

I turn around, looking down at her. "I'm capable, too." I say it more to convince myself than I do for her sake.

Opening the door, I'm hit with Dax's scent. The crisp, clean smell has me second-guessing washing the bedding. I don't want to wash it away. I like feeling that any day he'll be back. The realization and fear hit me all at once as I wonder if I'll ever smell it again, just like Lincoln's. The only thing I haven't washed so far is his pillow. That's the only time I'm truly able to smell him—when my face is pressed against it as I dream. His scent has been long gone, but I still tightly clutch his pillow every night.

I sit down on the bed and mentally berate myself for how I'm feeling about him being gone. *It's his job, Lynsie.* I say over and over in my mind as if it's a mantra. He'll be fine. It's just training. The same one Lincoln was supposed to go to.

The same training Lincoln was supposed to go to.

My heart sinks to my stomach. Why am I just now realizing this? Of course that's the only reason he's going. He has to fill the missing spot. How horrible that must be for him. Not only did he lose his best friend, now he's filling in where he's absent. Will everything in my life come full circle back to Lincoln? If that's the case, I may never fully recover.

I walk back downstairs empty-handed. "Change of plans. You can sleep in my old bed."

The rest of my day is spent curled up on the couch, listening to the rest of the book I started, while my mom sits close by, watching

DIY shows. I love my mom. I really do, but having her here seems a bit redundant. The little snacking I've done throughout the day hasn't received my mother's approval, so I give in and agree to sit and eat whatever she cooks for dinner.

"The spaghetti is good," I say as I fork it around on my plate.

"Have you even taken a bite?" Her words are laced with a mix of frustration and concern.

I sigh to keep from saying something I'll regret later. My phone rings, saving me. My fork clanks against the glass plate as I drop it and shove my chair back. Knowing it's Dax has me jogging to the living room to grab my cell off the table.

"Hey," I answer, half panting.

"Hey to you, too." I can hear the smile in his voice. "Have you been running or something?"

I laugh because there is no reason I should be breathless. It was a light jog from my dining room to my living room, yet I'm trying to catch my breath.

"I don't run," I throw back, chancing a glance at my mom. She has her back to me as she cleans up the mess from dinner, and a pang of guilt hits me. Still, I stroll up the stairs and shut myself in my room.

"Well, I'm all settled in my motel room." He lets out a relaxed sigh.

"How was the flight?" I scoot myself onto my bed, resting on my back.

"It went rather fast. Once I got here, I had to get my rental car stuff figured out, then head to the base."

"Sounds fun," I say, only a little sarcastic.

"Hardly." He laughs. "How're things with your mom?"

I groan. "Awkward. I feel like I have to watch everything I do in my own house. Not to mention the fact that she's on me about eating."

"Someone needs to be, Lyns," Dax says with concern.

"I eat, Dax." I lower my voice to a whisper. "Just because I'm pregnant doesn't mean I need to start eating like a sumo wrestler. Heavens, I'm going to look like one soon enough."

A deep laugh rumbles through the phone. I can feel it in my bones.

It's contagious and even has me giggling. "What's so funny?" I ask, laughing right along with him.

"You're not going to look like a sumo wrestler, Lynsie."

"We'll see. You probably won't even recognize me when you come home." The thought makes me sad. So much is going to change in the three months he's gone. I might be showing by then.

"Oh yeah?" he asks with humor. "Now you're being ridiculous."

"I know, but it's a possibility. Everything these days is a possibility," I say as I think about how nothing in life is set in stone.

"Yeah, I'm starting to see that myself," he says softly, sounding deep in thought.

"Three months is a long time," I huff. I hate how whiney I am, but man, do I already miss him. "I don't know how to function without my best friend around."

Dax is quiet on the other end. So much so, I can hear the TV lightly playing in the background of his room.

"Did I bore you to sleep?" I turn on my side, pulling my comforter over my shoulder.

"No." He chuckles. "I was just thinking."

"Don't keep me in the dark," I say, wondering what goes on in that head of his.

I hear him moving and picture him rolling over. Quietly, he asks, "I'm your best friend?"

"Yes," I say like it's nothing. Of course he's my best friend. "I mean, what you really are doesn't fully have a title because you're more than that, kind of." I sigh, not knowing how to explain it to him. "All I know is you're my friend, and you're the best. So it just made sense to call you my best friend."

"I accept that." I can hear the smile in his voice.

I yawn. "Good. If we do this every night, maybe I'll be able to survive this." *Maybe...*

"I sure hope so," he says tenderly.

THE WARM SUN on my face wakes me up. Out of habit, I pat the empty side of the bed. Some mornings when I wake from a dead sleep, I listen, expecting the shower to be on. Then reality slowly creeps in, reminding me I'm not in my bed. Those days don't come that often because I've become quite a light sleeper. One of the many reasons why I now sleep with the TV on in Dax's room. Watching whatever happens to be on when I do wake up at night tends to lull me back to slumberland.

This morning, I feel the empty spot and let my hand linger longer than normal. I'm reminded of the permanent and temporary loss responsible for the emptiness next to me. Sometimes I lie in bed longer than I should with my eyes trained on the ceiling. When I do this, I find myself getting lost in memories or daydreams I like to make up. For the most part, they put a smile on my face. Mainly the memories because they're real and the daydreams are not. The realness of what Lincoln and I had will always bring a smile to my face. The day that a smile is all it brings is a day I both look forward to and dread.

I finally pull myself out of bed and make my way downstairs, unsure what the day has in store for me. I'm sure it will consist mostly of me sitting around my house. First things first, I need some coffee. It may do nothing for my energy, but I crave it. Maybe Dax is right. I don't crave coffee necessarily, but the creamer and sugar I douse it with.

He's only been gone for a day, and I miss him. I'm so over missing people.

I open all the blinds and turn the TV on as I wait for the coffee to brew. I watch the weather, even though it has no effect on me since I won't be going outside. One day, I'll come out of my hermit shell. For now, I'm enjoying it.

Cup of coffee in hand, I walk over to the living room, sitting my cup down before I sink into the couch. The journal Dax bought me is sitting there, taunting me as I stare at it.

"What the hell," I mutter, bending over to grab it. I look in my end table drawer for a pen, but no such luck. Then I see the top of the pen that Dax must have slid into the spiral of the notebook-styled journal. *He thinks of everything.* I flip it open for the very first time, taking in the first page he has filled out for me.

This journal belongs to <u>Lynsie Pearl Fox</u>
You got this!
Love, Dax

I take a breath and flip the page, unwilling to let any emotions consume me. I need to do this. For Dax. For me. He says it helps and he hasn't steered me wrong yet.

I stare at the blank page with light lines. What am I supposed to write? Why does my mind suddenly feel so empty? I know it's not. Should I be writing all these thoughts down—these stupid questions I keep asking myself? They don't really seem journal-worthy.

I hold the tip of my pen on the very top line and let it linger momentarily before letting myself go with it. It's my journal, dang it. I can write what I want, even if it's dumb.

This sucks!
Writing sucks!
Feeling sucks!
Being alone sucks!
Being pregnant sucks!

I'm brilliant. Who knew? Then I place my hand over my stomach, regretting the last words I just wrote, and correct them.

No. Being alone sucks. Being pregnant doesn't.

Feeling silly about writing my jumbled thoughts out, I flip the cover shut and throw the journal down on my coffee table.

"This is stupid," I grunt in frustration as I grab my coffee and get up from the couch, not feeling any better about anything. Writing out your feelings is lame. It doesn't help.

"Maybe it helps Dax," I mumble to myself, "but it's not going to help me."

"What's that, dear?" my mom asks from the kitchen table. I had almost forgotten I wasn't alone. She's been so good at giving me my space these days that I temporarily forget she's around. I don't reply right away—something she's more than used to. Taking a seat at the table with her, I sigh. I need to open up to my mom, but I'm not ready.

"Dax gave me a journal before he left. He told me it helps him to write out what he's feeling." I break my eyes away from the steam-filled cup she's holding to look up at her. I study her, watching how her eyes flicker and her mouth twitches as she carefully works out what to say to me. I've made her this way.

"And you disagree with him?" It's more of a statement than a question.

"Well." I fold my arms against my chest and sit back in my chair. "Seeing that I've only attempted to write my feelings out once, and I royally failed at it, I do highly disagree with him." I stick out my chin, feeling like a child on the verge of a temper tantrum.

She looks down and carefully says, "The only things we fail at in life, honey, are the things we don't give one hundred percent."

I take a sip of my coffee as I let the idea bounce around in my head. I know exactly what she's saying. You can't expect conclusive results if you half-ass things.

"So you think that writing them out is a good idea then?"

She scoots her chair in front of me and grabs my hands. "What I'm saying is..." Her eyes start to get misty as she quickly looks away to recover, then gives me a weak smile as they meet mine again. She tries again. "All I'm saying is that if you aren't ready to talk about your feelings, then yes, writing them out is the best alternative. Holding that kind of pain in can break even the strongest person."

I gulp, my thoughts instantly going to Dax. He keeps so much in. I'm not sure if he does it for my sake or because he's really that quiet about his emotions in general. Everyone believes I'm too fragile to face what happened. The truth is it can't be any worse to think about it versus saying it aloud. It's constantly there, set on some sort of shuffle replay as I'm reminded daily. Tortured for what I lost. And blessed for what we had.

Chapter Twenty-Seven

DAX

I've been gone for a week and the longing to be back home hasn't lessened. Lynsie and I talk every night, occasionally sending each other texts throughout the day. It's always me initiating it, but she replies quickly. I know she doesn't ever text me first because she's trying to keep me from worrying about her. I sit on my bed, grab my phone off the nightstand, and shoot her a quick a text.

> Me: I miss you. Hope you're doing well.
> Good luck today.

Today is her second doctor's appointment. I hate that I'm not going to be there. She told me last night she'd be fine. Which is quite possible but still sucks. She at least needs to involve her parents.

> Lynsie: I miss you too, Dax.

I want to keep texting her, to pry into her plans for her appointment and tell her to keep me updated on how it goes as soon as she's done, but I don't. I'm trying not to be pushy where she's concerned.

I turn my phone off and shove it into the front pocket of my backpack. Flinging it over my shoulder, I head out of my motel room. Even if they'd had room on base for me, I would've paid out of pocket for the privacy. None of the guys would understand me staying up every night on the phone with Lynsie until she passes out. I have a feeling it's going to continue like this until I'm back, and honestly, it doesn't bother me one bit.

Class has become a nice distraction. I was losing hope that anything would be able to keep me focused and distract my mind. Of course, when I'm flying, I keep my mind on all the important components involved, but as soon as everything is checked and my copilot and I are safely in the sky, my mind has a habit of roaming. Not so much about the dangers, but more about the unknowns. We all face unknowns when it comes to life, pilot or not.

I try to keep to myself out here, but I swear, Zack Peterson is like an STD I can't get rid of. He's always following me around. I know he's capable of bullshitting his way into the hearts of these other guys, but I don't get why he's so determined to do so with me. Maybe it's because I'm the only one he really knows, or that we're borderline friends and he thinks we should constantly hang out. Whatever it is, it's becoming a nuisance. For some reason, though, I don't want him to stop trying. I have a feeling one day I might give in. He isn't that horrible of a guy; he just needs to grow up some.

I manage to scoot out of the classroom before Peterson or anyone can ask me to join them for lunch. Hurrying down the hall, I pull my cell out and turn it on as I head for my rental car. I wait for the phone to vibrate as I jog the last few feet. I'm hoping to hear something from Lynsie.

Nothing.

I quickly find somewhere to stop and grab lunch. Sitting in a booth at a sub shop on base, I scarf down a BLT and stare at my phone the whole damn time, willing it to go off.

It doesn't.

I let out a heavy breath. I need to pull myself together. I'm not going to hear from her until I call tonight. I already know this. I put my phone in my front pocket as I gather my trash to throw away. I get back into the black Toyota and crank the music up along with the AC as I lean my head back to clear my mind. My phone vibrates in my pocket, startling me. The anticipation causes a zing of happiness to run through me.

> Mom: How's training going, son?

Happiness zing gone.

> Me: So far so good. How's everything going at home?

I don't ask about Dustin. I quit asking about him a long time ago.

> Mom: Your dad and I are fine. We miss you. Really wish you'd come visit sometime soon.

I sigh. I do miss my parents. They have good intentions, but they aren't happy with my career choice. They hoped I wouldn't follow in my brother's footsteps, and I didn't. Not really. I didn't join the Army because of him. He's actually the reason I didn't want to join. I saw what being in the military was doing to my brother and I was scared it'd do the same to me. Even though I'm settled where I'm at now, my mother is constantly reminding me of the job that will always be waiting for me at the aviation school back home.

Me: I know.

I should've added more to that text, but I'm not about giving people false hope. I could've told her I'd come see them soon, but I don't have any intention to, even with the holidays coming up. Does that make me a bad son? Probably, but my parents have each other. They aren't my concern now. I've heard the first holidays, coping with the emptiness of a missing loved one, are the hardest. Not that the rest of them aren't, just the newness is still there.

Heading back, I get my second wind, knowing that the last part of the day is actual flight training. There's so much to learn in The Fixed-Wing Multi-Engine Instructor Pilot course. I can't afford to let my mind roam. There's a good bit of role-playing involved. My instructor teaches me how to be an instructor, and I have to act as the instructor training another pilot. Sometimes the Check Pilot will do role reversal, where he acts like the student, and I'll have to evaluate and critique his performance so he knows I know what the hell I'm doing.

Usually, the day is divided into classes and the flight line. Classes include: Instructor Pilot Fundamentals (How people learn and all the things that affect learning so you can teach them), Physiology (How the body works and things that affect people, from types of Hypoxia to Nutrition and Drug interactions, Eyeballs and the Inner Ear), Aerodynamic so you can actually explain them and how they apply to flying, Aircraft systems, Airspace, Weather and a few more.

The flight line is where I'll learn to describe each maneuver as I'm doing it, based on the Aircrew Training Manual. I'll start off with the basic maneuvers and eventually move on to the complex ones. Of course I'll have to learn all the systems limitations for the aircraft, as well as emergency procedures, which *have* to be committed to memory, along with everything else we learn.

AS SOON AS we land for the day, I pull my phone out. I need to know how her appointment went. My phone chimes, alerting me of a voicemail. Assuming it's from Lynsie, I hit play.

"Dax, this is Cindy at Doctor Marx's office. I've been trying to get ahold of Lynsie today and haven't had any luck. She missed her appointment, and she will need to reschedule. If you'll have her call us ASAP, that'd be great. Thanks."

Shit!

I impatiently scroll through my recent calls, knowing Lynsie will be high up on that list.

She doesn't answer. "Lynsie, it's me. Answer your phone."

I call again. No answer. She's avoiding me.

Taking a break, I grab something to eat for dinner and pull out my notes from class to start studying. Unless she calls me back, I'll wait until later tonight.

Two hours and a shitload of studying later, I pick up my phone and dial. It's not our normal time, but I need to hear her voice.

"Hello," Lynsie answers hesitantly.

Relief instantly washes over me. "Don't worry me like that, Lyns."

"Sorry," is all she says. A moment of silence passes. She's being too quiet. More than usual. This isn't good.

"What happened today?" I don't need to explain what I'm referring to.

"I don't know, Dax." Her voice cracks. "I really planned to go. Then, last minute, I just couldn't do it," she sniffles.

I sink against the uncomfortable motel chair. "Lynsie, I know it's hard, but you can't miss your appointments. If you won't tell your parents, then you need to tell Echo so she can go with you."

"No," she quickly interjects, "I can do this on my own."

"Yes, but you shouldn't have to. No one thinks you're incapable, Lynsie," I clarify.

I decide to stop lecturing her, and we spend the rest of the night chatting about random little things, such as the books she's been listening to lately, but the whole time we talk, something nags at me. I need to tell someone, anyone, that Lynsie's pregnant.

After we hang up, I pace back and forth, contemplating what I should do. I don't want to put my loyalty to her on the line, but I also can't sit back and do nothing. I hate myself for agreeing I'd keep my mouth shut, but something's got to give. She might end up hating me, but it'll only be temporary. I hope. I have to do what's best for her, even if she doesn't see that my intentions are pure.

I grab my wallet off the dresser and pull out the folded piece of paper. I stare down at the name and number for what feels like forever before finally letting out the breath I've been holding, then I grab my phone.

The phone picks up after three rings. "Hello."

"Hey, it's Dax Adams. I'm sorry to call out of the blue, but I really need to talk to you." I add hesitantly, "I need a favor."

After I get off the phone, I feel a hell of a lot better, but I still worry. Having the best intentions isn't always enough. I just hope, in this case, she realizes I'm only doing it to help her since I can't physically be there to do it myself.

With so much on my mind, I pull out my journal. But I can't slow my thoughts down enough to put them on paper. Instead, I start doodling this idea that's been overwhelming my mind lately. I used to be into drawing, which led to my obsession with wood carving. Ever since I joined the Army, I haven't really had the place to keep up with my second passion.

The drawing part I catch myself doing every now and then, but it's not like I used to, where I'd have an image pop in my head, and I couldn't stop scribbling until I captured it perfectly. This idea, however, is amazing and I know one day I'll have to bring it to life. Just the thought of finding the perfect piece of wood and sawing it down just right, then chiseling the rest of the details into it, has me pumping with excitement. This will be the most meaningful thing I've ever designed.

I start with a large swoop of an angel's wing and lightly shade it in with my pencil as I figure out how to transport what I'm seeing in my head into a physical image. My goal is to incorporate an aviator wing and join the two wings together. They'll be connected but separate enough to make out what they each are. The idea behind this image makes me sad, for Lincoln mostly, but I also think about all the pilots who've lost their lives flying—doing what they loved.

When this idea came to me, I had every intention of strictly dedicating it to the memory of Lincoln Fox, my lifelong best friend. Now, there's no way I can only dedicate it to him and him alone.

As I scratch out a few lines here and there, I think about how I really should be studying. A loud knock startles me and I glance at my clock. I roll off my bed, grab my shirt, and throw it over my head as I walk to the door. Whoever it is bangs on it again.

"Hold on. I'm coming." I peep through the tiny hole, seeing Peterson on the other side. I groan. I'm not in the mood for company.

"Let me in, Dax," he slurs from the hallway.

He's drunk. I'm so not in the mood for a drunk Peterson gracing me with his sloppy presence.

Sighing, I turn the bolt. He looks like a hot mess with glossed over eyes, leaning against my doorjamb, unable to stand on his own. I wonder what the hell his problem is. I've never seen him like this— even when I've seen him drunk. He's one of those happy, loud, obnoxious drunks. Not sad, like someone ran over their puppy. It's going to be a long night.

"Thanks," he says, shuffling past me into the room. He stops next to my dresser and grabs a handful of Jelly Belly's. "Dude, what's up with all the jellybeans?" He eyes the empty packages lying near the bowl. Ignoring his question, I turn my back to him as he throws a handful of candy into his mouth. "Are you pregnant?"

I can barely understand him with that giant wad of candy in his mouth. As I whip around, I see him waving the pregnancy book I bought to gain a better understanding of what Lynsie will be going through. "Yeah." I yank the book from his hand and throw it on the other side of my bed. "The cat's out of the bag, Peterson. Your mom and I are having a baby."

"Not funny, Dax." He grabs another handful. Thank God I already took the ones I needed out. I don't trust where his hands have been. "I don't even know my momma," he says while fishing out the pieces stuck between his teeth.

I debate apologizing, but he's so drunk, he probably won't remember any of this in the morning.

I watch Zack pace back and forth a few times before he stops, facing me. "I know you can barely stand being around me because of what happened with Lincoln. I've never talked to you about it because, honestly, I carry so much guilt around. I see how miserable you are, the pain you try to hide, and I know I'm responsible. Maybe it's dumb of me to keep trying to be friends with you. Maybe every time you see me, you're reminded of that awful day. But shit, man, I know it should've been me." He sits down on my bed, holding his head in his hands.

I sigh and grab a chair from the desk and sit, facing him. "I don't blame you. It was a freak accident. If you had stayed on that plane, you would've died. You wouldn't have been able to keep it from crashing into the crowd. That's why they made the call to take it down. No one's to blame."

He looks up at me. His face is serious, but the undertone of what he says isn't. "Then why won't you just be my friend? I know I'm trying too hard, but damn, I don't know anyone here and I don't want to." *Hello, my name is Needy Peterson.*

"I'll be your friend, Peterson," I say, exasperated, and slap his shoulder.

His face lights up. "Thanks, Dax." Then he falls back on my bed and passes out. Some friend.

"Peterson." He doesn't reply, and I try again. "Peterson." I kick his leg.

Nothing. He doesn't move.

"Peterson, get off my damn bed."

I kick a little harder this time. He lets out a few snores, confirming that I'll have to push him off my bed, onto the floor. No way am I sleeping in a bed with a guy, or on my hard floor. I told his drunk ass I'd be his friend. That doesn't include waking up next to him. We aren't that close.

Chapter Twenty-Eight

LYNSIE

I expected Dax to be mad at me last night. He wasn't. It was almost stupid to think he would be. For some reason, I don't want to disappoint him. I should've gone to my appointment. I was scared. I thought I could do it, until I couldn't. Then the rest of the day, I stayed in bed, ignoring everyone's phone calls, even his. Not intentionally, but I decided to silence my phone while I took a nap. I hadn't expected him to call sooner than normal, but I also hadn't expected him to know I ditched my appointment. It made me thankful that I listed him as my emergency contact. That wouldn't have been fun to explain to my parents.

I don't know why I'm keeping this to myself anymore. I don't have any viable reason. It's a selfish one, I know. I just feel that once everyone knows, it'll change everything. They already treat me like I'm fragile. Once they know, I won't be able to ward it off, and right now I like keeping people as close or as far as I want.

I lie in bed, staring at my ceiling as the TV plays in the background. My nightly routine has turned into me coming to bed with my phone, journal, and remote to Dax's TV. Those three things manage to keep my mind in one place.

It's ten minutes past 9:00 p.m., and I'm getting antsy, wondering why Dax hasn't called yet. He's an hour behind, but that's why we settled on nine because I wanted to give him enough time to wind down after being in class all day. I'm never the one who calls him, but my finger is moments away from scrolling through my phone of its own accord and pushing call.

The doorbell rings, stopping my finger in its tracks. I look at my phone, double-checking the time. Who would be at my house this late without even calling? I sit up, throwing my legs over the bed as I wait a minute, debating on answering. Maybe they'll leave if I don't.

Wrong, I know, but I'm not up for company, especially when I'm waiting for Dax to call.

Dax! Would he surprise me?

I don't know, but the possibility has me springing to my feet and jogging down the stairs. The bell rings one more time as I reach the bottom of the steps.

"Coming," I yell, my bare feet padding across my wood floor. I flip on my porch light and fumble with the locks. It shouldn't take this long to unlock my doggone door.

Finally! Smiling, I fling the door open, expecting Dax on the other side. My smile falters, but only temporarily before clinging to my visitor.

"Rebecca!" I throw my arms around her, hugging her tightly. *She's at my house.* Relief instantly washes over me.

"I hope you don't mind me showing up unannounced," she acknowledges.

I pull back, holding her at arm's length. "You don't know how good it is to see you." I let out a sigh of relief.

She looks tired. I take in her black yoga pants, neon green T-shirt, her auburn hair thrown on top of her head. I'm sure she's been driving all night.

I look behind her at her car. "Where are your kids?"

Her face brightens. "I left them with my parents for a couple days."

She steps in and I close the door behind her. Heading into the kitchen, I turn on every light I pass. There's no way I'm going to be able to fall asleep now. Not that I don't enjoy seeing the few visitors I do get, but I finally have one who gets me more than even Dax does. I begin to make us an extra strong pot of coffee. I sense a long conversation on the agenda.

I press start on the coffee maker, then turn around to Rebecca. She's watching me intently, but her eyes aren't filled with pity like most people's. I'm sure that's a look she despises as well, but I can tell she's concerned. Who isn't?

"So what brought you here?" I lean back against the counter.

She lets out a light sigh, shaking her head. "Lynsie." She takes a few steps closer. "Are you supposed to be drinking caffeine?" Her sincere eyes search mine.

"Yeah." I cross my arms, trying not to look defensive. I have no reason to be. "Why wouldn't I?" Then it hits me. "Dax." I let out a sarcastic laugh. "That little shit."

Rebecca lets out a light chuckle. "Don't go getting mad at him." She yawns.

She's defending him. He betrayed my trust by telling someone, and she's defending him. I look off to the side, toward the dining room. I can't stand the idea of letting her see my pain. She has enough of her own. I can't even pinpoint where this pain resonates from.

"He cares deeply about you," she says gently.

That makes my head snap in her direction. "And that makes it okay? I told him not to tell anyone. I would do it when I felt the time was right. I trusted him."

"Lynsie." She places her hands on my shoulders to ease the tension as she rubs them up and down. "He called me. He didn't call your parents or anyone you know around here. More than anything, he wanted to throw in the towel and rush back to you. That's how much he cares about you and this baby, but he called me, a complete outsider, for guidance. He's loyal to a fault. Many would say he should've told your parents when he first found out, but he didn't. And he won't." There are tears in her eyes. Her compassion is filled to the brim. "But, honey, you need to."

I nod, tears filling my eyes.

We stay up for the rest of the night, talking about anything and everything, weaving in the parts of our continuing grief, how we've both been trying to truly move on from what we've endured, and how I feel about being pregnant.

"You never fully move on," she admits, fully accepting that fact with a sad nod. "I mean, it's only been a few months. Don't get me wrong, it's getting easier, but the ache is always there. You'll have good days and really bad days. The bad days eventually start to taper off."

I nod in agreement, knowing exactly what she means. For the first month, I felt like I could barely breathe. Very few stolen moments throughout the days, I felt normal. The rest, I was numb. And I didn't mind. It was more bearable than feeling.

"What I hate most is how I push everyone away. Dax is the only one I haven't. I don't know why. I just feel like we both loved Lincoln so much and that connects us. When he's around, I don't have to put on a front or pretend to be dealing with it well. Even though he hides it better, he's feeling what I'm feeling, and I take comfort in that. Not sure if it's wrong or not." I'm silent, deep in thought after saying that out loud. Speaking it puts it all into perspective. Am I using Dax?

"He needs you just as much as you do him." Rebecca rubs my knee, pushing my negative thoughts away. "But you do need to start opening up to those around you. They want to help you, too. I can attest that it's a huge relief once you do. You can never have too much support."

She's right. I've just needed someone who could be objective. Anyone else and my mindset would've been to rebel.

I grab my phone off the coffee table and shoot Dax a quick text. He never called. Now I know why. Somehow, he always knows what I need. It's late, and he's probably in bed, but at least he'll have it first thing in the morning.

> Me: Thank you!

I go to sit my phone back down, but before I can, it instantly buzzes in my hand. I grin as I look down.

> Dax: I will always have your best interests at heart. Night, Lynsie.
>
> Me: Night, Dax.

I look over at Rebecca, whose sleepy eyes haven't moved off me. "Will you do me a favor tomorrow?" Not that I can't do this on my own, but if I can't have Dax by my side, I really want her to be with me. Mainly to keep me from backing out.

She sits up a little straighter. "Anything."

"Will you go with me to tell my mom?" I rub my hand across my still flat stomach. Sometimes I forget that I'm even pregnant.

"Of course I will." She smiles in relief. I'm sure she's doing a small victory dance inside. Her reason for coming has been accomplished.

I offer Rebecca my room, but she reassures me the couch is fine. I hear her light snores as my foot hits the bottom step. Tonight will be the first night I fall asleep without hearing Dax's voice. The thought has me wanting to speed-dial him, but I think better of it as I crawl into bed, yawning.

* * *

THE NEXT MORNING, I wake up tired as hell but with a sense of determination. The dread I expected to weigh me down isn't there. I throw some clothes on and brush my teeth before making my way downstairs. Rebecca is still asleep on the couch where she passed out. I told her she could sleep in my room, but I think she was so worn out from her drive, she didn't have the energy to climb the stairs.

In the kitchen, I pour the old coffee out from last night and get the pot ready to brew a new batch.

"Tsk, tsk," I hear a groggy voice coming from the couch.

I get a drink out of the fridge and make my way to the living room, standing in front of her. I open my small bottle of orange juice and take a long drink from it.

"The coffee is for you." I shake my OJ proudly, displaying my healthy drink of choice. "Even though my doctor did say I could drink a cup a day."

"Better watch out." She scrunches her nose, sitting up. "Some pregnant women get sick from orange juice."

I frown at the bottle when I think about it. "Hmm, I haven't really gotten sick since I found out I was pregnant. I just figured the few times I did were all trauma or stress-induced."

"I'm sure that didn't help it any. So." She stretches her arms above her head, letting out a yawn. "You ready to do this?" This woman doesn't waste any time.

"I guess it's now or never."

AN HOUR LATER, the two of us are standing on my parents' front porch. Even though I'm their daughter, and I usually exercise their open-door policy, I find myself standing here, knocking as if I'm a stranger. My mom answers the door, giving me a confused look. I would too if I were her. The things I do lately don't always make sense.

"Hey, Mom." I take a deep breath as I fidget with my keychain. "I hope you don't mind us showing up without notice."

"Of course not, honey." She beams, giving me a quick smile, holding the door wide to let us in.

Inside, I introduce Rebecca to my mother. "Mom, this is Rebecca Robinson."

Rebecca smiles warmly. "It's nice to meet you, Mrs. Clark. I'm Travis Robinson's wife. He was good friends with Lincoln and Dax. He died a few months ago in a plane crash as well."

The happiness falls from my mom's face, and I'm sure she's expecting this visit to be a solemn one. "I remember hearing about your husband. I'm so sorry for your loss." Her condolence is genuine.

"Thank you." She nods, giving my mother a faint smile. "It's been rough, but it's a day-to-day struggle. Each one gets a little better."

"Can we sit down?" I interject. Feeling a sense of unease pushing through, I know I need to do this before I lose my nerve.

"Of course." My mother turns to lead us into the living room. She sits down in the recliner, and I sit down on the couch with Rebecca beside me.

"Rebecca showed up at my house last night." I look over at her and smile before returning my attention to my mother. "Dax actually got ahold of her without my knowledge. He figured that speaking to someone who's going through what I am would help, and it did." I look down, fiddling with my fingers.

Rebecca places her hand on my shoulder and lightly rubs it. "You can do this, Lynsie," she whispers, reassuring me.

I can feel my mother's curious eyes on me. I let out a breath, looking back up as a few tears slide down my face. Her eyes are full of concern as she patiently waits for me to open up.

"I'm pregnant." I smile as more tears stream down my face.

My mother's eyes twinkle as her whole face lights up with excitement. "I'm going to be a grandma," she cries through her happy tears.

"Yes." I beam, letting the excitement and relief that I've been pushing down take over. My mother jumps up, throwing her arms around me. I knew the idea would excite her—excite everyone—but that's why it feels so wrong. I have this beautiful miracle growing inside me that I can't wait to hold, but with that comes an overwhelming amount of guilt. That's why I've wanted to keep it to myself. Because it takes the focus off what we've lost, putting it on what we are to gain. I can't help but struggle with these two polar opposite emotions that are fighting me for control.

WHEN MY PHONE rings, I see Dax's name on the screen and a thrill of excitement takes over. A lot has happened today. He'll be so proud of me, which makes me even happier for some reason.

"Hey!" I answer with enthusiasm. "I've been waiting all day for you to call. It's been crazy and I've been dying to tell you all about it." I stop, finally taking a breath.

Dax laughs on the other end. "Whoa there, Lynsie. Good to talk to you, too."

"Shut it," I threaten with a laugh. "I really want to thank you for sending Rebecca. That was pure genius on your part. You never cease to amaze me," I admit as I fall back on my bed.

"I will always do what's best for you. Even when you don't see it, your best interests will always be what drives my decisions."

I let out a sigh of contentment, realizing how much lighter my chest feels after finally telling my parents about the baby. I'm still dreading the call to Lincoln's parents. I'll wait a little longer for that one.

"Well, I told my parents." I smile, remembering how ecstatic they both were.

"And?" Dax urges. "How'd that go?"

"Amazing. We cried. We laughed. We all hugged. And it kind of broke something, whatever reason I've been keeping them at arm's length," I add quietly as I rub my flat tummy. "I'm going to make it through this, Dax. I can feel it. I'm carrying a piece of him now. Hearing the baby's little heartbeat again today...wow."

"I'm so glad to hear that." His voice is as quiet as mine. "Like I've always said, you'll be an amazing mother." He lets out a heavy yawn, and I picture him staying up late last night, worrying about me. Worried that I was going to be mad at him for sending Rebecca to my house. Sometimes I wonder if all this man does is worry. "Wait. You went to the doctor today?"

"Yeah, at my parents' house, I went ahead and called to reschedule. They had a cancellation this afternoon, so we went."

"Who's we?" he questions with a hint of jealousy.

"Just me, my mom, and Rebecca before she left to head back home."

"Oh, well, that's good. I'm glad your mom was able to be a part of it." His voice is low.

"Don't be over there worrying," I say, feeling the need to reassure him.

"Worrying about what?" His voice is now laced with curiosity.

He thinks I don't know him, but I do. Like the back of my hand.

I've picked up bits and pieces of him and his moods from the last six years.

"You're still my number one, Dax," I say tenderly. "Just because I'm slowly opening up doesn't mean you're getting pushed to the side—unless it's mine," I add. I say it like a joke, but I'm dead serious.

"I need you too, Lyns," he says sleepily as he yawns again. I know it's only a matter of minutes...seconds before he passes out. "When do you plan on telling Lincoln's family?"

I've been battling this idea all day. I feel like I took a huge leap today and I'm not sure how soon I'll be ready for another, but I know I need to. This might be good for them. To know a piece of their only child will live on. To know they'll get the grandchild they've always wanted. They deserve to know—sooner rather than later. It will hurt them if they do find out and realize I've been keeping it from them.

"Soon," I tell him. "I plan on telling them real soon."

* * *

THE NEXT DAY, I decide to go for it. I haven't talked to Lincoln's family since the day after the funeral, and I feel horrible about it. I've ignored every attempt his mom has put out. Lincoln would be disappointed in me. He wouldn't want me shutting out his parents when they're hurting just as bad, and he certainly wouldn't want me keeping this precious gift from them.

For Lincoln, I'll be strong. For our baby, I'll be strong.

On the second ring, Julie answers. "Lynsie!" she exclaims. "I'm so glad you called."

A pang of guilt hits me as I contemplate hanging up and playing it off as an accidental call. Then I remember why I'm doing this and for who, and the courage I need comforts me.

"Hi, Julie. I'm sorry I've been distant lately. I've kind of, umm," I stammer. "I've been distant with everyone, not just you guys." I don't want her to take it personally.

Julie lets out a breath. "It's understandable, honey," she reassures. "Dax has been keeping in contact, so I knew you were in good hands. But I know he's been gone for training, and I couldn't help but worry about you."

"Yes." I swallow hard, squeezing my eyes shut. "It's been rough without him around, but..." I pause and take a deep breath. "It's also time I quit pushing everyone away. So I guess you could say his training has been sort of a blessing in disguise." I hate saying it, but who knows if I would've come to terms otherwise.

"I'm really glad to hear that."

"Umm, I have something to tell you." I pause, replaying the words I want to say in my head.

"Oh?" The curiosity in her voice urges me on.

"Julie, you're going to be a grandma," I blurt out.

"What?" She gasps, and her voice cracks as the emotion takes over. "I'm going to be a grandma?" she chokes out through her sobs.

"Yes." I smile, crying a little quieter on my end of the phone.

"Thank you, Lynsie," she sobs. "Thank you so much. You have no idea how much this means to me. I have to go call Jim. He will be so thrilled."

Oh, but I do, I think, absently caressing the same spot on my belly over and over. I've been doing that more and more lately. It's real. This is real. And carrying Lincoln's child means the world to me.

The doorbell chimes, yanking me out of my daydream, and I wonder who it could be. I run downstairs, barely being able to contain my excitement. I unlock the door and fling it open. A UPS man is walking off, heading toward his truck. I glance down at a medium-sized box and pick it up yelling, "Thanks."

With no return address, I quickly make my way to the kitchen to cut the tape off. I open it and gasp. I start pulling all the different snacks out of my box. Everything from beef jerky and dill pickle chips to caramel popcorn fills the box up. It isn't until I see the note attached to the Ziploc bag at the bottom of the box that I begin to get choked up.

I pull the bag out and all my favorite flavors shift around inside. Watermelon, tutti-frutti, bubble gum, green apple, and red apple Jelly Belly's, just for me. I smile, wondering how in the world he knows me so well.

Lyns,

I really hope these are the ones you like. I know I can't be there for your crazy pregnancy food cravings, so I hope everything else will hold you over until I can be.

Love,
Dax

I start crying and I have no idea why. Maybe it's because he's so good to me. It also could be pregnancy hormones setting in. Either way, I grab my phone to call him, then think better of it when I see the time. He's still in class, but I can't wait, so I text him.

> Me: You really think of everything. You never cease to amaze me. Thanks for being such an incredible person. All the goodies will hold me over, but next time just send yourself :)

He quickly replies, causing me to giggle.

> Dax: If that's what you want.

Chapter Twenty-Nine

DAX

It's been almost three months since I arrived in Fort Hood, Texas. My time here is almost done. From what Lynsie tells me —and anyone else I talk to—she seems to be doing well. As well as she can. I think calling Rebecca was the smartest thing I could've ever done. She offered her something I couldn't—a kindred spirit.

Now that Lynsie is finally opening up, she's also starting to heal. Relishing in the support system she's surrounded with instead of pushing them away has been the best thing for her. She's not back to who she was, but she's on her way, and so am I.

I nailed the last bit of training earlier today, just in time to celebrate before heading home for Thanksgiving tomorrow. The guys have decided to drag me out tonight. I hesitated at first, but they got the best of me. As we walk into the bar, the four guys I've been training with these couple months start hooting and hollering with excitement. It feels good. Something I've been missing. Friendship outside of the Fly Zone is a balance I need to regain in my life, too. No one will ever replace Lincoln, but I do need to start letting people in and getting back into the social aspects of life. It's all a part of the healing process.

I was so worried about the tests today—the one in the classroom, along with the physical one. I'm more than thankful that Lynsie's dad made sure to prepare me the best he could before I left. There's no amount of training that can prepare your heart for such traumatic loss. I believe that quickly getting back in the sky was a form of therapy for me. Lynsie's dad holds a heavy burden when it comes to Lincoln's death. He blames himself. He knows Lynsie wishes Lincoln had been the survivor. He wishes himself that had been the case.

"Drinks on me." Aarons elbows me on his way up to the bar. A few minutes later, he's making his way back with two pitchers of beer in one hand and cups in the other. For a Monday night, the bar is crowded. I'm surprised the five of us even found a spot to sit.

"Man, I can't wait to get home to my girl tomorrow," Carter says, pouring his drink.

"What girl?" Jones smacks his arm. "You've been hitting on everything in sight since you've been here." He laughs.

"Gotta scratch my itch somewhere." Carter shrugs.

I tilt my glass toward him. "Pretty sure that's what gave you an itch in the first place."

Everyone at the table laughs, except Carter.

"Oh, yeah. Well, what's your story, Dax?" Carter demands. "You got you a special lady at home?"

All eyes are now focused on me. "Something like that," I disclose, trying to keep it vague. No way in hell am I explaining anything to his cocky ass.

"Well," Carter quips, "she must be pretty damn special if you're able to keep it in your pants for so long."

"What's that saying about your chick back home, Carter?" Peterson dives in to the rescue.

Carter waves his hand. "Nah, she knows how I am. She's the

same way. We're just exclusive when I'm home." He says it like it's nothing new.

Peterson doesn't back down. "All I'm saying is, if you have someone special back home, you should cherish it. You're just abusing it."

I stare at him, shocked. "Are you sick, Peterson?" I place the back of my hand on his forehead. I've never heard him talk about caring for a woman. And he's never struck me as the type to ever settle down.

"Screw off, Adams." He swats my hand away.

I continue laughing. He sounds like an article from Dear Abby.

After a minute, the tension diminishes, and everyone joins in to laugh at Peterson. Maybe everything that was said hit Carter a little too close to home. That's usually the reason people get offended. Not because they don't agree, but because it's true. They just don't want to acknowledge it.

"Let's play some darts," Aarons says, looking at me.

I more than happily agree, eager to get away from this conversation.

"Thanks," I tell him as we weave around the tables to get to the dartboard.

"No problem." His eyes are understanding. "I could tell you were uncomfortable back there. I finally got you to come out with us." He grins. "No way am I letting that douche ruin it."

"I needed to get out." I sigh, moving behind the taped line on the floor.

A few games and a couple of beers later, I feel my phone vibrating in my pocket. When I see Lynsie's number on the screen, I push through the heavy crowd, toward the front door as fast as I can.

"Hey, Lyns," I answer, barely in time.

"Dax! You had me worried." Her voice is panicky.

"I'm so sorry I didn't call," I say as I sit on the curb. The realization that I let the time slip by pisses me off.

She's quiet, and I can tell I hurt her feelings. "It's okay," she says through light sniffles.

"Dammit, Lynsie." I press a hand to my forehead, feeling like such a jackass. "I'm really sorry. We just had these tests today and then the guys wanted to celebrate." The front door opens, exposing the loud music.

"Are you at a bar?" she stutters.

"Yeah. The guys wanted to come here."

"Oh." She recoils. "Well, I'll let you get back to your celebration."

No! No! No!

"Lynsie, wait."

"Congrats on your test, Dax," she says before hanging up.

I shouldn't have broken my routine. How could I deviate from our nightly ritual? I feel like shit right now. Going out with friends is fine, but I let down the most important person in my life in the process. I have to make this up to her somehow.

The door opens and out walks Aarons. "Everything okay?" he asks, eyeing me. "You kinda just took off," he states, sitting down next to me.

"Far from it." I sigh.

"Maybe you should talk about it."

I squint my eyes, looking at him like he just lost his mind. From what I've gathered, Aarons seems like a decent guy. I admire his 'no shit taking' attitude. He's also the only guy here besides Peterson who has put out an effort to get to know me, which I haven't made easy.

He laughs. "I'm no expert or anything, and I have no idea what you're going through, man." He holds his hands up in defense. "But from the two months I've known you, I can tell you've been going through something deep. People talk, so we all know the basics. Just know if you need to talk about anything, I'm here." Then he motions between us. "And it will always stay here."

I sit, kicking at the gravel and staring out at the road as cars zoom back and forth. I've never really opened up to anyone. There are too many moving parts. So, besides writing in my journal, I hold it all in. But now, I'm thinking about it. It can't hurt to tell one person, an outsider, a portion of what I'm dealing with.

"My best friend died in that plane crash on the Fourth. That special someone back home"—I sigh, readying myself to say it out loud—"is his wife." I look over at Aarons, waiting for him to give me a look of disapproval, but he doesn't, so I continue. "We've kind of become each other's lifeline during all of this."

"Was that her who called?" He points to my phone that I'm still holding.

"Yeah." I nod. "Ever since I've been here, I've made it a point to call her every night. I guess she's become reliant on that. I've become dependent on her, too. So she kind of freaked out when I didn't call."

"Shit," Aarons mutters, shaking his head. "And us talking you into coming tonight totally jacked you up?"

"Yep." I sigh heavily. "I think I'm gonna call it a night. That cool?" I push off the curb and stand up.

"Course. Let me give you a ride to your motel." He stands, pulling his keys out of his front pocket, forgetting that Peterson and I met them here.

"I'm good to drive my rental, but will you do me a favor? Make sure Peterson makes it back?"

"Of course, man." He stands and turns to walk back in.

"Yo, Aarons," I call out, stopping him. "Make sure Peterson doesn't overdo it. He tends to turn into a big sap if he does." I laugh.

"Right." Aarons snickers. "Thanks for the warning."

"Oh, and make sure he makes it to his room this time, not mine."

I GET BACK to the motel and pack my bag, more than excited to get back home. I know she isn't happy with me, but I refuse to avoid reaching out.

I shoot her a text before crawling into bed.

Me: I miss you.

At least she'll know I'm thinking about her. Still, I wonder about things. What if I've messed everything up tonight? Will she still be excited to see me?

But another question makes my heart beat faster. What if she doesn't really need me anymore? She's doing a lot better than I expected since I've been gone.

A minute later, I get a reply.

Lynsie: Me too.

That's it. Two words. Lynsie is never that short with me. *Great!* She's pissed. I run a tired hand through my disheveled hair, really hoping this surprise gets me back in her good graces.

WHEN THE TAXI pulls away, I'm suddenly hit with a jolt of nerves. Standing here on this all too familiar porch, it's the last thing I should be feeling. Sadness, depression, guilt—all feelings that should be flooding me in an overwhelming abundance, yet they're not.

I ring the doorbell and wait. What feels like ten minutes is only a mere five seconds. My finger presses against the little round button one last time. I pull my keys out of my pocket when I hear the lock flip over and watch the knob turn. My pulse pounds in my neck and I swallow hard as the door slowly opens and Lynsie peeks her head around.

Once she sees me, the door flings open and she's in my arms.

"I missed you, too," I say, the sound of it slightly muffled by her hair. It feels so good to have her back in my arms.

"You weren't supposed to be back yet," she squeals, pulling away from me with tears in her eyes.

"We have a mini break for Thanksgiving, so I wanted to surprise you." I shrug sheepishly. "Plus, I messed up last night and needed to fix it."

Lynsie backs up, allowing me in. "There's nothing to fix, Dax. You didn't mess up. I overreacted." She tries to play it off.

I grab her hand and pull her back to me. "No, Lynsie. I messed up. What you felt last night...I never want you to feel that again. Not because of me, anyway."

She gulps, staring at my chest. "You're allowed to have a life."

"I know that." I squeeze her shoulders. "Don't ever think I don't care. Truth is, I never realized how important my calls were to you until last night."

"I didn't either...until you didn't call." Her eyes shift nervously. "Are you still tired?"

"Yes, I barely slept on the plane," I admit. She grabs my hand, leading us up the stairs. Lynsie hesitates as we both stand facing each other, about to turn and go our separate ways. I know she's been sleeping alone since I left. She doesn't need me to lie with her, but it doesn't mean I don't want to. I want to fall asleep with her in my arms so bad.

"Well, guess I'll see you in a few hours." Lynsie's tone is full of uncertainty. I can tell by the way she fiddles with her fingers and doesn't head for her room right away that she's feeling the same, but I can't be the one to bring it up. I don't want her to regress just because I'm here. I'll have to go back for a few more weeks once the holiday is over.

"Kay." I smile. "See you in a few. Get some rest." I quickly shut myself in my room before I change my mind. I toss my bag on the floor and kick my shoes off, then flop down on the messy bed. I look over at the bedside table, noticing her journal on it with her phone sitting on top. Even with me gone, she's been sleeping in my bed.

I hear light footsteps and a quick knock on the door. My pulse quickens with joy as a smile spreads across my face. Lynsie doesn't wait for me to answer before she lets herself in and crawls into bed next to me. I smile as she grabs my hand while we both lie on our backs next to each other.

"Just because I can deal with everything while you're gone doesn't mean I don't need you anymore." Her voice drops to a whisper. "I'm always going to need you, Dax."

My heart soars with those last few words, putting all my stupid fears to rest. "Good." It's the only word I can make myself say. I don't want to say too much.

"Thank you," she says, squeezing our joined hands.

"For what?" I rub my thumb along the top of her hand.

"For just being you." She yawns.

"I'll be whatever you need, Lynsie," I tell her, just above a whisper as she starts to finally doze off and I fall close behind her.

SUNLIGHT FILLS THE room as I slowly peel my eyes open. The brightness quickly shuts them. I rub the back of my hands over my face, willing myself to wake up and adjust to the light. Glancing over at Lynsie, I smile, noticing we're both still lying in the same position we passed out in, except we aren't holding hands. I quickly rectify that as I take her delicate hand in mine, which makes her stir next to me.

With the light in the room and her on her back, I'm able to see the little pooch of her stomach that I didn't notice earlier. Her T-shirt must've hidden it.

She looks over at me and notices where my eyes are and pulls my hand, resting it on her stomach. "Maybe the baby will move for you." She smiles.

I keep my hand as still as possible. I've never felt a baby move inside someone before. The bump she now has makes it even more real than it seemed when we heard the heartbeat at the doctor's office. I can only imagine how much more real it can be feeling the baby move.

Nothing happens and she sighs. "Sometimes this works better." Lynsie rolls onto her side, pulling me with her. I lie here with my arm draped over her side, almost as if we're spooning. Her body fits perfectly against mine. I stare down at the bare skin of her neck and swallow hard. I want to place light kisses all over it before tilting her face toward mine, giving me access to claim her mouth.

I'm doomed. These feelings I have for her only intensify daily. She grabs my hand and holds hers over it, slowly rubbing them both over her stomach. "Did you feel that?" She peeks excitedly over her shoulder.

"No," I say, disappointed.

"Well, quit breathing." She snickers. "Just kidding, but be real still and focus on any sudden movement under your hand."

I nod. Being as still as I can, I focus solely on my hand and the warmth of Lynsie's skin beneath it.

Then I feel it—a sudden shift in her abdomen. "Whoa! Was that the baby?"

Her face is brightly lit with excitement as she nods.

"That's so cool!" I'm simply amazed at how it all works.

"Yeah," she breathes, content. "It is amazing. It just started. I mean, I thought at times I'd felt it before but never knew for sure.

Now I know without a doubt it's my baby." She beams as she talks.

I rub my hand over her bump a few more times before pulling away. The more I have her in my arms, the more painful it becomes to pull away. If it were up to me, my arms would never leave her.

"It's incredible, Lyns. I've never felt that before," I say as Lynsie quickly rolls over, facing me. We're both lying on our sides.

"You can go with us today." She gives me a hopeful look.

"Go with you where?"

"The ultrasound. At the last appointment, the baby was shy, and we couldn't see the sex, so my mom set up a three-D appointment at an outside place. Us girls are going"—she pats my shoulder—"and now you can, too."

Sure, because being a fifth wheel has always been my dream. "Ahh," I start awkwardly, pushing the covers back. "As much as I want to be there, Lyns, I'm not trying to interfere with your girls' day. I'm not trying to put a kink in your plans."

"Seriously, Dax." She smacks my shoulder, bringing back a part of the Lynsie I know so well. "You just made this day a hundred times better." She rolls off the bed and stands next to it, looking down.

I can't help but chuckle at her messy hair. It's something else I wasn't able to fully notice when I got here.

She rolls her eyes at me. "Yeah. Yeah. I know my hair is a mess." She brushes her fingers through it. "I'm gonna go get ready. I suggest you do the same."

I watch her practically skip out of the room. Her disposition is far better than when I left, almost three months ago. She always says that it's me and that she can't survive without me, but I have a sneaking suspicion this baby is the true lifesaver. Maybe for all of us.

Chapter Thirty

LYNSIE

"*It's a girl!*"

The words keep playing over and over in my head as I lie here, looking at the precious face on the screen. My mom and Echo have tears of joy running down their faces, while Dax sits next to me, holding my hand and staring at the same screen.

When he finally does look at me, I see the tears in his eyes. If I didn't know any better, I'd think he was sad, but he's just as excited.

"Congrats, Lynsie." He leans over, placing a gentle kiss on my forehead.

"I'm so glad you were here for this," I whisper, brushing a tear from my face.

"Me too." He rests his forehead against mine. I see so many emotions whirling in his eyes before he tightly shuts them.

"Now we can go shopping!" My mother claps her hands excitedly, sitting on the other side of me.

The heartbeat made this real. Feeling the baby move made this even more real, but seeing the chubby face, features and all—and finding out she's a she—makes it the most real.

I look over at Dax, feeling guilty because I know he's not going to want to be a part of our shopping excursion, but I don't want to ditch him either. I've missed him so much.

Before I can even say anything, Dax senses what I'm thinking and comforts me as always.

"You go shop and spoil this little girl rotten."

I start to speak, but he stops me with a warm smile. "Don't worry about me. I'll find something to do."

WHEN I ARRIVE back home, Dax is sitting on the couch with his journal open on his lap. I walk up behind him and glance at what he's doing. I can tell he isn't writing by the way he's holding his pencil at an angle, like he's shading something in.

I gasp. "That's gorgeous."

His face stays focused on the picture and tilts to the side. Dax is in the zone, and I'm enjoying getting to witness it. He erases a few parts and reworks them as I lean over the couch, watching intently. I'm glad he doesn't mind me being nosey. I never knew of this talent.

"What is it?" I ask. "I mean, I can see the aviator wing and how it turns into an angel wing." As I say it out loud, it hits me. This isn't just any doodle; this picture is one of semblance.

At my silence, Dax stops drawing. He closes his journal and places it on the table, turning sideways so he's now facing me. "I've had this image stuck in my head for months. It's hard for me to get it perfect. I want to carve it into a chunk of wood and see if they'll let me put it at the hangar as a memorial. Not just for Lincoln," he adds quietly, "but for all the guys who've died doing what we love."

I let out a sarcastic laugh. "Lincoln said that when Robinson died. I remember how I justified it, thinking he was right. That the best way to die would be doing what you love." I bite down on my bottom lip. "I don't know if I believe that now."

"I'm sorry, Lyns," he says with understanding. "I wasn't trying to upset you. I just wanted to explain my idea, but if you don't want me to go through with it, I won't." His eyes are serious, letting me know it's up to me.

I stare at him for a moment, then sigh softly. "No. I love the idea. The meaning behind it is beautiful."

"Okay, good." He lets out a heavy breath and leans back into the couch. "Now all I need to do is find a piece of wood that'll work and buy a new set of chiseling tools. I can rent a chainsaw," he thinks out loud.

"I'm pretty sure my dad has a chainsaw," I offer. "He might even have a chunk of wood you could use. One of their trees was struck by lightning or something during a storm last week."

* * *

IT'S HARD TO be thankful when you're in a season of grief. It can be difficult to see through the thickness of despair weighing you down. But it's slowly lifting, allowing bits of light to shine through, and for that, I'm thankful.

I stand, scraping my chair back against the floor as it slides against the tile. All conversations cease as all eyes are now focused on me. "First"—I let out a breath as I now have everyone's full attention—"I want to thank you, Mom and Dad, for your unconditional love. I haven't been easy to be around these last four months, but thank you for being whatever I needed you to be."

My dad wraps his arm around my mother, giving her a little squeeze as they both watch me with nothing but love in their eyes. Tears form in my mother's eyes, and I quickly turn my attention else-where before my own take over.

"Dax." I turn sideways to face him. "There are no words to describe what you've been to me during all of this. No words could even grasp what it meant to have you by my side. Even though you haven't physically been here the last couple months, you'll never know how important hearing your voice every night is to me." I gulp hard as a few tears stream down my cheeks. He places his hand over mine, giving it a light squeeze as he looks up at me with a face full of reassurance. "If it wasn't for your selflessness and putting your feelings on the side, I wouldn't be where I am today. From now on, I promise to return it back to you." I turn back, not facing anyone in particular as I wipe away the few stray tears.

"And I'm thankful for this baby girl growing inside of me." I rub a protective hand over my stomach. "More than anything, I'm thankful for Lincoln's memory that will live on through her." I glance over at Lincoln's parents, who are sitting at the end of the table. "Thank you. I'll forever be thankful for the man you raised. I was lucky to have him for the short amount of time I did, and now, we have a little parting gift to share on his behalf."

THE MEN HEAD to the living room to watch the game, leaving the women to clean up the mess and converse.

"Do you have any names yet?" Julie asks as we rinse the dishes off.

I shrug, my arms elbow deep in soapy water. "I've played around with names here and there, but nothing has stuck. I have a feeling the perfect name will come once I see her gorgeous face." A mixture of nervousness and excitement settles over me. I can't help but wonder which of Lincoln's features our daughter will be blessed with.

"Yeah, I didn't have Lincoln's name picked out until I held him in my arms for the first time." She looks up, scrunching her brows like she's deep in thought. "I take that back. I had a name picked out for him, but once I had that boy in my arms, I knew it wasn't the right one."

"What was it?" I ask curiously. I can't imagine Lincoln being named anything else.

"Jeff." She laughs.

I scrunch up my nose. "I'm so glad you didn't go through with it."

We giggle together. It feels good to be able to do this. To talk about him and it not sting so deeply. I want to remember my husband and enjoy it as I do. I don't want to dread it, fearful that it'll only make me sad. Finally, I'm seeing the light at the never-ending tunnel. The light that proves that there comes a time when the memories of our loved ones make us more happy than sad.

"I miss him," Julie says, and my giggles cease.

The fear is back, but it's not as strong. "I do, too. I always will, but it doesn't always have to hurt."

Dax comes out of the living room, walking toward the back of the house, his phone ringing in his hand. I drop the rag I was using to dry off the dishes. "I'll be right back," I tell Julie as I follow him. I'm nosey, I know, but he didn't look overly thrilled.

I approach with caution. He's leaning against the wall at the end of the hallway. He gives me a crooked smile when he spots me. I slide down the wall across from him, trying not to rudely eavesdrop as he wraps up the call.

"Well, I'm going to let you go now, Mom. Tell Dad I love him. Happy Thanksgiving." He looks down at me jokingly, rolling his eyes as he continues to try to end the call. "Okay, Mom," he says impatiently, "I'll see what I can do." He nods a couple times. "Yes. Yes. Bye."

"Sheesh," he says, sliding down the wall across from me.

"You don't talk much about your parents," I say. It isn't the first time I've thought about it, but it's the first time I've voiced it.

He shifts uncomfortably, looking everywhere but at me. "There's not much to say."

"Tell me about them," I prod him gently. "I don't know anything about them or your brother." He snickers, and I add, "Humor me, why don't ya. You know basically everything about me. Tell me more about you. The stuff I don't get to see." I smile, inviting him to open up to me.

"Guess I'll start from the beginning." He sighs, scratching the back of his neck. "Dustin and I aren't close. He's not close to any of us. He enlisted in the Army right after graduating high school and hasn't really looked back since. He rarely comes home, even if he has leave. I can't wrap my mind around it, really."

He pauses, looking at me from the opposite wall. "He's only gotten worse since joining."

"Worse how?" I ask.

He glances at me. "Cold. Ice cold. I remember one time he did come home for like a week my senior year. Our cousin died in a car wreck."

I lightly gasp.

"Yeah, it was sad. She was only sixteen." He closes his eyes, shaking his head like he's trying to get rid of a memory. Keeping his eyes closed, he relives it instead. "I remember at her viewing, I was hesitant to view the body. I mean, I didn't want to see a dead body, especially my cousin's. I was sitting outside when Dustin came out. He patted my shoulder and said, 'Go ahead. She doesn't look that bad.'" He opens his eyes back up, and I see the pain from the memory.

I scoot up and grab his hands in mine as he continues. "Dustin is the reason I was so hesitant to join the Army. But Lincoln convinced me otherwise."

It warms my heart hearing Dax mention Lincoln, remembering when they were younger. In my mind, I can picture them together so clearly.

"What was it exactly that kept you from the Army?" I inch

closer, our knees now touching.

"His coldness." He shrugs like it's obvious. "I thought the Army was responsible. I know he's seen a lot of men and women die overseas. I was scared I'd turn out like him," he admits softly. "That if I joined, I'd wind up heartless and shut off from everyone."

I smile up at him, pulling our joined hands into my lap. "Dax, you couldn't be heartless if you tried."

He gives me that carefree smile I love so much. "I see that now, but I was young."

"I'm glad you did." I smile. "I can't imagine you not being a part of my life."

Dax's face is somber as he sits quietly for a moment. "We still would've met, eventually, but we would never have gotten to know each other."

"Exactly," I say, teasing him a little. "If you hadn't joined the Army, you would've jacked everything up."

He tilts his head, giving me a doubtful look. "What all would I have jacked up?"

"The part about you being a permanent fixture in my life." I stick my tongue out, trying to lighten the mood. "So what's the deal with your mom? I've gathered that she calls you often, and you never go visit. What's up with that?"

He clears his throat. "Umm. Well, I just like to avoid them if I can. It's bad enough that every time she calls, she practically begs me to leave the Army. Always reminding me about the instructor pilot job I can have anytime at the aviation school back home if I were to move back. When she doesn't get anywhere with that, she starts giving me a guilt trip to convince me to come visit. I know she hates that Dustin and I are both in the Army, and she's constantly worried about us, but she needs to give it a rest. You'd think she'd learn that bugging the shit out of us typically has the reverse effect. Especially with my brother."

"That sucks, Dax," I blurt.

"All right." He stands and pulls at our joined hands, raising me to my feet. "Enough about my crazy family. I hear that pumpkin cheese-cake calling my name."

"All yours, buddy." I laugh, scrunching my nose.

* * *

"IT'S NOT ANY easier this time." I look down at the concrete, concentrating on Dax's shined-up black boots.

His finger under my chin lifts my eyes back to his. "Yes, it is," he says tenderly. "This time I'll only be gone for a couple weeks. I'll be back before you know it." His words help, but they don't make me feel any better. I'm going to miss him all over again.

"Whatever." I take a step back, crossing my arms over my chest. This jacket can't keep the despair from shivering through my body. "Just hurry back. I'm going to miss you no matter how long you're gone." Then I grab onto him, holding him as tight as I can, while I still can.

He places a light kiss on my forehead just like he always does. The simple act is another thing that I've grown to expect from Dax. "See you soon, Lyns." He crouches down in front of me, placing both hands on my small bump. I instantly blush. "Hey, baby girl." He grins at my belly. "You be good for your momma while I'm gone. Keep her company for me."

"People are staring." I see the random onlookers in fatigues watching Dax talk to my stomach.

He looks up. "And?"

"People talk, you know," I say, suddenly feeling self-conscious.

"Oh, yeah. Gotcha." Hurt flashes in his eyes, but he tries to hide it.

"I'm sorry," I say, feeling terrible as I clutch my coat tighter.

Dax takes a few steps back, putting more than enough space between us. I can see the battle in his eyes. The hurt and the stoic look he tries to cover it with. Knowing that I did this to him breaks my heart, and I swallow hard.

I close the distance, grab one of his hands, and graze the side of his cheek with my other. "I shouldn't care what people think."

"It's natural," he says simply. He looks away, but his features relax beneath my touch.

"What we have is natural, too," I remind him, not wanting him to think I want anything to change. "I had a moment. It won't happen again. You mean more to me than anything they say."

"Love ya too, Lynsie." He smiles sweetly at me, his hazel eyes shining brightly.

Those words have come out of his mouth a couple times. They're words that don't even need to be spoken because every action has shown it. But I love hearing him say them because I love him too— he's my best friend. But the way they slip through his lips sounds so natural. Some guys holler and Dax looks over his shoulder, then back at me. "I have to go. I'll be back soon." He hugs me one last time before turning away. I stand and watch him jaunt away from me to the military plane that will take him back to Texas. It doesn't hurt as bad this time.

* * *

DAX AND I fell back into the same routine, talking on the phone every night and texting some throughout the day. When he was home for Thanksgiving, he told me how he and Peterson have been hanging out some. I was somewhat wary about it at first, but Dax promised he isn't a bad influence, which made me laugh. Dax needs friends. I think he feels guilty about getting close to anyone, especially the man who was part of the accident. I have a feeling he looks at it the same way I do—if we let someone get close, as close as Lincoln was, we're replacing him. Truth is, that's a spot that can never be filled.

Besides the one time I cut Dax's, today is the first day I'm attempting to do anyone's hair since the accident. Echo practically begged me to touch up her roots. I'm not dumb. She could do it herself as per usual, but I have a feeling she's pulling what my dad did with Dax and trying to get me back into the swing of things. She probably thinks all I need is a nudge in the right direction, and this is it. I do miss it. I'm just not sure I'm ready to go back to the salon. I'm not ready to face everyone's pity-filled faces.

Echo arrives and an overwhelming sensation of happiness sets in as she walks through the door, supplies in hand. I feel like it's been so long since I've seen her, and I really miss our daily interactions at the salon.

"Hey, girl." She squeezes me, avoiding my stomach. She steps back and squeals as her hand covers her mouth. "Eek! I just can't get over your precious baby bump." She places her hand on my middle. "Is she moving?"

I shake my head and laugh. "Not at the moment."

"Bummer." Her face falls with disappointment. "Well, maybe Miss Priss will move for Aunt Echo before I leave."

"I love the sound of that." I beam.

Thirty minutes later, Echo and I sit across from each other at my kitchen table while we wait for the dye to process.

"So how are things with you and Dax?" Her eyes are wide with curiosity.

"Things are great." I smile, shrugging my shoulders. Echo has never been good at being nonchalant. I can tell she's been wanting to ask me about Dax since the moment she showed up. "He's been amazing through all of this."

"He's really a good guy. You're blessed to have him in your life."

I nod in agreement. Propping my elbows on the table, I rest my face in my hands.

"What's gonna happen when he gets stationed somewhere else?" She eyes me suspiciously as I quickly sit back up and shift in my chair, feeling uncomfortable. "Because he won't always be stationed here," she adds, driving the punch in harder.

"I haven't really thought about it." I stare down at my hands and start chipping away at my peeling nail polish.

"I wasn't trying to upset you, Lynsie." She places her hands over mine, stopping my nervous fidgeting.

"I'm not upset." I give her a weak smile.

"Yes, you are," Echo says in a low, comforting voice. "You can't hide it from me, and you don't need to. I know you care about Dax, and he cares about you, and you both have been helping each other get through this. I'm just wondering where that leaves y'all for the future."

I take her question into careful consideration. "Is it bad that I can't see a future without him? I don't want to lose him." Not for any reason. A job or a girl. That admission seems wrong, and the realization puts a knot in my stomach. I try not to think of the possibility, but one day I'll have to come to terms with it. One day, he won't be all mine.

Echo opens her mouth to speak, but my phone ringing snaps it shut. I feel relieved, a distraction from the dreaded questions I don't have answers for. My dad's number flashes across the screen, and I debate whether I should answer it.

My conscience gets the better of me, and I let my finger slide across the answer key before it goes to voicemail. "Hey, Dad." I try to sound somewhat excited. We haven't talked much these last few months.

"Hey, Lyns." He sighs, and a prickling feeling of déjà vu hits me.

I instantly straighten, my body covered in goose bumps. "Dax," I whisper, knowing something is wrong. Of course. I should've known he'd never call me unless there was a dreaded reason.

"Yes. Something went wrong during training today."

His words twist my stomach, and my throat restricts, keeping my remnants from lunch at bay.

Don't freak out. Don't freak out.

I'm freaking out!

"He's fine," he adds hastily. "He was able to land the plane, but I have a feeling he's probably shaken up."

Relief washes over me, though I still feel like I might puke. I relax against my chair, letting out a shaky breath. *He's okay. Dax is okay.* Someone really needs to school my dad on his delivery. Dax being okay should've been the first thing to come out of his mouth.

But I can't fully believe he's okay until I see it with my own eyes. "I have to see him," I say firmly.

Echo stands beside me, visibly worried.

My dad sighs again. "I figured as much. I had your mom book you a flight. She'll be there in an hour to pick you up. I'd ride with, but I'm stuck here on base."

I gulp at the idea of getting on another freaking plane, but I have no choice. I have to see Dax. "Thanks, Dad. I love you."

"Love you too, Lynsie Pearl. You bring that boy of ours home." Warmth fills me at hearing my dad's words. He knows how special he is to me.

I get off the phone and explain what's going on to Echo. We're both relieved he's okay. This incident right here just reminds me how uncertain the future can be. It doesn't matter what I plan out. At any moment, it can be yanked right out from under me. Lincoln's death is proof of that. Living in the moment with no expectations of the future seems more and more appealing.

Chapter Thirty-One

DAX

Once I'm checked out and released to leave the scene, I quickly return to my room. As soon as I walk through the door, I jump in the shower. A nice, hot shower seems like it will clear my foggy mind.

But the only thing it does is make the reality of today clearer to me and how truly frightening it was.

Under the spray, I crouch down and let my tears mix with the water. My body shakes as the sobs ripple through me. I lose track of time, not knowing how long I've been in here. I think a lot about what Lincoln had to have been feeling right before his plane crashed. If he had time to really think about it. I can't imagine that fear. You can't look death fully in the face and not be scared. When I finally turn the water off, it's cold, and my head is pounding from the number of tears shed. I dry off, throw on some sweats and a T-shirt, and lie down. I've been staring at this ceiling for God knows how long now, willing my eyes to shut, but every time I go to doze off, the events from today jolt me awake.

A knock on the door startles me and I silently curse myself as I get up to answer it, hoping to God it better not be a drunk Peterson or a sober one.

I slowly creak the door open, not even looking up as I do.

"Dax!" Lynsie is standing with a rolling suitcase in tow, her eyes big and round with shock and worry. Her voice does something to me. With one swift tug, it releases the knot I thought I meticulously tied my emotions up in. I release the door, not even able to fully look up before she crashes into me. I cradle her against my body as I begin to sob uncontrollably. If I'd known she was coming, I may have better prepared myself, but as of right now, there's no way I can hold it all in anymore.

She pulls one arm away just enough to shut the door before I fall with her to the floor. The one person I've never wanted to see me break down is the one here holding me as I do. I want to feel weak. I want to feel embarrassed. But right now, the only thing I feel as she holds me tightly in her arms...is loved.

After what feels like forever, I'm finally able to gain my bearings. I look up at Lynsie through glazed eyes, not sure what I'll see in hers. She holds my gaze with a knowing look full of sincere understanding. She brushes her hands against my cheeks, wipes the last few of my tears away, then leans in and plants a gentle kiss on my forehead. That simple act almost has me breaking again. Lynsie just used what I like to think of as my signature trademark, and all I can think is, I hope she feels half of what I just did when I do it to her.

"You flew all the way here to check on me?" I ask in disbelief, knowing how terrified she must've been.

"Yeah." She nods. "I had to see you." For a moment, she appears slightly embarrassed, but it quickly fades.

I let out a heavy breath as the last of my sobs ripple from my chest. "I'm okay," I say with a shaky breath.

She looks at me like she doesn't believe me. "It's me, Dax." She wraps her hands around mine and pulls them close to her chest. "You don't have to be so strong for me."

I nod, looking away and letting out a few more breaths to steady myself before I speak again. I turn back to her, my heart warming as she keeps her eyes fixed on me. "So you conquered your fear of getting back on a plane just because you had to see me?"

Her smile lights up the room as she realizes how huge this is. "Yeah, I guess so. My worry for you overtook the fear. Flying home is going to be a different story." She worries her lip between her teeth.

"How 'bout I go with you?" I offer. Like hell I'm letting her get back on a plane alone. I wanted to be with her when she took her first flight, but since she did it on her own, I want to be there this time.

"You can do that?" She pushes herself up on her knees, now eye to eye with me.

"Yeah, training is over in a couple days. I'm sure I can go a little early. Under the circumstances and all." I wink.

"I'm so glad you're okay." She finally flings her arms around me, and I rub my hands up and down her back, holding her against me. Lynsie pulls away, resting her back against the bed beside me.

"Me too. You have no idea." I'm so glad she's here. With me. Right now.

"You wanna talk about it?" She inches closer to me, making my heart beat a little faster.

I close my eyes, letting the familiar smell of her shampoo drift through my senses, temporarily blocking today out. Her hand lightly grazes my face, causing a chill to rush through my body. It's a chill that any other time I'm able to hide, but in this weak state, all my vulnerabilities are transparent. I just can't. Right now, I want to forget how close our plane was to crashing. I can't relive it just yet.

I look down and shake my head, hoping she understands. "Not yet."

She grabs my hand and rubs her thumb along the top. "It's okay. Whenever you are ready, I'll be here."

"How 'bout we go grab some dinner?" I suggest. Dinner should help.

Lynsie's stomach growls.

I laugh. "I take that as a yes."

Ten minutes later, we're waiting to be seated at the mom-and-pop restaurant I've grown to love nearby. While we sit side by side, waiting for a table, I spot Carter and some chick making their way toward the exit.

"Well, hey, Adams," he says, walking up to shake my hand.

"Carter." I nod, as neutral as possible. It's not that I don't like Carter, but he doesn't rank high on my list of guys I'd choose to be friends with.

"I heard what happened today."

I dread where this conversation is going with him, of all people, but then he surprises me.

"Man, I just don't know what I would've done in that situation." He shakes his head and for the first time, I see a sincere side to him.

"Adams, party of two," the hostess says.

I stand and pat him on the shoulder. "Well, man, I'm sure you would've come up with something. Take care."

He goes to speak but stops when Lynsie stands. His goofy, crooked smile takes over and I instantly wish we'd gone somewhere else—or he had. That night at the bar and our talk is coming back to me.

He points at Lynsie. "Ahh, so this must be that special person you mentioned." He looks back and forth between her and me like he just unlocked some big secret. "Now I see why you were so gung-ho about not giving any female the time of day." He chuckles and I want to deck him.

The chick, who is obviously his date, rolls her eyes from behind him and yanks on his arm. I use that as my cue and move Lynsie in front of me, hollering back, "Have a nice life, Carter."

"What was that about?" Lynsie eyes me suspiciously as she grabs her water, taking a long drink from the straw.

"Let's just say Carter and I have different outlooks on life." I laugh to lessen the tension. All I wanted was to get out and have a relaxing time with Lynsie.

"I'd say so." She rolls her eyes. "He had total douchebag written all over him. I felt bad for his date."

"See." I motion to her. "You, on the other hand, totally get me. The way he sees women is irritating." I shake my head, exasperated.

She nervously fiddles with her straw wrapper. "What was he talking about?"

"Hmm?"

"He said you mentioned a special girl." She pauses, eyes on the table. "Was he talking about me?"

I wish to hell I could gauge her state of mind, but I'm having a hard time reading her.

I sigh as I search for the right way to explain it, finally settling on the truth. "The night we were at the bar, we were all joking around and harping on him for his ho-ish ways."

Lynsie laughs.

"Anyway," I continue, narrowing my eyes at her. "He got all defensive and flipped it on me, asking about my situation, and I told him I have someone special back home."

Lynsie's smile drops as she turns her attention to the piece of paper she's been rolling up.

"Hey." I reach my hands over to hers, but she doesn't look up. "Lynsie, look at me."

She slowly raises her head and there's a hint of sadness in her eyes. I can see her features working to cover it.

"I was telling him the truth," I admit softly, noticing her shoulders sag even further.

Well, that didn't help.

"That's good, Dax. I'm glad." She forces a weak smile.

She's not getting it. Lynsie still has no clue what she means to me.

"Lynsie, you're the special person."

"Really?" she whispers as if it's so hard to believe.

"Yes. You mean so much to me. I'm so thankful for our friendship." I hate belittling what we have to a friendship, but it very well could be all that becomes of us.

"Best friendship," she corrects me. "You know, I've been thinking about our situation lately." Her eyes are cast down, her voice barely above a whisper.

"Oh yeah?" I ask, encouraging her to continue.

"Yeah." She finally looks up, holding my gaze. "I have a lot of feelings when it comes to you. I don't want to keep you from truly finding your someone special. Sometimes I question if I'm being selfish, holding on so tightly to you." She gives me a weak smile.

I say the first thing that comes to mind without hesitation. "Don't loosen your grip."

THERE'S SOMETHING ABOUT Lynsie that calms me. With her by my side, I lie in my bed, today still playing out in my mind. I've tried to be strong. I haven't talked about it, and I've been pretending it was no big deal. It was anything but no big deal. I need to talk about it, get these thoughts out and the feelings before they suffocate me.

"I was really scared today," I say out of nowhere, lying underneath the covers with Lynsie by my side. "When I thought the plane was going down, you know?"

"I can't even imagine." She rolls onto her side, and I do the same so we're facing each other. "I was so frightened when my dad called. What exactly happened?"

I close my eyes, visualizing how it all unfolded. "Everything was fine. Peterson and I were flying. Today was the first time we've ever flown together." I smirk as I keep my eyes closed, hearing Zack and his joking ass before the first bird hit the plane. "Then everything wasn't fine. Suicide birds, I swear."

"Birds?" Disbelief coats her voice.

I shake my head at how crazy it must sound...how crazy it was. "The first one flew into the engine on my side, stalling it out. Then, like a damn torpedo, one crashed through the front glass. There was blood everywhere." I open my eyes.

Lynsie's watching me intently, horror in her eyes.

"Zack was out." I shake my head, remembering the image. "I thought he was dead. It's not like I could tell with all the blood, you know?"

She nods, rubbing her hand up and down my arm.

Again, the feeling calms me. "I called the control tower. I tried to keep my cool, but I was flipping the hell out. I was terrified I was going to crash—that there'd be no way to land safely. I mean, I had one engine out and a broken windshield letting air into the cockpit. I thought I was seriously screwed." I let out a huge breath, feeling all that fear all over again.

"How'd you manage to land safely?" she asks softly.

"I started thinking about you and how I couldn't die." My voice is shaky. "That if anything happened to me, on top of everything else, it'd destroy you. I couldn't let that happen. The plane wasn't out of control, so I was still able to glide it, but it was the where part. Everything around us was residential. Then out of nowhere, an opening appeared. I saw a field and knew it was that or nothing. I put everything into that emergency landing, pulling out all the tricks we had just learned again, but honestly, I really believe I had a guardian angel with me. The odds were truly against us. I shouldn't have been able to safely land that plane," I admit, still not believing it.

Lynsie now has tears streaming down her face. I didn't want to tell her that part, but I don't like keeping things from her. I shouldn't be here right now, and every fiber within me screams that Lincoln was there with me today.

"I'm so thankful for that guardian angel," she says, her voice thick with sadness. "Losing you would break me. I miss him so much, Dax," she cries, leaning into me.

I slide my arm beneath her neck, cradling her into me. "I miss him too, Lyns. So much." I let the tears fall freely. Today was a close call. One I wouldn't wish upon anyone. Today I got a glimpse into how Lincoln felt during his last moments. His last thoughts were of Lynsie...just as mine were.

She sniffles a few more times and pulls back. "Wait. So, what about Peterson? He's okay, right?"

I run my hand down her hair. "Yeah, he's fine. The bird just knocked him out." I chuckle at the hilarity of a bird hitting him. "All the blood was from the bird, too."

"Good." She sighs in relief.

"That hard head of his came in handy today." I snicker.

"Glad it was good for something." She giggles back, finally joining me. I love the sound of it. I soak it up every time I hear it.

Her stomach presses up against my side when I feel it. "Did she just kick me?" I turn my head her way.

"Yeah." Her eyes are full of delight as she smiles brightly. I get lost in those emerald eyes of hers, but my gaze momentarily shifts down to her lips, wondering what they'd feel like pressed against mine.

She moves her head and snuggles against my side, draping her arm across my chest. "Thank you for everything you do, Dax. It means the world."

"You are my world," I whisper against her forehead before lightly kissing it.

* * *

IT TOOK ME a long time to come up with what to buy Lynsie for Christmas. It's impossible to buy for someone who wants nothing but her deceased husband back. It proved to be difficult, but I refused to give up. Really, there isn't a thing I can buy that'll mean anything to her. Nothing I can think of anyway, and I want to give her something full of meaning.

We agreed to do our own little private gift exchange after dinner with her family. They had a big get-together at their house, which turned out to be a good distraction. Lincoln's family even showed up. All I have to say is this baby girl is already spoiled beyond belief and rightfully so. I knew today—just like any holiday the first year after losing someone—would be extremely tough, but I also knew that being around loved ones would lessen the blow.

When we get back home, I have two gifts for her sitting in my room. One is wrapped, one isn't, and I paid for neither of them. It sounds cheap on my part, but like I said, money couldn't buy what I'm going for. I'm nervous, praying my plan doesn't backfire. That's the last thing I want, but I'm taking the risk.

"You're the only one I bought a gift for this year," Lynsie admits as she sits the box down on the coffee table.

I make my way to the couch. "I feel special." I smile brightly at her.

She returns the smile. "You're very special, Dax. Maybe I'm not there yet, but I wouldn't be where I am today if it wasn't for you."

"I think we are each other's form of therapy," I say, plopping down beside her.

"I concur," she says, attempting to sound super sophisticated.

She sits up, grabs her box off the table, and turns to me. "Open mine first."

I loosen the ribbon tied across the top of the wooden box, letting it fall to the floor. Placing the box on my lap, I slide the lid off. I'm literally stunned at what I see.

My silence worries Lynsie. "Oh no," she says, disappointed. "You don't like it. I should've asked."

I shake my head. "No, Lyns. I love it. How did you even think to get me this?" I'm still shocked as I look down at my new set of chiseling tools. They don't look anything like the cheap random pieces I've acquired and lost over the years. This set is prime and most likely cost a pretty penny.

Her smile returns, and she bites her lip shyly. "Well, let's say I'm eager to see you bring that drawing of yours to life. Plus, I'm really interested to watch the process of turning a chunk of wood into something beautiful."

I take a breath and just stare at her for a moment.

Her excitement and faith in me make me want to start my project right this second, but it's winter, and I don't really want to freeze the entire time. No one knows about my crazy hobby. Lincoln knew I was artistic, but he never saw where I took it. It's something I've always kept to myself. My own little secret, and I liked it that way. Now that Lynsie has unlocked it, I like the idea of sharing it with her even better.

"I'll make you something someday," I say as I carefully place the beveled-edge chisel back in its place. "Now it's your turn." I reach behind the couch, grabbing the gift that's wrapped.

She reaches for it as I face her, but I pull it back, feeling a bit uneasy.

"What is it?" she asks, not about the gift but my sudden shift in mood.

"I'm just worried it isn't the right thing to be giving you."

She tilts her head. "Seriously, Dax? You, of all people, put so much thought into things. It'll be perfect." She gives me a reassuring smile and I reluctantly hand the decent-sized box over.

The shiny snowflake wrapping paper flies everywhere as she shreds through it like a child. Once she knows what it is, she stops and stares at it, realization hitting her as the first few tears seep out.

"See? I knew it." I run my hand through my hair in frustration.

"No, Dax," she whispers, "it's perfect." She pulls off the note that's been taped to the box of the remote-control airplane for the last six months. The note Lincoln wrote before he hid it in my closet.

It reads, *You better not find this, and if you did, I still love you. – Lincoln*

She looks up at me through her watery eyes and I see a bit of confusion.

"For Christmas, I knew there wasn't anything I could buy you that would make you happy or that you would actually like." I sigh as I bend over, resting my arms on my legs. "I wanted to give you something that was full of meaning. I knew I needed to give you this gift he had bought you, but I didn't know when or how soon. So this seemed like the perfect time. I figured the best gift I could possibly give you would be a gift from Lincoln."

"I love it," she says, reaching over to give me a hug. "Quit doubting yourself," she whispers in my ear.

"I have one more gift for you," I say hesitantly, hoping I'm not overdoing it with the emotional gifts tonight.

She pulls back, smiles, and wipes her tears away as I hand her the gift that I could only cover with a trash bag. I slowly pull the bag off, careful not to break any of its now fixed parts. She gasps, throwing her hand over her mouth.

"Is that what I think it is?" she asks in disbelief with a sparkle in her eyes; this time not caused by surfacing tears.

"It is." I gently place Lincoln's now fixed remote-control plane in her hands.

"You had it fixed." She inspects every inch, looking for evidence of the destruction it endured. "I can't even tell. It looks brand new." She smiles at me. "Thank you so much for fixing it. It means more than you'll ever know."

* * *

THE NEW YEAR has come and gone, and Lynsie is now seven months pregnant and gorgeous as ever. I only tell her that on days she's self-conscious of her perfectly round stomach...which is practically every day. After Christmas, she decides to go back to work—for at least a few days a week. She's been going stir-crazy being in the house all the time.

I fully support her going back. She needs to start living again and what better way than through her passion in life? After getting my chisel set for Christmas, I could no longer put off bringing my design to life. I'm obsessed with it, spending every free moment pouring myself into it. In return, I end up with very calloused and blistered hands, but a masterpiece more amazing than I even imagined.

With the baby's due date quickly approaching, I came up with an idea. Not only for Lynsie but the baby as well. It came to me when I was carving last Saturday evening. I'm stopping by Lynsie's parents' house today while she's at work. I can't let her find out what I'm doing. It's a secret. I knock quickly, alerting Lynsie's mother that I'm here before I let myself in. I used to wait at the door, but Lynsie's mom has lectured me enough about how I'm practically family and don't need to be let in.

"I'm in the kitchen," she yells. She's sitting on a barstool, going through some pictures spread out over the counter. "This is all I could find." She picks one up, holding it delicately in her hand as she smiles. Flipping it around, she says, "I think this is the last one of Lincoln. All three of y'all look so happy."

I take the picture from her hand and smile as I remember that night. "Lynsie hated my date. I'll have to cut her out of the picture." I laugh and hand it back.

It was from the night Lynsie's dad was promoted to colonel. Someone caught a picture of us without our knowledge. Those are the best kind. They're rare and real. And the moment we were all caught smiling at each other is now going to last forever.

She hands me a small box. "Here they are. Just bring back the ones you don't use."

I grab the box and nod. "Yes, ma'am. Thanks for getting them for me."

"No, honey." She smiles. "Thanks for all that you do. You're a godsend." She pats my arm and I hurry to leave and make it home before Lynsie.

* * *

IN THE ARMY, we have what we call a transition. It's when a pilot goes from one particular aircraft to another. It can be switching from one type of helicopter to another or switching from helicopter to airplane. Any change in the type of aircraft you are flying is called a transition.

The inscription hits me as I'm putting the final touches on the carving. I don't want it to be some typical 'In Memory' memorial. I want this to be something that gives every pilot chills when they see it. I want every person walking past it to stop, read it, take it in, and fully grasp the concept of what we go through and the dangers that surround it. No matter what, we're one, a united front of pilots who devote our lives to our passion. We know the dangers that lurk, but with our wings at our sides, we continue to fly.

So many things we go through in life could be considered a Final Transition. To most, that statement screams death. As I etch the title near the bottom of the aviator wing, I let the meaning play in my head. In this case, Final Transition is death, but it's so much more. This transition isn't one we seek as pilots, but it is one we wait for, prepare for. Trading in our mortal wings for immortal ones is the grandest promotion we will ever receive. Now all that's left is the inscription I need to have made for it.

Final Transition: Inspired By Tragedy, This Sculpture Was Created To Symbolize The Final Transition From The Wings Worn In Life As Mortals To Those That May Be Found In Death As Immortals.

CW3 Lincoln Fox
&
CW3 Travis Robinson

And All Other Aviation Crew Members That Have And Will Make The Ultimate Sacrifice While Doing Something They Love.

Chapter Thirty-Two

LYNSIE

There's something about returning to work that feels like a missing piece of me is no longer lost. It fills a void I didn't realize I even had. I thought I'd feel out of place or like I didn't belong, showing back up to claim my workstation again. Much to my surprise, it was set up as if I never left. My name was even still on the wall. I'm sure I have Echo to thank for that. She'd never let anyone replace me. She continues to prove she's got my back through and through.

I don't want to be stuck at work today on Dax's day off, but Echo needed me to fill in last minute and I can never tell her no. But I'd much rather be spending time with him and working on the nursery. Her nursery will be in Lincoln's and my old room. Painting, putting furniture together, organizing clothes, diapers, and every other odd and end I've already received as a gift has proven to be time-consuming, but I wouldn't trade it for the world.

I feel like a whale and probably resemble one, too. I look down at my stomach as I wait for my shift to end. Even though I'm all belly—as many keep informing me—I feel like my whole body is pregnant and expanding. I've thickened up a bit all over. If I get any bigger, Dax may have to roll me out of the house. Visions of Veruca Salt from *Willy Wonka* assault my mind.

With Echo not here, it's been rather boring today. Now that I'm about to be a mother, I sympathize with her even more, having to take care of a sick child. She doesn't have any family here to help. I'm not sure I'd survive without a good support system—even more so now that I'm about to have a baby.

On the way back home, I stop to grab me and Dax some lunch. He's been so busy with that daggum carving of his, he probably hasn't eaten. I can't wait to see the final product. Patience isn't my strong suit, but I know how important this is to him, so I respect his privacy surrounding it. I know the end result will be worth it. Pulling into the driveway, I'm met with an eager Dax, who promptly walks up to my car and opens my door.

"How was your day?" He grins, practically bouncing with excitement.

"Slow." I barely finish what I'm saying before he grabs the food from my hands. With his free hand, he pulls me out of my car. Not an easy task these days.

"I have something to show you." He grins like a little kid.

I eye him suspiciously, wondering what in the world has this man so eager. I've never seen him so excited. He doesn't let go of my hand, dragging me into the house. He sits the food on the table and steps behind me, covering my eyes with both hands. I smell the lingering scent of wood and it clicks. Excitement starts to bubble within me, but I keep it hidden.

"It's outside," he says. "Slowly start walking."

I do as he says, taking small, even steps.

"Let me open the door."

I stop and he removes one hand as he leans close to reach the handle. My head turns. His face is right next to mine as I take in the lingering scent of his cologne. It's become one of my favorite smells. Maybe it's just Dax. He could probably bathe in dirt, and I'd love the scent.

After he opens the door, he puts his hand back over my eyes. Both hands aren't necessary. The one hand is big enough, but I'm sure it's more for effect than necessity.

"Watch out for the step," he whispers close to my ear.

Instant chills sweep over my body. I play it off as the cool wind that's whipping around outside, but I know it's him.

He slowly pulls his hands away. "Tada."

My eyes pop open and I'm almost brought to my knees. "Oh my, Dax." I cover my mouth as I walk up to it in complete awe.

He stands back, gauging my reaction as I make my way around the beautiful memorial. It's a good four feet tall and two feet wide. The details in the aviator and angel wings are stunning. The way it blends together, starting as the aviator wing at the bottom, then swooping into an angel wing is simply flawless. I'm speechless.

Until I read the inscription.

The words bring me to tears. They're perfect and capture the very essence of what these pilots do every day. I turn back around to a worried Dax standing with one arm crossed over his chest, elbow of the other propped on it as he bites at his thumbnail.

"There are no words. It's..." I wipe the tears away as I trail off. "It's amazing."

"You really like it? You can tell me if you don't." He shoves his nervous hands in the pockets of his jeans.

I walk up to him and grasp his forearms. "I absolutely love it, Dax. It's so perfect. We're going to have to get some kind of case for it."

He lets out a sigh of relief. I have no idea why he'd be worried about me not liking it. His heart for those he loves is like no other. And his talents...unmatched.

"Yeah, I'll probably have to get one custom-made," he says absently, still studying his own handiwork.

"Well, bring it in so I can stare at it while we eat," I say jokingly, but I'm completely serious. It's so eye-catching that you can't help but be taken aback by it. There won't be a single person who'll be able to look at this without it tugging at their heartstrings.

"Yes, ma'am." Dax starts to walk past me, but I grab his arm, stopping him. He looks down at my hand and then up at me. I turn into him, holding him as tightly as my big belly allows.

"Thank you, Dax," I whisper in awe. "I know you didn't do this for me, but thanks for being you and for caring about people as much as you do. You have one of the biggest hearts I've ever known. I'm lucky to have you in my life."

"I'm the lucky one, Lyns." His hand combs through my hair a few times. I see something in his eyes that I can't quite place before he cups my face and kisses my forehead.

I love the feel of his lips when they touch my skin. Sometimes I find myself wondering what they'd feel like pressed against my lips. Maybe this thought should bring guilt, but it doesn't, and I don't want to question it. I smile against his hoodie.

THIS IS MY last week at work. I'm thirty-eight weeks along, and Dr. Marx recommended it since I'm on my feet all day. At my last weekly appointment, she said everything looked perfect. I was even dilated to a one. It doesn't mean much since you can stay at a one forever, but I'll take what I can get.

While she was checking me, she asked about baby names and if I've picked one out yet. I haven't. Coming up with the perfect name is starting to stress me out. I've thrown around a few: Avery, Emma, Jenna, Reagan...nothing sticks. So I've put off trying for now. Surely, it'll come to me as soon as she's in my arms. That's how it happened for Lincoln's mom.

"Thank God she didn't name you Jeff." I laugh out loud, crinkling my nose.

Maybe it's in the blood—that our babies want to be present for the naming process. All I can do is hope this precious little girl's appearance strikes some sort of epiphany because, as of now, I got nothing. I can't even name my own kid. I'm already failing as a mom.

The door chimes and I pull myself from my pity party for one. When I look up, I see Dax walking my way and smile. I quickly give him a once-over, taking in his jeans and fleece pullover. Why am I just now starting to fully notice how good he looks—in everything. I've always been aware of his looks. They just never affected me like they seem to now.

"You getting paid to just sit around?" he teases.

"No, the customers pay me." I gesture around the salon. "No customers, no getting paid."

"Well, in that case." He sits down in my chair and makes himself comfortable, grinning at me through the mirror.

I shake my head and grab the apron. "You don't even really need a haircut." I finger the length, gauging how much to trim.

"I have a hot date tonight," he brags, wiggling his brows. "I need it to be perfect."

I look up in the mirror, watching his smile grow, and I'm shocked into temporary silence as I try to figure out why Dax saying that affects me, and not in a good way. As my heart beats faster, my cheeks heat.

Am I jealous that he has a date? Or am I jealous of his date? Either way, whatever I'm feeling will be kept on lockdown until I'm able to figure it out.

"Anyone I know?" I ask nonchalantly, refusing to make eye contact. My eyes would undoubtedly give my emotions away.

"In fact, yes," he responds cheerfully.

I swallow hard as my stomach drops. He's going on a date with someone I know. Why do tears prickle at the back of my eyes? Why does this bother me? Did I think I'd always have him to myself? Yes, yes, I did. Of course I couldn't keep him forever and it's stupid of me not to think he'd want to start dating again.

It's been close to a year since he really has, and that's because of me.

I muster as much control as possible and finally look up in the mirror, taking a break from my trimming. "That's great, Dax. You should start dating again. I'm happy for you."

His smile falters.

Maybe he was expecting me to tell him it's a bad idea and try to convince him against it. If I tell him otherwise, he'll back out. I can't take the risk. Dax deserves to be happy, but why do I have this strange sensation that I only want him to be happy with me? I try to shake the crazy thought out of my head. It must be these crazy pregnancy hormones messing my mind all up.

Nothing more is said since there isn't much to be done to his hair. He hands me a twenty. "Keep the change." He winks.

I roll my eyes as I shove it in my pocket. "You should've saved it for your date. It's not like you needed a cut anyway." I try not to sound snooty, but the more I think about it, the more irritated I am. Mainly at myself for being jealous.

"Nah, now my date can treat me." He shrugs.

"You're hot and all, but I don't think your date is going to be splurging on you, buddy." I pat his chest as I walk past him to get my broom.

"So"—Dax flashes me his pouty eyes—"you wouldn't splurge on me?" He leans over the counter, propping his head in his hands as he watches me carefully sweep up his hair.

"Well, yeah." I shrug, crouching down with my dustpan. "But I'm different. I already like you."

In an instant, he crouches down in front of me, grabbing the dustpan and broom from my hands. "Good. Be ready by six." He swiftly sweeps the hair up and finishes my job, then dumps the hair in the trash.

I frown in his direction. What just happened? "I'm not going out with you and your date." No way in hell will I ever play third wheel.

Dax starts laughing. Annoyed, I prop my hand on my hip and stare at him.

"Lynsie, you are my date. I want to take you out tonight."

"Oh." I drop my arm, a strange sensation of relief flooding me. "Well, why didn't you just say that?"

"Because I wanted to see your reaction," he says, walking up to me.

"What reaction?" I ask, realizing it was all a test.

He palms the side of my face, gliding his thumb up and down my cheek. "I had to make sure," he says softly. Something familiar in his eyes is making me nervous.

"Of what?" I whisper, caught in those hazel eyes of his.

A warm smile lights up his face. "You do have feelings for me."

Blinking, I look away, a traitorous blush taking over my face. I should've known I couldn't hide anything from him, even jealousy.

"Look at me, Lynsie." His voice is gentle. I look back up and I'm trapped again. "I was wondering the other day. Today... I guess I was testing you a bit." When my brows pull together, he adds, "I wasn't sure if you'd figured it out yet, and I thought"—he pauses—"that maybe if you thought I wasn't yours anymore..." He looks away, quickly rubbing the back of his neck. Then his eyes pierce mine, and I can see everything as clear as day. "I thought you'd realize what you feel for me."

He places his other hand on my face, forcing my gaze to stay on him. "But now you know that I will always be yours...always have been." He whispers the last part as he bends down, placing his signature kiss on my forehead. His lips linger there longer than normal. I find myself wanting to lean in, wanting to melt into him, but I'm frozen. I want to lift my face to his, but I'm scared. I want a lot of things, but I can't reach for them quite yet.

He pulls away, walking backward to the door. "Don't forget. Be ready by six." He flashes me his sexy smile, then swivels on his heel and he's gone.

I'm glued to the floor, stunned by what just happened...and the fact that I just used the word 'sexy' to describe his smile. *What the hell is happening to me?*

"What was that about?" Echo comes up behind me.

"I've got a date," I say in a daze.

"Umm." I hear the grin in Echo's voice, though I'm still gawking at the door. "I'm pretty sure whatever just took place is way more than a date, honey."

That pulls me out of my Dax-induced trance. Still baffled, I turn around to face my entertained best friend. "I think he just told me he likes me." I quickly cover my mouth, hiding the smile tugging at my mouth.

She laughs. "'Like' is an understatement."

"What's that supposed to mean?" I ask, completely naive. I sit down in my chair as she makes her way to her workstation.

"Lynsie, that boy has it bad for you. He's had it bad for you for a while now."

I frown again. *He has?*

I EXPECTED TO be nervous going on a *date* with Dax, but I'm not. We grab a quick bite to eat from the sub shop before we head to the movies. When we arrive at the theater, his movie choice shocks me.

"You seriously think of everything, don't you?" I look up, expecting him to give me his cocky smile, but he doesn't.

"I try." He shrugs, attempting to play off his thoughtfulness. I know better. "I remembered you saying you really liked the book, so when I saw it was coming out, I knew I had to bring you."

"Well, thank you." I smile, grabbing his hand. "Let's hurry and get good seats. My pregnant self needs a good aisle seat."

"Isn't my date supposed to splurge on me?" He looks down at me with pouting lips.

I chuckle. "Fine, cheapskate. What do you want?"

We walk into the theater with our arms full of goodies. I can't remember the last time I saw a movie here. All I know is the last time I was here, these awesome recliners were not. This is a pregnant woman's dream. I have snacks and comfort galore.

Dax and I hold hands throughout the movie. It's something we do regularly anyway, but tonight it feels different. He has to feel my rapid pulse as we sit silently with our hands tightly clasped because I can feel his.

WHEN WE GET home, I can sense Dax's hesitancy about the sleeping arrangement. We've been sleeping in the same king-sized bed this whole time. I don't want to stop just because he voiced his feelings and exposed mine.

He has an uneasy look on his face when I ask him if he's ready for bed. "Yeah, sure. I'll be up in a bit." He's acting a little off, but I go ahead and take myself upstairs to change and brush my teeth. He's already in bed with the light off when I climb in.

"Dax?" I ask in the dark.

"Mmmhmm," he says, his back facing me.

"Nothing has changed between us, okay?"

"Okay," he murmurs.

"Will you please face me?"

He turns over and I can barely make out his features in the darkness. I grab his hands, holding them between us.

"When I thought you were going on a date today, it made me jealous." My eyes start to adjust to the darkness just in time to see the slight curve of his lips. I leave it at that, already feeling exposed enough.

"Good," Dax replies against my skin before kissing my forehead and holding me as close to him as the barrier between us allows. I can't wait to meet this human barrier of mine growing inside me. I smile at the thought as I begin rubbing my belly. "I love you, Lyns," Dax whispers against my ear as his hand runs through my hair, and my smile doubles.

"I love you, Dax." I've said those words many times throughout the six years we've known each other, but something feels different saying them aloud now.

Chapter Thirty-Three

DAX

Lynsie's in labor and I'm freaking out. She assured me this morning the pains were nothing. Oh, how wrong she was. I would've never got on this damn plane if I thought she would go into labor. Now I risk the chance of missing the delivery, and that thought kills me.

But thank God I'm flying with her dad because he's just as freaked out as I am. We safely turned our plane around once we both simultaneously got the call. I know Lynsie, and I know she's panicking that I won't make it back in time. Truth is, I have to make it back in time. I have to be there. I promised her. We've practiced for this day.

We fly in silence, and I pray for the baby to wait, but the closer we get, the antsier I become.

"Can't we just fly to the hospital?" I half tease. Surely there's some sort of runway nearby.

Dan shakes his head. "Boy, do I wish we could, but we're almost there."

Almost isn't close enough. I'm breathing a sigh of relief that I at least put the baby gift in my car the other day. The car seat is also in my car since I'll obviously be the one driving them both home.

Us home. Wow, the idea of driving Lynsie and the baby home has me anxious with excitement and nerves. Thirty minutes later, we land and quickly run through our post-flight log sheet. Unfortunately, we can't just hand it over to someone else.

"You riding with me?" Dan asks as he tosses the clipboard on his desk.

"No, I have to drive my car. It has the car seat and stuff." We rush to the parking lot, keys in hand.

"See you in a bit." He smiles before we split off in different directions to our cars.

When I arrive and park, I practically run through the sliding doors of the hospital, remembering where the Labor and Delivery area is. We took a tour a few months ago. The Lamaze and breast-feeding classes we had were in a wing nearby. Echo is in the waiting room, thumbing through magazines. Her son sits next to her, playing a handheld game. He glances up, and a sense of familiarity strikes me again. I shake it off and run an anxious hand through my hair when I realize Lincoln's parents aren't here yet. They weren't planning on heading down until this weekend, but Lynsie went into labor three days early.

"What room?" I ask as I jog past them.

"Three-thirteen," Echo hollers back.

Coming up to the closed door, I slow down. I don't hear any screaming, so I must not be too late. I give it a couple knocks, pushing it open before I get a response. Lynsie's lying on her side with her hand gripping the bed railing and her eyes pinched closed. Her mom is standing behind her, rubbing her back. I quickly make my way to Lynsie's side and grab her hand tightly in mine.

She looks up and smiles through the pain. "You made it."

"I promised you I would." I let my knuckle graze her damp

cheek. These contractions must be kicking her ass. "Have they given you anything for the pain?"

Her mom shakes her head. "Lynsie said she wants to do this naturally. Plus, she's already dilated to a seven, so by the time they get anesthesia down here, it'd be pointless."

Lynsie shudders. "I don't want them digging that crazy needle into my back—" She cuts off as another contraction hits.

"You're about to have a baby coming out of your..." My voice trails off as she glances up at me, giving me the meanest look she can muster—which, in this moment, is pretty damn mean. And cute. "Well, you know where," I finish weakly.

"Please don't remind me." She groans in pain as she holds her breath.

I drop her hand and work my way around the bed, stepping in front of her mom. "You have to breathe, Lynsie. Remember what we learned in class."

I massage her back the best I can with her lying on her side. Whatever I can do to alleviate the pain or maybe distract her.

"Thank you," she says as her heavy breathing lessens. Before I can say something clever in response, she tightens as another contraction hits.

Her mother steps toward the door. "I'm going to get the nurse. She needs to be checked again."

Moments later, the nurse comes in, followed by Lynsie's parents. Dan has more of a look of fear instead of joy when he sees Lynsie.

"Okay, Lynsie, the baby is ready," the nurse says, walking over to Lynsie's other side. "I'm going to need you to turn onto your back. Remember to breathe and when you feel your contraction starting, push with everything you have."

Lynsie only acknowledges her with a nod.

The doctor walks into the room and sits in front of Lynsie.

"I'm going to wait right outside the door," her father says as he walks backward like he might pass out if he doesn't get out quickly enough.

I help Lynsie as best as I can through each contraction. I'm hunched over her with my head next to hers, telling her how great she is as she grips my hand tightly.

She lets out a cry as she pushes her head deeper into the pillow. "I can't do it!" she grits through clenched teeth.

"You're doing amazing, Lynsie," Doctor Marx praises her from where she's sitting between her legs.

"You got this," I tell her again soothingly. "You can do it. You are so close to holding your baby girl." I run my free hand—the one not in Lynsie's death grip—across her dampened forehead, pushing back the strands that have escaped the messy bun on top of her head.

"Okay, Lynsie," the doctor says in a commanding tone, "one more big push. On three, give me the biggest push of your life. One, two, three."

Lynsie leans forward, screeching with that last push, and tiny little cries fill the room. Lynsie's body relaxes as she lets out a sigh of relief, falling back onto the bed. The emotion is overwhelming. I feel the prickle of tears in my eyes as I look down in awe at Lynsie. She has the face of an angel, glowing with happiness and tears, just as I am.

I bend down, pressing my forehead to hers as she looks at me. Then, without thinking, as if it's the most natural thing ever, I press a light kiss on her lips. "You did it," I whisper.

She doesn't pull away from the closeness or even act affected by what just happened. She just smiles, and I feel like I'm soaring.

"We did it, Dax," she corrects me. "I couldn't have done any of this without you." She pulls at my dog tags, bringing my lips back to hers for one more kiss.

I slowly pull away, swallowing as tears stream down my face. Tears full of hope instead of loss.

We stare at one another before our attention is drawn to the nurse standing near us with a wrapped bundle in her arms.

"Lookie who I have, Mommy." She coos down at the bundled baby. "Congratulations, guys," the nurse says, slipping the baby into Lynsie's eager arms, and we're entranced by the gorgeous, bundled beauty.

Lynsie's crying. I'm crying. Lynsie's mom is crying as she comes back into the room with her husband. It's a very emotional experience, but a happy one.

"She's perfect," Lynsie says as she gently touches the baby's plump cheek.

I want to touch her, but she seems so fragile. My hand is bigger than her head. I've never held a baby. What if I break her? I mean, I'm sure I can't break her just by holding her, but still. I'm so big and she's so tiny and beautiful, and I can't help but trace her tiny, bunched up fist with the tip of my finger. She lets out the most adorable sigh as she snuggles her head into Lynsie. She's perfectly content. And in this moment, so am I.

Echo comes in and I take a seat, allowing her to be introduced to Lynsie's daughter. She gushes over how beautiful she is, and I silently agree.

Lynsie's mother announces, "We're going to grab some dinner and swing by the house so Dan can change. Then we'll be back. Dax?"

Everyone looks at me. I don't plan on leaving anytime soon. Even though I'm still in my flight suit. I'll keep it on until I take Lynsie and the baby home if I need to.

Lynsie's mom asks, "Do we need to stop by y'all's house for some clothes?"

I relax a bit in the chair. They know I'm not leaving Lynsie's side.

"Ahh. Yeah." I sit up, pushing my legs out so I can grab my keys out of my pocket. "Let me get you the key."

"No," Lynsie says, shocking me. All eyes turn to her. She looks at me and smiles, then shrugs, dropping her gaze back to her baby. "I already have some clothes here for you."

A LADY FROM medical records stops by, needing Lynsie to fill out the birth certificate form. She places it on the side table and leaves, letting us know someone will be back for it. It's just Lynsie and me. Her parents are still gone, and the baby is having her newborn tests done.

I watch her glance at the form, then down at her fidgeting fingers.

"What is it?" I ask softly, stepping over to the bed to take her hand.

Sobs ring out as she opens her mouth to answer. "I just—" She drops her head, continuing to cry. I unlock the bed bar, letting it fall to the side, and sit on the edge, then I wrap my arm around her and pull her to me, rubbing her back as she cries into my chest. Her warm tears soak through my shirt.

"Whatever it is, it'll be okay," I whisper.

"No, it won't." She shakes her head against my chest. "My daughter doesn't have a dad. What am I supposed to write on that stupid piece of paper? Do I leave it blank, a constant reminder of what she doesn't have? Or do I fill it in, a constant reminder of what she should have? Either way doesn't really matter. It doesn't change anything. She'll never know her real dad."

"You're wrong, Lynsie." I shake my head, determination in my voice. "She will know him."

She looks up at me, her tear-streaked face frowning with confusion. I climb out of the bed and walk to the backpack I carried in. I unzip it and pull out the gift I made. It's mainly for Lincoln's daughter, but I know Lynsie will love it just as much.

I hand her the photo book. Trying to pick out the perfect one was difficult. I stared at baby-themed ones for a while. I was about to go with a girlie polka-dotted one when the perfect book caught my eye. That's when it hit me—this is a memory book—one I was going to fill with nothing but memories of Lincoln. It needed to capture him. I picked up the photo album that's covered in all sorts of airplanes. Putting it together did a number on me. I worked through so many emotions and feelings I had been holding back. It was quite therapeutic.

I watch Lynsie giggle and cry her way through every picture, something I've already done, so this time I just enjoy watching her. She works her way from the end to the beginning, which is filled with pictures of Lincoln when he was younger—which naturally included me.

"I love seeing how close you boys were. What you had was so special. It's not easy to find that best friend who you can stand the test of time with," she says without looking up as she continues to flip the pages.

There's a light tap at the door. "Come in," Lynsie says.

"Someone's hungry, Momma," the nurse says as she pushes baby girl in. "I have everything you need to feed her on the bottom rack. If you change your mind or feel she isn't getting what she needs."

Lynsie smiles. "Thank you."

The nurse leaves and I walk around the bed, gazing down at the sweet baby girl with big blue eyes. I can only hope she'll share her daddy's eyes one day. I'd give anything to see those perfect brown eyes every day of my life again.

"You can hold her." Lynsie nods at me while flipping the page.

"Ahh, I'm not sure," I say hesitantly.

She's about to flip the book shut but stops. "There's nothing more beautiful than a blue sky." She's reading Lincoln's quote I wrote in the front. Her bottom lip quivers as she traces her finger over the words. Lynsie looks my way with tear-filled eyes as I very carefully bend over to pick up baby girl. "You're a genius, Dax," she says, holding her arms out for me to place the precious bundle in.

She glances at me and smiles before looking down at her precious baby, who has her tiny palm wrapped around her finger. My heart warms as I stare at both of my girls, who have my heart in the palm of their hands. In this moment, I gladly accept that they own me.

"I think your daddy was onto something, baby girl," she proudly coos, kissing her tiny little fingers. "There truly is nothing more beautiful."

A look of total peace comes over Lynsie's face as she says, "Welcome to the world, Blu Skye Fox."

Chapter Thirty-Four

LYNSIE

I chuck the breast pump across my bed in pure frustration. I groan loudly, throwing myself back against the pillows.

"Easy there."

I cut my eyes to the doorway and watch Dax tread with caution. He bends over, picking up the pump I tossed.

"What'd this thing ever do to you?" He drops it onto the bed.

"Where do you want me to start?" I ask, raising a brow.

He sits on the edge of the bed, crossing one leg over the other. "How about from the beginning. And tell me how you really feel?" he teases.

I roll my eyes and let out a giggle. "Seriously, though. I'm so over pumping. Blu doesn't get what she needs on her own when I breast-feed and I can't get crap out with the stupid pump. I'm so over it. I fail! I can't even feed my baby," I whine.

Dax laughs. "You don't fail, Lyns. Every baby is different, and every experience is different. It won't make you a bad mother to switch over to formula. I'd actually be able to help out with her more if you do."

"I know." I pout, still not convinced. "But all the books are like 'breastfeeding is best' and everyone I talk to agrees." I point to my chest. "Except my boobs. They disagree."

Dax throws his head back, bursting with laughter. "Did they put their foot down? The three of you had a discussion?"

I laugh. "We should. Maybe they need to be coerced." I look down at my sore chest. "Boobs, why don't you feed my baby?" They don't reply.

Blu starts to cry through the baby monitor. We've only been home for a few days. During the day, I try to make sure she naps in her room so I can use the loud pump in my room without disturbing her.

"Great!" I smack the bed. "My boobs are broken, and my baby is hungry." I start to scoot off the bed, but Dax stops me with his hand on mine.

"How about you and your broken boobs take a nice, long shower and maybe a nap. Let me change out of my uniform real quick and I'll take care of her. You take a little break."

"Fine," I grumble, knowing I can't argue with him. Even if I could, a hot shower sounds good right now. I look down. My boobs agree. "The little premade formula bottles the hospital sent home are on the counter."

Dax smiles and shakes his head. "I know, I know."

He bends over and unlaces his black boots. He slides each off, then sits them at the foot of the bed before standing and unzipping his flight suit. His back is toward me as he slides it off, and my jaw drops as his back muscles flex.

I've seen Dax in nothing but his boxers many times, but there's something intimate about watching him undress.

Holy hell, these hormones are gonna be the death of me.

"Ahem." He peeks over his shoulder. "See something you like?" He winks, giving me a smirk.

I gulp and clear my throat. "Nope, not at all." I throw my legs over the bed and rush to the bathroom, shutting the door behind me.

What is wrong with me?

"You're horny," my boobs reply.

"Oh thanks, now you talk back."

I turn the shower as hot as I can stand before inching my sore body under the spray. I rest my head back and enjoy the warmth spraying down my body. Thoughts start flooding my mind about this past year and how far I've truly come. I would've never thought it possible. Then I start piecing together the people who've been essential to my progress. Everything that's taken place comes full circle back to Dax.

I stand in the shower until the water cools and my hands and feet are wrinkly, analyzing my feelings for Dax. Do I care about him? Of course I do. Do I love him? Yes. I've loved him for as long as I've known him. Has that love turned into something more?

I tightly wrap the towel around me, tucking the piece of cloth into itself, and then blow-dry my hair. Throwing on some clothes, I yawn and really debate crawling back into the big, comfy bed. But the smell of food and the cooing coming from downstairs make me think better of it.

Walking down the stairs, I see the back of Dax as he bends over and baby talks to Blu.

"Our plan worked. Now I can help your momma more. High five."

As I walk up behind him, I see him gently pushing his giant hand to her tiny fist, and my heart melts. The answer clicks into place—*I'm in love with him.*

I sit down next to them, and he looks over, giving me a slightly embarrassed smile. "How much of that did you hear?"

"Oh, you know. Just the part where you and Blu sabotaged my boobs." I laugh.

"Yeah, about that. We had a little pow-wow just now and agreed it's for the best. Seeing that we both need our time, while you have your alone time."

I tilt my head and look at the two of them. "Well, I've come to the conclusion after a nice, long shower that I agree with both of you."

"It's all about teamwork." He winks before returning his attention back to Blu.

"Dax," I start carefully, my emotions welling up inside of me.

"Hmm?" He continues to play with Blu's feet.

"I don't expect you to stick around."

His body tenses, but he doesn't look up.

I continue in a rush, "I mean, not because I don't want you here. I feel like you're putting your life on hold to help me. Don't get me wrong, you'll never know how much everything you've done and continue to do means to me, but I just don't want to hold you back." I pray that's not how he feels about this, but I can't just assume otherwise. Especially now, realizing I have feelings for him.

He sits still for a few long seconds as if he's collecting his thoughts. Blu starts to drift off in his arms. I'm all too familiar with the comfort they offer.

Dax looks at me and I hold my breath in anticipation. "You don't hold me back, Lynsie," he says quietly. "You move me forward."

I nod, letting out the breath I was holding. Dax has a way with words. Always knowing exactly what I need to hear.

The smell has my stomach growling. "What're you cooking?" I ask as I peek into the oven.

"So far, baked chicken. I haven't started the sides yet."

He stands up with Blu, walks her over to her bassinet, and lays her down, then comes into the kitchen with her empty bottle.

The love he holds for my little girl tugs at my heart.

"I'll take care of the sides." I smile.

"You don't have to do that, Lyns. You're supposed to be taking a break, remember?"

"Teamwork, remember? Does that ring a bell?" I tease as I dig out a side item to cook. I close the cupboard and turn around. He's leaning back against the counter with his arms crossed, watching me.

"Plus, I want to be down here with you." I shrug like it's no big deal. I might've just come to terms with the fact that I have deep feelings for him—feelings I never expected to have for anyone again, but that doesn't mean I have to disclose that yet.

IT'S BEEN TWO months since Blu was born. Keeping these thoughts and feelings from Dax has been torture. When we snuggle in bed at night, or he's holding my daughter like she belongs in his arms, my heart screams for me to tell him.

But I can't. Not yet.

Instead, I've been writing my feelings and emotions in the journal he bought me so long ago. Sometimes I sit and flip through it, perusing the things I've written these past months. Doing so makes me realize just how far I really have come.

I slam my journal shut. I've been writing the same thing in here for the last couple months. It's like a broken record. Writing it over and over obviously isn't helping me. Everything just builds until I almost can't stand being near him without spontaneously combusting.

Sighing, I grab my phone and start scrolling through my contacts. I see Echo's name first and ponder calling her. She always has great advice, but I have a feeling she'd be a little biased on this matter. I can hear it now. "You're already sleeping with him, Lynsie. Now *sleep* with him."

I'm debating on tossing my phone to the side when Rebecca's

name pops up. She's someone who would know the reservations I'm struggling with firsthand.

I push call and eagerly wait for her to answer.

"Hello?"

"Hey, Becca." I smile.

"Hey, Lynsie." I can hear the smile in her voice. "How are you doing? How's that gorgeous baby of yours?"

"I'm good. Blu is perfect."

"Glad to hear it."

"How are your kids doing?"

She's mentioned the older one has been asking more questions about his dad.

"They are great. Randy just turned five. And Maddy is just jabbering like crazy these days. It's amazing how fast they grow." She sighs.

"I agree." I glance over at Blu, who's peacefully sleeping, and I sympathize. A lot has changed in two months. "I need to talk to you about something. Do you have a minute...or thirty?" I nervously laugh.

"Of course. What's up?"

"It's Dax." I pause. "I think he has feelings for me."

"He most definitely does," she replies without hesitation.

"What makes you say that?" I sit back on the couch.

"A guy like him wouldn't do everything he does if he didn't love you. If you ask me, he's loved you for a while." She seems to choose her next words carefully. "Possibly even when Lincoln was still around."

"Really?" I find that hard to believe. I would've known if Dax was in love with me, even back then.

Suddenly, I'm questioning everything.

"What he feels for you is genuine, Lynsie. I have a feeling, and that's just me being an outsider."

I take everything in and think back on all the dates I attempted to set him up with and how he always found something wrong with each one. I remember him playing it off, like he was still hung up on his ex, but could he have been hung up on me?

"So what do I do?" I rub my sweaty palm against my sweatpants.

"That depends on what you want to do," she says so logically. "Do you have feelings for him?"

I tightly close my eyes, willing my mouth to cooperate with what the rest of my body is screaming. "Yes. I do. I'm in love with him, and it's terrifying."

"What scares you about it? You feel guilty about moving on? Or you're scared to lose someone you love again?" she asks like she knows because she does.

"Both," I whisper. "It's too soon. And I'm scared of losing Dax. I'm scared one day the Army will take him. I'm scared if I don't tell him how I feel soon, another girl will take him. I'm scared that if I do give in, and something goes wrong, I'll lose my best friend." My cheeks dampen as the first few tears fall freely down my face.

"No more living in fear, Lynsie," she tells me quietly but firmly. "You've already experienced the most traumatic event anyone should have to endure. And look at you. You've come through it."

"Because of Dax."

"Because he loves you," she corrects me. "Who better to spend the rest of your life with than the man who will never try to wash away Lincoln's memory? Dax doesn't want to forget his best friend, just as much as you never want to forget the husband you lost. Both of you together, raising Blu Skye, will keep Lincoln's memory alive."

TALKING TO REBECCA was not only an eye opener but a soul opener. I needed to hear this is okay. That it's okay to love again. Now I just need to figure out when to tell him.

"Lynsie," Dax hollers from downstairs after shutting the front door.

"In the bathroom," I yell back as I squirt some soap on the washcloth.

I listen as he jogs up the stairs and down the hall, wondering what's got him in such a hurry.

"I got some news today." He stands in the doorway, smiling and out of breath.

"What kind of news?" I ask hesitantly.

"Ever heard of the Broken Wing Award?" He makes his way toward me, getting down on his knees next to me. Leaning over the rim of the tub, he tugs on Blu's wet toe. "Hey, baby girl."

She looks toward his voice and smiles. I could get lost in her tiny smile. Watching him reminds me of what Rebecca said. I'm staring at him when he finally looks back up.

"Ahh," I say awkwardly. I was caught.

The smile on his face proves it, even though he doesn't call me out.

"Yes, I've heard of it before," I finally tell him.

"Well, I'm getting one." As if his smile couldn't get any brighter, it somehow does.

"Dax! That's incredible." I throw my arms around him.

He holds me tightly to him and I almost melt into his arms. Blu starts getting fussy before I'm able to, and I silently thank her for it.

Pulling away, I gulp as my hands stop on his biceps. I've never noticed how defined they are until this very moment. They flex under my touch as he places his hands on both sides of my face and bends down to kiss my forehead. The idea to lift my head so our lips meet crosses my mind, as always.

My lips tingle as I'm reminded of the two kisses we shared when Blu was born. If I'd had time to analyze it before it took place, it never would have. Thank goodness for spontaneity. I have a feeling that's the only way the next one is going to happen since I seem to overthink everything.

"I'm pretty excited, too." He grins. "The ceremony is going to be this weekend. I want you to be my date."

I let my hands fall to my sides and he grabs them, holding them loosely in his.

"Are you asking me or telling me?" I ask, seeking clarification.

He shakes his head and laughs. "Lynsie Pearl," he says, all humor gone and something lingering in his eyes that I'm too scared to name. "Will you be my date Saturday night?"

I bite my bottom lip to keep my grin from taking over my whole face. "Dax Lance Adams, it's a date."

He wastes no time. "Did you hear that, Blu? Your mommy said it's a date. You're my witness, little girl." Then he struts out.

As I'm wrapping Blu up in her towel, I think back to when Dax took me on a date. He told me he liked me that night. He saw that I was jealous and smoothed it out by opening himself up to me...and he hasn't done it since. Maybe it's my turn to do the same.

Chapter Thirty-Five

DAX

I don't fully understand why I'm being awarded. It isn't because I'm wickedly talented or did something no one else in my situation would've done. Everything happened so fast. The only thing I had time to do was keep us from crashing. The same thing any pilot would've tried doing.

This isn't an award they hand out to everyone like a participation trophy. Since I "survived the odds" and managed to land a damaged plane, I'm considered this year's *"most outstanding example of a military pilot"*. It's with great honor that I'll be accepting the Broken Wing Award tonight. In my opinion, it should go to Lincoln. He paid the ultimate sacrifice. He died a hero.

I wait impatiently in the foyer while Lynsie finishes getting ready. I dropped Blu off with her mom, but her dad will be attending the ceremony. My heart begins thumping harder as Lynsie makes her way down the stairs. I rest against the back of the couch and watch in awe. She looks stunning. Her black dress has a transparent design that starts right above her chest, stopping at the base of her neck. It's a delicate, lacey material, with intricate beaded flowers perfectly placed along her shoulder and collarbone. The rest of the dress is solid and has the same beaded designs flowing down the fitted length that hugs her amazing curves. Her hair is up and to the side in some sort of bun, and her makeup makes her eyes shine brighter than I've ever seen. I've never had the urge to kiss her so bad, but I can't... not yet.

Because once I start, I might not be able to stop.

"Well?" she says uneasily as I gawk at her.

I can't help the audible gulp as I search for the right words. She's breathtaking.

I swallow hard. "You look amazing, Lyns." I grab her hand and lift it to my lips, placing a kiss on the smooth skin. "Thank you for going with me. You don't know how much it means to me."

"That's why I'm doing it." She reaches up and places a quick peck on my cheek. I see the sly smile she tries to cover with her hand as she pulls away. The cute gesture quickly passes when she notices my messed-up tie. "You boys and ties. I swear."

I chuckle. "I believe it's a trick we've all learned to master."

"And what kind of trick is that?" She steps back, inspecting the tie's symmetry.

"To have an excuse for a pretty girl like you to get close."

She blushes, and I see a faint smile. "You don't need excuses for any girl to get close." She pats me on the breast of my jacket as she passes by, heading for the door.

"But I don't want just any girl." I grab her hand, stopping her in her tracks.

She nods, then looks back over her shoulder at me. "Come on, handsome. We can't be late." She tugs my hand, pulling me out the front door.

She called me *handsome.*

"OH, GOD," LYNSIE mutters under her breath, causing me to follow her gaze. She tightens her grip around my arm, and I look down at her, hiding my amusement in her protectiveness. This simple motion tugs at my heart. I know she cares about me, but this...it's starting to feel like more.

"Oh my goodness, Dax. Look at you."

I cringe when Haley grabs my hands, holding them between us, forcing Lynsie's arm to break away from mine. Lynsie huffs. From the corner of my eye, I see her cross her arms over her chest and shoot Haley a death glare. I pull my hands away from Haley, but it only encourages her to step closer.

I knit my brows together. "What's your name again?"

Lynsie giggles. If messing with Haley makes her feel better, game on.

"Like you could ever forget my name," Haley says seductively, running her finger down my chest.

Before I can even shake her off, Lynsie steps in closer and grabs her by the wrist. "Are you blind, honey?" she snaps.

Haley sputters, pulling her wrist out of Lynsie's grasp. "What's that supposed to mean?"

"It means," Lynsie replies sharply, "that you need to check out this man next to me. He has females lining up for days to get with him, and you really think, out of all of them, he'd remember anything about you? Girl, please."

Lynsie lies through her teeth, but this reaction from Haley is priceless. I'm stunned and speechless as Haley looks back and forth between me and Lynsie, her mouth hanging open. I push my shoulders back, standing a little straighter. *That's my girl.* I covertly glance down at her.

Lynsie links her arm in the crook of mine again and looks up at me with her beautiful smile beaming. "You ready, baby?"

Shoot. Am I ever. Her term of endearment makes me feel like putty in her hands. "You better believe it." I grin at her, wondering what else is in my eyes that I can't hold back. For the moment, I don't care. I look back at Haley, who's still standing in front of us, and shrug my shoulders before we step around her.

I pull Lynsie off to the side. "That was the best thing I've ever seen."

"That was the best thing I've ever done," she says, laughing. "I hope I didn't overstep, but that girl has had it coming for a while."

Cocking my head to the side, I reply, "Even though you made me sound like a complete man whore at the expense of sticking it to her, it was worth it."

"I hope you don't think that's how I feel about you." Her tone turns serious.

"Nah, I know you think better of me than that." I graze her cheek with my knuckles. It's getting harder every day not to kiss her. The touch makes her shiver. "You could've just told her I was taken."

"Yeah." She shrugs. "I could, but it was more fun the other way." I give her a questioning look, and she explains, "Girls like her, they like competition. I mean, if you want her all up on you" —she scrunches her nose at the idea—"we can go back and tell her."

"Please don't." I shudder at the thought. "There's only one girl I want."

Suddenly, the noise seems to dim. It's quiet around, and it's just us. It feels as if time has stopped and we're the only ones aware of this moment. Her eyes search mine, and I see a lot of questions there... questions I ask myself daily. Ones that hold no right or wrong but can only be answered in time—by feelings.

I want to pull her into me and kiss her so hard she won't be able to breathe. I want to show her what I feel, make her reciprocate. I want to tell her it'll be okay, that we can be happy and it's not wrong, but I can't do any of that here. This is not the place. There's so much riding on it that I'm starting to question if the risk is worth the possible outcome.

"Ahem," I hear from behind, and the moment between us is broken.

I turn around, seeing my brother making his way to me.

No way. I can't believe it. I see my parents as they stand back, watching Dustin and me from a distance. I knew they were coming, along with Lincoln's parents, but I haven't seen my brother in years. Emotions flood my senses and I make the conscious decision to shove them down. I quickly close the distance and pull him in for a hug. When I tighten my hold, his body slackens, and I feel his reserves dissipating as he embraces me back. I don't care about the distance and time between us. He will always be my brother.

"Man, you've grown up," Dustin admits, staring up at me as if he's trying to burn my features into his memory...as if this might be the last time we see one another.

"Take a picture. It lasts longer." I snicker and Dustin laughs, pulling me back to our childhood.

We pull apart, and I eye him up and down. The Army hasn't been too shabby on him. He stands about two inches shorter than me, broad shoulders filling out the uniform he's wearing. His hair is shorter than he used to keep it, and the stubble on his face is something unfamiliar to me.

"We got leave for a month. I wasn't going to come home," he admits with no sign of regret, "but when Mom got ahold of me and told me about this award..." He looks away for a moment, trying to hide the emotion that quickly flashes in his eyes. "I couldn't miss it." Maybe his heart hasn't fully turned to stone yet.

I smile. "I love you, too."

"I'm really sorry about Lincoln. I know how close you both were."

I nod, accepting his condolence.

"I have someone I need to introduce you to." I pull Lynsie to me, and she melts into my side like she belongs there. "This is Lynsie Fox."

"It's nice to meet you, Dustin." She sticks her hand out to shake his.

He quickly glances at me for answers I can't explain in front of her. His big hand closes around hers as he gives her a genuine smile. "It's nice to meet you too, Lynsie."

With Lynsie by my side, I catch up with my brother for a moment. People start to make their way into the room where the ceremony is being held, and we slowly meander in that direction.

"Lynsie," I hear coming our way.

I smile when I see Echo in a full-length, red dress that has one thick strap going across her right shoulder, leaving the other bare. It's very elegant and the blond and black of her hair, which I'm seeing down for the first time, contrasts against the dress well. Lynsie told me she invited Echo and her husband since he was home on leave.

"You look gorgeous, girl." Echo smiles down at Lynsie, hugging her.

Dustin stops in his tracks, seeming to have tensed up. I look back, eyeing him momentarily as he stares at the girls. He runs his hand through his hair, resting it at the crook of his neck. Looking all around, he begins to appear antsy. Like he's looking for the closest escape route. But why?

Before I can ask him what's wrong, Echo's attention is on me. "Look at you, Dax. You sure clean up nice." She playfully smacks my cheek.

"You don't look so bad yourself, Echo," I reply.

With a wide smile, she's about to reply, but her eyes look past me, falling on Dustin. Now I'm looking at two statues. Lynsie and I are both glancing back and forth between the two of them, trying to figure out what's going on. Echo and Dustin stare at each other in silence for what feels like an eternity.

"Dustin," Echo whispers with a hint of disbelief. From my peripheral, I see Dustin's stoic face soften. She looks back and forth between me and him, piecing it together. "Y'all are brothers?" she asks, voice slightly cracking.

I nod.

"How do you and Dustin know each other?" Lynsie asks, watching Echo carefully.

Dustin clears his throat. "We went to high school together," he flatly replies.

I observe Echo, intently trying to place her. Dustin is four years older. By the time I made it to high school, he had already graduated and was gone. It's possible I never saw her. I look back and forth between her and Dustin as realization from the night of Lincoln's crash sets in. "Oh shit," I mumble. Now I know who her son reminds me of.

Dustin starts to say more, but Echo's husband, Brian, walks up, and she cuts her eyes at Dustin, silencing him.

"I see you've met my new Platoon Leader?" Echo's husband asks before placing a kiss on her cheek.

She musters a smile. "Seems so."

"Brian, this is Lynsie and Dax. Dax is Dustin's brother," she introduces us, keeping her eyes on Dustin. I have a feeling there is way more between them than just going to high school together. Knowing Dustin, I'll never find out.

"All right," I say, hoping my voice will slice through the thick tension. "I think it's time for us to take our seats."

I'M CALLED TO the stage to accept my award. Lynsie's dad stands on the stage, alongside another colonel who's holding the plaque. He moves away from the microphone, allowing me to speak.

"I'm at a loss for words," I start, buzzing with nervousness. "Though I'm extremely proud and humbled to be getting this award, I'm just happy to be alive today. I believe every pilot will fight through a bad situation, to the best of their abilities, but there are times when it's beyond our control." I look down at Lynsie and smile. "As you all know, it's been almost a year since we lost someone important to me—someone who was like a brother. When I got word of this award, I thought what better night to reveal the memorial I made for that dear friend of mine, along with every pilot we've lost and will lose along the way. I dedicate this Broken Wing award to them. May they forever be our guardian angels. Thank you."

I turn around and take a few pictures, holding my plaque while I take turns shaking each man's hand. I make my way back to my seat to watch as they pull the sheet off the memorial I hand-carved. I grab Lynsie's hand, lacing our fingers together.

"That was amazing, Dax." She looks up at me, searching my eyes before glancing at my lips.

I hear gasps, and we both return our attention to the stage, where my wooden carving sits in an enclosed glass case. When the ceremony ends, everyone seems to head for the stage to take in the details and read the inscription. Looking up at it, I'm still amazed I made it— that my hands were capable of making something so beautiful.

"I'm going to the restroom," Lynsie says, pushing her chair out.

I turn my head to where her gaze is and see Echo taking off. Maybe Lynsie will be able to get some answers. "Okay." I pull our joined hands up to my lips and place a kiss on her hand. "I'll be waiting."

She swallows, staring at my lips again before nodding, then takes off in the direction Echo just went.

Dustin approaches me. Just when I'm about to ask him for his side, my parents come up from behind. I narrow my eyes at the look of relief that crosses his face. He might've dodged the bullet this time, but I'll find another chance.

"We are so proud of you, Dax," my mother says, throwing her arms around my neck.

"Thanks, Mom." I pat her back.

My dad grasps my shoulder while my mom is still latched on. "Very proud of both of my boys."

I look over at Dustin. He's wearing a slight smile, something that hasn't graced this family in quite some time.

"Yo, Dax," I hear Peterson's booming voice heading my way.

My parents move to the side, allowing me space to make my way to him.

"Hey, man." I go to shake his hand, but he pulls me in for a bear hug instead.

"I think we're past the handshaking," Zack says.

"Oh, are we dating now?" I tease, patting his back.

"You saved my life, Dax," he recalls, pulling away.

"You would've done the same thing."

"Yeah, I guess, but still. That was my second close call. Suicide birds." He laughs, but I can see the insecurity in his eyes.

"For real." I chuckle.

"Anyway, I'm heading out. Just wanted to say congrats. You deserve it." He pats my arm and turns to leave.

I turn back to my brother and Dad, who are sitting at the table talking, while my mother is standing facing me. I have a feeling she has a lot of talking to make up for, and I'm not getting out of it like I usually can on the phone.

"How're things with Lynsie?" she asks.

"Great." I can't help my grin. "The baby is doing well. Everyone is fine." I try not to go into detail. No matter how perfectly I describe it, my mom has already made her mind up. I'm not living the life intended for me.

"That's nice." She clears her throat. "So when are you going to find yourself a nice woman and settle down? Maybe retire from the Army and move back home?"

I barely refrain from rolling my eyes. "Seriously, Mom. This again? No matter how many times I tell you I'm happy, you don't get it."

"You're right," she replies snidely, crossing her arms. "I think you're only sticking around here, helping her out, because it was Lincoln's dying wish."

"For shit's sake," Dustin mutters from behind our mother.

"You're kidding me, right? Maybe it was his dying wish, but that's not why I'm sticking around." I hear a gasp behind me, and my mom's eyes go wide. My stomach drops.

I spin around to Lynsie and my heart drops as well. A shaky hand covers her mouth as she eyes me. "Lincoln's dying wish was for you to take care of me?" she chokes out.

My mouth opens, then shuts. I don't know what I can say to make it better. "Yes, but..."

Her eyes widen, and her chin trembles. "So that's the reason you've been around? Because it was your best friend's dying wish? I've just been some promise you vowed your friend to keep?" The last part she all but whispers as the tears begin to fall.

I shake my head, reaching out for her. "No, that's not why."

She pulls her arm away, taking a step back.

Panic sets in at the distance she's keeping between us.

"Lynsie, wait." My voice is full of desperation. She can't leave. Not like this.

She keeps walking backward, away from me. The devastation I see on her face almost brings me to my knees. I want to tell her I love her—that I'm in love with her—but she'll never believe me. Not under the circumstances. She turns around, running off, and I don't chase her like I want. Right now, my words don't mean anything to her. She's going to need proof.

I quickly make my way over to Echo across the room and tell her, "Lynsie's upset and ran out. Will you give her a ride home?"

Without hesitation, she stands. "Of course. Tell Brian for me."

I watch her weave through the tables with ease. When I glance back, I see Dustin, his eyes fixated on Echo as she departs.

"I'm so sorry, Dax," my mother claims as I make my way back to our table.

"No, you're not," I grit out through clenched teeth.

Lynise has been on the upward climb the last few months. She's so strong and no longer lives every day consumed by grief. The pendulum has finally shifted. Things with us seemed to be shifting, too. Lincoln's one-year memorial is right around the corner, and now she thinks I've only stuck around because I feel like I owe it to my best friend. *She's so wrong.*

"I gotta go," I say, giving my parents a hug.

Dustin clamps a hand on my shoulder, and I see something in his eyes I've seen before—determination. "Go get your girl." He uses the words I used on him so long ago, and I'm hit with the gravity of it all.

"Is that... Is Echo..." I start, then shake my head. It can't be.

"Yes," he all but whispers, devastation lacing his voice. It all makes sense now. The reason he took off, leaving his promising base-ball career in the dust. Leaving me in the dust. "Now go get your girl," he repeats, with a sense of urgency this time. I see the war in his eyes, and I want to tell him to go get his girl, too. "Now," he commands, all but yelling, pulling me back to my current circum-stance and not back to when my world was turned on its axis when I was fourteen. "Before we're both cold-hearted assholes," he admits, solidifying his situation.

"Please come see me before you head out." We have so much

catching up to do. He nods, but the sincerity doesn't reach his eyes. I know he'll be gone before I know it. So I pull him in tightly. This time, he doesn't tense, and I tighten my arms, holding him longer than I should, not knowing when I'll have the chance to do this again. "I love you, brother."

Chapter Thirty-Six

LYNSIE

"You wanna talk about it?" Echo asks as we pull out of the parking lot.

"Do you wanna talk about what was going on between you and Dustin?" I ask, using both hands to wipe my remaining tears away. If I'm going to talk, then so is she.

"No," she whispers.

"Then neither do I." I cross my arms and look out the window. It's dark out, but I enjoy looking at all the lights lit up in the distance as we make our way closer to town.

She sighs heavily. "Dustin and I went to school together. It was our senior year and my parents moved me back to Oklahoma before graduation."

"I call bullshit. There's more to this story." I angle myself toward her in my seat.

"You're right," she quietly admits. "I loved him." She looks at me with tears in her eyes. "And he loved me."

"Oh wow," I whisper. Her story is doing nothing but twist the pain and confusion I'm already feeling even more.

"I never got to say goodbye," Echo says, gripping the steering wheel. "It was really hard."

"I can't imagine what it was like, seeing him tonight after so long."

"I tried to find him after graduation." She glances over, her eyes holding so much sadness and regret. "But that was before Facebook and everything was available at your fingertips, but I guess seeing him tonight answers that he must've joined the Army right out of high school. Brian mentioned a new Platoon Leader but never a name. I'm just glad to see he's alive...and well." Her voice becomes a whisper.

I think about the vague details Dax mentioned about Dustin. "Maybe alive...but I don't think the guy is well."

Echo looks at me, worried. "What do you mean?"

I sigh, not sure if it's my story to tell. "From what Dax has said, Dustin is kind of stone cold. That ever since high school, he distanced himself, and being at war has only intensified it."

"I did that to him," she cries.

I grab her free hand, squeezing it. "People make their own choices," I tell her firmly. "If he chose to cut people off, it's not your fault. That's just how some people deal. If they don't have to feel, they seem to think it's easier." *At least, I thought that when I first lost Lincoln.*

Her sniffling comes to an end, and she says, "Dax is really worried about you. What happened?"

I silently replay what I overheard as I was walking back from the bathroom.

"Well," I mutter hastily. "Dax doesn't care about me the way you think he does, or the way I was starting to believe he did. I overheard him and his mom talking. Apparently, Lincoln's dying wish was for Dax to take care of me. Can you believe it?" My stomach knots, and tears begin to form all over again.

"Yes, I can," Echo says softly.

"What?" I shriek.

She shrugs. "Dax and Lincoln were best friends. Lincoln probably knew Dax harbored feelings for you. He also knew you both were close. Who better to watch over his wife than someone he knows will deeply care for her? It makes total sense. It also proves just how much Lincoln loved you."

I HAVE ECHO drop me off at my house. I run inside to grab my car keys and kick my heels off. I need to think, and driving seems to help with that. I arrive at the lake twenty minutes later and park near a bench with a light pole over it. It's so dark around, but I somehow find comfort in it. Every so often, I can hear the hushed lapping of the water in the distance, and it makes me sad.

"I miss you so much, Lincoln," I say out loud as the tears begin to fall. "Why'd you have to leave me!" I yell. My body hunches over as I whisper, "I'm so confused."

My mood follows my words. "I feel guilty for having these feelings for Dax. I'm not trying to forget about you. I could never forget you," I choke out. "I love you so much. What if I can't love anyone the way I love you? How am I supposed to move on?" I shake my head. "Now I'm questioning everything. Everything I thought Dax felt, even the things I was starting to feel." Speaking this aloud makes me feel like I'm crazy. I know Lincoln isn't here, but being here makes me feel closer to him. "Please, Lincoln. I need you to show me. I need some sign that it's okay—that what I feel is real."

I let my head hang down, silently praying for an answer. I hear the crunching of gravel in the distance and see the headlights hitting the trees. I don't even have to look to know who it is. He knows me too well.

Slow footsteps and a cautious voice come from behind. "When you weren't home, I figured you would come out here."

"Yeah," is all I say. I don't feel like talking to him right now.

He sits down beside me, running his hands over something. When I look over, I see his journal sitting in his lap. "I told you one day I'd let you read it." He hands it over, looking at me with his heart in his eyes, and whispers, "I'm in love with you, Lyns. So read this." He nods to his journal, now lying in my lap. "You'll see why I've stuck by your side."

He gets up and walks off. I hear his car start and just like that, Dax is gone.

I stare down at the worn leather journal in my hand. Do I want to know all of Dax's thoughts? He just handed me his most valuable possession.

I open it a few pages in. It starts with him talking about being transferred here and how happy he is to be close to his best friend again. He writes about how he enjoys the Army and how the fear of it changing him is a thing of the past. I continue skimming through and flip over a few pages. He talks about his parents and what they want from him—mainly his mother. Then I come across a poem.

October 2011
My heart is torn, she just doesn't get it.
I could never make a move, I'd be sure to
regret it.

I shouldn't be having these thoughts going
rampant.
He's my best friend, why won't they just go
away, dammit?

How wrong this is, is very clear.
One day surely, these feelings will disappear.

That was only six months after he transferred here. I scurry through the pages, taking in all the proof. Proof of his struggle through the years. He's had feelings for me this whole time.

June 2012
Lynsie doesn't get it. I can't tell her that playing
matchmaker won't work. How in the world did I
manage to fall for the one woman who's completely
off-limits? These feelings are so wrong, but I can't
control them. I don't want to want my best friend's
wife, but I do. There are times it pains me to see
her with Lincoln. During those times, I attempt to
keep my distance, and it's still impossible. I'm
drawn to her. As crazy as that sounds. You can't be
drawn to your best friend's girl.

June 2013

I picked the worst possible date I could for her dad's promotion tonight. It was shitty on my part, but I was trying to prove a point...which I don't think worked. If I had known my date would wound up hurting Lynsie in the process, I never would've taken her. Her asking me not to sleep with Haley shocked me. She's never seemed to care how far things went with any of the girls I dated. In fact, it's usually the opposite. Yes, I've been burned in the past, but I didn't turn into a jaded man whore because of it. Not like it matters. None of this does. I really wish these feelings would take a hike already. I'm seriously thinking about looking into being transferred. Maybe being away from her will help me get over her.

He writes about being pissed that he stupidly broke his hand and couldn't fly in the show. As I read it, I think about how close he would've been to dying if it were him. Dax wouldn't have ejected. He would've been too worried about the plane's trajectory, worried it might hit the audience. Reading about Lincoln's death and all the emotion he held in just to be strong for me damn near breaks my heart. He was dying inside, but he kept it to himself—for me. Everything he's done has been for me.

July 2013

Hearing your best friend's dying wish to watch over his wife is the hardest thing to hear. He trusts me with her. There's no reason not to, but it makes me wonder if he knows just how deeply I care for her. Were my feelings that transparent? I'd be by Lynsie's side even if it wasn't his last request. Maybe it's stupid of me to think that I'm the only one who can help her in the way she needs right now. All I know is I need to be strong for her. She needs me and I'm going to be whatever she needs, even if that means putting the feelings I have for her on the back burner. I can't help but feel I was made for her. Whatever capacity that may be.

I'm crying as I read about Dax's love for me. If anything, these last eleven months have only intensified his feelings.

March 2013

This is it! My life was complete once I saw Blu in Lynsie's arms. Lynsie was amazing, and I'm so proud of her. She's so strong. She never ceases to amaze me. I'll never forget the glow on her face and the shimmer of love in her eyes as she gazed down at her baby. I thought she could never look more beautiful, but I was wrong. The moment her sweet baby girl was placed in her arms, my heart stopped. The happiness that washed across her face is a look

I'll never forget. That was the happiest I had seen her over these last nine months. This is my family, Lynsie and Blu. Even if I haven't been able to claim them yet, in my heart, it's what I feel and that's all that matters. I love them both. I don't know what I'll ever do if Lynsie doesn't want the same. All I can do is keep showing her how I feel.

I flip the book closed and look down at the journal. This was my sign. Lincoln brought me my sign. "I'll always love you, Lincoln." I wipe away my tears and stand up. It's time to go home.

On the way, I'm feeling eager and nervous and a million other things, but when I make it into my driveway, I stay in my car, contemplating my next move. I flip down my mirror, checking my face. I wipe my eyes to rid the evidence of my tears. As I go to push my visor back up, something catches my eyes, and I finger the chain around my neck. It's been hidden by the neckline of my dress.

I've held onto Lincoln's tags as if they were some sort of lifeline. Surely, they had to hold some part of him since they were all that was left of him. Knowing that he was wearing them when he died was reason enough for me to never take them off. It made me feel closer to him.

Taking them off now doesn't mean I'm choosing to replace him. Tonight, I'm letting go of Lincoln, and I'm taking flight with Dax.

Chapter Thirty-Seven

DAX

I'm a wreck. What I did was smart, right...leaving Lynsie there with my journal and her thoughts? I'm convinced it was the only way to make her see. Still, this is torture.

Most people put their heart out on the line in the form of words spoken, not written. My every thought has been shed in ink in that leather binder. My deepest, darkest feelings. There are good times I never wanted to forget. The battle my heart and mind have fought over the years as I dealt with my feelings for Lynsie. The fears of flying I had after Lincoln died. My feelings in general after he died. How I'd be by Lynsie's side no matter what—that I didn't need it to be Lincoln's dying wish for it to happen. I truly only believe he voiced it because he wanted me to know it was okay.

I lie in bed in my gym shorts, listening to my playlist on my laptop play on repeat. Tossing my tennis ball in the air, I try to stay positive, hoping I didn't just scare the woman I'm in love with away. I really don't know what can happen with us if she doesn't feel the same. I don't know what will happen to me or my heart.

"Stupid. Stupid," I say out loud. My heart and mind are in a full-blown battle. I shouldn't have given it to her. Yes, I should've. I trust her. I trust that woman more than I've ever trusted anyone. I have to have faith in her and myself. I don't believe I could've handed my written soul over to her if I didn't think she would handle it with care.

A light tap on my bedroom door pulls me from my torturous thoughts and my heart takes a dive.

"Dax?" Lynsie says as she slowly pushes the door open. Completely forgetting about the ball I just tossed in the air, I quickly sit up and it thumps me on top of my head.

"Ouch." I rub my head, then glance at her. "Yeah."

Lynsie tries not to giggle. Still in her dress, she makes her way to my bed and sits next to me. I gulp at the closeness, my mind going crazy as I wonder what she's thinking. The lamp lets off just enough light in the room to see the tears falling down her face.

"What's wrong?" I lean into her, using the pads of my thumbs to dry the tears away.

"You," she cries.

My thumbs still as I stare at her, begging her for answers. I'm ready, and I need them. I can't wait anymore.

"Why me, Dax?" She hesitates, blinking in confusion. "You're so amazing. You could have anyone you want, and this whole time you've wanted me. I never knew." She whispers the last part.

I go to speak, but she stops me.

"And all this other stuff in here..." She grabs my face. Her eyes are gentle, full of concern—and so much more. "You should've told me. You shouldn't have gone through it alone."

I softly trail my knuckles down her cheek. "You were already going through so much, Lyns. There's no way I was going to throw more on you."

She leans into my hand, quivering from the touch—*my* touch.

That alone tells me all I need to know. Things between us will never be the same.

Her full green eyes search mine. "Promise me something."

"Anything," I say without hesitation as I revel in the feel of her hands holding my face. I position mine on her wrists, holding hers in place. If I could freeze us in this spot, I would.

"Let me be your journal from now on," she says softly. "Your feelings are just as safe with me as they are on paper...but unlike this"—one of her hands breaks away to pick up my journal—"you speak them to me, and we can bring them to life."

"You don't know how bad I've wanted to."

She waves the journal at me, and I swallow.

"Well, maybe you do know, but I just couldn't risk it. It wasn't just my heart on the line. It was yours, too. I couldn't risk hurting it once you were finally putting it back together."

Her eyes are hooded and full of emotion. "Do you think I would've been able to mend the pieces back without you in my life?"

"We were both left with broken wings, Lynsie. I completely lost mine that day, too, but it's up to us to decide if we're going to leave them broken or pick them up and learn to fly again."

She drops my journal and presses her hand back on my face. "I want to fly again, Dax, but only if you're by my side."

I move my hands to her face as we stare at each other, begging the other to initiate. We both glance at each other's lips before quickly meeting eyes again. This is the moment I've been waiting an eternity for. I lick my lips as I close the distance between us, pulling her face to mine as I lean in.

"I'll always be by your side," I breathe against her lips before gently placing mine against hers. Emotions I've never quite felt before take over, and the kiss deepens. This feels so natural, yet so scary. And all too soon, Lynsie retreats.

"Is this right, Dax? Is what we're doing okay?" she asks as if she's seeking permission to move on.

"I don't know, Lyns," I tell her honestly. "I know it should be more than okay for us to move forward, whether that be together or not. I ask myself daily if what could happen between us would be right or wrong."

"And?" Her eyes are full of hope.

"Well... If we do this because we both want to feel again, then it's right, but if we're only doing it because we want to keep from feeling, then that's when it will only end badly for one or both of us."

"What do you feel, Dax?" she whispers.

I graze my finger across her cheek. "Like being with you is the most natural thing ever. I don't question how I feel about you. I only question you and your feelings."

"Why do you question mine?"

"Because..." I grab her hand. "The way I feel, I've felt since I met you. So I know it's real."

"Dax, I love you," Lynsie says tenderly.

It should be music to my ears, but it's not. "I know you love me, Lynsie, but it's never been the same kind of love I feel for you." My heart pounds hard in my chest.

"Only because the heart is designed to feel that kind of love for one person, Dax. I'll always love Lincoln. Always. I do have feelings for you, but what if I can't love you like I loved him?" she whispers as tears slowly find their way down her cheeks.

Using my thumbs, I wipe them away. "I don't ever want to replace what Lincoln meant to you." I search her eyes before I continue. A hint of sadness is visible, but it gets overshadowed by love and understanding. "I want to be the one who makes you happy. The one you can always count on...lean on. I don't want you to love me the same way you loved Lincoln. I want you to love me differently." I press my lips against hers, reclaiming her mouth with hunger and raw need.

No longer holding back, Lynsie kisses me with urgency. She slowly pulls away, leaving my mouth, begging for more. She stands up, extending her hand out to me. I take her hand in mine as I stand up next to her. Lynsie kisses my hand before letting it go as she turns her back to me.

She tilts her neck to the side, glancing back at me. "I need help," she says with a mischievous smile.

"You don't have to tell me twice." I quickly close the distance between us, wrapping my arms around her slender waist as my lips find her neck. Her head falls back against my bare chest, granting me better access. My mind is going nuts, and I can barely breathe as I work my way from the base of her neck to where her dress is zipped. A sense of eagerness takes over. I start to pull down the zipper, realizing her neck is completely bare.

She took the dog tags off. My finger traces where they used to rest.

"I took them off after I read your journal." She turns her head up, gazing into my eyes. "I'm ready to move on with you, Dax. I'm ready to feel again. Make me feel."

I don't need any more convincing than that. My lips crash into hers, wanting her to feel every fiber of my being. How much I've wanted her, how much I love her, how I'll do anything for her. With her hand against my cheek, her lips part, granting my tongue entrance. A taste I've been craving for as long as I can remember; better than I could've ever imagined.

Barely having the strength, I untwine our tongues and start scattering kisses all the way down her chin. I lift her head up as I make my way back down, kissing as I go. I savor the sound of her soft moan. I want to taste every inch of her. I could gladly spend the rest of my life doing so.

My hot breath leaves a wake of goose bumps everywhere it

touches, and it makes my heart beat so hard, I'm almost worried it'll explode in my chest. I slowly push the fabric of her dress over each shoulder, kissing the newly bare skin. Inch by inch, my lips savor the taste all the way down her tan, toned body—a body I've been longing would belong to me.

Never in my life have I had the desire to take my sweet time with a woman or put so much attention into every single detail, but everything is different with Lynsie. It always has been. She does something inside of me I can't explain, reaching places no one has ever come close to.

Lynsie takes a step away from me, inhaling a deep breath, then pushes her dress the rest of the way down before she turns around and faces me. My gaze drops from her eyes to her shoulders, to her chest, focusing there a beat longer than the rest before continuing my downward surveillance. I take my time returning my eyes to hers. She's so beautiful and perfect. She's so... MINE.

Raising her arms above her shoulders, she pulls out the pins that are holding her hair tightly in place, allowing her curls to flow down her back. Her lacey black panties are begging me to take them off, but I don't. Not yet.

The sight of her, bare and vulnerable just for me, makes my heart stop. I knew I loved this woman, but this is a whole new level. It's a level I thought was unreachable.

I keep my eyes planted on hers instead of scanning her beauty that's beckoning me to roam my hands all over. "You're so gorgeous, Lyns." I take a step closer, placing my hand on her cheek.

She runs her hands up and down my bare chest, causing me to shiver. Her hands still and she lets out a sigh that worries me.

"Are you okay?" I whisper in the dimly lit room. "We don't have to do anything." Even though my body is screaming right now, I don't want her to feel any pressure.

She looks up and a glorious smile takes over as she shakes her head. "No, that's not it at all. It's..." She pauses. "It's just that I've been fighting off the idea of having feelings for you for a while. I questioned if they were real. I questioned if they were right, but now, being this close to you, I realize they're more real than I thought possible. I had no clue how much my heart could feel again, but finally caving to them has opened something deeper inside." She waits a second, then says, "I'm so in love with you, Dax."

"You don't know how long I've been waiting to hear those words." I crash my lips to hers to keep the overwhelming emotion I'm feeling from spilling over. My mouth curves into a smile as I hear the song playing on my laptop. It wraps up everything I feel for this woman and what I want her to feel for me. I can't help but let the words drift from my mouth as I run my fingers down the side of her face, looking deeply into her eyes as I sing to her. The words talk about giving your heart over to the person you love, asking them to take it when they think they can't. Letting them know that once they let go and just go for it, it'll open their heart up.

I wrap my arms around her, molding our bodies together as we very slowly sway to the song.

I continue to whisper the lyrics, hoping they find their way into her soul. Somehow this song sums it all up, but in a way I'd never be able to vocalize. It's sexy and sultry, everything I'm feeling in this moment with her. This isn't just about physical exploration. The emotional journey we're both staking claim on tonight is more abundant than the pleasure factor.

Lynsie looks up at me as the song comes to an end. Just like I did earlier, she runs her fingers up and down my cheek. "I want you, Dax. I want you to make love to me. I need you to make love to me. More than I've ever needed anything in my life, I need this," she says, almost begging me.

"Only if you're absolutely sure, baby." Man, it feels good to call her that.

Pulling her down to the bed, I can't help but get caught up in the beauty of this moment. I tuck Lynsie beneath me. Everything I've ever wanted is right here. It's a lot to take in when we've both been through so much.

"I love you," I whisper, pressing my nose to her forehead. "I love you more than I've ever loved anyone or anything in my entire life. You own me, Lynsie. I never even had a choice."

"I don't think I did, either," she says as overwhelming emotion takes over. A single tear trails down her face. It's a tear that signifies letting go but never forgetting. I slowly push my way inside her and kiss the evidence of that single tear away.

Chapter Thirty-Eight

LYNSIE

e lie in silence in each other's arms. He's on his back and I'm tangled up against him. My hand dances up and down his chest as I think about what just took place. I'm glad he can't see me right now. I'm sure I have the most cheesy, girlie grin across my face. Happiness is to blame.

"What are you thinking about?" he asks.

I sigh contentedly. "You."

"What about me?" I hear his smile as he twirls a piece of my hair around his finger.

"Just how happy you make me...and how amazing that was." I feel the heat of a blush moving across my face.

He sighs this time. "Amazing doesn't do it justice."

"You're right." Because there are no words for it. Other than perfection.

Dax snatches my hand up from his chest and brings it to his lips, placing light kisses across it. When his mouth reaches where my wedding ring is, he pauses.

I explain, "I took it off when I took the tags off. I can't keep holding onto him when I'm ready to move on with you."

He places a kiss on my empty finger, then holds my hand against his heart. "Moving forward doesn't mean we're forgetting. We'll never forget...and we have each other as a reminder."

I glance up into his eyes. "I have a feeling you were made just for me." I yawn as I start to happily drift to sleep.

"I was," Dax whispers, placing his signature kiss on my forehead.

I WAKE UP bright and early, and my motherly instincts kick in. *Where is my baby and why isn't she crying?* It's a knee-jerk reaction. Then I remember Blu stayed the night at my parents'. I glance over at Dax, who's lightly snoring, and smile. I place a kiss on his forehead and quietly crawl out of bed.

Throwing some clothes on, I make my way downstairs. Coffee is needed. Strong coffee at that, with lots of sugar and creamer.

I grab my phone and shoot my mom a quick text.

> Me: How's my baby girl?
>
> Mom: Perfect!
>
> Me: We'll be there in the next hour or two.
>
> Mom: No need to rush. We'll be here when you're ready.

I pull out my headphones, grab my coffee, and head to the couch. I'll listen to some of this book I bought while I let Dax sleep in. I put my headphones on and I'm about to push play when I get a text.

Echo: First off, I need an update ASAP.
And second, you have to watch this.
Dylan showed me. GURRL, I. Am. Dying.

I follow the link to YouTube and, without even knowing what I'm about to watch, I hit the play button. *What is she making me watch?*

This video is dumb. I roll my eyes as my finger hovers over the stop button. Then I hear it, and I start laughing. I laugh because it's ridiculous. I laugh because it is dumb, but mainly I laugh because now I get what Dax meant so long ago. I'm laughing so hard that my eyes are tearing up.

I feel the couch dip and look over to see a worried Dax beside me. I push my headphones back, trying to calm myself, but I'm in hysterics.

"Are you okay?" he asks, thumbing the few tears away.

"Yes." I giggle. "I finally get it."

His brows pinch in confusion. I pull the cord from my phone so the song that has me laughing can play loudly.

Dax joins in on the laughter. "So now you know what the fox says, Mrs. Fox."

"Yes. I'm definitely in the know now." I turn the video off and sit back on the couch, finally catching my breath. "I told my mom we'd be there in an hour or two."

A look I'm not used to seeing flashes in Dax's hazel eyes. A look of desire that's pointed directly at me and boy, does it look good on him. Not to mention the tingles it sends through my body.

"Glad to hear we have plenty of time before we need to go pick up our girl." His voice is husky as he closes the distance between us, pinning me underneath him. The fact that he just referred to Blu as 'ours' has me melting into him even more.

"Time for what?" I squeak out as his eyes pierce mine.

"This," he says as he moves his hips between my legs.

I moan at the friction. "Yep." I pant. "We definitely have time for that."

"I'm taking you back to bed," he says gruffly. Then he stands and scoops me up, carrying me back to our room.

WE WALK IN, hand in hand. My mother quickly inspects our joined hands but says nothing.

Dropping his hand, I walk over to where she's holding Blu. "Hey, baby girl," I coo. "How was she?" I ask my mom without looking up.

"Perfect," my mother says, with so much love in her voice. "Woke up once during the night."

"How you doing, son?" My dad walks up behind Dax.

"Couldn't be better." I hear the goofy smile in Dax's voice and glance over my shoulder and smile. Looking back up, I see my mom eyeing me suspiciously.

"Was that your brother I saw last night?" my dad asks Dax. "I didn't get a chance to meet him. It seems like everyone left out of thin air." He laughs, and then I remember how I took off without telling anyone. I can only assume Dax did the same shortly after.

"Yeah, I haven't seen him in years." Dax looks off in thought. "To say I was shocked is an understatement. That reminds me, I really need to get a hold of him and see if he's still in town."

I grab Blu and snuggle her against me. "Yeah, maybe he can explain what the deal was between him and Echo. I was only able to get some of the story, but I have a feeling it has a lot to do with him taking off right after graduating."

"Hmm," Dax says, deep in thought, then shrugs. "He's not going to say anything. I can guarantee that." He returns his attention back to my dad about some flight they have coming up this week. I tune them out as I walk to the living room.

"Oh hey, by the way, you boys just received last-minute overwater training orders scheduled in Pensacola, Florida. You, Peterson, Connelly, and a couple more will be heading down to Florida for a week."

I flip back around at my dad's words. "What?" I shriek at him.

"It's only for a week, Lynsie Pearl. I think you'll be fine." My dad walks past me, giving me a quick side hug and Blu a kiss on her forehead before making his way to the couch.

Of course I'll be fine. It has nothing to do with my emotional state like the last time Dax had training. This time is different. This time I'm in love with him.

My mom stays in the kitchen, gathering all of Blu's baby stuff while I walk to where Dax stands. His eyes are focused on me, gauging my reaction as I make my way to him.

I lean into his side, and he wraps his arm around me. "I know it's only a week, but I just got you," I whine.

He sighs. "I'm not thrilled either, but your dad is right. One week should fly by. It'll be easy this time."

I look up, cutting my eyes at him.

"Okay." He smiles. "It'll be *easier*. Leaving you will never be easy."

Chapter Thirty-Nine

DAX

I had never heard of "overwater survival training" until a week before I was scheduled to go, along with five of our guys. It's apparent that this type of training is only relevant if shit goes wrong over water. Which, before Lincoln's crash, I would've thought the likelihood of that would be slim. I've learned to accept that there are some cases that no amount of training can save you from. And with the uncertainty of where my career in the Army is going to take me, I'll gladly take all the training I can get.

I'd rather be safe than sorry.

One thing is certain, it wasn't any easier leaving Lynsie this time around. It was harder. I've never allowed myself to grow any attachments the whole time I've been in the Army until Lynsie. Now that she's mine, leaving her was torture.

This training I'm at in Pensacola, Florida, is only for a week, which doesn't seem bad now, but what happens if I get sent away for another three-month training? Or if I'm relocated to another base? Lynsie's parents live here. She won't take herself and Blu away from them. Where does that leave us? I hate these feelings of doubt. Now that I have the woman of my dreams, I have this nagging feeling that something is going to creep in and pull her away from me.

We cover a lot of classroom material before they have us jump out of a plane into the bay. Everything from repairing your parachute, deploying certain gear, quick release of your chute as you enter the water, and inflating your raft and getting into it while waiting to be rescued. A ton of useful information that, besides the parachute part of it, hasn't crossed my mind.

Peterson and I have grown closer than expected over the year. At times, I can tell he still feels responsible for Lincoln. He hasn't voiced it again since that one drunken night, but he doesn't need to. It's still written on his face.

After the classroom part of our training, Peterson and I walk side by side as we head to grab something to eat on our lunch break.

"Dude, when is your term up?" he asks me. "You don't have that much longer, do you?"

"I don't know exactly," I lie. I know exactly when, down to the day, but I'm not admitting that to him. "Less than six months." It's a date I've been dreading as it closes in. It's stupid for me to give a date so much power, but I can't shake the feeling that so much of my future relies heavily on it.

"What're your plans?"

I stop mid-stride. "I don't know, Peterson." My annoyance is evident. My sunglasses not only block the bright Florida sun, but the worry in my eyes I'd rather him not see.

"Don't get your panties in a wad, Dax. Shit." He turns back around and takes off ahead of me.

A minute later, I'm by his side, quiet, and I have a feeling it's more than just my attitude that's caused it. He sighs and turns to me before reaching the door of the cafeteria. "I've heard talk." He looks around, making sure no one is listening.

The dread in my stomach just got bigger. "What kind of talk?"

"Talk of our battalion getting sent overseas. Talk that the whole reason we're here on this training is that very possibility."

"Shit!" I shove my hand through my hair, wanting to pull it all out in frustration.

"That's exactly why I was asking how much longer you had."

"Don't beat around the bush next time, Peterson." The door flies open and out walks Connelly.

"Oh, I'll show you bush," Peterson teases to lift the seriousness of the mood that Connelly just stumbled upon.

"I'm pretty sure everyone has seen your bush," Connelly jokes as he passes.

"Not true," Peterson growls. "I'm still holding strong that your mom will come to her senses."

"Oh snap," I say as Connelly stops dead in his tracks, quickly turning around with a look of disgust covering his face.

"Dude, that's just gross. Nothing against my mom." He shakes his head as if he's imagining it. Connelly visibly shudders, muttering gross one last time before making his way back to the hangar.

I look at Peterson, appreciative of how he's always able to lift the heaviness of a dreadful situation. Even if it's only temporary before that weight comes smashing back down. Sometimes all you need is to take in a fresh, new breath until you find the relief again. Peterson has become my metaphorical bench-pressing spotter. He stands behind me, ready for me to falter so he can catch the bar before it crushes down on me.

He's managed to squeeze himself in when I was trying to guard myself from getting close to anyone. After Lincoln, losing someone else I cared about, a fellow pilot no less, was the last thing I wanted to experience again. Lynsie understands my reservations where Lincoln and even Dustin are concerned. My best friend is dead, and my brother is emotionally unavailable. I don't want to become either. For a while, I believed those were my only two options. I would die, or I'd lose myself from seeing everyone I'd grown attached to through the Army die off around me.

"Connelly is fun to mess with." Peterson chuckles.

"Yeah, about that." I raise my brows. "We really need to work on raising your standards."

He starts laughing, almost choking. "I was joking about his mom, dude."

I clamp a hand on his shoulder. "His mom is probably hot compared to some of the women you pick up, my man. Standards. We need to find you some."

"Are you calling me a ho?" he sarcastically huffs.

"More like borderline desperate." I smile, pulling open the door.

"Damn, that cuts me deep, bro."

He gives me his wounded pride look, walking past me, and I roll my eyes, muttering, "I highly doubt that."

* * *

TODAY IS OUR last day and final test. Thank the *Lord.* Thrilled doesn't even capture the half of it. Yes, it's only been a week, but boy, I've missed my girls, which just makes me dread more and more what Peterson told me. I know what I need to do first thing when I get back. As much as I want to run home to Lynsie, I need to talk to her dad first. He'll shoot me straight.

"That'll do it." Peterson pats my back as he checks my harness for our last parasail.

I jump out of the plane and enjoy the freefall sensation. My stomach seems to have disappeared as I release my parachute. Floating through the air is such a thrilling feeling. I hold my breath, hitting the water. When I come to the surface, I start to gather my parachute, but as I'm pulling it closer, I see signaling red dye around me.

What the hell? Where'd all this come from?

I climb into my raft and there's even more red dye. I look out at the water a few hundred feet and see Peterson climbing into his raft. When he spots me, he busts out laughing.

"Hey, Adams!" he yells. "You got a little something on you." He falls back, laughing at his wittiness.

When he looks my way again, I give him a one-finger salute before lying back in my raft and looking skyward as I wait to be picked up. Out of nowhere, the Navy's Blue Angels cut through the sky. I envy people who live here and get to watch them year-round.

I simply stare up in amazement. It makes me proud to be a pilot. I don't think I can ever not be one. Lying here, I get a crazy idea to put something together for Lincoln—for the one-year anniversary of his death. It's next month. Just another thing I'll need to bring up when I talk to Lynsie's father.

AS SOON AS we land, I head back to his office. I knock a few times before barging in. I walk in after I hear him tell me to come in and he looks up, shocked to see me.

"How'd training go?" He leans back in his chair.

I sit down in front of his desk, leaning back as I stretch my legs out. "Really well."

"Well, what can I help you with?" He's cutting to the chase because he knows me well enough to know Lynsie would normally be my first stop.

"Are we getting deployed?" I ask nervously, studying his schooled features.

His chair squeaks as he bends forward, resting his arms on his desk. He sits in silence, searching for the right words. "I can't say for certain, Dax. There is a highly probable chance it could happen."

"Shit," I mutter, closing my eyes as I lean my head all the way back.

"You love my daughter?"

Startled by his question, I quickly sit back up straight. "Yes, sir, I do."

"You'd do anything for her?"

I keep my eyes trained on him and my tone of voice sharp. I want him to fully believe I'm answering him truthfully. "Anything and everything."

"You'd give up your wings for her?" He raises a brow.

Flying will always be a passion of mine, but...

"Sir, Lynsie and Blu are my life. If she ever asked me to give up flying, I would." Lynsie would never do that, but if it was a choice between my life and my passion, my life would easily win.

"So." He leans forward on his desk, keeping his expression neutral. "You're saying you'd leave the Army for my girl?"

"With all due respect, sir, the Army has never been my calling. It only led me to her."

"I figured as much." He sits back in his chair, crossing his leg and looking deep in thought. "I knew you loved Lynsie. I've known for a long time."

I nervously bite my thumbnail, waiting for something tangible to come out of his mouth.

"Honestly, there's no one else I could ever fully trust with her and Blu." He sighs, and there's a flash of pain in his eyes as he debates his next words. "Take her, Dax. Take her and Blu and get out. You both deserve a lifetime of happiness. I'm not saying it's not possible if you were to stay in the Army. I'm just saying you both have had enough hurt associated with it. Now, I think you need to take this opportunity to take my girls somewhere and go start a life together."

I nod, taking in his blessing. Where would we go? I can think about that later. "Thank you. That means a lot coming from you. I know Lynsie is a daddy's girl."

He laughs. "That she is." Another look of sadness comes over him. This time, it's wistful. "And now it's time for her to leave the nest."

"LYNSIE," I YELL, letting the door slam a little too loud.

"Shhhh," I hear her as she comes down the stairs.

Without another word, she runs to me and jumps into my arms. I hold her tightly against me as I walk us back up from where she came. We both giggle as I hit the wall a couple times on the way up.

"You're going to wake our girl up," she whispers.

I tiptoe us down the hall and lightly shut our door behind us. I bend over, laying Lynsie on the bed, and crawl over her. As much as I want to take her right now, the conversation I had with her dad weighs heavily on my mind. I roll off of her and sigh as my back hits the bed.

"What's wrong?" she asks, rolling onto her side. Her eyes are concerned.

"There's some stuff we need to talk about." I tilt my head toward her. "Some decisions that need to be made." I roll over, facing her, and grab her hands. "Decisions I'm not making without you."

I see dread flash across her face. We both knew this day would come, but I'm thankful it waited until after Lynsie realized she had feelings for me. I'm not sure how this would be ending otherwise.

"Okay." Her body moves as she releases a heavy breath.

I bring my hand to her face and caress it down her cheek. She closes her eyes and presses her face closer to my hand.

I smile and pull my hand away. "There's been talk that we might be getting deployed."

She gasps, tears instantly welling in her eyes.

I quickly try to calm her. "I have no idea when or if it's definite."

"No," she says over and over, shaking her head, tears already streaming down her face. "No, Dax. I refuse to lose you, too."

I cup her face with my hands to steady it. "I don't want to go either, baby. I don't want to go anywhere without you. Here's where the decision part comes in." I carefully eye her. I need her to listen carefully. "I have the option of being honorably discharged in about a month. My term is coming to an end."

Hope spreads across her face as she begins nodding excitedly. "Yes. Do that!"

I chuckle at her. "But here's the thing. If I leave the Army, I'm not staying here. This place isn't my home. So we need to come to a decision." I pause, letting out a breath. "I want to move back home and take the offer to become a pilot instructor at the school near my hometown. Maybe one day I'll start a little wood carving business on the side."

A smile tugs at her lips as she leans into me.

"But I want you by my side, Lyns. I know your parents are here, and I hate that you would leave them behind."

She's torn. I can see it in her eyes.

"I want you to really think about this, okay? Don't rush it. I want it to be what you want, too." I kiss her forehead and smile against her skin as I hear Blu waking up through the monitor.

"She missed you," she whispers. "We both did."

Chapter Forty

LYNSIE

I spin around in my chair, waiting for my client to show. Echo sits in hers, texting in her station next to mine.

"Dax's birthday is coming up. I have no idea what to give him," I tell her and sigh. Finding him the perfect gift is proving to be stressful.

"I know what you can give him." Echo snorts.

I roll my eyes. "That's not a gift, dork. It has to be something special and meaningful like he does for me. I want to show him I'm ready to move on with him. That wherever he goes, I go too. He's so worried that I won't ever be able to fully let go or leave my parents."

"So basically you want to show him you're ready to spread your wings and fly?" She eyes me, cocking a brow.

"Yes, exactly. Now how in the world do I do that?" I ponder as my chair slows to a stop.

"I have an idea." Echo gives me a sly smile as she leans across the cabinet that separates us, holding her phone out.

"I become a Victoria's Secret Angel?" I ask, confused by the picture of the half-naked woman in high heels and wings that are bigger than her.

"No, dork. Come with me Monday. I'm doing a boudoir shoot."

I grab her phone and start scrolling through the different pictures on the photographer's website. They're stunning...and sexy. Very sexy.

Doubt creeps in as I hand her back her phone. "Ahh, I don't know if I can do it."

"Let me ask you this." She props her hand on her hip. "How close are you and Dax? I mean, you guys are serious, right?"

"Yes. He's a permanent fixture in my life. I just don't know if I have the balls to do the sexy thing."

She lets out a cackle. "You definitely don't need balls. The panties you'll be wearing wouldn't be able to conceal them."

I laugh at her assessment.

The door chimes and in walks Echo's ten o'clock. "Think about it," she says before turning around to greet her client.

I push off on the floor one more time, spinning around and hoping when I come to a stop, my mind will have an answer. After a minute of spinning, I'm getting dizzy, and still no answers.

After a few more spins, I slam my foot down and throw all my reservations to the side. "I'll do it." My eyes are shut as heat rises to my cheeks. I'm unsure if it's the idea of having pictures taken or the spinning. I slowly peek my eyes open.

Echo is standing in front of me, smiling. "You sure?"

I nod like a maniac as excitement about this and what it signifies starts to bubble over. "It's perfect!"

* * *

WE ARRIVE DOWNTOWN in front of an older three-story brick building. The area looks pretty secluded, with 'for sale' signs on every other building lining the street. The emptiness of the surroundings has me feeling slightly more comfortable since I'm about to get undressed inside this building. We grab our bags filled with lingerie and make our way to the door.

Echo pushes the doorbell and I instantly hear the inside lock click as she pulls open the door. She gestures for me to walk ahead, and I gawk at all the distressed furniture as we mosey through the front area. I'm in heaven. I love everything about distressed furniture and all things Pinterest.

"Up here, guys."

I see a gorgeous brunette with heavily highlighted hair bending over the third-story railing. Glancing around, I notice that the second and third floors seem more like loft areas. I keep my eyes on the ceiling as I admire the original tiles lining it. This building holds so much character. I could see Dax and me owning a place like this someday, filled with all his wood creations. He's so talented.

Bags in tow, we trod up the wooden staircase. I take in all the photos that adorn the wall and truly admire this lady's talent. They're gorgeous, and so far, they're mainly family pictures, with a few senior pictures thrown in.

I can do this, I tell myself for the hundredth time. No matter what, I know the shoot will come out beautiful with Casey behind the camera.

On the third floor, my steps slow as I gulp at the surroundings. The lighting up here is low and seductive, but what has me stopping is the unmade bed against the wall. I have a feeling I'm going to be on that bed, which is making me reevaluate this whole idea. Then I look at the wall next to me, and again, I'm lost in the beauty. These women look beautiful. Nothing about these photos screams at me to run. In fact, they summon me to stay. Looking at each one, I see the love these women are showing as they put their bodies on display for the men they love.

I want this. Dax knows I love him, but I want to show him. He knows me well enough, and he'll know how much I care by this simple act. Imagining the expression on his face as he opens his present is all the motivation I need.

Okay, where do I strip?

Echo goes first and I sit back and watch. She has gorgeous curves. Baby got back is an understatement. I smile as I watch her work it. She's a natural and a pro by now. As she rolls over on the bed in nothing but a lacey red matching bra and panty set, she seductively places her finger in her mouth, giving the camera a sultry look.

"Sexy momma!" I hoot from the side. She smiles, and I hear the camera click. It's got to be a gorgeous shot. Shoot, every shot so far has been stunning, I'm sure.

Echo looks in my direction but doesn't make eye contact as she keeps her eyes barely open. I take in her high rosy cheekbones, perfect round nose, and plump lips with a hint of gloss. Seeing her like this is like seeing her for the first time. My beautiful friend is so gorgeous. Something about being stripped down allows your natural beauty to shine.

"Give me that gorgeous, playful smile of yours." *Click. Click.* "Now that sexy nail bite you've mastered." *Click. Click.* "Perfect!" Casey turns to me. "You ready?"

I suck in a deep breath and slowly exhale. "As I'll ever be."

I peel off the robe covering my barely clothed body. I bought a few special sets to wear just for today. The first one I decided to go with is the classic black look.

"How do you feel about doing a couple window shots?" Casey asks. "The natural light gives the photos an amazing touch."

I glance over at it and remember how secluded it is around here. I feel safe that no wandering eyes will see me in front of a wide-open window on the third floor.

Nodding, I pad over to it and Casey has me standing at an angle, resting against the window frame. My body is mainly facing her, but my face is sideways, looking out.

She pulls her camera down. "Now I want you to stand completely in front of the window but looking out with your arms raised up like you're stretching them. You have great legs, and those heels accentuate them."

"You still have those wings, don't you, Casey?" Echo asks, sitting on the bed in her robe. "I think Lynsie was really interested in doing some photos with them." She smiles my way, and I'm thankful for her. I'm so overwhelmed with the newness of this that I completely forgot the wing theme that brought me here to begin with.

"Yes, I do," Casey says, snapping a few more pictures of me at the window. "And they'd look amazing on you in front of that window." She crosses to the far side of the room and returns with a pair of medium-sized black wings in one hand and a pair of long, shimmery, white wings in the other. Dangling from her fingers appears to be a bag filled with feathers.

"These"—she holds up the bag—"will look amazing scattered on the bed with you lying on top of them."

Echo snickers. "Who needs a bed of roses when you can have a bed of feathers?"

I weave my fingers through the feathers as Casey holds the wings in her hands. Echo nudges me from my side, and I look up, catching Casey's bright blue eyes trained on me.

She smiles. "You ready to fly, Lynsie?"

My eyes barely glaze with tears. If she only knew.

Chapter Forty-One

DAX

Lynsie has been a sneaky little thing this past week. I'm pretty sure I know what the deal is. My birthday is today, and she nonchalantly told me happy birthday before I left for work. I could tell she was antsy, trying to push me out the door.

"Happy birthday, man." A hand clamps down on my shoulder from behind. I turn around to face a cheesing Peterson. "So whatcha say about letting me take you to the strip club tonight? Since it's a special occasion and all."

I choke on my laugh. He would think taking me to a strip club just because it's my birthday is a swell idea. "Nice try, buddy." I pat his arm as I shake my head.

He shrugs. "Never hurts to try. Anyway, I need you to come to the back with me. I have something I need to show you."

"Dude, I'm not interested in seeing your bush." Now it's him laughing as I remind him about his bush talk in Pensacola. "Your secret's safe with me." I wink.

He turns around, shaking his head with laughter. The blinds are shut in the back office as Peterson pushes the door open. I follow right behind, not really paying attention.

"Happy birthday!" all the guys yell in unison, catching me off guard.

I push the lump in my throat down, refusing to show my emotion, but it's overwhelming. Who would've thought something as simple as a surprise from my coworkers could make me tear up? But it does. No one has ever really done anything for my birthday. Other than when I was younger, my birthdays have just come and gone like any other day.

"Thank you, guys. You have no idea how much this means," I manage to say without squeaking or getting caught on my words.

The rest of the morning is spent around the break table, eating cake and drinking coffee. I sit back and enjoy the conversations. More than anything, I'm enjoying hearing the stories. I realize I've grown attached to these guys. We all tend to get so caught up in our own lives and what's going on, that we never take the time to fully get to know each other.

And sometimes life just moves too fast to allow it, even if we wanted to. Right now, I'm silently vowing to start appreciating life more and being thankful for what and who I have.

That's what's important.

MY PHONE BUZZES as I make my way to my car.

> Lynsie: Let me know when you're on your way home.

I smile, knowing she's got something up her sleeve.

> Me: I'm heading home now.

The sunset on my drive home is breathtaking and I can't get this shit-eating grin off my face, knowing what's waiting for me when I get home—more like who. It's nothing new. I drive home to this amazing woman every day with the same grin plastered on my lucky face. For some reason, though, I feel today deserves the biggest one I can muster. It's beyond my control. I pull into the driveway and all but run through the front door.

Only a few lamps light the living room. I hear music playing upstairs and head in that direction. Something on the floor slides under my boot as I step forward, causing me to look down. That's when I notice the trail of feathers...leading to the stairs, and that's not all. Every few steps, there's a framed picture placed in the trail of feathers. I walk up and bend over, picking up the first frame. What I see has my pulse spiking into overdrive. She looks unbelievably gorgeous. Her face is turned, looking out a window, and it's the sexiest thing ever.

I take a few more steps and grab the next frame. I groan...loudly. It earns me a distant giggle that echoes down the hall. She's laid out gloriously on a bed. A bed covered in feathers. Her hands are twisted above her head as she stares into the camera. I know it's me she's staring at because it's me she took these for.

Taking the stairs two at a time, I grab each frame and take in every sexy detail of each picture. Every detail of my beautiful Lynsie. At the entrance to the bedroom, there's one more. When I pick it up, it stops me in my tracks and almost brings to my knees.

Wings. She's wearing wings. They're black and make her look like the goddess I've always known her to be. The only thing covering her fine body is a pair of red lacy panties and some "I'm going to rock your world" red heels.

"Come here, Dax." I hear her sultry voice from the other side of the door.

I twist the doorknob, slowly inching the door open. The music playing is slow and sensual, much like the first time we made love. Bright red heels catch my eye, and I take my time, slowly gazing up as I memorize every inch of her tanned legs. My eyes come to a halt on her panties. *Unwrap me* is written across them.

I groan.

She closes the distance, pressing her hands flat against my chest. "Happy birthday, Dax," she breathes against my neck, kissing her way up to my lips. This woman of mine is on a mission. A mission to please me...or completely destroy me.

Happy birthday to me indeed.

She slowly starts to unzip my flight suit while paying careful attention to my mouth as she caresses her tongue against mine. We're both breathless when she pulls away.

"Did you like your photos?" she asks with a sly look as she inches down, taking my zipper with her.

"Hottest thing ever," I grit out, hissing as her hand grazes over me.

"Just for you, baby." She looks up at me from where she's perched on her knees, undoing the laces of my boots. "I wanted to show you"—her voice falters only for a second—"what you mean to me." She pulls each boot off and slowly stands back in front of me. "I wanted to show you that I'm ready."

I scrunch my eyes in confusion, and she grabs both of my hands, holding them in front of us as she intertwines our fingers together. Much like I imagine our bodies will be soon.

"I love you, Dax," she whispers, her heart in her eyes. "And I'm in this with you for the long haul. Those pictures are me letting go...and free falling with you. Wherever we land, I know you'll catch me and that's the best feeling ever." She beams.

I drop her hands and tangle mine in her hair, crushing my mouth to hers. She's mine. She's giving herself over to me, trusting me.

We're about to move on from this together, stronger than we'd ever be separate.

I move one hand down, pulling her tightly into me.

"What's this?" I ask, grabbing at the fabric on her backside.

She looks up and bats her eyes a few times, smiling. "I'm your present. You own me. Now it's time for you to unwrap me." She slowly peels away from me and turns around.

"Best present ever." I moan as I take in the black bow on the back of her panties and bra. "Do you have any idea how gorgeous you are?"

"You make me feel beautiful," she whispers.

I stand up, turning her to face me. "And you make me whole, Lynsie." Holding her gaze, I wrap my arms around her, slowly undoing the last bow and staking claim. She's mine. Forever.

WE LIE IN bed, tangled in each other's embrace, too excited for what's to come to find sleep.

"So how much longer are we going to be here?" Lynsie props her arm up on my chest, looking down at me.

"I'm not sure. I know there's a process. I haven't started it because I was waiting for your answer before deciding anything."

"You always knew what my answer would be." Her fingers dance up and down my chest.

"Yes, but I needed *you* to figure it out. I needed you to know what all you're giving up by going with me."

"I'd only be giving something up if I stay." She blinks down at me.

I shift beneath her, suddenly worried. I should've told her my plans before, but there was no good time. Now, I can't put it off with the day nearing. "Before we pack up and leave, there's still something I have to do."

"What's that?" She shifts, trying not to show concern.

"Well"—I let out a breath—"the Fourth of July show is right around the corner."

Her body tenses and I pull her closer to my chest, running my hand through her hair down to her back. I repeat this movement over and over, easing Lynsie's worries away one by one as she slowly loosens, melting into me even more.

I hear light sniffles. I knew this would ultimately upset her. It's going to be a hard day, no matter what, but this is something I have to do. "Lynsie." I sigh. "What you did, proving you're ready to let go and take off with me, was amazing, and it was what you needed to do. This is what I need to do. It's so much more than closure for me. It's," I stammer, searching for the right words, "it's me paying my respect to my best friend one final time. I need to do this." I pull back. Using my finger under her chin, I tilt her face up to mine. Her tear-filled eyes almost have me reconsidering. Almost. "This is me letting go. This is the way I need to do it. Please understand." I scan her eyes, looking for some sign of reassurance.

She closes them, allowing the tears to spill over. When she reopens her big green eyes, I take in the sincerity that now fills them.

Lynsie places her hand on my cheek, and I lean into it. Her touch is magnetic. It pulls me in. "If this is what you need to do, then I'll be there. Wherever you are is where I'll always be."

Chapter Forty-Two

LYNSIE

A year later, here I stand, in the same place where my world came crashing down around me. This time, I don't have a husband to lose. Instead, it's the person who has taken up residency in my life. The person who has become such a dependable fixture that I know without a shadow of a doubt I wouldn't recover if something ever happened to him. It's not that I care for him more than Lincoln, but how would it be possible to recover from losing love twice?

My stomach is in knots, my palms are sweaty, and it has nothing to do with the Alabama heat. My emotions are running wild.

A year ago, my husband flew into the blue sky above, never to return. Today, his best friend, the man who has been a heaven-sent angel, is flying into that same sky where pieces of my late husband will always live on. I still have to remind myself that he died doing what he loved.

Echo walks up behind me a few minutes later, holding Blu. She was giving me a few minutes alone to process the memory today brings. She's been so good to me this past year. Lincoln's death brought us closer. She was another one of those God-sent angels.

"Hey, Lynsie." She wraps her free arm around my shoulder, pulling me to her side. "You okay?"

I turn to her and smile, wiping the few tears away. "Yes." I shrug my shoulders as I look back out toward the sparkling lake. "This could be as good for me as it will be for him."

Echo hands a very sleepy Blu to me, and I hold her against me, resting her head near my shoulder.

Dax approaches, and I take in his tall, lean body filling his flight suit and can't help but smile. I'd be lying if I said he didn't look good, strutting over with his messy, dirty-blond hair and shades on. Dax pulls his sunglasses off as he comes to a stop right in front of me. His hazel eyes and grin cause my heart to momentarily skip a beat. My Dax. The guy who has loved me for so long. The one I'm so deeply in love with.

"Why are you looking at me like that?" he asks, giving me his cocky grin.

"Like what?" I play innocent, licking my lips.

"Mmmhmm." He stares at my lips, then bends down and places a sweet kiss on my mouth. "How are you doing?" He looks deep into my eyes, searching for the truth.

"I'm trying," I tell him honestly. "For *you*, I'm trying not to freak out. I know this is something you need to do."

"You know how much I love you, right?"

I see nothing but adoration in his eyes.

"If this is going to hurt you..." He looks down, shaking his head. "Then let's go."

I press my hand to his face. "No, Dax. I get it. This is something we both need to face. You need to face it up in the sky. I need to face it down here. I will be here, waiting for you when you're done."

"Thank you," he says tenderly, tugging me and Blu against his chest. He kisses my forehead before saying, "I just can't shake that this is what I'm supposed to do. I feel like it's my way to really honor Lincoln. And you being here supporting me means the world." His face softens even more. "More than the world."

"Just be careful. I don't know what I'd do without you." I hold back the sob threatening to take over. I have to be strong. If he sees how worried I am and the dread of déjà vu taking over, he'll back out. I won't let him do that.

"Always," he says, smiling down at me, brushing a piece of hair behind my ear. Then he bends down and places a kiss on a now sleeping Blu tucked into my arm. "Sleep tight, beautiful girl. I'm going to go tell your daddy 'hi'."

Those words do something unexplainable to me. I choke back the sob that threatens to break loose as he tenderly kisses my lips one last time. Resting his forehead against mine, he places both hands on the sides of my face. "I love you, Lynsie."

"I love you, too."

He pulls back, giving me one last smile. I nod before he turns to walk away, just in time for the first wave of tears to trickle down my face. These tears aren't just sad ones. There are many emotions behind them: sadness for what today and this place represents and worry. Because I'm scared out of my mind right now. But there's also a sense of letting go and moving on, and I feel as if my soul is lifting as each tear slides out. There's so much I've been holding onto and carrying around this last year.

Looking up at the perfectly clear sky, I suddenly feel warmth surrounding me, as if someone is wrapping their arms around me in a soothing manner. Maybe it's Lincoln. Maybe he's reassuring me it's okay—that he's okay. I know he'd only want what's best for me, but it's still hard when you feel like your best was ripped away too soon. Now that I have Dax, though, I see that it's possible to have something so amazingly great more than once in your life.

We take a seat on the blanket, and I glance over at Echo, who's rather quiet, staring off into the distance. Dylan's playing catch with some other kids, and I examine his features. Something about him always stumped Dax. There are days, every so often, I catch Echo spacing out ever since Dustin showed up. I'm constantly wondering where her mind goes and if it has anything to do with him. I have a keen suspicion it has everything to do with him. There has to be a story there, and it obviously didn't end happily. It makes me sad for my best friend and sad for Dax's brother. It explains a lot on his part, but thirteen years later, what can really be done? She's now happily married, with a son.

I sigh, wishing I had the answers to everything.

Someone places their hands on my shoulders as they kneel down behind me. I look back to see my mom, and I smile. Even though my father is flying again this year, I wasn't sure she'd come. Last year, she was sick with a migraine. I was afraid this year she'd be sick with worry. Nonetheless, I'm glad to have her by my side.

"Y'all wouldn't be having a party without us, would you?" a deep male voice says from the side.

I look over and see not only Dax's parents, but Lincoln's as well, and my eyes swell with tears. I'm a lucky girl, indeed. I know this has to be difficult for Jim and Julie, but I can't help the relief I feel that they're here. They've never stopped supporting Dax because of Lincoln's death. If anything, they're more supportive, and they never pass up a chance to see their grandbaby.

Dax's parents sit off to the side. I'm sure it's more his mom's choice. She's probably a bit nervous because of what took place last time they were in town. For her son's sake, she meant well, and it wasn't a personal jab at me, but the way she's standoffish, I sense she's feeling guilty. I'm not sure if Dax has even talked to her since, or if he's mentioned anything to them about leaving the Army and moving back to his hometown. It makes me giggle, picturing his stubborn self not telling her since she always bugs him about it.

I hear the sound of planes in the distance and train my eyes on the sky. Excitement bubbles inside me as I see the first plane coming into view. I'll never get tired of the sight. As much as I want to hate it, I can't.

One plane is heading in our direction, and then out of nowhere, two others show up on each side. This happens again and again until there are seven planes flying in a V. I can't fully take in what they're doing until they get closer, but once I figure it out, I throw my hand over my mouth as I take in the synchronized motion they're all doing.

"Oh my. They're all doing the wing dip," I whisper in awe.

Echo throws her arm around my center and my mom leans her head on my shoulder. "They're doing that for Lincoln," she says with tears in her eyes. I can hear the amazement in her voice.

I'm amazed myself. It's beautiful in so many ways. The whole time they fly toward us, they dip to one side and then slowly dip to the other. They truly look like wings flapping from down here.

I sniffle and use my free hand to wipe away the tears. My mom is the only one who knows the significance behind it, yet I can hear others around "oohing" and "aahing" all around me in amazement. They knew that was a signature move of his and they all collaborated on a way to bring it together as one. What a beautiful tribute they just gave Lincoln.

Looking up, I can almost picture Lincoln side by side with Dax, smiling down, his arms outstretched and flying beside his best friend. The idea makes me smile. I'm so proud of Dax right now and the rest of the guys. Peterson is up there, and it has to be equally hard for him. I have a feeling this isn't just a memorial for Lincoln, but a rectification for Dax, Peterson, and my father.

Today, we're all letting go.

Final Transition

DAX

Carrying a box down the stairs, I stack it at the bottom against the wall next to the others. Before running back up for the rest, I pause to watch Lynsie as she stares at the case in the living room. It holds all of Lincoln's model planes. I scratch the back of my neck and shake my head. Boy, did he love his model planes. Many of those were from his childhood—meaning, I helped put them together.

I walk up behind her and wrap my arms around her. "What's on your mind?" I kiss the top of her head.

"It's just hard packing his stuff." She sighs.

"Does it make it better that you also get to unpack it?" I ask, hoping she realizes the packing part of it is only temporary.

Silent for a few seconds, she lets her head fall back against me. "Yeah, actually, it does. Thanks, I needed that reminder."

She looks up at me, and I lean in to kiss her. I pull away, pointing toward the stairs. "I have a few more boxes that I'm going to bring down. If you need any help packing these, I'll be done in a bit."

"Nope, I think I got it." She smiles.

Even though I didn't want to, Lynsie convinced me it would be good to give my mom a heads-up that we're moving there, and to warn her that Lynsie and I are a family. I agreed it wouldn't be good for my mom to find out through the town gossip...or running into her at the local grocery store. I do love her, but she can be overbearing at times. Okay, all the time.

I warned her that she needed to get it under control by the time I moved back, and she assured me she would. Only time will really tell if that's the truth. I also asked her about Dustin. I never got to say goodbye or ask him about Dylan. Just like normal, he took off without giving anyone a lick of notice. I wish I could sit him down and get to the bottom of things, but like always, he's running. He's bound to get tired of it sometime—I hope.

It's been one month since Lynsie agreed to move back home with me. Right after she told me, I put in for an honorable discharge. I don't have a negative outlook on the Army because of everything I've been through. I wholeheartedly believe it brought me to where I was meant to be, and that my journey in uniform has come to an end.

We're almost packed up and, since it's our last night here, we called our friends over for a 'see you later' celebration. The Army can be finicky and the chances of seeing these people we've grown close to depends on us to put in the effort, but also a bit of fate. None of us are promised tomorrow. We've all managed to pull through this past year. It's been a group effort, but bonds were formed I never expected, and now we're about to put them to the test. Bending, but never breaking them.

Lynsie stands with a slice of pizza in one hand and her Solo cup filled with soda in the other. "Ahem," she says, gathering everyone's attention, "I just wanted to say something real quick while you all are here." She looks down at me, and I nod, urging her to continue. "It's sad to say that sometimes we don't know who our closest friends are until tragedy strikes. Sometimes it takes tragedy to bring us together. Sometimes it brings people that you fight to let in, but eventually lose the battle." She raises her eyebrows at Peterson, and we all laugh, knowing how hard he's had to work to get on Lynsie's good side.

She continues, "I can honestly say, as I look around"—she does a clockwise glance, starting with her parents sitting to her left and ending with me sitting at her right—"that each one of you played an invaluable role in my survival this past year, and I wouldn't have made it out without each and every one of you." Her voice starts to tremble. "I love you guys so much, and I'm going to miss you," she chokes out, then adds, "Even you, Peterson."

We all laugh again.

"No need to play hard to get, Lynsie." Zack walks up to her and pulls her into a hug. "It just wasn't in the cards for us." He looks down at her with a seriousness I'm not familiar with. "But don't you worry your sweet little ass. You may not have got this"—he motions his hands down his body before looking my way and winking—"but at least you got second best."

"I guess I'll take what I can get," Lynsie teases Zack, but when she glances over at me, all I see is undying love in her eyes. The kind of love that can survive anything. The love we have makes me feel invincible.

Lynsie and the girls huddle together and cry through their good-byes as everyone makes their way to the door.

Once Blu is fed and asleep, Lynsie and I lie on the air mattress. This feels surreal. Tomorrow, we'll start a new journey in our life, and there's no one in this world I'd rather have by my side.

"IS THAT THE last box?" Lynsie asks, striding toward the mailbox, and bends over to put the 'For Rent' sign in the grass.

I look down at the model airplane box I'm carrying—Lincoln's last gift for Lynsie. "Yep. When we get home, I'm going to have to teach you how to fly this."

She smiles dreamily at me and nods.

Lincoln's parents told me about a house for rent with a couple acres. They said the owners would probably sell if we ended up loving it. Lynsie fell in love as soon as she saw pictures showcasing the big front porch and huge yard for Blu to play in once she's older. She also pointed out that it's the perfect space for me to start up my carving business. I might just take her up on the idea.

"I'm just going to do one final sweep through," she says, pulling on my arm as she pushes up on the balls of her feet to kiss my cheek.

She knows the house is completely empty and there isn't anything to sweep through—except memories. Leaving this house that holds so many memories for her, of Lincoln and their life together, has finally arrived. This final walk-through is Lynsie letting go of her past and trusting me with her future. I no longer question why I was so drawn to her. There was a purpose behind it, and I'm living it now.

I snuggly slide the last box into the truck, pull the door down on the U-Haul, and lock it. I walk back into the house to check on Lynsie, only to find her sitting on the bare living room floor. I'm instantly by her side, pulling her into my arms. I don't ask what's wrong because I already know. Saying goodbye is hard. There are things and places that will always connect us to people, and when we see them, we'll instantly think of them. This house is a major one for Lynsie.

As we sit here, a memory comes to me. "Remember that time when you guys had that pool party, and Lincoln came running through the back door, soaking wet, trying to pull a *Risky Business* scene and fell on his ass instead?"

Through her sniffles, she giggles. "Yeah, I do. That was so funny."

"I'll never forget that." I pull back slightly and lift Lynsie's face up. "*We* will never forget him. We have each other to always remember him. Anytime you're missing Lincoln, you come to me. If you need to cry, I'll cry with you. He's gone, but he'll always be with us."

She leans her head against my chest. "I love you so much. It's crazy how things work out."

"What do you mean?" I ask, running my hand through her hair.

"You're the only one who truly understands what I lost, what we lost. There's no one else who would be so willing to keep my dead husband and child's father's memory alive. I wholeheartedly believe you were put into my life for this purpose."

"I used to fight the whole fate idea." I smile to myself. "Not that I didn't like it or hope for it, but in the beginning, I hated what it represented. To me, it basically said that Lincoln was destined to die. I guess that could be true. We all have our day, but I didn't want it to be like he was supposed to die so we could be together." I grab her hands and hold them between us.

Worrying her lip between her teeth, I rub the pad of my thumb over that full bottom lip of hers. She instantly releases it, and her wide eyes look up, capturing mine.

Lynsie's mouth slowly curves into a determined smile.

"I've come to the conclusion." She runs a hand through my hair, and I close my eyes, reveling in her touch. Her hand trails down the side of my face, resting against my cheek. I open my eyes, and my heart stops. "That everything happens for a reason, and with that, I know I can face anything with you by my side."

"Well, are you ready, pretty lady?" I stand up and hold my hand out to her. "We have to go pick up our girl, make one last stop, then we're hitting the road."

"Ready," she says. With no sense of hesitation, she firmly grips my hand as I swiftly pull her up and toss her over my shoulder before she can argue. "Whoa there." Lynsie starts laughing as I carry her out of the house.

I slowly let her slide down, but I don't want to let go of her just yet. She wraps her legs around my waist as I wrap my arms around hers. "I love you, Lynsie."

"I love you too, Dax." She gives me a cheesy grin. "You are the wind beneath my wings."

Who would've thought that a clichéd phrase could hold so much truth? But, in our case, it's words to live by.

LYNSIE FOLLOWS BEHIND me as we make the twenty-minute drive to Lake Tholocco. The sun is shining brightly, and the wind is nowhere to be found. I'm able to see the beauty that resides in this place instead of a constant scene of destruction.

I get out and make my way to Lynsie's car, waiting as she unstraps Blu. She hands her over to me and shuts the door. I start walking around with Blu, wanting to tell her stories about her father, even though there's no way she'll understand what I'm saying.

"Has your mommy ever told you where she got your name from?"

Lynsie grabs my free hand as she comes to my side.

"Your daddy used to always say, 'There's nothing more beautiful than a blue sky'." I look down at Lynsie, who's wiping a tear away but smiling. I grin at the girl I love, then at my little girl in my arms. "When your mom first laid eyes on you, she knew your daddy was right. That indeed, there was nothing more beautiful than our Blu Skye."

"I'm going to miss him every day of my life," Lynsie says, staring out at the water where the only remains of Lincoln, if any, have found their final resting place. Her grip on my hand tightens. "But it doesn't hurt anymore...not often anyway."

I pull her hand up to my lips, placing a kiss on it.

"Goodbye, Lincoln," she whispers, letting go of my hand and wrapping her arm around me. I drape mine along her shoulders, pulling her closer to my side as we stand in silence.

We turn to walk back toward the U-Haul, stopping in front of the metal statue replica of the Final Transition piece I made. It's only been out here for a couple weeks. The original still resides in our hangar, but they loved my idea so much and thought there needed to be some sort of remembrance of where the crash took place. Being the colonel, Lynsie's dad oversaw it.

"Wait a minute," I say to Lynsie, handing over Blu. "I just need a moment if that's okay."

"Of course. Take all the time you need." She reaches up, kissing the corner of my lips.

I watch them make their way back, then I pull the piece of softly folded paper out of my pocket. The paper that was once rough is now soft because of the number of times I've unfolded it to read it, scratch words out, and add to this poem I wrote for Lincoln. Knowing it's finally perfected, but not knowing if it will be heard, I need to read it here as if he can hear me. It's not something I should keep on a worn piece of paper. They're my final words to my best friend, and I want him to know he'll never be forgotten.

"You said goodbye, from way up high.
You left us broken, unable to fly.
You held no doubt, no time to spare.
You knew what had to happen, while flying in
the air.

Very slowly we began to mend the pieces back.
Feather by feather, wings now fully intact.
Your last wish I guard and will keep in my
heart.
Till my dying breath, it never will part.

Blu Skye's a calling. I can hear her now.
Your memory lives on. That's my number one vow.
We miss you, Lincoln. That will always be true.
Take care up there, Wings. We love you."

Acknowledgments

First and foremost, I want to thank God. Thank you for your grace and being ready for me with open arms when your prodigal daughter returned. Thank you for this insane passion for storytelling and this creative mind you've blessed me with. I'm where I am today because of you, and where I go from here on out will be because of you. I put this book and these characters in your hands for you to do as you please. May your will be done, not mine. I know it's by your grace I've found my passion again and I want it to glorify you. Shut the doors not meant for me, and I will walk through the ones you open. In Jesus' name, Amen.

Second, I need to thank Ena Burnette. I honestly can't say that Broken Wings would even exist if she hadn't told me I needed to write an Army book.

I was an Army brat growing up, and my dad was a pilot. My father lost many friends as a pilot. Until writing this book, I never fully grasped it. The Final Transition piece is a real carving that my father made when two of his close friends died. The inscription in BW reads straight from it (except the pilot names, which I mixed up and incorporated in the book). I told my dad I needed just enough detail to make my book believable. What's funny is that almost all (except both Fourth of July air shows) are deviated from stories my dad told me. I titled the book Broken Wings because of the double meaning. It fits with the pilot aspect as well as overwhelming grief—feeling as if you are broken and unable to fly again. When my dad later told me there is a Broken Wing Award (before he even knew my title) I felt as if it was fated. The whole story was perfect. So without the help of my father and the twenty-eight years he was a pilot in the Army, Broken Wings wouldn't exist. I'm sure the idea would have been there, but I couldn't have made it into what it is. So CW4 Kirk Hosp aka Daddi-o, thank you for your service and all your late-night emails. I couldn't have done it without you!

There are too many people to thank for helping me make Broken Wings what it was in 2014 and now what it is ten years later. If you read, loved, critiqued, shared, or had any part in the publishing process, this 10th Anniversary Edition is for you!

About the Author

ERIKA ASHBY GREW up an Army Brat, spending most of her childhood in Oklahoma, where she finally put down roots in 2003. She currently lives in Edmond, OK where she faithfully attends NORTH.CHURCH with her kids. She's a blessed mom of four who loves Jesus and serving others. Her hobbies include attending dirt track races, concerts, reading, DIY, and making red dirt shirts. Erika is an advocate of 'it's never too late to go after a dream'. After all, it wasn't until the ripe age of twenty-seven when she realized she had a hidden passion for reading. Up until that point in her life, she claimed to have hated it. Six months later, she was hit with another revelation: the desire to tell stories. Knowing she had failed all writing assignments in school, she set out on this journey mainly to prove to herself she could do it. So here she is today, claiming she's an author. Erika wants to encourage anyone with a dream to go for it. "We are our biggest obstacle, and only regret the chances we don't take."

Facebook: @authorEAshby
TikTok: @authorerikaashby
Instagram: @authorerikaashby
Website: Authorerikaashby.com